A MAX AHLGREN NOVEL

EXISTENTIAL

The Mission: To Survive

RYAN W. ASLESEN

It was supposed to be just another mission...

Buried deep in the rugged Alaskan wilderness lies a secret that could alter the future of mankind–a secret that billionaire Elizabeth Grey has invested millions in solving. When the dig goes silent and all attempts at making contact fail, an elite team of battle-hardened military contractors are brought in led by former Marine Max Ahlgren, a warrior haunted by his past. The mission: to make contact and rescue a team of scientists and engineers working on the secretive "archeological" project.

Once on the ground, the team discovers the grizzly truth that this is no ordinary rescue mission. In what was supposed to be an easy payday, Max and his men find themselves in the fight of their lives against a nightmarish enemy like nothing they have ever seen. The mission becomes a struggle for survival as the world's greatest soldiers encounter the universe's ultimate terror in a battle that puts all of humanity at stake.

Cover Illustration Copyright © 2017 Ryan Aslesen
Cover layout by Deranged Doctor Design
www.derangeddoctordesign.com

Book design and production by BookBaby

Editing by: Tyler Mathis
               Leigh Hogan
               Ashley Davis

Existential
Copyright © 2018 Ryan Aslesen.

ISBN (Ebook Edition): 978-1-54391-958-5
ISBN (Print Edition): 978-1-54391-959-2

www.ryanaslesen.com

To my father, thank you for being there to

pick me up when I fell, and for teaching

me not to be afraid of the dark.

Acknowledgments

A lot of work goes into writing a book and this book is no exception. I couldn't have done it without the help of a lot of talented people. I first would like to thank my writing coach and developmental editor, Tyler Mathis, a fellow Marine and brother-in-arms, for being my constant guide on this journey and helping me achieve one of my life dreams. Tyler this book wouldn't have become what it has without your professional guidance and expertise.

I would also like to thank the rest of my editorial team that helped me sharpen and improve my manuscript. Leigh Hogan for all the time and energy put into copy editing my manuscript and helping me make it the best it could be. Ashley Davis for the excellent line edit and improvements to my manuscript. And Laura Wilkinson for the final proofreading of my work. I also wish to thank Garrett Cook for the creative input and suggestions that gave my manuscript the extra edge I was looking for. Any mistakes or shortcomings that remain in this book are mine and mine alone.

A book isn't complete without a cover and I want to thank Kim and Darja with Deranged Doctor Design for the final cover design and marketing materials. I appreciate your patience with me during the design and review process. If I am your typical customer, I don't envy your job.

Last, but certainly not least, I want to thank my beautiful and brilliant wife, Amy. You gave me the courage and support to go through with this project. What started as some scribbled notes on a legal pad has become so much more because of your encouragement and unwavering belief in me. I also want to say thank you to my two wonderful sons, Darien and Mason. Darien for listening to my rambling ideas in the car and always being supportive and making me feel hip and cool when I'm not. Mason for reawakening my imagination and showing me what it means to be a kid again. I apologize for any time this project took away from you guys. You were the motivation to keep pushing on when I thought about giving up. I hope this book, as humble of accomplishment it is, inspires you to pursue your dreams.

I'm absolutely convinced. . .There has been and is an existing presence, an ET presence [on Earth].

-Robert T. Bigelow

Whoever fights monsters should see to it that in the process he does not become a monster. And if you gaze long enough into an abyss, the abyss will gaze back into you.

-Friedrich Nietzsche

1

IT WAS THE GREATEST DISCOVERY IN THE HISTORY OF MANKIND.
A discovery that could alter the course of humanity and perhaps
even the evolution of the species, and Greg Ramone had signed on to
be a part of it. Yet, as he practically sprinted from Research Pod 1 into
the unseasonably warm chill of the Alaskan wilderness, a greater
motive hurried his step through Base Camp.

A brilliant ray of sunshine slanted into his eyes from just over
the tree line, only to be extinguished a moment later behind the leading edge of a flat gray cloud spanning most of the heavens, with no
end in sight. The scene made him think of the overworked cliché, "If
you're tired of the weather here, wait five minutes," though it didn't
appear as if the gray sheet would be moving out anytime soon.

He consulted his titanium sports watch: four eighteen p.m. It
would be full-on dark in less than an hour. Around Base Camp, auto-
mated lights atop towering aluminum poles illuminated in response

to the dying daylight. In the background, the generators hummed, straining to keep the camp lit and heated, a constant reminder of man's intrusion into an otherwise pristine wilderness.

Even though emotions of any sort seemed frowned upon within the Greytech empire, Greg couldn't help but feel as if he'd been blithely oblivious when he'd jumped at the opportunity to join this expedition, more than happy to fly to Alaska on Dr. Lawrence's white coattails. He needed to gain field experience, anything to gain an edge while writing his doctoral dissertation in biochemistry. It would look great on his résumé, provided the fruits of this project were ever revealed. He had signed a strict non-disclosure agreement, forbidding him from revealing any details of the expedition or its findings.

The money was good as well. Despite having been on the project for a little over a month, other researchers still considered him an outsider. The project excited him, like most of the scientists on staff. Everyone had their reasons for being there, but all wanted to somehow capitalize on being a part of this truly revolutionary discovery.

A horn weakly beeped, failing to trump the guttural grumble of a powerful diesel engine. Greg was startled from his reverie and jerked to a stop. A massive orange wheel-loader trundled by with a shipping container on its forks. Its driver, who wore the standard silver-gray jumpsuit of a Greytech employee, shot him a face full of annoyance as the machine passed. In the other direction, an ATV passed with a uniformed Greytech employee in front and a researcher in back.

Greg finally had a clear path across the wide, muddy track that passed for a main street. He crossed and turned uphill, headed east, ever mindful of being observed and recorded by the dozens of security cameras placed atop the light poles around camp.

Greytech's top-secret Base Camp stretched east to west for over a half-kilometer along the south bank of a marshy stream that flowed down from Boundary Peak 171, a four thousand-meter mountain that neatly bisected the border between Alaska and the Yukon Territory. The glacier that created the valley had receded since the last Ice Age. Only a fraction of it remained at the head of the valley, high up the slope of Peak 171. A grid of pre-fab research buildings and dormitories comprised the eastern end of Base Camp, closest to the dig site. The west end of camp housed logistics: equipment storage, maintenance and fueling facilities, a diesel-powered generating station, and a cluster of helicopter pads adjacent to several stacks of metal shipping containers that had been flown in, packed to bursting with vehicles, provisions, and sensitive monitoring and research equipment. Science for profit at its most grandiose. The CEO and majority owner of Greytech, Ms. Elizabeth Grey, had spared no expense in her quest to unlock the mysteries of the alien craft.

As it should be.

Greg walked up the gentle slope into the gathering twilight. He still considered himself an idealist, and certain aspects of Greytech's culture bothered him, despite the hefty sum on his contract. The company had taken the vanguard in solar R&D, but this operation was anything but green. A pall of diesel fumes hung over the valley at all hours of the day and night. Greytech's scientists were a different breed from the academicians he had grown accustomed to at Stanford. These were brilliant men, of course, but their loyalties lay with Greytech. They made all their discoveries in the interests of Elizabeth Grey and her bottom line. The way of corporate science, he realized. Though he had never witnessed unethical behavior by any Greytech researcher, something about the atmosphere in Base Camp smacked of callousness and moral disregard.

An alien object, buried half in the glacier and half in the mountain, served as the entire reason this remote valley had been transformed into such a hive of activity. Not yet a doctor of biochemistry, only a research assistant, Greg had been kept in the dark regarding the happenings at the dig site. But today, he'd assisted Dr. Lawrence in examining some data samples of the organic life that had been found aboard the ship—a black organic substance that the head researcher, Dr. Jung, suspected might be sentient.

At this moment, Greg couldn't have given a shit less about the substance, sentient or not. He had work to do, yes—a perfunctory check of some ambient radiation sensors just south of the camp. The true purpose of his hike, however, was to make a simple phone call. Only nothing was simple about communications from the camp. First off, the NDA he had signed strictly forbade contact with the outside world. Second, cell phones were useless a hundred miles from the nearest signal tower.

He hoped instead to raise Elana on the satellite phone burning a hole in his pocket. A fellow doctoral student had artfully secreted the phone within a shipment of highly sensitive equipment that had arrived from the university that morning. Greg's career would be over before it started if he were caught making even this innocuous call to his girlfriend back in Palo Alto. However, there were things about the project that were starting to bother him. The more the company seemed to uncover, the less communicative the doctors became, and the fewer questions they would answer. He was feeling alone. Lonely enough to violate the NDA.

He needed to hear Elana's voice—a task that necessitated this trek into the woods. The handful of personnel trusted enough to carry sat phones found they were useless within the valley and around the dig site. Even Greytech's satellite communication technology, light years more advanced than any cell phone, had patchy reception when sending and receiving transmissions. Additional IT men had flown in this morning to analyze the problem and fix it, or so he'd heard in the mess hall.

Greg came to the camp's eastern perimeter and felt a knot of nervousness form in his stomach as he approached the security checkpoint. It was manned by a Greytech security guard cradling an assault rifle and appearing alert for the surveillance cameras. All of his gear—helmet, body armor, weapons—was camouflaged in a pattern of white, green, and gray. Faceless behind polarized goggles, the security man said nothing as he scanned the barcode on Greg's ID badge before waving him through the perimeter.

Headlights bore down on Greg from up the hill as a dump truck whined its way downgrade with a load of dirt from the dig site. He stepped off the road and cut south, first through leafless scrub and then into a stand of towering firs. He switched on an LED flashlight and picked his way between the trunks. The wind picked up slightly as bad weather moved in, but from the reports he'd seen, he had a couple of hours before things really turned to shit, though around here one never knew. He made his way diagonally up the ridge, skirting drifts of snow that hadn't melted since the last storm three days ago. It had been piss warm since then, thirteen degrees Celsius for the high yesterday, which was downright sweltering for Alaska in early November.

Upon reaching the first sensor atop the ridge, Greg found it reading the same as it had the previous two days. He would have been cursing if not for the phone. Greg looked to make sure no one had followed him, then pulled the phone out and consulted the screen. He frowned, no signal. Stowing the phone, he jogged to the top of the next ridge. He checked it again and smiled. Not one bar, but two!

He dialed Elana's number in Palo Alto. She would be home from class by now, likely indulging in a glass or two of pinot noir before she cooked dinner for herself. *Better be just her, anyway.* His smile didn't waver though he worried at times. She was devastatingly attractive, after all, and they weren't quite married yet.

"Come on," Greg urged as he awaited connection with Elana's phone. After an interminable time—roughly fifteen seconds or so—he heard a ring, followed by two more. "Shit, be available..." Apprehensive, he bounced on the balls of his feet and stared down into the mud at an odd grouping of puddles. *What the heck?* A *click* drew his attention back to the phone. "Hey, hon, it's me!"

The reply came after a moment of lag. "Greg!" Elana's voice echoed a bit, but the connection was better than he'd hoped for. "Oh my god! Oh, hon, I miss you so much!"

They'd been separated for over a month which was the most time they had spent apart since their engagement. She sounded ecstatic to hear his voice, just as he'd been until the odd puddles formed a footprint.

Six toes?

Indeed, two smaller toes graced either side of the footprint in the mud, with four longer toes between. Greg concluded this impression had come from the right foot, though he found the very idea absurd since this alleged footprint appeared to be just shy of a meter long, not counting the two triangular impressions driven straight down into the muck directly behind the heel.

Avian? Talons? What the fuck am I seeing here?

He stood dumbstruck with the phone at his ear. Elana had become a warble, like Charlie Brown's teacher, the voice Greg loved reduced to a bleating trombone. He crouched and moved forward.

Another track in a patch of slush, the left foot, lay about two meters beyond the first. The bipedal creature, certainly no mere animal, had slipped a bit here. There were no triangular marks behind the heel but the nails—*claws*—on its front toes had dug deep into the snow to find traction.

Greg followed the tracks as Elana nattered on, something about the absurdity of her best friend doing her Master's thesis in philosophy on the works of Sartre. The fourth and fifth footprints he discovered showed the prominent marks of two talons emanating from the heel. In making the sixth footprint, the creature's front claws had sliced right through a fir root over two inches in diameter just by treading upon it.

"I mean, *Sartre*? Nobody takes him seriously anymore. She'll be laughed right out of the department! I told her she should—"

The anatomical details of the footprints had piqued his interest to the point where all other instincts and thoughts shut down. Having grown up in suburbia and not in the woods, he failed to consider the most pressing question presented by his find: when had the tracks been made? Had he have known, he would have abandoned Elana, Sartre, and the sat phone and would have gotten the hell out of there.

"You're awfully quiet, *Doctor* Ramone." Elana laughed. "How's it going up there? I know, it's all hush-hush; a simple well or poorly will suffice."

When something nearby snapped, Greg felt like screaming at the phone, the distracting device dulling survival instincts he never knew he possessed. In that instant, when he first comprehended the danger, he dropped the phone to his side, Elana still squawking.

Greg hadn't heard the grizzly coming. He'd just known something would be there when he turned. Muscles in the bear's shoulders bunched and relaxed in metronomic rhythm as the golden-brown beast ran on all fours straight for him. He pissed slightly in his Gore-Tex trousers and opened his mouth to scream, though no sound came from his throat. *Elana.* The bear closed upon him in a flash, within arm's reach.

Greg had thought upon sighting the bear that his life was over. Instead, he whirled around and watched the bear run on into the underbrush, moving quietly despite its size and speed. He gazed down. One of the bear's paws had tracked next to one of the gargantuan footprints.

"Can you hear me all right?"

Bewildered by the phone and Elana's voice, so incongruous in his primal surroundings, it took Greg a few seconds to seek out the phone. "Yeah, uh, everything's great, hon."

He again felt a presence nearby and scanned the dimming landscape amongst the firs. Elana's voice continued making inquiries through the receiver. Every pore on his body had turned to gooseflesh. He was alone, standing atop a ridge in the vast wilds of Alaska. Alone and, yet, not alone. The creature's tracks, the bear...

It all made sense. *Walk or run?* He knew—at least he'd heard—one should stay calm and move slowly when escaping an apex predator. *Couldn't the fucking thing smell fear?* It would sure as shit smell the mess he'd made in his pants.

And so it had. Greg didn't turn his head. He couldn't yet bring himself to look. But he knew it was there. His newly discovered instincts served him well, albeit for only a brief time.

From the right came a vicious, gurgling noise.

Greg's boots rooted where he stood. With running no longer an option—if ever it had been—he turned and gazed upon the horror rising over his shoulder. A kaleidoscope of blackness overtook him. Greg had never thought the color black could vary in shade and brightness, black being the absence of all color. Yet there it stood, a fact Greg's mind was still trying to fathom. Its alien eyes gleamed, large flat orbs of polished jet that saw only death and reflected only the same.

He didn't suppress his scream this time. Even so, no sound came. A great pressure pushed against his chest, presaging an instant of the most intense pain imaginable. When it came, he felt as though his chest had been split open with one mighty blow of a giant ax. He stood on his feet an instant longer before crashing backward into the mud.

Steam rose and clouded the air as a tepid rain pattered down on him in fits and starts. Opening his eyes one final time, Greg witnessed his own death from afar. His heart lay in the creature's palm, still beating, each pump spitting blood from the ragged ends of lacerated arteries. The creature, in rapt fascination, examined the organ with its gleaming jet eyes. Greg Ramone left the world as billions before him had done, thinking of the one he loved most, his image of Elana slowly fading. She called faintly from the phone's speaker, more urgently now, sensing something amiss. "Greg! Greg!"

MAX AHLGREN COULD FEEL THE BEADS OF SWEAT FORMING under his combat shirt as he crouched in the shadow of some bushes waiting for the cartel sentry to pass. Past midnight, the temperature still hung close to a hundred degrees. The guards would be finished changing, just settling in for their shift.

For the past two days, Max's team had surveilled the compound. He had grown familiar with the habits of the man about to approach. As the sentry walked past, nearing the entrance to the compound, Max uncoiled his muscular six-foot-four frame and rose up from the shadows, stalking his prey like a panther.

The sentry started to turn around.

I must be getting old, Max thought, disgusted that the man had heard him. It wouldn't matter much but it was inconvenient. Max took a final step, shot his left hand up to cover the sentry's mouth, and jerked the man's head back violently. He stabbed the sentry's throat with the razor-sharp KA-BAR in his right hand, pushing the blade forward and around viciously. He pulled the sentry down and back into the darkness as he thrashed. Max held him in an intimate embrace as the blood sprayed in spurts from his throat. With a faint gurgle, life seeped from the sentry with every pulse. As he completed his final death throes, Max gently eased the guard to the ground. He did this all as if it were a matter of routine.

Max reflexively wiped the blood on his ATACS camo pants, not out of disgust, but knowing the blood could cause the blade to stick in its Kydex sheath.

The second sentry, Miguel, stood about ten feet away, guarding the main gate. Max's team had identified him by his cell phone calls during their previous surveillance. Standing inside the makeshift guard shack, he was pouring himself a cup of coffee from a thermos and listening to mariachi music on a small radio next to him. Max silently observed his movements for a few seconds and raised his suppressed HK416 rifle as he strode toward him. Though a gunshot in Mexicali, Mexico was like a lightning strike to the people of Florida—a deadly force of nature but commonplace, familiar, and harmless as long as you weren't standing helplessly in the open— he'd chosen suppressed gear to make the other guards misjudge the distance of the shots. Max shot the man in the head twice, never breaking stride, firing so quickly that the two shots sounded like one. The spent shell casings dropped by his feet as he observed the man fall back, painting the wall in blood and brain matter. There were few constants in the business of warfare and killing, yet in all but the most elite units, one maxim usually held true: the shitbags pulled watch in the dead of night, ironically the most likely time for an attack.

Mexican drug cartels weren't elite units, but they still could be a formidable force. They recruited many of their members from the Mexican military. Rather than tactics and skills training, they focused on intimidation. No one in Mexico had the balls to silently storm one of their compounds in the middle of the night. Or perhaps they possessed common sense enough not to do so.

Max sprinted the few feet to the dead cartel enforcer, picked him up, and sat him on a milk crate, slumped over as though he'd fallen asleep on watch. Reaching inside the guard hut, Max pressed the green button on the control board. The gates opened a couple feet and Max hit the red button.

"Main gate down," he whispered into his headset.

He then ran for the closest cover—an old Mercedes sedan that sat on blocks, slowly rusting from the wheels up. He scanned for movement. The compound appeared to be a construction contractor lot and conducted business like one during the day, all as the front for a cartel's kidnapping safe house, like a wolf hiding in sheep's clothes.

"LT, status?" Max asked.

"We are in position. Moving to west side."

Max glanced behind him and saw Sugar and Diaz emerge from the shadows to slip through the gate. They eased toward the Mercedes.

The main building consisted of a two-story, run-down, flat-roofed square of crumbling cement blocks, very typical of modern Mexican construction except for the lack of windows on the ground floor. Max ran a few feet, took cover briefly behind a small bulldozer, then sprinted for the southwest corner of the building. Glancing back, he spotted Sugar's shadow crouched behind the Benz, his Mk 48 machine gun leveled at the steel double doors of the main building. Since a guard inside could potentially sense something amiss and raise an alarm, he would remain posted there in hopes that someone inside would first see the watchman "asleep" at his post and open the doors to investigate. Bottom line: move fast and control the action.

"Tango, that's two," Red said through the headset, busy clearing the north side of the compound.

Max adjusted his night vision goggles, NVGs, since their recon showed the west side of the compound had poor illumination.

He peeked around the corner and came face to face with another sentry. Normally, Max would have reflexively raised his rifle and wasted the guy in an instant. Except this guard was just a gangly kid, who couldn't be more than fifteen. The kid jumped back in shock, dumbstruck, mouthing soundless gibberish as if Max had been a demon of death emerging from the darkness. Then he fumbled for the M16 strapped across his back.

Max put a 5.56 round through the kid's forehead. The back of his head exploded like a melon. The kid crashed to the dirt on top of his M16, the body and weapon raising an awful clatter in the still night. *You picked the wrong friends, kid.*

In his line of work, those who hesitated died, or worse yet, they second-guessed their buddies into a rubber bag. Max cursed his hesitation as he put another round into the body.

"Tango, another down," Max whispered into the headset.

"You owe me a coke," Red replied.

"Location?"

"Northwest corner."

"Copy that. Got a visual on you, Red. Move up. I'll cover you."

Red moved carefully forward. Max watched him somehow duck his massive frame behind some fifty-five-gallon drums of God-knew-what. He swept the area in front of him with his silenced Sig, then moved forward again. Max spied Diaz posted at the northwest corner of the building, covering Red from behind.

Max's headset crackled just as the three men were meeting at the southwest corner. "We've got company, Chief!" The transmission came from Coach, the team sniper, stationed some six hundred yards away, atop an abandoned warehouse. Coach had started the party a few minutes earlier by taking out the two sentries posted atop the compound's main building. "We got two inbound vehicles approaching at high speed."

"LT, your twenty?" Max asked.

"East side of the compound, ground level."

Max heard a cell phone chirp faintly inside the building. *Fuck!* "We are compromised. Breach immediately. LT, do you copy?"

A moment of silence followed.

"Copy that." LT didn't sound amused, but he would get his breach team into position ASAP. They all knew from experience that plans usually gave way to improvisation.

Coach asked, "Take out these vehicles, Chief?"

"No, let them come. Sugar and I will give them a welcome out front. You pick off the ones who hide behind the vehicles." Max knew that Coach could, with a high degree of probability, take the drivers out even at that speed and distance. However, once the passengers dismounted, they would become more problematic. Max preferred to know where his enemy was going to be.

"Copy, Chief," Coach replied.

"Let's move!" Max urged Red and Diaz.

He ran back to the rusting Mercedes and took cover behind the engine block as a stream of automatic fire erupted from a gun port through one of the front doors. The sound of men cursing in Spanish emanated from the building. Two more short bursts of fire came from the front doors, rounds pinging on the Benz and the bulldozer as they either lodged or ricocheted. The car's glass shattered. Bullets whizzed over Max's head. Bits of shattered adobe wall rained down on him and Sugar.

"Shit!" Red grunted.

Max knew he'd been hit, but didn't have time to help. Diaz was with him; if the wound needed treatment, Diaz would see to it. Sugar opened up with his machine gun on the front doors in a vain attempt to squeeze some lead through one of the gun ports.

"ETA fifteen seconds on those vehicles!" Coach warned through the headset.

Fuck! "Let's go, LT! Breach that wall!" Max urged.

Within seconds, the breaching charge replied. Max had complete confidence in LT's ability to handle the dirty work inside.

When the firing from the door stopped for a moment, Max peeked around the car and saw the front door swing open to the courtyard. Max spotted LT's fireplug silhouette crouched in the entrance dropping a green chem light, signifying that room was clear, before disappearing back inside. Johnny Gable, the team's other breach specialist, moved along behind him.

But for some frantic cursing within the building, the compound grew eerily silent for an instant. Then the maelstrom erupted. Vehicles screeched to a halt outside the front gate of thick wrought iron. Firing resumed inside the building.

Max turned his attention to the barred front gate and the action outside. He then peeked back to make sure Red continued covering him and Sugar. Max wouldn't have done so, except, with Red hit, he needed to know his back was covered before he turned to the cartel crew outside. Indeed, Red had his weapon pointed at the building. Diaz gave Max a thumbs-up to indicate the wound was superficial and Red was still operational.

Shots echoed from inside the building as LT's team engaged the men behind the double doors, taking the pressure off the men in the courtyard. Max couldn't see outside the front gate, but he heard a hell of a lot of voices shouting in Spanish—a language he was far from fluent in. He'd spent most of his time in the Corps stationed in Iraq and Afghanistan, and, alas, knowing some Arabic and Farsi was doing jack shit for him right now. A few Spanish words stood out though, chief among them *muerto*, dead, Coach's handiwork.

Now it was showtime for Max and Sugar.

"Y'all ready for this?" Sugar asked, teeth gleaming in his black face. The other seven members of the team had blackened their faces for this mission, but Sugar's deep complexion didn't require that precaution.

Max nodded. He traded his assault rifle for the custom 40mm pump-action grenade-launcher slung across his back. With any fire from the building now suppressed by the breaching team, Max stepped into the open and fired a grenade at the front gate. The following blast ripped the gates off their track. A cartel doorman, armed with a pump-action shotgun, knelt dazed before the gates. Sugar cut loose with his machine gun, taking him out.

Cartel thugs poured from an ancient Ford Bronco and a Toyota pickup that wasn't much newer. Sugar had them running for cover. Pinned behind the vehicles, they made easy prey for Coach's sniper rifle. Max fired a grenade into the Bronco. It exploded in a shower of flame that ejected three smoldering bodies into the air.

Shouts quickly turned to screams. Realizing the Toyota no longer presented safe cover, cartel men took flight from behind it. Max pumped the launcher, fired, and destroyed the pickup, taking out two cartel men who had moved too slowly.

Max estimated five or six cartel thugs still stood, including one man at the rear shouting orders. Two men split from the group, one going left and the other right to provide flanking fire. The rest of the men stormed the gates, ready to take on Max and Sugar as opposed to Coach's sniper fire, which they hadn't any hope of countering. Max and Sugar took cover behind the adobe walls on either side of the gate, ready to turn the cartel's attack into a suicide charge with their crossfire.

* * *

Lance Thompson, LT to the team, peered around the corner and saw stairs leading upward through his NVGs, which painted the tiny, tenebrous world of this cartel outpost in varying shades of ghostly green. The interior of the compound lay cast in dark shadows to unaided eyes after Max's team had blown the power.

The first bullet cut a swath through his communications earpiece, ripping his helmet from his head and burning his ear. LT ducked back behind the corner as more gunfire rained down the stairwell. He stood stunned. The bullet hadn't even grazed him; he'd merely been burned by its velocity. Irish, who was stacked up behind him, picked up LT's helmet and handed it back to him. LT put it back on but found his headset dead.

"Fuckin' AK up there," Gable growled from behind him, his Alabama drawl yowling and practically incoherent.

All three men recognized the gun's distinctive metallic clatter as the cartel man emptied a magazine. And then he stopped, likely to reload. Not about to wait for confirmation, Gable jumped out onto the landing, his AA-12 shotgun at the ready and pointed up the stairs, with Irish right behind him. Not for the first time, LT felt impressed by the balls on the former Ranger, which were fortunately backed by solid instincts. If not for the latter, Johnny Gable would have been wasted years ago.

With Irish and LT following, Gable took the stairs two at a time. Two blasts from Gable's automatic shotgun tore apart the corner of the wall at the top of the stairs where the cartel thug crouched. The man cried out in pain and did not return fire.

Gable charged on up the stairs. The top landing consisted of a hallway that ran to the left. He paused on the penultimate step with his shotgun leveled at the corner. LT pulled a flash-bang grenade and tossed it over Gable's head to carom off a wall and down the hallway. The blast would temporarily deafen anyone hiding up there, but the breaching crew had the corner protecting them.

The grenade exploded. Gable rounded the corner and shot the AK man twice as he lay bleeding from his upper chest, disoriented from blood loss and the flash-bang. LT took point again, having recovered from the shock of his very near miss a few seconds before. He caught a glimpse of the dying cartel member, two fist-sized holes punched through his chest by the shotgun. He added a 5.56mm round into the guy's head as he stepped over him.

LT assessed the hallway: thirty feet long with four doors, three spaced evenly on the left wall and one on the right wall about ten feet away. The situation reminded him of a game show. Their prizes were behind one of those doors, but they had a clock to beat and no time to open the wrong ones. With winning being their only option, the consolation prizes were a trio of shallow graves in the Mexican desert.

Unlike the other three, the one on the right seemed to be some exotic wood. "That one," LT said. "Cover us, Irish."

"All over it," Irish acknowledged in a voice that rumbled like distant thunder over the Texas plains.

Posted to the opposite side of the door from Gable, LT brushed his fingers over the wood—teak or mahogany. The man in charge likely worked behind it, and therefore the women would not be held in there. He was just about to rescind his last order and search for the victims behind the first of the other doors when he heard an unmistakably feminine scream from within.

"Well, whaddaya know," Gable observed. "You the boss for a reason."

LT didn't have time to congratulate himself on his own instincts as they now screamed at him that this was a trap. "Watch it," he cautioned.

Gable nodded. "Feelin' it too." He reached for the knob. It turned in his hand.

Trap, indeed.

Gable pressed his large frame against the wall as he bashed the shotgun butt into the door, which swung inward. Electric light poured from inside. Both men instinctively stepped back, successfully dodging the brunt of the explosion. Temporarily deafened by the blast, LT scanned the wall opposite the door, now blackened and pockmarked with several hundred small, smoldering holes. There were seven hundred bb's in a M18A1 Claymore mine, LT recalled from his training years before, and it looked as though every single one had missed him and Gable.

LT and Gable donned their NVGs and put their weapons to their shoulders, then rushed back to the door in a heartbeat. Bullets smacked into the doorframe, fired by two cartel men crouching behind a flipped desk of heavy wood that would have been at home in a lavish New York office. Instincts took over now. The two men had ascertained in nanoseconds that there were no women in this room, only the enemy, and they took them out accordingly. Gable used his shotgun to bore through the desk, taking one hostile out with the fourth blast. LT squeezed a burst into the other as he dove from behind the desk in vain.

This section of the office lay in ruin. They moved inside, flowing like water; LT and Gable up front and Irish covering their backs, movements choreographed by years of training and experience. Another section of the room lay to the left, partially screened off by a row of decorative mahogany pillars ornately carved into alluring female figures. Beyond the pillars stood an actual billiard table, the sort with no pockets and only three balls, centered within a ring of leather couches and chairs. LT fired three rounds into the back of one couch, moved forward, then eyeballed the floor space beneath the billiard table. The room was empty.

He noticed another door to the right on the far wall.

A muffled female voice screamed again; this time, LT could make out the word *please.*

"Bin-go," Gable stated.

There was nothing to it but to do it.

The two men posted on either side of the locked door. A single shot rang out, followed by a scream. Gable blasted the lock with the automatic shotgun.

LT's brain registered details as they moved in: a windowless room, maybe eight by fifteen; one bare bulb hanging from the ceiling providing dim illumination; three women in various states of life and death. A filthy, older man with an ancient Uzi sprayed bullets at them, two of which hit LT in his body armor, center mass, just after he squeezed off a burst with his rifle. LT's aim proved superior—one of his rounds found the man's larynx, another found his jugular vein, causing a fine red mist to spray across the room. LT dropped to his knees and gasped for breath after the punch of the bullets, but far from his first time getting shot, he knew he'd be fine.

His focus zoomed in on the other cartel thug, who held a

shapely yet battered brunette woman hostage with a pimp-chromed .45 pressed to her temple. LT recognized her from the mission briefing as their main objective, Diane Laird. Her two friends, likewise kidnapped, lay at opposite ends of the room on thin, filthy mattresses saturated with blood. One woman, obviously dead, was missing half of her blonde head; the other might still be alive. The thug's eyes latched on Gable, who had his shotgun leveled at the man. LT knew he wouldn't fire—no way could Johnny Gable engage the tango without killing the woman. The AA-12 wasn't designed for precision work.

"Come on, *pendejo*," the Mexican taunted Gable.

The sweaty cartel member's gold toothed smile and wide eyes would have appeared maniacal to eyes less seasoned than LT's. In truth, the man was scared shitless and doubtless resigned to his fate. He would blow Mrs. Laird's gorgeous head off within the next few seconds. LT had his weapon on the guy but didn't have a shot.

"You ain't winnin' this," Gable growled, taking a step closer. "I want what we came for."

Something arced over LT's head. It landed on the wooden floor with a solid *thunk* and rolled toward the thug and his hostage. For an instant, the Mexican took his eyes off Gable and LT, who at the last second shielded their faces as the flash-bang grenade exploded.

LT heard cursing from both men in the room and a scream from Mrs. Laird, followed by a shot from the .45 as he tried to regain his senses. He gazed up and saw Max stride through the door as he fired two silenced rounds from his rifle. The thug's .45 dropped with finality to the floor. Mrs. Laird lay on the floor, sobbing and holding her ears. Gable had dropped to his knees, shaking his head.

Irish joined them at the door. "Strike three," he called flatly, though one corner of his lip curled up in satisfaction.

LT released a pent-up breath, his ears still ringing. "Yeah... You can still pitch 'em, Irish."

Max took in the room with expert eyes, noting that Gable wore an irritated expression and hadn't transitioned to a more precise weapon. "We done wasting time, gentlemen?" Max strode out of the room, yelling over his shoulder, "Grab the bodies and get her ready for transport."

THE IMAGE ON THE GIANT FLAT-SCREEN MONITOR FROZE ONCE again.

Elizabeth Grey gritted her teeth and growled. She had several million dollars invested in this new satellite-messaging technology and, as of yet, it didn't function any better than Skype or Facebook Messenger. Her IT director would receive an earful of bile in the morning.

"Say again, Dr. Jung," Elizabeth instructed when the doctor's image reanimated. "I didn't get any of that."

"Sorry, Ms. Grey. Now, let's see..."

Elizabeth's eyes darted to the other monitor as she waited for the doctor to collect his thoughts. The live video feed showed faceless men in white rubber HAZMAT suits trudging into an ice cave. The video shifted to another camera inside the ship. There, two scientists attempted to squeegee a puddle of the black matter into a container

for further study. The substance separated into several black iridescent blobs that seemed to roll effortlessly across the shiny metallic
floor, forcing the scientists to give chase. Its consistency reminded
Elizabeth of mercury. The goo didn't have a name yet—simply 'the
substance' to all concerned—but its discovery would rock the scientific world. A living specimen of primitive extraterrestrial life made
for the greatest discovery in mankind's short history on the planet,
along with the extraterrestrial ship they were still exploring.

Elizabeth thought of the hundreds of millions of dollars in company funds and her own fortune she had dumped into this project.
She'd paid five million to silence the hermit trapper who had found
the narrow ice cave leading to the derelict spacecraft buried deep in
an isolated Alaska mountainside. The trapper took the money and
promptly disappeared. Her investigators confirmed he'd abandoned
his shack in the wilderness for a condo in Aruba. They would continue to surveil him to ensure he kept his silence. And that trapper
constituted only the beginning of her expenses.

The most loyal foremen and workers from her construction
division had built Base Camp and widened the ice cave to allow
easier access to the ship. It had taken months to even gain access
to the ship's interior. Her team had tried all sorts of high-tech tools
and substances to cut into the hull. In the end, high-pressure water
eroded a breach in the ship's hull. Greytech's top scientists presently
swarmed throughout the spacecraft, gathering samples of the goo
and earmarking other alien technologies for further research.

They had gained access to only a small fraction of the ship.
What they'd discovered already presented a lifetime of research.
Secrecy was paramount, and her entire security apparatus, both
onsite and here at corporate headquarters, remained constantly on
full alert to spot any potential information leaks. The field operation

had been impossible to fully hide. All moves by a Fortune 500 company such as Greytech were observed by the business media, and the government had likely taken an interest in her project as well. So, she hid the project in plain sight and billed it as an archeological expedition. She even went as far as making a generous donation to the archeological department at her alma mater, saying that it had always been one of her passions.

*If the government were to find out what I've got...*Elizabeth's eyes fell on the portrait of her son, Edward, propped up on her glass desk. *No. No, that's not going to happen. It's locked down tight. I just need more time.*

Dr. Jung, haggard from lack of sleep, continued, "The mere longevity of the organic matter is astounding, considering the spacecraft crashed before the last Ice Age. That it remained alive and active with no apparent life support is nothing short of a miracle. And if more specimens are preserved in the cargo hold, they may be even healthier. This substance has presented some very unusual cellular qualities. All indicators support the likelihood of sentience." He smiled, the crooked slant of his lips matching that of his thick, horn-rimmed spectacles, likewise askew. Though extremely intelligent, Ms. Grey insisted that he keep his comments brief and free of scientific jargon, which tried her patience.

She tried not to show her pleasure at this information. "What about the other specimen, the passenger?"

"Dr. Rogers has informed me that her team needs more time to study the passenger and the life-support technology sustaining it before attempting revival, or they risk losing this one as well."

"I won't have this one dying, Dr. Jung. Impress upon Dr. Rogers the urgency of the passenger's survival. If you don't think she's up to the task, let me know and I will find someone who is." The passenger could save her years of research and clear up all mystery of the craft's origin, provided they could communicate with it.

Dr. Jung grimaced before he continued. "Dr. Rogers wishes to spend another ninety-six hours examining the life support technology before attempting to revive."

"She has seventy-two, no more. What were the DNA results for the dead passenger?"

"Inconclusive so far. Dr. Rogers's people are working feverishly, I assure you."

Elizabeth sighed and took a moment before confirming a course of action. As important as the passenger was, the goo remained even more so. *Such longevity. Does it have curative properties as well?*

She would never find out if the government stepped in.

Elizabeth Grey had never been one for extracurricular interests. Her passion involved developing new technology, her lifelong work. Her only other interest, alien phenomenon. Now she had reason to pursue it, as well as specimens to study—specimens that might provide a cure for terminal illnesses. Hell, specimens that might unlock the very secrets of immortality. Finally, her billions and resources might have found a cure for Edward.

"Right now, the substance concerns me more than the passenger, Doctor. All scientists, with the exception of Dr. Rogers's team, will concentrate on collecting and qualifying the substance. We need to learn all we can as fast as we can. We're running out of time. I can't keep this quiet for much longer."

"Yes, Ms. Grey. All available resources are being brought to bear, I assure you."

"I want progress, Doctor, not assurances. Contact me with updates every eight hours. There is another delivery of advanced test equipment arriving tomorrow morning, along with more scientists and engineers. Find suitable work for all of them. No one sits idle on this project."

Dr. Jung nodded emphatically. "Yes, Ms. Grey, I will see to it."

"Is there anything else?"

Dr. Jung hesitated and peered off-screen. He swallowed hard before he spoke. "Yes, we are missing a researcher. There may have been a security breach. Mr. Salerno will brief you on the details. I will update in eight hours as requested."

"Very good, Doctor."

Nicholas Salerno, Director of Security on site, appeared on screen, his visage tired as well. His dark, spiked hair showed more grays than she remembered. "Ms. Grey, we are unable to locate Greg Ramone, Dr. Lawrence's research assistant." A file readout and a picture of the young man appeared on the other screen. "He left the camp late this afternoon to check some perimeter sensors and never returned. This is the most recent footage we have of him." A video of Mr. Ramone checking out with the security guard played on the screen as he spoke.

He continued, "We conducted a search and found some... remains...but no body. It appears that he may have been attacked by some sort of wildlife, perhaps a bear." A grainy picture of some trampled ferns covered in blood appeared.

"We also found this." He held up a satellite phone in front of the camera. "It isn't one of ours. It appears to have been smuggled into the site."

Ms. Grey took a breath before responding. "No one leaves the camp alone anymore, and they all must be cleared by you. Find out how he got the sat phone into camp and who he contacted ASAP. You assured me you could keep this site secure, and I'm holding you to that. Take care of this loose end personally. Record it as an accident, but do whatever it takes to keep OSHA out of this."

A nightmare scenario played out in her mind: the entire area sealed off; the spacecraft dismantled and shipped to Wright-Patterson Air Force Base for studies, the results of which would never be revealed; the goo's healing properties isolated and put to use, though only to keep certain select people alive. Her Edward would die, but David Rockefeller might live another hundred years courtesy of her discovery.

Enough. There would be no government intervention. Besides, she had already taken steps to avoid that. She would go viral with her discovery when the time was right. After that, the government could try all it wanted to deny the existence of extraterrestrial life, but it could never bury the technology. She suspected that this might not be the first time humanity had found evidence of alien life.

Elizabeth tapped the keyboard on her desk. Mr. Salerno disappeared, replaced by an overhead view of the ship's cargo hold, packed full of gleaming spherical containers, each the size of a compact car. They were seamless and appeared to be chrome plated, though Elizabeth knew they were constructed of a stable, super-dense isotope, unhexquadium-482, a substance well beyond humanity's current scope of manufacture. The engineers roaming the hold examined them closely, searching for a way to crack one open.

Elizabeth watched the monitors, toggling continuously through over three-dozen live camera feeds covering both the ship and the base camp. Everyone moving; no one goldbricking. As she watched, she mentally noted some minor improvements in procedure that she would relay to Dr. Jung in the morning.

Her gold watch read one thirty-two a.m. "Lights dim." She swiveled her chair around and examined her reflection in the window. Considered beautiful by any standards, she could see only fatigue and age in her countenance. Raindrops trickled down the smoked glass windows of her corner office, the lights of Seattle's skyline setting them agleam like so many cats' eyes. All furniture and appliances in the room were streamlined and ergonomic. The office was spacious enough, though hardly the huge workspace preferred by most CEOs of Fortune 500 companies. Elizabeth concentrated better in a limited workspace, always had. She'd composed her most brilliant academic works in a squalid ghetto apartment a few blocks from the University of Chicago, back in the days when she had to scramble for grant and scholarship money while waiting tables thirty hours a week. She still practiced austerity in her personal habits. No lasting success had ever been founded upon overindulgence.

Likewise, no one had ever become rich by sleeping eight hours a night. Elizabeth slept when she had to, and never for more than four hours at a stretch. She had a private bedroom, bath suite, and fitness spa built next to her office, accessible by a concealed door. Though she owned a lavish home, she lived at work for all intents and purposes. Her home served for entertaining, but there had been little to celebrate as of late.

Yawning, she rose and started for bed.

Faintly, as she began falling asleep while typing notes into her tablet, Elizabeth remembered she had neglected to call Edward. She hadn't seen him in several days, with the alien project consuming all her time. She thought about calling—her phone beside her on the nightstand within easy reach—but did not. He was likely on morphine and asleep for the night. Besides, she wanted to contact him with solid information, with *hope*. Would she have it in eight hours? Likely not. *But by tomorrow evening...*

She fell asleep thinking of Edward in the full vitality of his youth, cured and prepared to conquer the same world she had.

MAX NEGOTIATED THE SUBURBAN THROUGH THE NO-MAN'S-
land of abandoned buildings, vacant lots, and scattered slum housing that made up the far west side of Mexicali. Riding shotgun, Sugar
gave him directions to the airport via the Google Earth app. Sugar
remained in fine spirits, though he had been injured in the firefight
when bullets chewed up the remains of the front guard shack, propelling wooden shards through the air at a deadly velocity. He and Max
each had several small splinters sticking out of their camo utilities,
but Sugar had taken a six-inch shard in his left bicep. He'd pulled it
out himself after the battle, but if he remained in pain, it didn't show.

"Bang a left here, Chief," Sugar instructed.

"Gotcha." Max turned accordingly.

He glanced into the rearview to check on Diaz and his patient,
Mrs. Laird. He didn't bother asking her condition since she'd been
tortured and raped multiple times and forced to watch both of her

friends die from the same treatment. LT's crew had extracted the bodies of the other women as well, so their families would at least have the comfort of laying them to rest. Their corpses lay folded in body bags in the SUV's cargo section amongst weapons and some remaining ammunition. The dead were never left behind, if at all possible. From day one of his Marine training: never leave a man behind. It wasn't good for morale, Max knew, but more importantly, it wasn't good for business.

"All right, make this right, and that should take us out to the main road," Sugar instructed.

Max turned. Coach, piloting the SUV at Max's bumper, followed. This dirt road was an improvement, relatively flat and somewhat free of holes. Max dropped his foot, eager to put Mexicali and this goat fuck of a mission behind him. *May I never return to this hellhole again.*

"Sweet, sweet pavement!" Sugar pointed ahead to the next intersection. "Right here takes us straight to the airport."

Max slowed to make the right. Partway onto the road, he stopped the Suburban dead.

"What's goin' on?" Sugar asked, his voice dropping an octave.

Max pointed right. The distant horizon grew brighter, though not from the dawn, as it was only one in the morning. Lightning strobed red and out of rhythm, beating the night sky from behind a rise. It crested the horizon two klicks distant and broke into a myriad of flashing red.

"Federales," Max said as he wrenched the steering wheel left and floored the SUV.

Coach's voice crackled in Max's headset. "Chief, what the fu— Never mind." He followed Max onto the highway.

Mrs. Laird began to panic in the back seat. Diaz busied himself trying to calm her.

"Sugar, find us a spot down this highway, a nice straightaway just past a bridge if there is one."

"On it." Twenty seconds passed before he announced, "Got it."

Max tapped a contact on his phone and dialed, the tone coming over the speakers via Bluetooth. "Yeah, Max?" answered a deep voice appropriate for a radio host.

"Jay, we got unfriendlies. Can't make the airport. Get the bird in the air and fly to the following coordinates. Max relayed the info as Sugar read off the coordinates for the stretch of highway he'd chosen.

"What the fuck, Max? Am I landing in a beet field or some shit?"

"It's hardball, an asphalt highway. And if you wanna get paid, you'd better land there and pick us the fuck up. Understood?"

"Uh, no. You're going to get my FAA license revoked. This is a Learjet, not a Harrier. There's more to landing a jet than..."

Max took a deep breath before responding. He'd worked with Jay Andrews, a former Marine aviator, on several missions during his time in the Special Activities Division of the CIA. Cautious but possessing rock-steady nerves, Jay balked at risks not previously calculated. Max thought, not for the first time, that Andrews just wasn't cut out for this business, despite his unmatched excellence as a pilot.

"Just get the bird up and land her at those coordinates. You owe me. You seem to forget that."

A deep-throated growl was the only response for several seconds. "Fine. On my way. Out!"

"Asshole," Sugar muttered as the call ended. He glanced at the passenger-side mirror. "Shit, Max, these motherfuckers are gaining on us."

Max had the SUV floored, but the excessive weight in the vehicle made it unresponsive. He and Sugar were a quarter-ton by themselves, then add two more passengers, all their gear and ammo, and two corpses. Coach's vehicle came in even heavier; his SUV had fallen behind by a half-klick with the Federales closing fast.

"We're taking fire, Chief," LT announced through the headset.

"Roger that, LT. We got a plan. Just keep following. The bird is gonna meet us on the highway."

After a brief pause on the line, LT replied, "Understood." The *thump* of an M203 grenade launcher followed.

Max watched in the rearview as a Federale car careened off the highway in flames, flipping several times before coming to rest on the desert floor.

"Man, this is one fucked-up country," Sugar commented as he readied his machine gun for more action.

Max didn't respond, though he couldn't have agreed more. Nothing needed to be said regarding the cartels and Federales working hand-in-hand in many Mexican precincts. Corruption and collusion between governments and criminal elements were standard operating procedure worldwide. The big difference in Mexico: nobody tried to hide it.

"How much further, Sugar?"

"Maybe ten klicks to the bridge."

Sugar's ten klicks turned into twenty, though, to Max, the distance could have been measured in inches for the time it took to drive. Coach remained in constant contact, relaying their battle with the pursuing police who had backed off considerably beneath the rain of bullets and grenades loosed upon them. His prior work consulting SWAT teams made him downright encyclopedic on police procedures. Yet still, they came, secure in the knowledge that Max's team could never make it back across the border through a checkpoint. They could afford to be patient; to their knowledge, they had nothing but time.

"Here we go." Sugar pointed ahead to a bridge maybe fifty feet across that spanned a steep-sided gulch.

"LT, block both lanes of this bridge with your vehicle and then abandon it in flames, copy?"

"Affirmative."

Max stopped the SUV at the far end of the bridge and got out. Coach pulled up and blocked the bridge about a minute later. Both teams piled out with Red laying down suppressive fire with his machine gun. They had maybe forty-five seconds on the Federales. LT wrestled a folded spike strip from the cargo area and unfolded it across the highway at the end of the bridge. The rest of LT's team sprinted for Max's SUV. No way would the car hold five more men and their weapons.

LT laid the spike strip in place. Red tossed a grenade into the SUV, then he and LT ran for Max's car. The SUV exploded in a fountain of fire, glass, and metallic shards.

"LT, Coach, get in," Max ordered. That left Gable, Irish, and Red, who were all over six feet tall. "You guys are luggage. Let's do it."

"We're like clowns with guns!" Gable said with a laugh as he climbed onto the roof. Irish and Red joined him as they stood on the running boards and held onto the roof rack.

The Federales pulled up behind the burning car and opened fire. Gable responded with his grenade launcher as Max tore off down the highway.

Sugar dialed Jay. "Where the fuck are you, man? You see our marker?"

"Yeah, you're kinda hard to miss. ETA one minute."

Two klicks later, Gable confirmed over the headset, "Bird's inbound."

No one greeted the good news with cheers or whooping. They were still a long way from getting out of this shit.

"They've moved our car," Irish announced.

"Acknowledged." Max drove on for another klick, then stopped the SUV so it blocked the road. No orders were necessary—gear and bodies exited the SUV as if it were on fire as well. The grenade tossed in as if it was a mere afterthought.

The Federales broke past the first burning SUV as Jay touched down and reversed thrust on the turbojets. Max's full team shuffled down the road to meet the plane, LT leading the way while Max hung back with Sugar, who carried Mrs. Laird in addition to his gear. Irish and Red, the other two massive men in the group, each had a corpse slung over their shoulder and were likewise trudging slowly.

A horn honked from behind them, a Mexican motorist pissed off at the flaming SUV blocking his path.

"Blow it out your ass, Pablo," Irish bellowed, not bothering to look back.

Seconds once again stretched to eternities. The plane came to a halt amidst the roar of the jet engines, drowning out the sirens of the approaching Federales. Max figured they had about half a minute to board the plane and take off before it got shot all to hell.

The plane's passenger door dropped, revealing a flight of stairs, atop which stood a copilot Max had never seen—a short, nondescript, bearded fellow in a leather jacket who kept peering back at the approaching red lights as if another look would reveal them as a mirage. He said nothing as the team loaded up. Only once did he show any emotion—revulsion at the sight of the women's corpses.

Max didn't like him on sight, mostly because he didn't like dealing with unknown people on a mission. This guy had little or no experience in life-or-death situations, which could get people killed.

"I got this. Get back in the cockpit."

He moved off without a word.

"You assholes loaded yet?" Jay shouted from the cockpit.

The instant LT cleared the step, Max replied, "Yeah, get us out of here." As the plane jerked forward, he raised the stairs, sealing them inside. He moved toward the cockpit as they gained speed.

Max watched as Jay taxied the aircraft midway down the improvised runway, the lights of the police cars growing in the cockpit window. He deftly spun the aircraft around and aimed the nose of the plane away from the oncoming pursuers. Max felt the plane surge ahead as Jay rammed the throttles forward to their full stops, the plane quickly picking up speed.

"We're taking fire," LT shouted.

The plane suddenly lost a bit of speed on its takeoff run.

"What the fuck?" Max growled.

"Lost number two engine." Jay maintained a veteran's veneer of calm, but Max sensed rising tension in his reply.

"We're on fire!" LT announced.

"Shit!" Jay cut the fuel to the burning engine.

"Can you get her in the air?" Max asked.

"Eh, yeah. If we don't take any more damage. Got to get over this guy first."

Headlights approached from dead ahead—the guy who'd been honking his horn had driven overland around the burning SUV and now headed straight for them.

"Is this fucking guy out of his mind?" the copilot asked.

"Shut your pie hole, dumbass," Jay replied.

Playing chicken with a plane, Max thought. *Yeah, this guy's on something.*

The nut didn't deter Jay in the slightest. Simple wisdom finally prevailed, and the car swerved off the road a split second before it would have collided with the plane.

"Fuuuck this!" The copilot's voice suddenly unnaturally high.

"Here goes jack shit," Jay muttered as they approached the burning SUV a hundred yards away.

Seventy-five...

Fifty...

Twenty-five...

The plane lifted into the column of smoke and flame. Max estimated they'd cleared the car by maybe three feet, tops. He remained standing in the cockpit entryway as they gained altitude at an agonizingly slow rate.

Fuck it, we're flying. Nothing else mattered at the moment. "Nice work, Jay."

"Go strap in, Max," Jay demanded balefully. "And you can consider us even now."

Max nodded, turned, and headed for a seat.

"Hey, where's our peanuts, Andrews?" Gable demanded.

The cockpit door slammed in response.

* * *

A moderate yet relentless breeze off the Pacific Ocean blew across the vast stone patio, riffling the water in the swimming pool and occasionally rattling the cups and saucers in the coffee service. The canvas pavilion overhead snapped in the wind while protecting the three men from the searing Southern California sun.

Another man came and poured coffee in Max's cup.

Max poured the milk as fancily as he could, trying to remain at ease as he attempted to dilute the dark liquid into something palatable. *I hate coffee.* Max had sat through more of these after-action meetings than he cared to remember. He already wanted to forget this one.

"Let me make sure I understand this," said Everett Massena, Max's client. Approximately fifty-five years old, Massena seemed the prototypical nabob. Though not a physically imposing man, he sprawled out in his wicker chair to take up a lot of space. He wore a cream linen suit over a blue shirt with a white collar, white French cuffs and a red ascot knotted at his throat. *Like a millionaire at the racetrack.* "So, you were in the midst of this raid and reinforcements were called in?"

"No." Max choked down his exasperation. The guy kept spinning Max's statements, repeating questions and pulling new ones from a seemingly inexhaustible supply, expecting Max to step on his tongue. The elite business types all acted like that. "The reinforcements just showed up. That compound hadn't been alerted to our assault before they came in. Someone had tipped off the cartel that we were going to hit the place. If the call had come sooner, I wouldn't be here, and your wife, Mr. Laird, would still be a hostage."

"Yes," replied the third man at the table, Thomas Laird, Diane's husband. "You have my eternal gratitude, Mr. Ahlgren." The words fell flat—as wispy as the man who spoke them.

Everett Massena, a titan in the business world, owned the home and belonged in opulent surroundings. Max got the feeling that Laird, however, came from humbler stock, probably married into money.

"And mine as well." Everett leaned forward. "Nevertheless, Mr. Ahlgren, your mission ended in failure. You were supposed to bring back three women alive. Two are dead, and you claim they were shot at the last minute, is that correct?"

Max gritted his teeth, through being patronized. "One succumbed to torture earlier. One was shot as my men breached the room."

"But you didn't see this happen?"

"I was out front killing the reinforcements that mysteriously showed up."

"So how can I know that the ladies didn't die of negligence by your team?"

"Why don't you ask your sister, Massena? Does my explanation not corroborate with what she told you?"

Everett's face grew a shade redder. "I wouldn't know. She just came home from the hospital. I haven't had a chance to speak to her of this nightmare, nor do I wish to ask her. She's scarred for life as it is. I'm not about to aggravate the situation."

"You're going to have to." Now Max leaned his considerable bulk forward across the glass table. "Because you owe us money, Mr. Massena, and I'm not leaving here without it. Yeah, the mission could have gone better. But we saved your sister, and we brought back the remains of her friends. We did everything possible. Payment was not dependent on the success of the mission, if you recall. My men bled, and you're not about to stiff us on payment."

"You may wish to change your tone, Mr. Ahlgren. You're not the only man of violence on this patio." Massena flicked his eyes toward a fat, hulking Samoan in a Hawaiian shirt posted by the French doors leading into the house. "Now, in the business world, Mr. Ahlgren, payment is contingent upon success in all aspects of a project. You were to return three women safe and sound. You didn't. It's as simple as that. Not to mention I fronted expenses for your team to locate and surveille the cartel safehouse in Mexicali. No. No, I'm afraid your mission was a failure—"

46

"We were set up," Max repeated slowly. He'd stood up without realizing it and now towered over Everett, who didn't appear intimidated in the slightest.

The Samoan moved a step closer and Max noticed he held his right hand behind his back.

"Yes, you keep saying that. But by whom? Who set you up and why?"

"My evidence points to your brother-in-law."

Silence but for the ocean breeze.

"Preposterous!" Everett thundered.

"Indeed, it is," Thomas Laird concurred, still flat and unemotional.

Max rounded on Laird. "Really? Then why did you take out a life insurance policy on your wife three weeks ago?"

"I'm not about to answer to the likes of you."

Max pulled a sheaf of papers from his back pocket and slammed them down before Everett. "A private investigator's report, Mr. Massena. I had him look into the recent affairs of Mr. Laird. I think even a man as skeptical as you will find the report is accurate. I believe you've even used this same investigator a time or two yourself."

Everett reached a tentative hand forward, then snatched up the papers. He glanced at them. "Explain yourself, Thomas."

Thomas Laird laughed. "There's nothing to explain. Yes, I took out a policy on Diane recently. What of it? I have a policy listing her as my beneficiary as well. The timing is mere coincidence, I assure you."

"Really?" Max asked. "You know what I find amazing? The fact that this is our second meeting since I returned your wife and the only emotion I've seen out of you so far is some defensiveness regarding a big, fat life insurance policy. You didn't so much as smile or even appear relieved when your wife returned."

"That's because I wasn't supposed to come back," said an unmistakably female voice.

The men gaped at Diane Laird, who had just rolled onto the patio in a wheelchair. A nurse attendant pushed Mrs. Laird to a spot at the table, then left her patient with the men. Though she would bear her bruises for some time, Mrs. Laird's condition appeared much improved. Max figured the wheelchair was more a doctor's order than an actual necessity. She was one tough lady; he couldn't help but respect her.

Max nodded to her. "Pleasure to see you again, Mrs. Laird."

"And you, Mr. Ahlgren."

"Diane, you mustn't—" Everett began.

"Everett, please, this needs to be cleared up. Mr. Ahlgren is only partially correct. I wasn't supposed to die. As you well know, dear Tom has had his problems with gambling and drugs. He borrowed money from the cartel to pay his gambling debts, but when the time came to pay back his loan, he forfeited and offered me and my friends in return for his life."

Thomas edged toward her. "You're full of shit, Diane. You don't know what you're saying."

"Oh, but I heard it straight from the lips of Don Ernesto Aguilar, second in command. We were awaiting shipment to Sana'a, where our buyers were waiting." She paused to let that sink in.

All three men sat stunned—Max and Everett at this revelation, and Thomas as he struggled to construct some sort of plausible explanation.

Diane continued, "I'd been sold to a child prince. I suppose he prefers older women. Whatever the case, all three of us were broken in, multiple times, for our new duties as sex slaves." She gave her husband a scathing glare. "So, Thomas's debt had been paid in full, plus he had that life insurance policy worth several million dollars. By the time he'd dug himself into a new hole, I would have been missing long enough to be declared legally dead." She smiled at Thomas with soft lips but hard eyes. "Of course, that's all hearsay, inadmissible in criminal court. But I hope you get good at picking horses, asshole. You're about to owe me all sorts of alimony."

Thomas had lost his tongue somewhere between sex slavery and declaring his wife legally dead.

Diane motioned to the Samoan, who waddled over to the table. "Take me back to my nurse, please."

"Yes, ma'am."

As the Samoan turned her chair from the table, Diane added, "Pay Mr. Ahlgren, Everett. With a bonus, for the love you bear me."

Everett paused as he processed everything and nodded. "Consider it done." He turned his attention to Thomas. "You'd best leave my house before I have Loki extract your teeth via your rectum."

Thomas composed what passed for his dignity and departed with his head high; guilt just one of many things he'd lost at the casino.

"It appears I owe you an apology, Mr. Ahlgren."

"Don't bother. Let's get this over with."

Max departed the Massena estate with six hundred thousand cash in a briefcase—half a million for the mission plus the bonus. The team would be pleased. He knew better than to be so optimistic though. Word didn't always travel fast in the world of mercenaries and their employers, but it always got around sooner or later. A sloppy job like the Mexican debacle would tarnish his team's reputation, despite Thomas Laird's betrayal. *You're only as good as your last mission.* Max descended the front steps of the mansion. *And after a performance like that, we might not work again for a long time.*

ELIZABETH GREY'S SINGLE, RATHER STOIC CONVICTION—IF YOU don't lead with your feelings and work your ass off, you'll find success—was being tested. Sorely tested. And she sensed an uprising from that most pointless and deleterious of emotions: worry.

She pressed a prompt on the touch-screen of her glass desk. The flat-screen monitor on her wall illuminated and, for the fifth time, began playing a transmission recorded almost thirty-six hours earlier at the dig site.

"Ms. Grey, th—" Several seconds of garbled and pixilated nonsense followed before the person onscreen continued. Elizabeth forgot the woman's name, but as one of Dr. Jung's assistants, she held a Ph.D. in anatomy and cell biology. "—thing's gone wrong, Ms. Grey." The doctor gasped, taking a deep breath that lasted several seconds. She appeared ready to sob but held her composure. The camera twitched ever so slightly, indicating that someone had been holding it as opposed to having mounted it on a tripod. "Several people are missing: four research personnel, three from securi—"

An explosion interrupted the woman who cried out in terror.

"Jesus!" someone shouted, likely the cameraman. The camera pointed to the ceiling, then panned wildly across the laboratory before breaking into large pixels of slow-motion gibberish that lasted for thirty-four seconds before focusing on the woman again. The cameraman's shaking hands made it look as though the building was being rocked by an earthquake.

"Ms. Grey, we think the substance...that it might have something to do with the substance. Please! We need help. Now! Send more security. Send help!"

The final few seconds of the transmission included a crash, quickly followed by the tinkling of shattered glass. The woman jerked to her right in sheer terror. "Oh my God!"

The camera panned wildly again, punctuated by a man shouting, "Shit! Come on; let's go!"

The monitor went black.

Though disturbed, Elizabeth Grey hadn't been overly concerned when she'd first viewed the transmission. Shit had obviously hit the fan, but panic simply wasn't in her nature. In truth, she'd been most annoyed that progress on the operation had halted. She'd taken proper measures, dispatching a team of two medical doctors and fifteen seasoned security personnel to the site, along with a chopper full of emergency medical supplies, food, and ammunition. Her instructions directed the head of the security team to contact her immediately when they landed and to keep her updated as they ascertained and eradicated the cause of this delay.

She never heard from her security team. The helicopter hadn't returned. Attempts to contact Base Camp proved futile. The last satellite pass had shown no apparent movement or activity at the base, only the remnants of a couple small fires in some of the outer prefab structures. With the situation now officially out of control, Elizabeth Grey had almost reached the point of worry.

But damned if she wouldn't continue to fight. What she had discovered was far too valuable to let go. What if they had discovered a sentient alien life form? She had only recently begun to truly accept that as a viable option. From the beginning, the possibility had teased her imagination, but the overwhelming weight of responsibility for such a discovery had finally taken root. Dangerous or benign, it had to be contained, researched. Lives were at stake, not only at the site but in hospitals across the country. Her Edward. She hoped—no, she *knew* this life form held the key to saving his life and many others. Everything Greytech had discovered could advance scientific and technologic research centuries ahead. The ramifications were almost unfathomable.

This project would survive. She would see to that. After she had come so far and had invested so very much, no other option remained. She'd pushed her company ever closer to the financial precipice, cleverly hidden by hundreds of complex financial moves and accounting sleight of hand. This gamble had to pay out.

Elizabeth swiveled around in her chair and gazed at the Seattle skyline, though, in actuality, she stared through it, her mind a thousand miles away. *So, how to rectify this situation?*

Twenty well-paid, expert security personnel had failed to keep the site safe, and now fifteen more were missing. Overwhelming firepower alone wouldn't bring the dig site back to rights. She needed something more. She needed brains and balls, someone used to dealing with unusual and sensitive problems.

And I needed to hire them yesterday.

Greytech had numerous military contracts and a small army of military contractors employed across the globe. However, she had already deployed all her top security personnel plus all her immediately available assets to no avail. If she tried to pull more people from the business units to assemble another team, eyebrows would raise. No, she needed help, outside help.

She revolted at the thought; she hated asking anybody for anything. Wealth and power meant never being beholden to anybody. However, Elizabeth knew every second that passed marked the loss of more precious time and decreased her chance of regaining control of the situation.

She pressed another prompt on her touch screen to summon her go-to personal assistant, Cynthia Hilliard, who entered the office and stood before her desk within a matter of seconds. Though Elizabeth had several personal assistants, Cynthia had been with her the longest and was one of the very few people she trusted. Forty-one years old, Cynthia appeared to be roughly half her age, courtesy of an exhaustive workout routine and minimal cosmetic surgery. She kept her natural blonde hair short and possessed a delicate, rather Nordic physiognomy capped off by a striking pair of cobalt-blue eyes. Perhaps the highest-paid personal assistant in the world, Elizabeth found her indispensable.

"Yes, Ms. Grey?" Privy to all of Greytech's secrets, Cynthia had viewed the final transmission from Base Camp and had been a bit shaken by it. But she had recovered her bearing quickly, eager to implement whatever plan her boss had in mind.

"Call my government contacts: CIA, State Department, DOD. I need the most skilled tactical team currently available. Somebody that can work off the books. Be even more discreet than usual."

"Immediately, Ms. Grey."

"Thank you."

Cynthia turned and marched for her desk in the outer office. Despite the overnight hour in DC, she soon announced over the intercom, "Ms. Grey, I have Mr. Peter Banner on line three."

"Thank you, Cynthia."

Despite holding a mid-level position with the CIA, Banner had proven capable of bypassing much of the government's cumbersome and comically inefficient bureaucracy. She tapped the prompt to open the line. "Good morning, Mr. Banner."

"Morning, Ms. Grey. So lovely to hear from you again." Banner spoke with a down-home Oklahoma drawl. To the uninitiated, he sounded like a guileless country boy.

Elizabeth knew better. "I have a situation."

"Alaska?" Elizabeth heard his barely audible chuckle, confirming her fears that word had gotten out.

She stifled her anger at that fact. "I need a tactical team, the best available; I need a capable leader, no by-the-book tool; and I need absolute discretion. I'll see to it that you're well compensated, as always."

"Uh-huh. Well, I won't promise anything, gotta see who's available."

"The best, Mr. Banner. Nothing less. Pull favors to make this happen. If it takes further incentives, let me know." *And don't fuck with me.*

Banner laughed heartily, all for effect. "As you wish, Ms. Grey." A moment passed in rapid typing, punctuated by heavy thumps on the enter key. "It's your lucky day. Just so happens I have the perfect man for the job. We may be able to help each other out. Now, let's talk about Alaska..."

MAX SAT IN A PLUSH RECLINER IN THE DARKENED LIVING ROOM of his home—a rambling contemporary overlooking the city of Las Vegas. Through floor-to-ceiling windowpanes, he watched the twinkling lights of airliners stacked up in the night sky approaching McCarran International Airport in the valley below. He sipped on a cold glass of Diet Mountain Dew, grateful for a brief respite from the administrative side of his job, his eyes burning from the last two hours he had spent gazing at his laptop.

The numbers didn't lie. The team needed another mission. Though his team filled a unique niche, it operated like any other business. There were bills to pay, most recently for the repairs on the jet they had used to escape Mexico, and for the two SUVs they had destroyed in the desert. Max also leased a large warehouse on the outskirts of Vegas for training and storage. He had an assistant on salary to help with logistics, manage payroll, and oversee the generous benefits he provided for his team. To cover all his bases, he also kept a lawyer, a private investigator, an IT specialist, and an accountant on retainer. Max's business was killing; he had never expected to play the role of businessman, for which he found himself wholly unsuited.

He placed his glass next to the Glock 21 pistol and bottles of prescription pills on the end table. From the bottle of Ambien, he swallowed several pills, washing them down with the rest of his soda. That dose would have put down an average man for a couple days, but Max had developed a tolerance from years of use.

On his cell phone, he selected the picture gallery for his son, David. However, as he scrolled, the images soon morphed into the faces of the dead. Some were brothers in arms; others had died by his hand. Their faces had become more familiar than those of his ex-wife and son, as though they'd been seared into his brain with a white-hot branding iron.

Max had dealt fate to dozens of people. The only life he didn't have the nerve to take was his own. At first, he'd killed naively for his country, then for his fellow warriors, and eventually for his own reasons. Now, he simply sold death for cash. He still liked to think he was helping people, perhaps making the world a better place, but he knew deep down that he was nothing but a hired gun—a tool the wealthy used to solve their problems. Though a consummate problem solver, Max usually left a bloody, smoking mess in his wake.

* * *

A rocket-propelled grenade blasted the vehicle in front of Max's command car, an armored Humvee with a turret-mounted machine gun. The world seemed to slow down as black smoke poured from the burning vehicle. AK rounds smacked into the side of Max's Humvee. Iraqi insurgents poured down a narrow alley to his right, snaking their way toward the convoy.

Max yelled for his turret gunner to engage them, but received no acknowledgment of the order. Overhead, Lance Corporal Humphries slumped over his M2 .50 caliber machine gun, blood oozing down the front of his plate carrier. Max pulled the young Marine, barely nineteen, from the weapon into the bed of the vehicle. He applied pressure to the neck wound, the blood warm and sticky on his hands, but realized immediately that he couldn't possibly save the kid.

The sensation of slow forward progress dissipated. Max's panicked driver, Corporal Reynoso, shouted at him. It took Max a moment to make out his words over the maelstrom of combat. "Sir, what are your orders?"

They were boxed in behind the burning vehicle. Max's instincts returned to him. "Get out and find cover! Return fire!" He climbed into the turret and pulled back the charging handle on the machine gun. He got a bead on the insurgents and poured a steady stream of .50-cal fire down the narrow alley, taking out six men in the group.

One boy stopped, dropped to a knee, and aimed an RPG at his vehicle.

Max depressed the butterfly trigger on the weapon and fired a two-second burst.

The kid's head jerked back as though he'd been struck in the forehead with a howitzer shell. His anti-tank weapon fired in the same instant. The rocket shot a few feet over Max and his men to explode inside a building across the street.

His Marines returned fire with M16s as Max continued pouring bursts of lead into the insurgents. He heard the typewriter chatter of a SAW light machine gun and the slightly slower, bass drum rapping of another M2 .50 cal.

Max paused and took brief stock of the situation. Two of his Marines lay wounded beside the trailing vehicle with a Marine and a corpsman huddled over them. Far down the alley, more insurgents darted toward the rear of a building. The men toward the rear of his convoy were pinned down, taking fire from two buildings his vehicle had just passed. The enemy intended to flank his Marines. A simple mission to provide security for a broken-down supply convoy while it completed repairs had turned into a major firefight.

Max dropped down from the turret and picked up the radio handset. "Lima 6 Alpha, this is Lima 2 Bravo actual. We're under heavy small arms fire and need immediate air support and medical evac. How copy?"

After a long pause, a distant, garbled voice in the headset replied, "Copy, Lima 2 Bravo. We have two Snakes inbound to your position. ETA ten minutes."

Shit! We'll all be tits up in ten minutes. "Copy, Lima 6 Alpha. Marking our position with yellow smoke." Max dropped the handset.

Corporal Williams fired his rifle wildly over the hood of the Humvee, his first taste of combat.

It isn't like the movies, is it? Max got out of the vehicle, grabbed Corporal Williams by the shoulder, and barked in his ear: "Find Staff Sergeant Badger and tell him I have two Cobras inbound in ten mikes. Tell him to pop yellow smoke to mark our position. I'm gonna try to flank these bastards. If I'm not back in five, he's in charge!"

Max hefted his M16 rifle and charged down the alley, now clear of insurgents. Nearing a dumpster, he slowed. On the far side, an old man holding an SKS rifle crouched behind it. Max fired a burst into the startled man, who raised a futile hand to stop the rounds from tearing into his body.

By the time he reached the end of the alley, Max's heart pounded in his throat. He peeked around the corner into the next alley. When he saw no enemy, he cautiously continued down the backside of the building, spying an open gate to a courtyard ahead. He swept the courtyard through his rifle's sights, found it clear, then proceeded down the cracked cement path leading from the gate to a shadowed doorway. Though he could clear the room beyond that doorway with a grenade, he only had two remaining. He'd need them for the rest of the building.

Instead, he ran the last few feet into the doorway and slammed his shoulder into the door. The cheap lock held, but the door frame shattered. The door swung slowly inward. Max paused for a second, listening, then pivoted and ducked inside. He swept the room with his weapon and glimpsed movement in the corner. Tensing his finger on the trigger as his eyes adjusted to the gloom, he realized two women and some kids cowered in the corner. He pressed his index finger to his lips, hoping they would understand his silent order to keep quiet.

One of the kids pointed a finger straight upward before the older woman quickly grabbed his hand and pulled it down.

Max crept down a hallway toward the stairs. The chatter of weapons firing from rooms above grew more distinct. Atop the stairs were two doors; Max chose the door on the right. He crouched, pulled the pin on an M67 hand grenade, opened the door, and tossed it inside. He heard panicked cries in Arabic before the grenade detonated, a concussion that shook the adobe building as he hit the deck.

He jumped to his feet and kicked open the door, mindful to stay well clear of any windows in the room. Two insurgents lay dead on the floor. Max caught a glimpse of another man's legs as they disappeared behind an overturned couch. He rounded the couch and put three rounds in the insurgent's back. The room had no other exits.

Through a window, he witnessed the chaotic scene below as his Marines continued to take machine gun fire from the room next door.

Max returned to the hallway, then approached the second door. When it cracked opened, he fired his M16 into the door. Splinters flew. He felt the *thud* through the floor when the hidden insurgent fell. When Max slammed his shoulder into the door, he exposed two stunned insurgents reloading a Russian DShKM heavy machine gun. Max unloaded the rest of his magazine into them.

As he scanned the rest of the room, he ducked below the sight-line from the street through the window. He pulled a fresh magazine from the mag pouch on his chest. The door at the back of the room swung open, and with no time to reload his rifle, Max reached for his pistol. He completed his draw as an insurgent hastily fired into the room. When Max returned fire, the insurgent responded by feebly tossing a grenade into the room as the bullets struck him.

The grenade sounded like a bowling ball as it slowly rolled across the wooden floor. Max tried to stand, but his body stiffened up like setting concrete.

He moved impossibly slowly.

Then he saw movement in his peripheral vision.

Corporal Reynoso entered the room. "Look out, sir!" He shoved Max backward as he dove atop the grenade, smothering it with his body.

Max found himself falling over a flipped table, the only cover. The explosion rippled through his body before he landed. Three or four tiny pieces of red-hot shrapnel tore into his legs, each feeling like a particularly nasty hornet sting.

In the ensuing stillness, Max stood, limped over to what remained of Corporal Reynoso's body. Most of his legs were gone.

When Max rolled him over, scorched and shredded entrails poured from the corporal. He cradled his lifeless body and mumbled to himself, "No! You were supposed to stay down there, goddamn it! You were supposed to stay!"

His ears rang from the grenade blast, but he could still make out some sort of alarm sounding faintly through the firefight. The ringing continued until the dead Marine dissipated mercifully into the ether, but Max knew he'd not seen the last of that bloody, dusty street in Iraq.

Max opened his eyes. The digital clock on his stereo system read two thirty-one a.m. He'd slept a few hours. Most people—normal people—might have been pissed at someone calling in the middle of the night. Max, however, felt grateful. He'd endured many nightmare encounters with his past, haunted by the faces of dead friends and foes alike. He never died in his dreams. Yet he suspected the dead would take their vengeance on him some night, landing a killing shot that would stop his heart.

Max turned on the lamp and fumbled for the cell phone. "Yeah?"

"Hey, Max-a-million!" a drawling voice boomed into his ear.

It took a moment for Max's brain to identify the Okie, then he sighed. "Banner? Are you fucking kidding me?"

"No jokes about it. Long time, no see, old friend. This isn't a social call, unfortunately. I have something for you, if you're still in the game, that is."

Max sat up straighter, his interest somewhat piqued despite his distaste for Banner. "I might be."

Banner chuckled. "If you aren't, it might be in your best interest to cut short your retirement. Trust me on that; this job is a big one. You ever heard of Elizabeth Grey? Greytech Industries?"

"Sure. I happen not to live under a rock."

"Multi-billionaire, Fortune 500. And she wants to hire you for what might be your easiest mission yet."

"Yeah? And what's that?"

"An on-site security assessment. Nothin' to it, Max, and her money's good on Friday, as my daddy used to say."

"I'll bet."

"And you'd win. You interested?"

Max's mind shifted into overdrive while considering the offer. Was he interested? Why was Banner offering it to him? The two of them hadn't exactly parted on the best terms in the agency. The team had returned from Mexico only days before. Despite being in phenomenal shape, Max felt tired and achy. The sheer intensity of battle drained a lot from a young man, and in his early forties, Max no longer fit that demographic. His team weren't spring chickens either. No one had been seriously injured in Mexico, but Max doubted they could function at their best. His guys needed a break, even if the job proved to be as simple as Banner claimed, which it likely would not. He'd worked with Banner on many occasions as part of the CIA's Special Activities Division. Somewhat upstanding for a company man, he could dissemble and prevaricate with the best of them. Trouble seemed to follow him, though, and Max never got the best vibe from the guy. Plus, he tried to stay clear of jobs with ties to the Agency.

However, after the disheartening mess in Mexico, a slam-dunk mission, if that proved true, could do wonders for team morale. "I need a lot more info before I can commit."

"Understood. You'll receive an email with all the details in a few minutes. Trust me, you'll wanna take this one."

"You already said something to that effect. I'll judge for myself."

"You'll thank me, Max."

"We'll see."

Max terminated the call and pulled on some sweatpants and a t-shirt. His broad shoulders cast a shadow in front of him as he walked down the hallway. He was built like a professional athlete—sprinters legs, a muscular torso, with a barn-door-sized back from which hung long, burly arms, with biceps the size of softballs that ended in thick, calloused hands. His body a by-product of years of intense physical training that showed the scars of decades at war. His sandy-brown hair was cropped short and it framed a ruggedly handsome face with honey-colored eyes that took in more than they gave out.

He trudged to the kitchen. The room never saw much action since he considered cooking a tedious pain in the ass. Still, he could appreciate the stainless-steel appliances and the practicality of the pots and pans hanging over the center island. He opened the fridge and pulled a can of Diet Mountain Dew from the open twelve-pack on the bottom shelf, along with a single-serving container of no-fat cottage cheese. Max didn't drink coffee; an anomaly among Marines. He simply hated the taste of it.

Carrying his soda and the first of many small meals he would consume that day, Max made for his office. He passed through the living room, admiring the breathtaking view of the Las Vegas Strip before he switched on the overhead lights. He'd purchased the home in the Seven Hills section of Henderson, Nevada, in the hope that it would come to symbolize the sort of stability necessary to win back his son and perhaps even his ex-wife. A vain hope as it turned out.

There were thus no feminine touches evident in the decor. The sparse furniture was expensive and plush; the TV a giant flat-screen. And as much as he sometimes abhorred the duties of his profession, his home's decor bespoke of his fascination with fighting and warfare. A Spartan warrior's bronze helmet sat square in the middle of his coffee table. A mannequin dressed in an authentic Crusader's chainmail hauberk stood in the entry hall. An antique gun cabinet of glass and ebony displayed his prized collection of WWI infantry rifles with fixed bayonets, the Allied and Central Powers both represented.

Max took a last glance at the distant blinking neon of the Strip before moving along to the smallest of his home's five bedrooms—his designated office space. His curved Mameluke officer's sword hung prominently on the wall behind his glass computer desk. A painting of Smedley Butler leading Marines taking Fort Riviere, Haiti, adorned another wall.

Once he woke his desktop computer, he checked his email on his private server. An advertisement for Persian Rug Liquidators' clearance sale, this weekend only, had posted three minutes earlier. He clicked on it and the information from Banner came on-screen.

The mission statement appeared simple and vague enough: secure site and conduct security assessment for client, Greytech Industries. GPS coordinates of the site were provided, along with several satellite photos of the area. The mission needed to be conducted ASAP.

Max scrolled down and saw a number that shook the last vestiges of sleep from his brain: ten million. "God damn," Max breathed as he took in the figure, one million two hundred and fifty thousand per man, not counting expenses and his firm's cut. He shook his head. Simple missions didn't pay in the millions, but he vowed to withhold further judgment until he'd assessed all the data. He still pondered why the man had referred him this mission, his mind searching for a connection. Though it wasn't unusual to get referrals from contacts in the government, they typically got a commission from the client.

He downloaded the attached satellite photos and examined them closely. They showed the rough terrain of Alaska's heavily forested, high-altitude wilderness in November. *Perhaps this mission wasn't the softball it appeared to be. Not with that price tag. There's a catch, likely several.*

Max opened a search engine and spent the next half-hour researching Elizabeth Grey. She was of the old-school notion of hard work, apparently: brilliant student from a lower-middle-class background; a partial-ride scholarship to the University of Chicago followed by work as a low-level R&D employee at a green energy firm. She had perfected and patented a revolutionary photovoltaic process in her late twenties and used it to found the fledgling Greytech Industries, a corporation that now netted profits of over seven billion dollars per year. With guts, gumption, and genius to spare, Max couldn't help being impressed. And she was quite a looker too; a tight body with the best face money could buy. It might be worth a trip to Seattle just to see if she lived up to her photos.

The email listed Ms. Cynthia Hilliard as his contact at Greytech, available twenty-four seven. Max called her from the phone on the desk. Despite the early hour, the woman on the line sounded wide awake and a bit winded, perhaps getting in an early workout before reporting to work. He told her he was interested in meeting with Ms. Grey to discuss the mission. She reminded him that time was of the essence and assured him that transportation for his team would be waiting at the airport in Seattle. Max didn't ask her for any further details regarding the mission, and she likewise volunteered none. Their brusque conversation suited Max just fine.

He dialed Lance Thompson's home number, got no answer, and then tried his cell.

"What's up?" LT asked over club music thumping in the

background.

"Plenty. Where are you?"

"Luxor. Just finished playing poker with some friendly Japanese gentlemen. You should come on down." Female laughter tinkled in the background, followed by a mumbled remark from LT.

"Good take?"

"Eh, not bad, but I've done better." More mumbling as LT said something to the woman. "Sorry, I'm a little busy here, can I call you later?"

"No. We have a mission or a potential mission at least. We're flying to Seattle and we have to be ready to go immediately from there."

"Damn, already? We just got back." LT sounded annoyed.

"This is our biggest mission ever. Think over a million bucks per man."

LT laughed. "Well shit, why didn't you say so?"

"I'm serious. Get the team assembled with all their gear and book us a jet to Seattle, departing ASAP."

The line went quiet for a moment. "Gotcha. I'll call you with flight info when I have it." LT ended the call. If there was one thing he valued more than poker and pussy, it was earning the kind of money that provided for his prodigal lifestyle.

Max packed and loaded his gear before cramming in a quick workout in his extensive home gym. LT called at six twenty-seven. Their flight out of Henderson Executive Airport left in an hour. Go time. As dawn broke, Max climbed into his black Ford Raptor and headed off, his mind energized about the potential mission ahead.

MAX WATCHED THE HANGARS AT HENDERSON EXECUTIVE Airport zip past as the jet blasted down the runway, the roar of its powerful engines barely a whisper within the luxurious cabin. He knew Henderson well: the closest airport to his home and also the location of the helicopter flight school where he had been taking lessons for a while. With almost enough hours of supervised flight, he itched for his first solo. As it stood, he figured he'd learned enough to fly a chopper in a pinch if necessary.

The jet leveled off after making its initial climb out of the airport. Max swiveled his extra-wide leather lounge chair and gazed out the window at the barren desert and lonely brown peaks far below, pondering how it was the warrior's lot to travel. *How many flights to how many godforsaken places?* The nations, some of which no longer existed, rattled off in his head, the places where he'd faced the most intense violence rising first from his memory.

Maybe this really would be a skate mission. *No, nothing involving Banner is easy.*

Max turned from the window to face the luxurious cabin. There, seven men in various states of dress and coherence sat, waiting to be briefed on why he'd summoned them from bed—or, in Gable's case, from the floor of Sugar's den—to carry out another mission in some frozen circle of the world. The time for answers had come.

Mindful of the low ceiling, Max stood. He turned and faced the rear of the cabin.

The flight attendant secured her refreshment cart and hastily retreated into the galley. This particular flight crew had never flown his team before, and all of them seemed nervous about his men. Mostly bearded and covered in tattoos, they more resembled a biker gang than a band of elite professionals.

Max cleared his throat, then grasped for the right words. He saw no reason to reveal the client until they'd struck a deal.

Chris "Red" Bergman recited: "Friends, Romans, countrymen..." This elicited chuckles from a few of the men.

"Put a sock in it, Bergman," LT grumbled from his chair across the aisle from Max.

"Four score and seven..."

"Red."

"Ich bin ein..."

"Red, shut the fuck up."

Peevish as usual, I see. LT seemed a bit disgruntled of late and ripped from his favorite casino in the middle of the night, his demeanor had turned temperamental.

Max clapped his hands once. "Lend me your ears." This elicited a couple more laughs from the group. "I'll keep this brief, gentlemen, because I know about as little as you do. The job isn't a lock yet, but this could be our biggest mission yet, should we be fortunate enough to land it."

"Big how?" asked Johnny Gable, who had spent last night on the floor, a flag planted in his chest by Johnny Walker. His breath smelled flammable from several feet away. "'Cause that last mission was about the biggest shit storm I ever signed up for. We could stand to think small for a while."

Several nods concurred. LT, however, seethed in his seat, ready to pounce on Gable for the interruption.

"Big bucks." Max gave them a moment to roll their eyes in certainty that he was exaggerating. "One-point-two-five million per man, minus the firm's share and expenses."

"God *damn!*" Sugar gasped, while a couple of whistles accompanied his comment.

Max replied, "My sentiments exactly."

"And the catch?" Brian "Irish" McKern asked in his deadpan Texas twang.

"Hell, if I know," Max responded. "We're to secure a site and provide a simple security assessment."

Gable raised a single skeptical eyebrow. "Sounds like a Nigerian scam to me."

"Nobody asked you," LT snapped.

"Well pardon me for questioning why we're being paid millions for doin' nothin'."

Max had expected as much from Gable. Almost fifty years old, Gable looked the part of an out of the box GI Joe with his vintage sixties crew cut and faded forearm tattoos. On the job, he was a consummate professional, possibly the best breaching man Max had ever worked with. On the town, he was a terror, the sort of man that made commanding officers cringe whenever he went on liberty.

"Fair enough question," Max admitted. "I don't have the answer. The rest won't be revealed until we reach Seattle. So, rest up and enjoy the flight. I need bushy tails on every one of you bastards if we're going to get this done. That's all."

Since there were no more answers, the men had no more questions. General small talk took over. The flight attendant moved forward with the refreshment cart.

"Don't look so nervous, Diaz." Red dropped a meaty hand on the medic's shoulder.

"Don't get shot this time," Diaz responded to general laughter. This made former Navy Corpsman Javier Diaz's third mission with the team. Since Red had worked with him in Afghanistan years before, the Miami Cuban was a natural choice to replace Max's last medic and security man, Casey Collins, who'd gotten cut down on a mission in Georgia.

"Speaking of which, how's the arm?" Max asked.

"Tip-top, fer sure," Red replied in a thick Scandinavian accent. "Viking power!" Standing six-foot-five, with long red hair and two sleeves of Nordic tattoos running up his arms, Red certainly resembled a Viking, though he actually hailed from Montana. Max envisioned him, battle-axe in hand and one of those ridiculous horned helmets on his head, sacking an English village. The image never failed to crack him up. A retired Air Force master sergeant, Red served as the team's communications specialist, appropriate for a guy who didn't know when to shut the hell up. He was equally proficient with heavy weapons

"You best be tip-top," Sugar informed Red. "I ain't taking up your slack again."

"No problem." Red nodded toward Gable. "You got enough of a mess to clean up after."

Coach put in, "He cleaned up after him just this morning."

Max couldn't imagine sleeping in Sugar's den. Known to the team as the I-Love-Me Room, Sevelt "Sugar" Jackson displayed his various citations and awards from his distinguished career as a Navy SEAL in there. The Odd Couple came from diametrically opposed backgrounds: Sugar from the mean streets of Compton; Gable from the backwoods of southern Alabama. Something between the two men clicked, and it wasn't just a mutual love of soul food.

"No, my wife cleaned up after him this morning," Sugar corrected. "I swear, sometimes I think that woman loves him more than me."

"She is a glutton for punishment," Irish teased. Like Sugar, he'd served on SEAL Team Six, and the two men were familiar with each other. "Taking care of two misfit toys."

"A fly wouldn't land on that woman, saint that she is." Gable punctuated the comment with a pointed finger.

The flight attendant stopped her cart next to him.

"Bloody Mary," Gable requested.

LT shook his head. "I don't think so."

"Let it go," Max muttered to LT. Louder, he stated, "One hair of the dog, Johnny, no more."

"Thanks, Chief. You're quite the gentleman and a good judge of bad whiskey."

Coach snickered. "Ah, you bring a certain element to every mission, Gable. Uncertainty." Steve Thatcher had been an Army infantry officer and a member of Delta Force. He was also the team's de facto physical training instructor, hence the nickname "Coach", due to his obsession with dieting and fitness. His sniper skills had proven invaluable over and over. The battle in Mexico would have ended much differently if not for his uncanny accuracy with a rifle. Max had plucked the now retired police officer from NYPD SWAT where he'd grown bored as a marksmanship instructor.

"Here's to ya, Thatcher." Gable raised his freshly mixed Bloody Mary. "What would we do without you?"

"Feed the maggots in a bombed-out drug compound in Mexico?"

"You have an overly inflated opinion of your abilities."

Always ready to exchange insults, Coach grinned. "Stick to blowing shit up. It's the sort of slop artistry you're good at."

Gable tipped his head. "It's how wars are won, my friend."

"Just remember you owe me." Coach said it lightly, but he wasn't joking.

"You're not about to let us forget," Irish muttered. Coach's personality could wear on folks, and it grated on the big man from Texas more than the others. A bit laconic, the rare humor that passed from his lips came out desiccated.

Like any salty military officer, Max maintained an appropriate distance from his men, for familiarity did indeed breed contempt. LT and Irish were as close to friends as he had on the team. After putting in his twenty in the Navy as a SEAL, Irish had taken his breaching skills to the FBI's Hostage Rescue Team. It had taken some doing to pry him away from lucrative government work, with its pensions and perks, but Max prevailed by touting the freedom to be had by working independently. In the end, after years of taking orders from martinets obsessed with SOP and brown-nosing, Irish gladly accepted Max's offer.

Red suddenly yowled like a cat, raising his hand and scratching the air twice, throwing in a couple of hisses to keep it real. "Such vanity! You girls should be rushing a sorority or something."

Max suppressed a laugh but couldn't help smiling discreetly behind a hand.

LT sighed. "The shit I have to listen to for one-point-two-five million dollars." He rubbed between his eyes as though dealing with a severe migraine.

"Get some rest, LT," Max urged. "I'll need that poker face of yours in the meeting." He could brief his second in command on their client later.

LT shook his head, comically small atop his thick, bullish neck. "No, I'm good."

Max nodded. "You know what's best for you."

"Put in many a marathon session at the card table, my friend."

"I suppose that's true enough. But I have a feeling you're about to meet your shrewdest opponent to date. Be mindful of the stakes."

"Always."

Max nodded and then reclined his chair. *Man's strung tighter than a hillbilly's banjo.* Thankfully, Max didn't have that problem. Like most Marines, he could sleep anywhere anytime, so long as he had nothing else to do. The swiveling, oversized lounge chair on the private jet served him as well as his bed at home. He drifted off into his waiting nightmares.

* * *

LT fumed in silence as Red ordered a double Jamison's, neat, all for LT's benefit. Like Gable, Red considered it his duty to needle LT whenever the opportunity arose. At least Gable didn't take notice of Red's order; he would have been screaming for another Bloody Mary if he had.

On his tablet, LT studied the files Max had provided, stopping occasionally to switch windows and play a game of poker against the computer. He pulled his vape mod and tank from the inside pocket of his sports jacket and started puffing away. Diaz joined him, and the two began steaming up the cabin.

After pronouncing the food on the breakfast cart unhealthy, Coach made the mistake of saying he was considering becoming a vegan. Gable and Red wasted no time pouncing on that.

Meanwhile, LT tried to mentally drown them out as he vaped. He hated people in general, and the incessant talking battered him. Someone was always running their suck. On top of that, Red was too fucking sarcastic by half. Gable annoyed the piss out of him too, but a mutual respect lay buried between them, only to reveal itself when they were under fire. They'd gone through a lot of shit together, not that anyone would guess from the way they spoke to one another.

When did it devolve into this? LT mined his memory, digging deep shafts as he searched for a clue to when things had changed.

LT grew up in the Low Country of South Carolina. Half-Thai and half-white, he harbored strong Buddhist leanings courtesy of his mother. A gifted student of mathematics and statistics, LT had graduated in the top five percent of his class at The Citadel. He received a commission as an Air Force officer shortly after graduation and spent most of his military career working in G-2 intelligence.

LT didn't see much combat until his third tour in Afghanistan, when he was assigned as a liaison officer working with a company of Marine Raiders led by Capt. Max Ahlgren. Though he enjoyed the mental challenge of working in intel, LT found it child's play compared to carrying out actual operations against the enemy. The crucible of combat felt liberating and thrilling at first, before it became addicting and mentally taxing. LT felt a grim satisfaction after every mission. He'd done his part to spread freedom and make the world safer, just as he'd been taught to do since his first days as a plebe at The Citadel, though with each mission, he found it increasingly harder to feel good about the work.

The Air Force promoted LT to major as a reward for his faithful service and ordered him stateside to a position at the Pentagon. After one week at the Five-Sided Puzzle Palace, he realized just how little he'd known of the big picture on the War on Terror—a war that, by its very design, would never end. He resigned his commission four months later, fourteen years into his career.

From there, it was a short hop to a higher-paying job as private security director, first working for casinos in Atlantic City and then on to Las Vegas. The jobs were cush; the action practically nonexistent. He became bored and disillusioned once again. At the end of the day, he preferred a good time and a stimulating life to the trappings of wealth.

Then Max Ahlgren found him, put him back in the field, and crammed his wallet with blood-soaked cash. Times were good, *were* being the operative word. And now? The combat, the travel, the bodies strewn across the earth in the team's wake.

LT had seen enough and knew men in this profession didn't age like scotch.

One-point-two-five million. He watched Gable bullshitting with the team, pausing in his storytelling every now and then to spit dip juice into his empty Bloody Mary glass. *If only I could be that oblivious.* At forty-two, LT had one course of action open to him. *Get it on one last time. Then get out.*

Across the aisle, Max stirred in his sleep. He jolted awake, staring at the ceiling and breathing heavily as if he'd just run several miles.

Sleep, where our demons cavort.

Max caught him watching. LT gave him a knowing nod and turned to gaze out the window at the patchy white clouds far below.

MAX AND LT ALIGHTED FROM THE REAR OF A LINCOLN STRETCH limousine outside the headquarters of Greytech Industries. They had left their sidearms in care of the team who were holding up in a posh collection of suites at a five-star hotel downtown. Meanwhile, aware of Ms. Grey's concerns about espionage, Max and LT anticipated a short arm inspection before security would clear them.

The Greytech campus presented the public façade Max had expected: lots of well-manicured green space buffering soulless, boxy buildings of smoked glass. The grounds spoke of a progressive utopian workplace where the brightest minds came not to toil, but to create. It embodied the typical face of the tech sector, both necessary and symbolic. Also symbolic was the flag featuring the Greytech logo, a silver sun casting its rays across a black field, each beam of light morphing into a flying dove. Sixteen stories up, it flew below the American flag, an innocuous, ubiquitous symbol, boastful of its solar roots.

Like the swastika, Max thought.

LT followed his gaze. "Well, we're not likely to forget where we are."

"Yeah, I'd say. Get ready for the VIP treatment." Max subtly nodded at a tall man with a shaved head exiting the smoked-glass revolving door.

Decked in a black suit, mirrored sunglasses, and wireless earpiece, the man intercepted them, extending his right hand at the last second. "Good morning, gentlemen," declared the suit. "Michael Stewart, chief of Greytech security."

Max introduced himself and LT, pondering what government agency Elizabeth Grey had shanghaied a man that polished from.

"Ms. Grey awaits," Stewart announced. "I'll process you through security as rapidly as possible."

Rapidly proved to take about fifteen minutes. Guards manning the security checkpoint in the lobby scrutinized their IDs and issued bar-coded visitor badges before marching them through a metal detector. On the far side of the metal detector, Stewart rejoined them.

Then, four security guards flanked the trio, all tall muscular men sporting holstered Glocks, standard-issue buzz cuts, and body armor beneath their black uniforms. No rent-a-cops, these were hardened products of elite military and law-enforcement units. Not one of the seven men said a word as they stepped into a cavernous elevator that appeared to be fashioned of titanium and zipped only to the highest floor.

The elevator doors opened directly into another security checkpoint guarded by four men and featuring a millimeter-wave scanner similar to the whole-body imagers found in airports. Before Max and LT could enter the beast, they first had their handprints recorded on a biometric scanner.

Though even some in his line of work might have called Greytech's security measures a bit excessive, such prudent precautions impressed Max. The CIA had trained him to enter office buildings undetected during his time at Camp Peary- aka The Farm. This security would have been a tough nut to crack.

The security detail remained in box formation at the scanners while Stewart led Max and LT across a lobby of glass and gray Italian marble. Though tiny security cameras monitored both indoors and out across the Greytech campus, here at least two covered every square inch of this floor, the workspace of Elizabeth Grey and her top executives.

Past the lobby, Stewart led them into a hallway with soaring glass windows on one side that provided panoramic views of the Seattle area. Along the opposite wall, the paintings, presumably priceless works of modern art, reminded Max of the finger paintings David had once enjoyed sticking to the refrigerator. Between them stood ebony doors featuring gilded nameplates identifying the office holders.

They continued past a reception desk. The woman behind it, serious as a heart attack, uttered something into her headset as the men passed.

Stewart put his palm on a biometric scanner outside a door labeled "BOARDROOM" and entered a six-digit code into a keypad, carefully shielding the numbers with his hand. A lock clicked, and he ushered them inside. The narrow space extended all the way to an exterior wall, glass from floor to ceiling. A glass table some thirty feet long, lined with plush leather chairs, dominated the space. At the head lay a selection of breakfast pastries and two urns of coffee. A small ice bucket containing three cans of Diet Mountain Dew sat conspicuously before the first chair on the left side of the table. Max sat, and LT took the chair to his immediate left.

"Make yourselves comfortable, gentlemen," Stewart said, already making for the door. "Ms. Grey will be with you shortly." He departed. The door lock engaged behind him, effectively sealing Max and LT in the room.

LT took a cup and saucer and poured himself some coffee. Max popped the tab on a soda. Certain that Elizabeth Grey and her team were assessing them at that very moment via cameras and microphones, both men made vacuous small talk as they waited, volunteering nothing.

Max consulted his tactical black Tag Heuer watch. A half-hour had passed since his arrival. *Typical.* Most of their clients thought of themselves as potentates, which they were in their world. Their vassals' lot was to wait upon them. Max had learned to hurry-up-and-wait back at The Basic School, but it remained a thorn in his ass.

The lock clicked. The door opened.

Max and LT stood.

Elizabeth Grey strode into the room, imperious, another woman following her like a handmaiden. Simple elegance had never looked so rich. Her jet-black hair, cut in a stylish shoulder-length bob, neatly framed a countenance both patrician and tantalizing. Never one for poetry, words such as *exquisite* and *lush* nevertheless popped from Max's brain as he watched the long legs beneath her black kidskin leather skirt propel her lithe figure confidently into the room. She awoke within Max primal instincts buried years before by his marriage. A thin silver chain studded with diamonds, her only adornment, winked from the collar of her steel-colored silk blouse. With so many physical assets in her favor, Ms. Grey didn't need to rely on baubles for attention. Judging from the way her clothing hugged her curves, Max guessed she had received some cosmetic enhancements over the years. She did not merely live up to her photos—she made them a travesty.

Max read iron determination in her gaze. Her eyes danced, a sparkling dark green—the color lakes back in Minnesota would assume beneath the late-afternoon sun. He found himself caught off guard by the allure of their near-imperceptible movements—eyelids opening wider; eyebrows surreptitiously raised for just an instant.

"Thank you, gentlemen, for coming on such short notice." Ms. Grey then introduced herself and the other woman, her assistant, Cynthia Hilliard. "Please, be seated." She acceded the head of the table, Ms. Hilliard at her right hand.

Another head-turner, Ms. Hilliard had blonde hair, cut daringly short and spiked on top. She would have commanded the attention of any room were it not for the overwhelming presence of her employer. She opened a small Greytech laptop on the table before her with quick fingers, ready to take minutes of the meeting.

Elizabeth Grey cut the pleasantries appropriately short. "The non-disclosure agreement." Thanks to Ms. Hilliard, a pair of tablets appeared in front of her guests at precisely that moment.

"Understood," Max replied, stifling his surprise that no legal beagles or officious department heads would be joining the queen and her lady-in-waiting.

They want to keep this quiet.

He scrolled through the agreement, a clone of dozens over the years. He and LT signed the electronic forms with a stylus and returned the tablets to Ms. Hilliard.

Ms. Grey rose. "Our most sensitive scientific expedition has gone dark. The information we have is sketchy, but the terrain at the dig site is problematic for communication."

Sounds like someone went to a lot of trouble to upset your operation. Max asked, "How can we help?"

Her eyes burned with resolve. "Lives may be at risk or even lost. Assess the site. Take any necessary actions to secure it and all research data. Locate our staff. Over the next two days, we will assemble another team of Greytech security personnel to maintain the site. They will arrive via helicopter within seventy-two hours of your arrival. Your team and our staff will evacuate at that time."

"What's the nature of this expedition?" LT asked. "Why would you put people at risk this time of year?"

She acknowledged him with a nod. "Mr. Thompson, the expedition is testing for a rare and potentially priceless material. Satellite imagery of the site shows no activity at Base Camp in the last twenty-four hours. Nothing is happening up there, and that is our gravest concern."

Max noticed she used the word *we* as opposed to *I*, in the manner of royalty as he scanned the large digital display showing the most recent satellite feed. "Why haven't you contacted the authorities?" He already knew the likely answer but often asked such questions to gauge the response of his client.

"Due to the sensitive and proprietary nature of the project, we naturally do not wish to involve the authorities, as their attention will invariably attract the prying eyes of the media."

Max wasn't sure what to make of her answer. Was it merely the media she wished to keep in the dark, or did she fear government intervention as well? Depending on what exactly her people had discovered, Max could understand why she might.

LT asked, "You tried to contact your team via satellite communications?"

"Yes, of course." She paused, a microsecond wavering of

uncertainty. "A magnetic anomaly frequently disrupts communications from the site. We were sending helicopters regularly, courier and supply runs, a practice limited by the weather." She adjusted the displayed image to show the helipad. "The last helicopter we sent."

"Why not wait a couple of days and send your own people to secure the camp? Why send us?"

"We did. Two days ago. They haven't reported back, and time is of the essence."

That got Max's attention, though his and LT's faces gave away nothing.

Max asked, "Have you received any ransom or blackmail demands over the past few months? Any threatening emails or phone calls?"

"No."

"Were there any identified threats assessed before the current situation? Any disgruntled staff?" LT asked.

"None that we're aware of," Ms. Grey replied. "Initial assessments listed local wildlife as potential risks, bears, wolves, and mountain lions chiefly. Nothing more. And nothing new."

Max took a moment to gather his thoughts. "I understand your need to keep as tight a lid on this as possible, but anything you can reveal regarding your expedition can only be of assistance to us."

Ms. Grey pondered for an instant, then nodded. "Fair enough." For just a moment, weariness settled over her like a puff of magician's smoke, there and gone. "This expedition is checking the veracity of some older, inconclusive satellite scans that reveal the possible location of an undiscovered hyper-dense element that may potentially have ties to an advanced ancient civilization. Our research division found and extracted a sample for further study. They determined that the element is not radioactive or toxic, merely exceptionally rare, not just on Earth but within the known universe. Securing all research data on site—the computer hard drives in particular—is of paramount importance.

"Be advised: your team is not cleared to enter the actual dig site. Your job is to secure the camp and the research data only." She paused. "And rescue our staff, of course. The dig site is an extremely sensitive archeological area, not to be disturbed. Failure to heed this rule constitutes a breach of contract. Is that understood?"

"Very well, we'll stay out of the dig," Max replied, though the stipulation raised a red flag in his mind.

"As far as the camp, we leave that to your discretion," said Ms. Grey. "An incoming weather front will cut off transportation just after noon tomorrow, so you need to arrive no later than tomorrow morning."

Ms. Hilliard passed two thick manila file folders across the table to Max and LT.

Ms. Grey continued, "Those dossiers contain the latest satellite images of the area, along with the names and positions of all staff on site. We'll need your answer in the next half-hour. Buzz the intercom on the wall when you've reached a decision. Have you any further questions?"

"None," Max answered. He locked his stare on hers and the two played eyeball poker again. He opened this time, but she turned to give LT a final once-over, refusing to play.

"Very well. We'll leave you to make your decision."

Ms. Grey and her assistant gathered their belongings. Ms. Hilliard led the way out of the boardroom. Ms. Grey sashayed out slower than she'd entered, hips swaying.

Max smiled at her departing rear. *There's no mistaking that.* He leaned close to LT, who wore a cryptic smile. "So, what do you say?"

LT shrugged. He kept his voice just above a whisper. "Sounds like just another mission. How much do you think she's leaving out?"

Max sighed. "Oh, plenty I'm sure."

"Uh, yeah. A whole camp of scientists and two security teams gone black? There's some serious firepower involved here, and you know a woman like her has powerful enemies."

"Nothing we can't handle." Max instantly regretted saying it.

LT was right: they were headed into some serious shit if they accepted this mission. Yet he felt compelled to accept. Max lived for this. Besides, Elizabeth Grey awakened a puerile sense of chivalry within him. Max shook his head. *Damsels in distress? You need to grow up. Or get laid. Probably both.*

LT laughed, then leaned closer to whisper, "For the amount we'll be paid, you're probably right, it's worth the risk. Just another billionaire with too many toys and too much money. She probably doesn't realize how much she's overpaying us."

Max paused. "That's what worries me. She doesn't strike me as stupid."

"Me either. But this won't be the first mission we've taken without knowing all the facts. And you look pretty determined, so what the hell?" LT assaulted Max with a knowing smile.

Max stared at the wall and shook his head. "Christ, is it that obvious?"

"Eh, don't sweat it, Chief. You'll be well compensated." As Max's brow creased in question, he added, "Monetarily, that is."

Max chuckled. "That's what I like about you, LT. You always cut to the quick of things." Their banter filled the void as Max hedged, weighing the options and outcomes in his mind, hoping for some new information to materialize. Finally, he admitted, "After Mexico, we need this." He felt like a game show contestant as he punched the red intercom button to accept his fate.

DAWN HAD BROKEN, ALBEIT IN A HALF-ASSED FASHION. MAX watched the sky. One massive raincloud hung over their destination as flat, lumpy, and gray as a whorehouse mattress. Promising relentless piss drizzle, it spanned the heavens, allowing only remnants of light to filter through. *Ah, November in Alaska.* The temperature had risen a couple degrees since they'd landed. The brunt of the cold front wasn't due for several hours, by which time the team would be in the field, cleaning up Elizabeth Grey's mess.

Max turned to LT, who stood next to him by the hangar door. "Guess they weren't kidding about this front."

LT blew out a huge cloud of vapor through his crooked smile "It's like you jarheads say, 'If it ain't raining, we ain't training.'"

"Yeah, that's usually the way things go. Let's get 'em briefed and get a move on."

"Sounds good."

Max and LT retreated into the hangar, deserted but for the jet they'd flown in and the team who lounged on folding chairs, awaiting the mission brief. Visual aids had been provided: a PowerPoint projector and a portable movie screen. Max moved to the screen; LT pulled up the latest satellite image of the Greytech site on the projector. The team sat relatively quiet but for Red and Coach who were in the midst of a spirited political argument.

"Yeah," Red gibed, "you're an interesting paradox, a peacenik who shoots people for a living."

Coach leaned a bit left politically and wasn't afraid to make his views known. *As if it matters whether someone leans left.* Max knew America was embroiled in an endless war now, while nobody seemed to care, and things weren't likely to change no matter which side was running things. But Coach, Red, and countless other Americans still believed the fanciful promises of jackasses and elephants.

Before Coach could retort, Max announced, "All right, gents, shut your sucks and listen up." He stepped aside from the screen and pulled a laser pointer from his pocket. "You already know what we're here to do, so here's how we're gonna do it. This is a satellite image of the Greytech mining operation from yesterday. The whole shebang is located in a valley about two hundred klicks from here. The area is heavily forested, as you can see, at an altitude of about seven thousand feet, so I hope everyone's been keeping up with their PT."

Max circled the red laser dot around the mountain slope occupying the western edge of the photo. "This is Boundary Peak 171, which is neatly bisected by the US-Canadian border. And here is the Greytech mine." Max pointed to a glacier high on the mountain slope, punctuated by a gaping black hole in the ice. A couple of rectangular prefab buildings and several pieces of yellow heavy equipment surrounded the hole, parked in seeming disarray. "We're ordered to steer clear of their mine on pain of not being paid, so heed the warning."

Johnny called out, "Don't have to tell me twice!"

Ignoring him, Max moved the pointer down the valley, along the stream flowing from the glacier. "This cluster of buildings along the creek is Greytech Base Camp, our destination. The west end of camp appears to be largely logistics and support—helipad, storage structures, Conex boxes, motor pool, various repair facilities. Upstream, closer to the dig site are the living quarters and laboratories. Looks like something went down right here." Max pointed toward a building that appeared blackened as if by a fire. "Hard to say what happened, but things are definitely amiss, which is why we'll insert here, about six klicks from camp." Max pointed along a lengthy yet narrow break in the evergreen cover. "The coordinates where the Greytech expedition attempted to send its final transmission are about two klicks away, our first waypoint en route to Base Camp. Outside communications after we leave the drop zone will be damn near impossible, due to powerful, localized magnetic interference around the dig site. Don't be surprised if this anomaly affects our comm gear as well."

Irish asked, "You think that clearing is wide enough to land a chopper?"

"Maybe," Max said, "but be prepared to fast rope in. I don't want to jeopardize the bird or give the pilot a case of the ass—he's likely the guy they'll send to pick us up. We'll secure the DZ using our usual SOP: split into alpha and bravo teams, hasty three-sixty on the ground, then move out to the northwest side of the clearing. Then on to the first waypoint. Alpha team to consist of myself, Red, Irish, and Diaz; bravo team is LT, Sugar, Gable, and Coach. We'll re-form our usual breaching and security teams right before we move into

Base Camp."

Max hated like hell handing Sugar over to LT, even for a hike, but it couldn't be helped if he wanted a heavy machine gun on each team. LT would be tempted to frag Red, their other gunner, if Max tried it the other way.

"Once we find out what happened at the last point of contact, we'll climb this ridge to waypoint two and recon Base Camp before moving in to secure. Start at the east end and work our way west. A Greytech helo with more security personnel will arrive for extraction in two days, by which time we'll have the place sorted."

Max paused, using the moment to gauge the reactions of his team members. All appeared serious and contemplative as they thought things over, except for Red, who always appeared not to give a shit during briefings. No matter; he would have Max's back on the ground.

Max continued, "I won't pretend to know much about what we're getting into. We're pretty much flying blind here, but if you have any questions, fire away. I'll try my best to answer."

Sugar spoke up: "Chief, you were a company man. You think maybe the government is behind this? Our fine civil servants have been known to take whatever they can't buy. And if this new element has any use, they'll want every last ounce of it."

Max shrugged. "Crossed my mind a time or two on the flight up. But hell, it could be anybody: Russians, mercs for a rival corporation, natives pissed off about a violated burial ground. There's no shortage of potential bogeymen. Bottom line: secure the place, grab the data, and rescue any survivors. We aren't being paid to figure out what happened, and negotiating with un-friendlies isn't a condition of our mission. We take out whoever we have to. I don't give a damn who they work for."

Irish grumbled, "I been lookin' to tangle with some Russkis again since that mission in Georgia."

"Boy, you said it," Gable agreed.

"You'll tangle with whoever the hell is there," LT announced. "Don't go in with any preconceived notions."

A sliver of temper broke through Coach's game face. "Hope I don't have to shoot anybody I know."

Red grinned. "It's a distinct possibility."

"Did you not hear what the fuck I just said?" LT asked. "Keep pondering what you can't possibly know, and you'll be caught flat-footed by what you didn't expect."

Gable turned to LT. "Is that some kind of Buddhist bull—"

Max cut him off. "Knock it off. LT's right. Just concentrate on getting shit done, no matter what. Any more questions?"

Silence.

"All right then. Drop cocks and grab socks, we fly in half an hour."

The flight crew had gone somewhere to lay over, so they had the aircraft to themselves while they suited up. Max chose black digicam tactical gear as opposed to arctic; black would blend well with both the evergreen forest and the structures in Base Camp. He pulled on his vest, eight pounds of ceramic plates sandwiching his muscular torso. Knowing that it might be days before he took it off again, he adjusted it until the fit felt perfect. He checked his quick release tab, a cloth tab velcroed down on the front inside of the plate carrier. A pull of this handle would instantly release him from the vest. He, like the others, then repeated the process with each piece of their body armor.

Once clad in their basic combat gear, the team members found quiet corners of the plane to make last-minute calls or texts to loved ones. None of these communications revealed anything regarding the mission, including the team's present location. By this point, none of their relatives bothered asking for details.

Max pulled out his phone and opened the picture gallery, silently perusing photos of his ex-wife, Janet, and his son, David. Viewing their images jogged a memory of calling them before he headed out on a mission a couple of years back. He and Janet had still been married and the conversation immediately degenerated into the usual arguments—money, of course, and Max coming and going from their lives on an irregular basis, continually disappointing their son. He tried hard to get Janet to buck up and deal with the onerous aspects of being married to a professional warrior by reminding her of the good times they'd had and would enjoy again as soon as he came home.

"*If* you come home," Janet had replied. "Because one of these days you're not going to. What am I supposed to tell David when I never hear back from you? That Daddy won't be coming home ever again because he was blown up, burned to death, shot, beheaded by militants in some backwater shithole no one's ever heard of?"

"Janet—"

"Don't even, Max, because I won't be able to tell him anything since I won't know shit. Then I'll have to raise your son by myself. Not that I don't do that already."

"Look, I have to work; this is what I do. What do you think allows us to live the way we do?"

"It doesn't have to be this way. You could be a policeman or work for just about any branch of government. But you won't. Because you're addicted to combat."

"Oh, bullshit."

"No. It's the truth. You're not the man I married; he died in

Iraq. I'm stuck with a phantom now, but at least your son hasn't realized that. Yet. But he's learning in a hurry, a lesson taken from every ballgame, school play, and fishing trip that you miss. And I've had enough. Do things right or not at all—isn't that what you always say? Well, there's nothing right about this marriage. You can consider us over."

Max had tried to speak, only to find himself dumbstruck and stuttering. Janet's voice berated him, each sentence a mule kick to the head. Her final words shrilled in his ear: "Since you won't take your own advice and raise your son right, then you won't do it at all! We're done with you, Max. I'll have divorce papers drawn up and waiting. If you make it back, of course. Frankly, I couldn't give a shit less."

The line had then died.

Emotion was the first casualty of war. If it weren't, then every man on the battlefield would go insane at the first sight of a man being blown apart. But even now, two years since that phone call, Max nursed the hurt deep in his gut. The guilt weighed on his psyche, ruining his focus and causing his thoughts to drag before the most lucrative mission of his life. Max took one last look at David, the boy who symbolized all he'd ever wanted out of life—

Only you wanted something else.

He powered off his phone, which he stowed on the plane with the rest of his personal effects. The other team members were likewise removing all forms of identification from their bodies; a process known in the business as sterilization.

Max's memories of his family disappeared with his cell phone. He'd forced himself back on point. Proper and successful execution of the mission was all that mattered now.

"Hustle up," Max called. "Fifteen minutes to takeoff." He left the cabin, the first man dressed and off the plane. When Diaz followed on his heels, Max realized he looked physically ill. "Don't tell me my doctor is sick."

"It's nothing." The words were a croak, like a hiccup gone awry. Diaz coughed, then leaned over to spit a copious stream of saliva onto the smooth concrete floor.

"Bullshit, you look like you're about to throw up."

"I'm fine."

Max turned and stopped Diaz in his tracks. "What the fuck's the matter with you? If you're gonna hold us back, then you're damn well staying here."

That got Diaz's attention. He swallowed audibly, nodded. "I'm...I'm good, Chief. But I got some bad vibes about this mission."

"You need to secure those right now. This mission reeks like a stockyard at high noon. We all get it, and we're all dealing with it. If you can't, just say the word. I'll send you back to Vegas and hump the med kit myself."

Though Max had meant every word of his threat, that wasn't about to happen. Like every man on the team, Diaz was a pro, a man who often and proudly stated that more Congressional Medals of Honor had been awarded to Navy corpsmen than to any other MOS in the military. Bad vibes of varying degrees were unavoidable anytime lives were at stake, and though Diaz's were a bit worse than usual today, he appeared to be getting over them in a hurry. He just needed a friendly reminder of his importance as team medic.

"Got it, Chief," Diaz replied. "I'm ready to work."

Max nodded. "Good. Let's get loaded up."

Max and Diaz grabbed their weapons from the plane's cargo hold. Other team members exited the plane, either wearing solemn game faces—Coach, LT, Irish—or smiles worthy of the Joker—Sugar,

Gable, Red.

"Man, shut yo dumb country ass up," Sugar crowed to Gable, the two of them laughing at some quip as they walked over to pick up their weapons.

"No, I'm tellin' you..."

Max moved on, not caring to hear what Gable was telling anyone. *Better bad jokes than bad vibes.*

The munitions were on Greytech, which seemed only appropriate. Max usually had to provide his own munitions and supplies, problematic to transport. This airport even had an armory and barracks for the Greytech security teams, which currently consisted of the two men fortunate enough to be left behind guarding the fort. Steel boxes of ammo were laid out on the armory floor, along with wooden crates containing anti-personnel mines and various grenades: flashbang, smoke, high explosive, 40mm for the grenade launchers. Cardboard boxes held chem lights, various types of batteries, MREs, and basic medical supplies. Every man grabbed a pair of heavy leather gauntlets to wear over his combat gloves to provide additional protection for their hands when fast roping. The welding gloves would be discarded once the men hit the ground.

Max had to give Greytech logistics some credit. They'd laid out everything his team had requested and then some for this mission. There was even a six-pack of Diet Mountain Dew. Max only stuck two cans in his large combat backpack, however—one for each day in the boonies.

Once the team was provisioned, Max powered on his tactical radio. Their AN/PRC-152s all featured helmet-integrated headsets and optional GPS. Each man entered the coordinates for the DZ, the two waypoints, and Base Camp into their 152. Loaded with fresh batteries, each functioned properly during their comm check.

Every team member left the armory at least eighty pounds heavier, packs and pockets bulging with supplies and ammo, as much as each man could carry and still perform his duties. Due to all the unknown variables on this mission, the team packed everything they anticipated needing. There were no packing lists. Each man on the team had been hired for their combat expertise and was expected to bring what was needed to do the job.

Fog rose from the scant few inches of snow melting on the grass between runways. Two full-sized pickup trucks awaited them outside, transportation to their bird. Max climbed into the bed of the lead vehicle with LT, Irish, and Diaz. Sugar, Red, Gable, and Coach followed in the other truck. As they rode, Max sweated beneath his body armor and combat suit. *Christ, it must be forty degrees out here. Maybe the global warming boosters are right.* That was a debate best left to the likes of Coach and Red, and not one Max cared to listen in on.

LT craned his neck to peer around the cab. "Looks like we ride in style, Chief."

Max peeked around the other side of the truck and nodded his approval. Their transport to the drop zone was a massive Sea Stallion transport helicopter, military surplus still painted flat gray. The black decals of its civilian identification number were plastered over the ghost of the word "MARINES", still faintly visible if one focused hard enough. It was devoid of its former armaments, which might have come in handy at the DZ. As Max appreciated the pounding of the main rotor, he wondered if he could fly such a beast, many times the size of the small Bell helicopters he'd trained on.

"Just like the good old days," Diaz shouted over the rotor noise as he dismounted from the truck bed.

The good old days. "Yeah," Max agreed, not aware he wore a slight smile.

That touch of eagerness came innately in this situation, unable to be helped. Everyone reacted differently to the anticipation of action ahead. Boots were usually terrified when taking their first ride to confront the enemy, though some were all swagger, an action star ready to unleash a one-man symphony of death that rarely ran past the overture. Senior men were usually poised and quiet on the chopper; their thoughts impossible to read and nobody's business but their own.

But the elite warriors, the true professionals? They went in businesslike and impassive like Irish and Coach; pissed off like LT; nervous yet determined like Diaz; even laughing their asses off like Sugar and Gable, who didn't seem to give a shit whether they drank their next whiskey on the Vegas Strip or in Valhalla with Red.

Max felt only contentment as he pulled on his goggles and crossed the tarmac through the thunderous windstorm kicked up by the rotor. He boarded the chopper via the loading ramp at the rear of the aircraft, taking the foremost position on the starboard side, alpha team falling in behind him. LT and bravo team took the seats to port. The teams took up very little space in the cavernous cargo hold, spacious enough for three-dozen Marines in full combat gear. The fast rope was already clipped to the winch on the ceiling, coiled up on the floor atop the closed deployment hatch.

Max conducted the unnecessary yet customary headcount. *Old habits die hard.* All was in order. Everything checked out to his satisfaction, despite the vague factors inherent in the mission. As he sat across from his men, their faces streaked with face paint like Viking warriors with high-tech combat gear, he felt a sense of calmness flood over him. These were his brothers and this was his true home, his calling, and, for better or worse, the only place where he even remotely belonged.

*   *   *

Max stood in the cockpit doorway and watched as they approached the DZ, the pilots flying fast and low. On the satellite images, the clearing had seemed wider. Now it appeared to be only a hundred feet across and three hundred feet long. Max had his radio tuned to the same frequency as the pilot and copilot. Though he already knew the answer, eternal optimism demanded he ask, "You think you can touch down?"

"No," the pilot immediately responded, accompanied by a chuckle from the copilot.

Max didn't blame them. He wasn't sure what model of CH-53 they were on, but he knew the rotor diameter would fill three-quarters of the zone. No sane pilot would risk trying to land in a clearing with so little room for error.

"Very well. Put us in position," Max ordered.

He turned from the cockpit to the team, pointing toward the fast rope. Gable smiled; the old paratrooper loved this sort of shit. The rest of the team looked impassive, making their final preparations and gear checks in their flimsy canvas seats. A faint hydraulic whine accompanied the opening of the deployment hatch–a rectangular hole in the floor. The nylon fast rope dropped through the floor and uncoiled. Below, the rope whipped wildly in the maelstrom of the bird's rotor wash, the far end barely brushing the snowy ground.

Not gonna work. "We need another ten feet," Max informed the pilot.

The pilot paused. "Five is the best I can do. I'm damn near playing lumberjack as it is."

"Copy that." Five would have to do. But there was a definite element of danger involved.

Fast roping was a simple concept: don a thick pair of leather gloves, preferably with a pair of lighter gloves beneath for extra protection against friction burn, then grab the rope and slide down. His men would also clamp the rope between their boots to provide extra braking—a necessity for the amount of gear. In training, where the distance was never more than fifty feet and someone was steadying the rope, fast roping was as easy as it sounded. Eighty feet up with the rope swinging all over the place and barely contacting the ground made for a risky descent.

"Deploy when ready," the pilot conveyed.

"Deploying now." Max grabbed the rope, while his team stood nuts to butts, ready to follow. He believed in leading from the front, something that had been drilled into him since his earliest days as an officer in the Marines. Clamped on with his boots, he started to drop.

"Stand in the door. *GO!*" Gable called as Max dropped through the floor.

The first half of his journey went textbook smooth. For the last forty feet of the drop, he dangled from a rope in an epic tornado. With an especially violent whip, the rope freed itself from between Max's boot soles. His speed doubled under the weight of his gear, and even through the two layers of gloves, his palms seared. After near-freefall for the final ten feet, he landed hard despite the cushion of eight inches of melting snow with a wallow of mud beneath.

Nothing popped; nothing broke.

Not that Max had time to think about it. He rolled and sprang to his feet, found the dangling rope through the swirl of snow kicked up by the bird, and ran to secure it. He reached the end just as Gable touched down.

Crouched in the open and holding the rope, Max was a sitting duck for any decent sniper. Gable hit the ground running and took up a prone shooting position along the trail toward the camp. The others did similarly, filling in like points on a compass. About twenty-five feet apart, they scanned the tree line for any signs of the unknown enemy.

No bullets came before LT, the last man, hit the ground.

"All clear," Max radioed to the pilot.

"Acknowledged. Catch you in forty-eight. Good luck," the pilot replied through a garble of static. The winch began to reel in the rope. The rotor changed pitch as the pilot gunned the Sea Stallion straight upward, clearing the retracting rope over the treetops before he started back to the airfield. The team's last lifeline to the civilized world thumped away into the gray sky.

Max ran and dove into the snow, taking his place in the perimeter. "Report in," he ordered.

"Clear," each man reported in turn, no signs of anything moving.

Max pulled his binoculars and scanned the trees running the length of the clearing's northwest side, taking his time and lingering on areas of potential concealment. A whole lot of green tree boughs sagged beneath burdens of melting snow, but nothing appeared out of the ordinary.

Max secured his binoculars and grabbed his HK416 carbine rifle. "Let's move out," he ordered. "Double wedge to the tree line, two columns when we hit the woods."

The men fell into formation, still twenty-five feet apart. They jogged toward the tree line, weapons raised and ready. Radio silence ruled as the team awaited orders from Max and LT.

Max reported, "Nothing over here."

"Same here," LT responded.

The static wasn't enough to garble his words, but comm was definitely worse here than at the airport. Just as no one reported running across signs of recent activity or habitation in the clearing, the story remained the same at the tree line. Scattered animal tracks offered the only signs of life. A steady breeze kicked up, heralding the arrival of the weather front. For all its halfhearted bluster, the front wasn't pushing much in the way of cold weather. The temperature here hovered about ten degrees lower than at the airport; nevertheless, Max doubted it was cold enough to snow, at least not at the moment.

The two teams formed columns and headed into the woods toward their first waypoint. Max took the lead for alpha team while Gable did the honors for bravo, Gable's experience as a point man ever invaluable. They maintained about sixty feet between columns, the teams barely able to make each other out through the blanket of gloom cast by the towering evergreens. The men well accustomed to the outdoors moved silently through the dense brush, like big jungle cats stalking their prey. About thirty feet separated the men within their columns; those in the rear on the alert for hand signals from up front. Radio silence wasn't to be broken unless absolutely necessary. They stopped periodically to listen for any sound of movement in the forest. Moving carefully in this fashion, it took the team nearly two hours to make the first waypoint.

"I have visual on the clearing," Max announced.

After a pause of several seconds, Gable responded, "I have visual."

"Circle and secure the perimeter."

"Copy that."

Max reached the clearing, which he estimated to be roughly five acres in size, consisting of scrub and grass, perhaps created by a long-ago forest fire. A man in full battle dress lay near the center of the clearing in a mess of bloody snow with his neck ripped open and head turned at an impossible angle. "Visual on a body." Max waved Red forward and signaled him to set up with his machine gun at the clearing's edge.

"See it," LT responded. The static in their comm grew worse all the time.

Gable reported, "We got two dead on the ground, maybe more."

Red motioned to Max, then pointed across the clearing at something hanging in a tree. Max pulled his binoculars for a better view. The fir tree appeared sloppily bedecked in old silver tinsel that had faded to an unmistakable flat gray that Max knew all too well. All the boughs on one side of the tree had been snapped off to the level where the strands were hung.

"LT, you see that mess in the tree across the clearing?"

"Affirmative."

"Circle to the left. We'll take the right flank and meet over there. Leave Sugar to cover."

"Copy."

Though eager to confirm what he thought hung in the tree, Max took his time leading alpha team around the clearing. The ubiquitous animal tracks that had dotted the snow on their walk were conspicuously absent around the clearing, which was odd considering all the easy pickings for scavengers. The area fell eerily quiet. There was no ambient noise save for the occasional susurrus of the wind as the front moved in.

As he led his team through to the clearing, Max had an uneasy feeling, as if he could feel eyes upon him. He held the thought to himself, as he kept his head on a swivel, scanning the surroundings as they pressed forward.

Even having an inkling of what they would find in the tree did not prepare the team for the reality of it. The carnage began in the clearing. Spatters of blood and a trail of disrupted snow led to the tree, at the base of which Max made out the impressions of boots and some kind of animal tracks—perhaps a massive bear. Broken tree branches littered the ground, snapped like so many matchsticks from the tree trunk. Deep crimson smears, punctuated with the occasional scrap of viscera, stained the snow. A wild slash of claw marks led up the tree where a human torso lay wedged in a crotch at the trunk. No, more like half a torso, the entrails ripped from the gut and looped crazily over and around tree branches. The man's legs were nowhere to be seen.

Max followed the gory path up the tree and noticed that some of the claw marks were human as he saw the remnants of the man's fingernails wedged into the bark.

Gable arrived on scene and stared up into the tree. "What the fuck happened here?"

LT replied, "Fuck if I know. Looks like a bear attack."

"I ain't never heard of no bear with feet that big."

"They're called paws, Gable," LT corrected. "And now you have."

Max shook his head. *Do bears deliberately mutilate their prey? Make a spectacle of their killing?* Not a naturalist, he had no answers.

By this time, the rest of the team had arrived, minus Red and Sugar. All stared in disbelief at the remnants of the Greytech security man. Veterans of dozens of engagements the world over, killers in their own right who had seen bodies in every state of decay, murdered in just about every way—had ever seen anything this gruesome. The huge bear tracks, the extent of the carnage—it was all too unbelievable.

Diaz shook his head, first at the bear tracks and then at the headless half-man up the tree. *"No en talla,"* was his only comment.

LT sniped, "Denying it won't make him disappear."

"Not what I meant," Diaz said. "I lived in the Rockies for a bit. I worked on a victim of a bear mauling once, and the guy didn't look anything like this."

"You're the bear expert." LT took on the brusque tone he used far too often.

Diaz turned incredulous. "They don't make bears this big. Look at the size of those fucking tracks. The thing would be over twenty feet tall."

Irish added, "I've heard tales of grizzlies that big. Wouldn't surprise me up here."

"They don't do shit like this!" Diaz protested. "I'm telling you, bears don't decorate a tree with intestines and take off with the legs."

Max stepped in. "Keep it down. Maybe it didn't take off with his legs. Fan out, let's see if we can find any more of that guy." He peered up at the remains. *Poor son of a bitch.* Any form of death seemed preferable to what this guy had endured in his last moments.

Despite his opinions on the scene, Max held his tongue. A bear might be that big, but he knew Diaz spoke the truth. Scavenging animals on a battlefield invariably feasted on the entrails first, the most tender and nourishing flesh on a corpse. No animal would waste good guts decorating a tree. A hungry bear wouldn't chase down a man and then pass over entrails for leg muscle. It didn't add up.

Max transmitted over his headset. "Sugar, Red, move into the clearing and investigate those bodies. Try to preserve what you can around them."

Both men acknowledged the order.

"Let's fan out, boys, fifty-foot radius. Stay in visual contact and report anything you find."

Coach reported in first: "I got the bear's trail. Headed due north."

"Don't follow past fifty feet," Max repeated.

"Found a rifle here," Gable said. "HK G36."

About a minute later, Coach responded, "His lower body's here, just off the trail."

"Roger that," Max answered. "Check it out and then return to the tree. Sugar, Red? What do you have out there?"

Red snorted. "Got a guy with his heart ripped out and his head ripped off, otherwise he's just peachy."

"Five-five-six brass everywhere, Chief," Sugar reported. "Four men down out here, all stiffs and all mangled. All with G36 rifles."

Red added, "All their gear's top of the line. Fuckers were well equipped."

"Tracks," Diaz announced. "They lead to a pile of blood and tissue but no sign of a body."

"Ditto over here, tracks and gore but no body. Heading back," LT replied.

Back under the tree, Max asked Coach, "Anything special about his legs?"

"Not really. Ammo pouches still on him. I found these." He held up two thirty-round mags for the G36. "No ID."

"Rifle's empty." Gable proffered the G36 to Max. There appeared to be nothing unusual about the weapon.

"Pretty sure a grenade went off out here," Sugar added. "One of these guys has three, unused, still clipped to his vest."

"Dibs," Red called.

"Man, fuck you," Sugar replied.

"Cut the chatter. We're coming out to sweep the clearing." Max turned to Diaz. "Give me quick postmortems on each body."

"On it."

Into his microphone, Max said, "We need to do this quickly, fifteen minutes. Daylight's burning."

Diaz's verdict for the men in the clearing: death by rending and evisceration. "Never seen shit like this before." Max could hear the quaver in his voice.

"Not your worry, Diaz. Stay sharp."

All the rifles were empty, save one that belonged to a man down at the edge of the clearing who had apparently been the first to die. One of his arms had been ripped from his shoulder. Irish found the appendage about thirty feet from the body.

"Well, loo—" Static cut off the rest of Red's transmission.

Max turned his attention to where Red stood waving for him, then double-timed it over there. LT met him at the scene.

"Sat phone," Red informed Max and LT. "Found it right here." He stood about ten feet from the nearest body. The screen on the phone—a Greytech model, of course—was shattered, and the missing battery cover revealed an empty compartment.

"Let's find that battery," Max said. "Red, check his body. We'll check the snow, LT."

Red came up empty, save for more magazines; one loaded and two empty. Max found the battery cover lying atop the snow and then noticed a tiny depression in the snow several feet away. He carefully dug around it with his hands, revealing the battery. It appeared none the worse for wear. Max wiped all moisture off the contacts and snapped it into the phone. He powered it on, and to his surprise, the cracked screen illuminated.

According to the phone's log, it had dialed a number listed as Greytech Alpha two days ago at sixteen fifty-six and been connected for a duration of sixteen seconds. Just because the call connected didn't necessarily mean clear communication, however, given the magnetic disturbance. Max shook his head. He'd been informed that this security team's final call had been garbled in some fashion, but given the fantastic carnage visible about the clearing, he now had his doubts. *Maybe they didn't want us to know what they heard during those sixteen seconds.* The final call was the only one made on the sat phone in the last two days. Max found no voicemails or text messages to provide any further clues.

LT apparently harbored similar thoughts. "I'll bet you they have that recording."

"Probably so," Max answered. "It's my bust. I shouldn't have taken their word for it."

"We'd be here, regardless."

"True. But we might have been a little better prepared."

LT didn't respond. There was no reason to ponder the miscue any further. Max felt certain the nature of the final phone call was only the first of many prevarications he would discover in the next couple of days.

"What now?" Red asked. "We've found about all we're likely to around here."

Max replied, "On to waypoint two."

"We're not gonna investigate that bear's trail?"

Max shook his head. "We're not here to track a bear."

"You think this has anything to do with Base Camp and the dig?" LT asked. "Because I'm thinking this is a separate incident."

After a moment, Max nodded. "Yeah, that seems the most likely explanation."

"Besides, that bear has got to be dead," Red said. "It totally fucked these guys up, but they had to have hit the thing a few times with all the rounds they fired."

LT clarified, "We don't know if it was a bear that did all this. It has all the signs of an ambush, except for the guy in the tree. Perhaps the bear came after the fact?"

"Good point." Max keyed his headset, "Anybody find anything else of interest? Other than body parts and shell casings?"

The team answered negative.

"We got places to be. Split back into your teams. Let's move out."

No one looked back at the clearing as they formed up at the tree line. They were on their way in less than two minutes.

10

"WAYPOINT TWO IS ATOP THIS RIDGE," MAX BROADCAST TO THE team.

"Say again, over," Coach requested, his words barely understandable.

Max repeated himself and so did Coach; his radio rendered officially dysfunctional. Max said no more. Coach, the rear man on bravo team, would have to follow along without the benefit of comm for the moment. Other radios were likewise malfunctioning, working one minute and completely garbled by static the next. Once in Base Camp, the team could rely on the hand signals they'd all learned long ago in the nascent years of their combat training.

It had taken the team almost five hours to cover the four klicks from the clearing to waypoint two. Shallow gorges cut through the thick forest in three places, costing the team time as they sought suitable locations to cross. Thick mist choked those micro valleys, forcing the teams to work in closer proximity to one another than usual. With comm so unreliable, Max conducted several headcounts to make sure he hadn't lost anyone. Max also noted that his GPS was no longer picking up a signal, forcing him to use a map and compass the rest of the way.

The first raindrop fell as Max emerged from the mist near the top of the ridge, mere feet from waypoint two. A gust of wind kicked up, stirring the cover of fir branches. The rain came hard, relentless and steady, the drops half-ice and half-water. From waypoint two, Max surveyed Base Camp below. He found an outcropping of granite jutting from the ridge and low crawled out to the edge where LT joined him moments later. The rest of the team spread out at twenty-foot intervals, taking cover from weather and potential foes wherever they could.

The valley below spread much wider than the gorges they'd crossed, cloaked in only a thin layer of mist that allowed for decent reconnaissance. Max and LT scanned Base Camp with their binoculars. The satellite pictures hadn't done justice to Greytech's efforts in the area. Trees had been cut down to make way for the larger prefab buildings, but a good deal of forest cover had been left standing about the camp, likely in hopes of concealing the operation from prying eyes in the sky. *A vain effort.* The remaining cover masked only the scope of Greytech's efforts.

This was no exploratory expedition, but a full-blown mining operation that had employed dozens of people. The area around the mine itself, a crude hole in a glacier about a klick up the valley from Base Camp, lay in total disarray. A bulldozer had been flipped over, one trailer partially burned and another knocked askew. He made out a body lying on the ice, the cause of death uncertain.

Though glad they could avoid the chaos at the mine, Base Camp appeared little better. Several buildings had crumpled, with dents in spots. Doors were missing. Max discerned two major explosions. A ragged hole gaped in the side of a large maintenance structure. The disarray of several Conex boxes brought to mind giant building blocks strewn about and then abandoned by titanic children. A Sea Stallion sat on the nearby helipad, regal and appearing undisturbed amidst the devastation.

"I count seven corpses." LT continued to scan through his binoculars. "Make that eight."

"And exactly zero signs of life," Max replied.

"This is fucking crazy. I've never seen anything like it."

Max leaned toward LT to ensure no one else could hear him. "It's what I'm not seeing that bothers me—no sign of who or what made this mess. Every body I see down there looks to be Greytech civilian or security; not one dead aggressor that I can make out."

"Do you remember the camp we cleared in Liberia? They probably removed their dead to cover their tracks."

"Perhaps so. But how do you explain the hole in that building?" Max nodded to the left.

"Rocket launcher."

"Where are the blast marks? I don't see a single sign of an explosion near that hole. And look at those jagged rips in the metal. Explosives don't do that. Someone did a really sloppy job of cutting through the side of that building."

"Yeah, I can't argue with you with there. I don't like the looks of it."

Max raised his binoculars for another peek. "There, on the ground just to the east of that second large building on the admin side of camp." He pointed in the general direction. "If you look closely, you'll see corpse number nine. He seems to be missing a leg."

"I see it," LT replied. The tone of his voice, even flatter than usual, informed Max that he likewise considered that a possible connection to the mutilated corpses back in the clearing. "What the fuck are we dealing with?" He whispered, still scanning through his binoculars.

"Wish I had an answer, buddy." Max took a minute more to recon the camp, finding nothing else of interest. "Well, this camp isn't gonna secure itself." He keyed his radio. "Bring it in for a pow-wow, gentlemen."

Max and LT fell back from the outcropping into the forest cover. The team assembled around them, still keeping an eye on the surroundings as the rain poured.

"Grab some chow while we go over this, you might not get another chance for a while."

Everyone ate hurriedly as Max explained the relatively simple plan: split into security and breaching teams and sweep the camp for survivors and data, starting in the logistics section at the west end and working east into the lab and living areas.

"And then on to the dig site."

Gable jerked to attention. "Whoa, hold on, Chief. Thought that was a no-go."

"We aren't going inside, but I want to check every inch of this camp for those hard drives and any potential survivors. Remember, there could be friendlies in there, so identify your targets."

"Let's hope we find some answers in camp then," Coach grumbled. "Hate to think I walked all the way out here not to be paid."

LT took a pull from his hydration bladder and swallowed. "Way it looks down there, I'd worry about walking out first."

Max could have smacked LT. It was the wrong thing to say and typical of his second in command, just LT being LT. Max brought the briefing back on point. "We'll see what happens, but that's the plan for now. All of you, lens that logistics area carefully before we depart. We'll be paying special attention to that building with the gaping hole in its side. Diaz, you got anything on your toys?"

Diaz checked his nuclear, biological, and chemical detection equipment. "Negative, slight increases in radiation levels, but nothing out of the norms for background stuff, especially in these mountains."

Max was about to ask if anyone had questions but decided against it. He was just as clueless as everyone else about what they might find down there. "We move out in fifteen."

The team stuffed their mouths with various delicacies from the MRE pouches silently as they scanned the area below. Max found the damp scene oddly comforting—a reminder of simpler days as a lieutenant in the infantry companies. Since then, his life had grown gradually more complicated and had taken a hard turn toward incomprehensible that morning, when he'd slid down the fast rope to face this phantom enemy.

Max checked his watch: fifteen fifty-five. Chow was over; the team was ready to go. "Form up. Let's do this."

Daylight faded, goaded faster into temporary oblivion by the heavy downpour. The two teams moved down the hill in wedges, pausing at the bottom to don night vision goggles. Poles topped with powerful spotlights stood about Base Camp, but the generators that supplied their power had died.

Their sweep of Base Camp began at the helipad, where Max inspected the Sea Stallion and found the helicopter had been intentionally disabled. There didn't appear to be damage to any of the craft except for the large tail rotor, which had been cut clean off with some sort of explosive cutting charge. *It appears someone doesn't want us going anywhere.* It was a bit of a disappointment. He preferred a backup plan for their getaway, even if he wasn't sure that he could fly the chopper.

Next, they negotiated the scatter of upset Conex boxes, most of which had popped open before coming to rest in disarray, making the breaching team's work much easier. Supplies littered the ground, dozens of different items ranging from cleaning supplies to auto and machine parts.

"...marks..." LT related.

Comm had degenerated to where Max could barely decipher anything. He silently worked his way over to where LT stood by one of the upset containers.

"Check these out," LT whispered, pointing to a gash where the metal container had been sliced open. He produced a small LED flashlight and shined it into the box. Partially dried blood reflected back, stark on a white background of busted cardboard boxes and scattered sheets of printer paper. Max saw a hand and forearm—hairy, male, wearing a gold wedding band—lying amongst the paper, though its owner was nowhere to be seen.

The déjà vu wore on Max's nerves.

"We—" Sugar this time, his transmission abruptly cut off.

Max double-timed over to him, crouched in cover next to another Conex box. "What do you got?"

"I don't know. Tracks maybe? There's three of them in the mud right around here."

"The bear?"

Sugar shook his head. "Fuck if I know, but it ain't no bear."

Max saw Red nearby and waved him over. They examined the first track. The water-filled indentations in the mud formed a nearly perfect impression. Max couldn't believe what he saw: a sole some two feet long with what appeared to be six toes. In front of each toe was a small triangular impression. *Claws*, Max surmised. Two more triangular impressions, much larger and sunk deeper into the muck, were visible a couple of inches behind the heel.

Max, Red, and Sugar stood dumbstruck gazing at the track. Without a word, Max moved on to the next impression. He noticed the difference between the position of the longest toe in the two tracks.

Right foot, now left, that next will be right. Now, what the hell made them?

"This is all real interesting," Red said.

Max noticed Red smiling. "Is there something funny about this?"

"Everything has its funny side, Chief. The funny thing about these tracks is that I've never seen a damn thing like 'em, and I've been hunting woods like these since I was five."

Sugar joked, "Maybe Diaz has a second opinion."

Max ignored him. The last thing anyone needed was Diaz further spooked by the mysterious tracks. Max didn't know when Diaz would find out about them; he just knew he had to delay that discovery for as long as possible. "So, what's your take?"

Red shrugged. "Who the fuck knows? Something unknown and really goddamn scary? Maybe he—*it*—was what Greytech really came here to find."

"Or maybe it found them," Sugar suggested in an ominous whisper Max had never heard from the man. He'd never seen anything rattle Sugar, not even the abattoir back at the clearing.

Max grumbled, "Or maybe it's just somebody trying to skew our impression of what really happened here. Putting down false tracks of some mythical beast to cover their own."

Red chuckled. "Like an episode of *Scooby Doo*."

"Yeah, something like that." *Fuck, it has to be something like that! Monster tracks two feet long? Bullshit! It's got to be a hoax...or some sort of reasonable explanation.*

"Man, I don't know." Sugar leaned closer. "Them tracks look awful real to me."

Red almost laughed. "Yeah, right away, how many animals do you know of with six toes and feet bigger than Shaq?"

Before Sugar could respond, Max stated, "We got enough to sweat right now without everyone thinking there's some sort of monster out here. Let's stay focused on the mission."

Sugar nodded. "You're probably right. Still, man, I don't know." He shook his head and walked away.

Max wasn't sure if he'd convinced his men of the truth, but he'd certainly planted a seed of doubt regarding this phony beast. That would have to suffice for the moment. *Might as well get this part over with.*

He called in the rest of his men to look at the tracks. "I don't care about these tracks or the bear. I'm only interested in the sons of bitches who attacked this camp."

"This is seriously fucking *punto tremendo*," Diaz stated. "I'm telling you—"

"And I'm telling *you* it's nothing. We don't know shit, so let's quit making shit up." Max stared him down. He'd shut more than a few mouths over the years with that stare. Though he didn't want to reprimand Diaz in front of the men, one more comment and he would have to put the medic in his place.

To his credit, Diaz didn't flinch under Max's gaze. He pursed his lips and nodded once. And that was the end of it.

LT broke the silence. "Not much else of interest here, Chief."

"Agreed. Let's check out these last couple boxes, then it's on to that maintenance building." Max gestured vaguely toward the building with the large hole ripped in its side.

Who's the joker behind this? Max hoped the man was enjoying his last few hours on Earth, whoever he was.

* * *

The team didn't have to force their way into the maintenance building—a prefab structure that had been converted into a three-bay heavy-machinery garage. The rolling overhead doors to bays one and two were closed, but the door to bay three had been ripped from its tracks. It now covered a good portion of the muddy ground outside the shop.

As Max moved forward, he kicked something. He bent down into the mist to examine the obstruction—a human head; the face and most of the scalp had been ripped off, leaving behind a tonsure of blond hair. The dead man's exposed facial muscles and clouded, staring eyes reminded Max of an anatomical dummy from a science classroom.

"What you got?" Red asked from behind.

"More body parts. Let's move on."

LT's breaching team moved up to secure the garage, and Max sent Irish in with them. Max brought up the other two men as the breaching team disappeared inside. Bay two held a dump truck and three an excavator, but Max gave them only the slightest glance. A nanosecond was all the time he could spare from what greeted him in bay one.

The carnage here wasn't half that at the clearing, but the confined space made it appear worse. Blood spatter and viscera covered damn near everything. Max found the face belonging to the blond gentleman outside. It hung on the dump truck's rearview mirror.

Said gentleman had likewise been disemboweled in gruesome fashion; ripped open from groin to throat, his organs scattered across the floor and workbench. His assailants had even broken his sternum and cracked open his rib cage. Nothing remained in his torso but bones, his skin covering the remains like a sagging tent.

The second man had likewise met a ghastly fate. His head was squashed flat like a road-killed squirrel. As Max approached, he noticed that both the man's knees were broken and forced backward until the joints snapped. As if all that hadn't been enough to kill the guy, someone had ripped his heart straight from his chest. Both men's hearts lay near each other on the floor. Max wondered which was whose.

The same strange tracks covered the bloody, sticky floor.

Max's headset crackled. He barely made out the word "clear".

LT's team met up with them in bay one.

"Nothing noteworthy back there," LT confirmed, jerking a finger over his shoulder toward the heavy equipment.

"Shitload of tracks," Irish observed, scanning the floor. "No evidence of who really made them."

Max pointed to the jagged rip in the metal over the workbench. "Looks like they entered via the hole in the wall, killed these poor bastards, and burst out that way through bay one's door."

"Yeah, they got a real aversion to doors, don't you think?" Diaz said. "Jesus, I need a fucking drink."

Max inclined toward Diaz and motioned Sugar to take him outside.

Sugar nodded. "Let's go, brother."

Diaz didn't resist as Sugar led him by the arm out of bay one.

"Tell you what, Chief," Gable said, "Whoever's behind this monster hoax is doin' a goddamn bang-up job of it. You really know how

120

to pick a mission."

Max didn't respond. To LT, he said, "I think we've seen enough Scooby Doo shit here. Let's keep it moving."

For a moment, Max swore he heard a whisper, short, incoherent, and far off, like his brain had been momentarily tuned to the right radio station and then the signal faded.

* * *

The team's work devolved into drudgery as the night wore on, a monotonous cycle of clearing buildings and sweeping streets. As Diaz had proclaimed, this demon apparently hated doors. Most had been ripped from their hinges and cast away, making life a bit easier for the breaching team.

In one prefab trailer that had served as barracks, the team found two men who had apparently committed suicide together. Gun shots through both of their mouths, the weapons still in their hands.

The inexplicable destruction and bizarre atrocities mounted as they swept Base Camp. Max checked his watch for what seemed like the hundredth time: almost midnight. He had been to almost every hell hole the world had to offer and had seen countless horrors and atrocities, but nothing he saw here made any sense. The scope of this mini-apocalypse began to fatigue him mentally; the feeling spreading slowly into his limbs. The dank air and steady rain seemed to press downward upon him, making him feel as if he were working at the bottom of a river.

Several charred bodies greeted the team in the roofless, burned-out remains of what appeared to be the Greytech security barracks. Like most of the corpses they'd found in camp, the bodies were all mutilated in some fashion. Melted metal blobs that had once been shell casings littered the ashes around the bodies. They had been armed with HK G36 assault rifles and had gone down shooting from the look of things.

Christ, how many bullets does it take to kill this—? Max almost thought the word *thing* as some of the men were already calling the persons responsible for these atrocities. *You don't know shit, so just keep moving.*

At first, it appeared that the fire had spread into the street from the barracks, but the exact opposite was true. Sugar found a man lying on his side in the mud, charred black and clutching the remains of a weapon. "I'll be damned, old boy got a flamethrower!"

"Didn't do him or anyone else much good," Irish observed.

From the look of things, the man had been trying to roast someone in the street and wound up setting fire to the barracks. The surrounding area reeked of napalm and burnt flesh.

Max bent down and flipped the body, exposing the tanks for the flamethrower—a small nitrogen pressure tank mounted horizontally up top with the larger fuel tank underneath. The fuel tank bent askew with one triangular puncture mark about an inch wide visible.

"Never seen a flamethrower like this," Gable commented.

Max studied the tanks. "It's based on an old German design, the *flammenwerfer 41*. But this is brand new, perhaps an experimental design by Greytech for the DOD."

The team nodded in agreement. The DOD officially denied keeping flamethrowers in their arsenal, but they were known to deny a lot of things. Veterans knew better than to believe any of the bullshit blathered from the mouths of high brass to placate civilian activists. Granted, Max had never seen a flamethrower on the battlefield, never even seen one in use, but he'd never doubted their place in the arsenal, stockpiled in case of a dire threat to the homeland right alongside the mustard gas and nerve agents.

"Looks like there's a computer built into the trigger mechanism," Red observed. "Pity this thing's no longer serviceable. We could use something like this."

"Better than he did, I hope." Gable pointed to the charred operator with his gun barrel.

"Got to be an armory around here somewhere," LT stated. "Maybe we'll find another one."

Finding the armory proved easy; it was two buildings down on the other side of the street, a small, hardened Quonset hut constructed of thick steel. The steel door, over an inch thick, had been cast into the middle of the street. LT's team entered the armory and reported it clear moments later.

Max entered and illuminated the room with a red lens flashlight.

A counter fenced off with reinforced wire mesh ran the width of the front room, behind which were racks for storage of rifles and pistols. Mostly empty, a few HK G36s were still in evidence, along with a selection of Glock and Sig-Sauer pistols, mostly in 9mm and all equipped with laser sights. Several Mossberg 590 tactical shotguns perched up in one corner. Three 7.62mm miniguns and an Mk 19 40mm grenade launcher sat on a steel table next to a door in the back wall.

The access door through the front counter stood wide open.

"What the fuck?" Coach asked. "These guys have better toys than we do."

Max was thinking the same thing as he examined the miniguns and grenade launcher, heavy weapons normally meant to be mounted on vehicles. *Mining operation, my ass. Why would they need this kind of firepower?*

"You got your wish, Red." LT stood at the entrance to a back room and motioned the team forward.

Ammo had once been stockpiled here, but only a few metal boxes of 12-gauge, 5.56, 7.62, and 9mm Parabellum remained, as well as one box containing a belt of 40mm grenades for the Mk 19. Optics—the latest in NVGs and range-finding binoculars—were stored here, alongside combat knives and highly advanced comm gear for both portable and base operations. Two wooden crates on the floor contained Claymore mines and white phosphorus grenades, respectively.

The object of Red's desire—a second flamethrower in pristine condition—hung like a trophy on the back wall. Max and Red pulled it down for an examination. The flamethrower tanks were mounted on a frame to be worn on the user's back. Red found a booklet in a pouch behind the tanks on the inside of the apparatus. The word "SECRET" was stamped in red ink diagonally across the cover over the words: "MANUAL: COMBAT ASSAULT FLAMETHROWER MARK 12 (Mk 12) Department of the Army". At the bottom edge of the cover, beneath a line drawing of the Mk 12, were the words: "Manufactured by Greytech Industries, Pat Pending".

Max ran a hand along the smaller tank. "They definitely borrowed from the German design."

"Better materials, though," Red said as he hefted the tanks. "This puppy looks all titanium. I doubt it weighs more than forty pounds full."

Coach chuckled. "Santa brings little Red his first flamethrower."

Red absolutely beamed. "And I'm digging this neato computer by the trigger. Hey, LT, think it's got temperature control like that vape thingy you carry around?"

LT even cracked a smile at that. "Could be. Scroll past Raghead and Russian until you find the setting for Unknown."

"Charge that sumbitch up," Gable urged. "There's a nitrogen tank right there."

Sugar glanced around. "Don't see any fuel, though."

"They wouldn't keep flammables in here," Max said. "Let's finish our sweep, gentlemen. We can play with toys while we're waiting for our ride back home."

The sweep continued, the team gradually working east into the research sector of the camp. As they progressed, the weather continued to deteriorate, the rain and wind increasing in intensity as the temperate dropped. Rounding the corner of the muddy road, they came upon the second largest building at camp the main research lab. Max knew from the satellite photos that an explosion had destroyed much of the lab. It seemed the best place to begin their sweep of the final few buildings in Base Camp.

The front door, though still intact, was partially blown off its hinges. LT's team entered while Max and the rest kept watch in the street. "—ear," Max heard through his headset a couple of minutes later. He led his men inside.

As in so many other buildings, the first thing to catch Max's attention was a corpse. The woman lay crumpled in a corner; her once-pristine white lab coat now mottled in a pattern of red and black stains. Her limbs jutted unnaturally. Blood and brain pooled by her smashed skull. An indentation in the wall, deep and human-sized, hinted at her demise: she'd been propelled into it with astonishing velocity, enough to break damn near every bone in her body.

Max moved into the next room, where the explosion and subsequent fire appeared to have started. Computers, monitors, and unidentifiable lab equipment—all melted or smashed to bits—choked the room. "See if the hard drives on any of those computers are still intact," he instructed Red, who nodded.

"Chief, you'll want to see this," LT called through the open door to the next room. "Bring Red with you."

Max called out, "Change in plan, Red; you're coming with me."

Red turned around. "Doesn't look like anything is salvageable here anyway."

Max almost tripped on what, upon closer examination, proved to be an airlock wheel in a steel door lying on the floor amidst the high-tech rubble.

"That's interesting," Diaz stated in a flat, dry tone.

"You read too much into shit," Coach told him.

Diaz didn't respond.

Max joined LT's team in a windowless central room about twenty feet wide that ran the length of the building. Portions of the ceiling had collapsed during the fire. A platform, roughly ten feet square and elevated about four feet above the floor, dominated the space. Titanium support posts at each corner of the platform had connected it to the ceiling. A gray substance had flowed down the sides of the platform like magma to pool in solid puddles on the floor—the glass that had once enclosed the platform. A hardened steel console of four computers lined one side of the platform with the screens and keyboards encased in melted gray glass.

"What do you make of it, Chief?" LT asked.

Diaz answered in a condescending tone worthy of LT himself: "It's an observation chamber. They were conducting medical experiments."

"What the hell?" Irish asked, pulling his hand back.

"Yeah. *Exactamundo*," Diaz said. "Don't touch anything."

Max ignored Diaz's sardonic demeanor yet heeded his warning to touch nothing. However, he noticed something as he circled the platform. "Take a look at this." He pointed toward the floor. "Most of the melted glass over here didn't run down the side of the platform. It's in spatters all over the floor for a good ten feet that way."

Gable spit tobacco juice on the floor. "That's prob'ly the side it broke outta."

"All right, we don't know that, okay?" LT cautioned. "Keep your speculations to yourself, Gable."

"We'll keep it in mind," Max noted. Though he'd seen more weird shit today than on any other mission—a lot more weird shit— he couldn't bring himself to believe that some sort of creature caused all this destruction. But the mounting evidence turned in his mind and began to overwhelm his logic.

Max focused his attention to the computer console. "Red, pry open that console and see if you can pull the hard drives."

"On it." A couple of minutes later, Red stood and dusted his hands off. "They're already gone. From the look of the smudges and finger marks around the housing, they were removed after the fire."

"Huh..." LT mused.

Max paused to contemplate that. "Interesting. Doesn't seem like the style of our perps, does it? All they've done is destroy equipment, far as I've seen. Preserving information isn't high on their agenda."

"There could be survivors here after all," LT realized.

Max nodded. "We need to be cautious, particularly the breach-ing team. I know there's nothing you guys would rather do than shoot first after all we've witnessed here, but just watch it. Dead survivors aren't about to tell us anything. And I want to know everything."

No one spoke. Gable released a huff of breath. As the point man on the breaching team, he would likely make the first contact with any survivors. Or any hostiles.

The team explored the rest of the research lab and found

nothing more of interest, just the same melted equipment and a few more people who had suffered agonizing deaths at the hands of the unknown enemy.

A gust of wind-driven rain lashed Max in the face as he led the team from the research lab. Next door to the lab awaited the largest building in camp, a mess hall conveniently located along the border of the research and living quarters. It appeared untouched by the aggressors.

"Front—vice entrance?" LT asked over the radio.

Max could barely see Gable through the pounding sheets of rain. He jogged over to him and whispered, "Front doors. Keep it quiet."

Crouched low, Gable moved along the edge of the building, his size-thirteen boots sinking into the mud. He halted beside the double doors, metal with large glass windows comprising their upper halves. Gable tried pulling them open. Locked. He broke the glass with the butt of his shotgun, then cleared away the larger shards and reached inside to unlock the doors, which he slowly pulled open. The breaching team moved inside, Max and his men a few steps behind. Something was up; these were the first locked doors they'd encountered so far.

The cafeteria reminded Max of a prison chow hall with the tables and chairs built as single units of furniture bolted to the floor. A few trays piled with decaying breakfast food occupied some of the tables, producing a rotten stench, but otherwise, the hall appeared unremarkable. The reek grew stronger as they approached the serving area, where large pans of food had been abandoned in the dead steam tables. The putrid food lay undisturbed; no signs of rats or even roaches in the mess hall.

In the kitchen, the only signs of disorder were some cooking utensils lying on the floor and more pans of moldering food.

Two wide, heavy doors, each secured with a pull latch, stood side by side in one of the walls. Max figured they were freezers and braced himself to inhale another noisome wave of putrefaction. Gable and LT moved forward to the right-hand door. LT pulled the latch; Gable stood ready with his shotgun to confront whatever might be inside.

Two quick shots rang out in the darkness, the bullets ricocheting off the freezer door.

"Don't shoot, we're friendly!" LT shouted, putting his shoulder into the door to push it shut.

His entreaty was answered by a third gunshot and the babble of terrified voices talking over one another.

Gable shouted, "Guns down! We're from Greytech!"

The anxiety in his voice as he struggled to control his hair-trigger temper jerked Max to action. "Cease fire!" he roared as he ran to the door. "Cease fire; we're here to help!"

No more shots came. A woman, perhaps more than one, sobbed.

Max traded places with Gable at the door, which was still open a crack. "We're Greytech security contractors here to secure this camp. How many are you?"

A sob and then, "Three."

"I'm going to open the door now. Do not shoot! Is that understood?"

More sobbing before another voice—weak, rasping, and definitely male—responded, "We understand."

Max pulled the door open. The room served as a pantry as opposed to a freezer, roughly twelve feet wide and twenty feet long. Canned goods and other non-perishable supplies filled shelves running the length of each wall. An institutional-sized can of sliced peaches sat open upon the floor.

He observed the three survivors; two women and one man. The shooter—blonde female, early thirties, dressed in a dingy lab coat—held a smoking Beretta 9mm pistol, empty, the slide in the loading position. Tears streaked her dirty face, and she broke down crying at the sight of her rescuers. The other woman, swarthy and older with a curvy matron's figure, likewise cried as she looked to the sky and chanted her gratitude in Spanish. Max recognized the word *"Dios"* but nothing else. Both ladies appeared to be uninjured.

Max turned his attention to the man. He sat closest to the entrance, propped up on a makeshift throne of cardboard boxes full of fair-trade coffee. Shaggy and disheveled, he had a wild salt-and-pepper beard and a long, bony frame, with a dark tan complexion. His drawn and creased face reminded Max of Abraham Lincoln near the end of the Civil War. He likewise wore what had once been a white lab coat, now torn to shreds and soaked crimson with blood from chest to hips.

"Injured man here, Diaz," Max announced as he moved into the room.

"I'm fine," the man rasped, though he was anything but.

Max wondered how best to console the survivors. He needed to put them at ease before he could extract any information from them. He was about to speak, was going to tell them that everything would be okay, that they would be fine. *No,* he realized, *I'm not about to make that claim.*

Finally, he reached for the Beretta. "Let me help you up, ma'am. You won't be needing that for now." The woman allowed him to take the empty pistol. Max helped her stagger over to where she'd apparently been sitting atop some boxes of condiments.

"Thank...thank you," she stammered.

Behind him, Abe Lincoln shouted, "No, I'm telling you I'm fine!"

"My pleasure," Max said to the woman. He stepped back to the center of the pantry and addressed the survivors, first introducing himself and the team. "We've been contracted by Elizabeth Grey to secure this camp and rescue all survivors. You're the first we've located so far."

"We're the last." The Hispanic woman remained borderline hysterical.

The blonde said, "We don't know—"

"Shut up!" Lincoln snapped. No rasp this time—steel in his voice.

Max needed info from all three survivors, but Abe obviously outranked the other two and would be privy to more secrets. And he hadn't been very cooperative thus far.

Max introduced himself and asked them their names. The Hispanic woman was Amelia Quinones, a food service employee. She was fluent in English though she spoke in a rapid-fire manner that made her difficult to understand.

The blonde introduced herself as Danielle Harlow, a research assistant from Stanford University contracted to the Greytech expedition.

"And you, sir?" Max asked.

"Doctor Darsh Kumar, University of Chicago." The man said haughtily as Max detected an Indian accent.

Jackpot.

"Dr. Kumar, why don't you let my man examine your wounds."

"I'm fine, damn it—"

"You're bleeding to death, Dr. Kumar." Harlow stated.

The team had shut the pantry door behind them. The chamber was airtight, but there was a pushrod mechanism that allowed the door to be opened from the inside. Several chem lights now illuminated the room where before the survivors had been hiding in pitch darkness.

"It's not that bad," Kumar insisted. "I'm a doctor of biomechanics; I think I'm qualified to judge."

Diaz knelt on the floor before Kumar with his medical kit open. "I need to look you over, sir."

Kumar glared at Diaz. "And what is your medical credential, sir?"

"I'm a medic, a former Navy corpsman."

"So, none." Kumar rolled his eyes.

Sugar drew his large fix-bladed knife and stepped towards Kumar before anyone could blink. "If you prefer, Professor, allow me to expedite the examination process because you're annoying the shit out of me right about now."

The two women gasped.

Kumar quickly deduced that he longer carried any authority in the room, though he'd likely been a key player during much of the Greytech expedition. He moaned once, somewhat effeminately.

"Put it away, Jackson." LT said.

Sugar kept the knife leveled near Kumar's head.

LT looked to Max, who returned his gaze with a slight shake of his head. Kumar needed to curb his arrogance and learn his new place in the pecking order. He was no longer in charge of anything and needed to obey. Max knew Diaz was close to cracking and treating a patient would calm his nerves and hopefully get him focused once again.

"Okay," was Kumar's final gasped capitulation to Diaz cutting away his bloody lab coat.

"Now then," Max said, still standing in the middle of the room, "we need to find out what happened in this camp. Does anyone know the identities of the men who perpetrated these crimes?"

Harlow, the blonde, began, "It's not hu—"

"I reiterate: *SHUT. YOUR. MOUTH!*" Kumar bellowed. "Neither of you has any idea what you're speaking of."

"Doctor, I worked on—"

"Enough! *Arggh, shit that hurts!*"

"Yeah, but the news is good." Diaz attended to the doctor's injuries, cleaning three slash wounds that cut diagonally across the professor's chest and gut. "The wounds on your abdomen are deep but only superficial muscular damage. You won't be doing sit-ups anytime soon, but your organs are untouched. A few dozen stitches and you'll be fine."

Kumar looked ready to tell Diaz that he already knew that but refrained.

I might be able to work with him after all.

"Excellent," Max said to Diaz. "Now, you were saying about the aggressors, Ms. Harlow?"

"There were no—"

"Don't do it," Kumar warned weakly, his endless protestations draining his strength.

"No aggressors, as you put it."

"Stop! You are working under a non-disclosure agreement." Kumar said.

"Don't be absurd, Dr. Kumar! These men were hired by Ms. Grey."

"It doesn't matter—"

Max needed to hear this. "No, it certainly does matter. If you want to make it out of this place alive, Doctor, then I suggest you begin cooperating and tell me what happened here."

Harlow continued: "Mr. Ahlgren, we were studying a substance—"

"That you're not qualified to speak on," Kumar protested. "And you really don't know anything, anyway. You can only speculate. You weren't on Jung's team."

"Bullshit. I know what I saw." She paused, shaking with anger. "I know what did that to you! Don't you want them to help us? Don't you want to get out of here alive?"

Kumar gave a raspy laugh that quickly degenerated into a felicitous coughing fit that almost made Max grin. The doctor wouldn't be able to interrupt Ms. Harlow again for at least a few seconds.

Max whirled back toward Ms. Harlow. "This substance—tell me about it."

She parted her lips to speak.

The back wall of the pantry exploded inward with a deafening *pop* and a screech of rending metal, flooding the room in a deluge of leaking cans, broken boxes, and smashed shelving. Max dove across the room in an attempt to shield the two women with his body, though he knew he was already too late.

It had found them.

And it sure as shit wasn't human.

11

ALL HELL BROKE LOOSE AS THE CREATURE STORMED THROUGH the sundered wall of the prefab building. Max hit the floor face-first, rolled to his back, and threw aside some boxes that had fallen on him. His ears rang from the noise of the back wall being punctured, muffling the ladies' screams and the team's curses as they took cover where they could.

Through the eerie chartreuse glow of the chem lights, Max saw an inky mass of shining black standing in the gaping hole—rain and wind whipping about. It moved with unearthly speed and agility. Huge and humanoid in form, it had to bow its head just to clear the eight-foot ceiling. Powerful coils of muscle rippled beneath the dark translucent skin as it took two strides into the room and lashed downward with black talons several inches long. A fine spray of vermillion blood misted the air as Coach let out a caterwaul.

Max and his battle-hardened team froze in awe, feeling for an instant man's primeval fear of the apex predator, the survival instinct of flight unfamiliar to them all. The team had seen mercs, terrorists, torturers, criminals, and all manner of earthly nightmares, but nothing compared to what they saw. Max backpedaled from the aberration until his warrior instincts finally kicked in and regained control of his mind. *Kill this fucking thing!* Max needed his rifle, but unfortunately, it was strapped across his back, which he was lying on. He thought of the pistol on his belt; then he thought better of it. This thing had killed a few dozen people, most of them heavily armed. A few measly pops from his .45 weren't about to waste this beast. Max rolled, came to his knees, and reached back for his assault rifle, all in slow motion from the adrenaline dumped into his bloodstream.

Coach had been lounging near the rear of the pantry, wiping raindrops from his sniper rifle with meticulous reverence. He tried to crawl away from the beast, his left leg dragging behind and leaving a streak of blood across the floor.

The beast shot out an arm with unearthly speed and impaled Coach's other leg like a meat hook. It effortlessly picked Coach up off the floor, further stunning Max. Coach, the lightest member of the team, still weighed well over two hundred pounds with his gear. He emitted a stream of terrified babble as the creature hoisted him off the floor. Stupefied silence reigned for an instant in the pantry as the creature stood before the team and stared them down defiantly.

Max supposed that was the case anyway; he couldn't actually make out any eyes on the creature's mask-like face, which vaguely resembled that of *Tyrannosaurus rex*.

Max put the red dot of his weapon's reflex sight where he hoped the creature's heart lay. "Shoot it!" he yelled as he opened fire on the beast.

Several other guns joined in. The rounds punching holes in

the creature, yet they seemed to only slightly faze it, as the wounds healed nearly as fast as they were created.

The beast bellowed a deafening roar, its mouth agape, revealing several rows of gleaming black teeth that all angled slightly inward. Its front teeth were massive, easily surpassing those of a great white shark.

Utilizing uncanny speed and a dancer's grace, the creature bolted through the hole in the wall and out into the raging storm, carrying Coach along with him. The team blasted a few chunks of black gore from the beast as it ran, but the rain of bullets didn't slow its departure.

Max jumped to his feet and made for the hole, his progress impeded by the jumble of boxes and cans on the floor. He heard the women wail and sob with greater clarity as the ringing in his ears subsided. Once he reached the hole, he pulled down his night-vision goggles. LT joined him a second later.

The green night world Max saw through his NVGs flashed a brilliant yellow for an instant as a bolt of lightning touched down on. a nearby ridgeline. It took his eyes a moment to adjust after the lightning strike. "There!" Max shouted, pointing into the dark. "Eleven o'clock, just before that line of trees."

Max could just make out the creature and Coach, already some fifty yards off and about to disappear into the woods. Shooting the thing several times at point-blank range hadn't fazed it in the least, so there was no point trying to take it down from a distance.

Instead, Max turned and shouted orders to the team: "Red, Irish, stay here with the survivors. Everybody else, move it!" He whirled and jumped through the hole to sprint after the beast.

Thick mud and deep puddles forced Max to slow his pace lest he slip in the muck. He saw the creature disappear into the tree line.

He heard Coach yell a moment later, the noise of his cry nearly swallowed by distance and rain. Two gunshots followed. Precious seconds ticked by as Max and LT tried to pick up the creature's trail.

LT pointed. "Some busted branches up ahead. It must have gone in there."

Max ran for the trees, dodging oddly shaped puddles which he realized were the creature's footprints. Coach yelled again, his voice distorted. Two shots rang out, muffled by rain and wind, followed by three more.

Max hit the tree line. Though the world darkened inside his NVGs beneath the firs, he could easily track the trail of deep footprints and broken branches the creature had made smashing through the woods. Coach fired three more shots, and this time Max could see the muzzle flashes of his pistol through the trees. Max and LT charged forward into a small clearing, the others strung out in a running column just behind them.

Lightning lit the scene for a heartbeat, yet the illumination divulged no further details of the black beast that blended almost seamlessly into the night. Coach writhed and screamed in the grasp of its talons. He managed to raise his Glock and point it roughly in the direction of the creature's head. He fired twice, both shots appearing to do little. Meanwhile gleaming blood poured from several wounds on Coach's body.

The creature twisted its head toward Max as he brought his rifle to bear. It dropped Coach in the muck and pinned him down at the hips with a large, taloned foot. Coach struggled futilely to crawl away, low and panicked grunts of agony accompanying his every move. The creature bent down and seized his neck in one massive six-fingered hand, yanked hard to the side and then violently upward.

Max's jaw dropped. His aim wavered, and he lost his bead on

the creature's head.

With one mighty jerk, the beast ripped Coach's head from his shoulders. The sound of the rending decapitation—a bass *crack*, like thick ice thawing on a lake in spring—followed by an equally dull tearing noise as his spine, still attached to his head, was pulled up and out of Coach's body. The creature reared back and roared as it pivoted to face Max and his team, holding Coach's head and spine aloft like a grisly prize. It then tossed the head and spine back at the feet of Max and his men as if discarding a chicken bone or an apple core.

No order was necessary—they opened fire as one. The muzzle flashes of four rifles and a machine gun lit the clearing to midday brilliance. The creature jerked in a macabre dance beneath the ruthless hail of bullets. Puffs of black blood and dark chunks of smoking flesh blended with the powder smoke clouding the air to form a miasmal smog.

Gotcha, you bastard! Max continued pouring lead into the beast on full auto, his finger squeezed down on the trigger as he fought the rise of the weapon. He felt a strange pride in taking the creature down, his team succeeding where Greytech's security men had dismally failed despite their superior firepower.

As the creature turned and ran for the trees that pride wavered.

"Uh-uh, motherfucker!" Sugar shouted as he cut loose with another burst from his machine gun. His tracer bullets—one in every five rounds fired—showed he was lighting up the beast, the rounds pounding into its back and shoulders. The final few rounds blew off the arm that had held Coach's head and spine. The creature howled in pain, a penetrating sound halfway between a woman's scream and the screech of a bat. The pitch of the shriek, like nails on a chalkboard to the tenth power, made Max flinch.

The beast ran at incredible speed, its gait a sort of bounding run that covered ten feet in a single stride. Its powerful legs propelling it toward the tree line.

Come on, die, asshole! Max pumped more lead into its back. He was certain they had it. No creature could possibly take so many bullets so quickly and remain among the living.

And then it was gone.

The team advanced into the clearing, firing blindly into the trees in vain hope of finishing the thing off. Bullets mowed down nearly all the underbrush and low-hanging limbs. Sugar had even felled a couple of small firs with his machine gun.

And Max knew none of it mattered a damn bit. They had failed to bring down the beast, and shooting blindly after it wasted precious ammunition they would need down the road, especially if there were more of these creatures running around. "Cease fire! Cease fire!"

It took a few seconds for the team to acknowledge the order through the roar of gunfire. As the shooting subsided, the clearing faded back into fuzzy green semi-darkness through Max's NVGs. Several moments of eerie silence followed. Max's heartbeat thundered in his ears, nearly eclipsing the sound of the pouring rain.

"That was no fucking bear," Diaz said, and Max thought he detected a hint of vindication in his tone.

"Yeah, no shit." LT replied.

"Shit, it's moving!" Gable shouted, pointing to the creature's severed arm writhing in the muck.

"What the fuck?" LT said as he leaned closer.

At first, Max equated the flopping arm to how a lizard's tail would writhe when severed from its body by a predator. Then the first leg—chitinous and jointed like a spider's—sprouted from the arm. Three more followed in the next second, and the bloody stump of the arm morphed into a round maw filled with fangs, a stinger protruded from the tail end. The severed arm now formed a killing machine in its own right. It began to scuttle through the muck toward the team on its long spider legs—ten and counting. Before Max knew it, the thing was moving with the speed and grace of a cougar.

"Fuck you!" Sugar cut loose on the scuttling arm with his Mk 48 machine gun.

The thing took a burst of fire yet carried on at only slightly diminished speed.

Max snapped out of his mesmerized state and opened fire with his HK416 rifle.

The arm kept coming. It launched from the muck at Max's face.

He kept firing, but his bolt locked back as he expended his last round. The damned arm, now too close for Max to transition to his pistol, moved faster than any animal he'd ever hunted. He instinctively clubbed the creature away with the buttstock of his rifle.

Sugar blasted the arm with a surgical burst of fire as it fell into the mud, nearly all his rounds hitting home. Spindly spider legs and black blood flew everywhere as the creature disintegrated at Max's feet. The rest of the team joined Sugar in a semi-circle as they fired into the remaining pieces of the creature which continued to writhe. Soon only scraps of the thing remained. The sound of gunfire echoed away into silence.

"Is it dead yet?" Sugar inquired. He stood like a wraith in the cloud of powder smoke.

Max nudged the pieces of the arm with the toe of his boot, half expecting them to leap up and attack his leg. The world didn't often do Max favors but apparently made a concession as the remains lay still, apparently dead.

"Looks like it," Max said. "Nice shooting, Sugar. I owe you one."

Sugar said nothing. The entire team stood silently in a state of utter shock and disbelief after dealing with the creature and its severed offspring. They stared at the remains of the creature and at Coach's headless body. Diaz threw up at the sight, and Max tasted bile in the back of his throat until he finally looked away. When he snapped out of the gruesome reverie, he realized his team was exposed in the clearing. "We have to get back to camp. Now."

"What about Coach?" Gable asked.

"We gotta leave him for now. Form a column and stay close, ten feet apart. Let's move out."

"Damn fine soldier," Gable commented as he took his place in the column.

No one responded, though they all thought just as highly of Coach. This was not the time for commiseration, however.

The team fell in behind Max and made for the mess hall, moving slowly as they scrutinized every sound and stared deep into every shadow, seeking any indicators of another attack. They saw no further signs of the beast. A few minutes later, they re-entered the pantry through the hole in the wall.

Max could see the shocked look of disbelief still painted on Red's and Irish's faces.

"What the fuck was that?" Red demanded upon their return.

"Did you kill it?" Irish asked.

Max shook his head. "No. And it might not be the only one out there."

"Shit in a hat," Irish rasped.

"Coach?" Red asked.

The look on Max's face conveyed all that needed to be said.

Red nodded solemnly.

"God dammit," Irish muttered. "Connie. Lucas."

Max ignored that haunting thought and turned to the three survivors huddled by the pantry door. "What the hell was that thing!"

They shrank back from his rage, the women in tears. Dr. Kumar shifted away and pulled further back into the corner, like a small child trying to make himself invisible to an enraged parent.

"I'm waiting," Max prompted. "What the hell have you people been playing with out here?" He closed in on Dr. Kumar, grabbed him by his dingy lab coat and yanked him off his feet before slamming him against the wall. "I'll bet you know what's going on, Doc. I suggest you start talking, like right fucking now."

12

"GO AWAY," EDWARD SAID AS NICELY AS HE COULD, YET IT CAME out as a growled order.

"Please, be still," Debbie, the cute nurse, pleaded as she and the older nurse attempted to make him presentable.

He felt like throwing up, but this was nothing unusual. Nausea had long been his natural state of being.

Debbie said, "You know your mother will be arriving soon, and you want to look your best, don't you?"

"This is as good as it gets," Edward informed her.

His hair gone, his frame deathly gaunt, he could barely pull himself up to a sitting position today. Mama Liz just had to come and visit on one of his bad days. He'd felt somewhat decent for the previous couple of weeks, but she hadn't bothered stopping by then, despite the several entreaties he'd left on her voicemail. *No, she decides to show up on a day when I can barely breathe.*

He shivered in his pajamas. It always felt too cold in the ICU for some reason as though they were preparing him for cryonic suspension. He vaguely remembered his mother talking about that. Frozen at death to be revived when they could cure his cancer.

Yeah, right.

Debbie pulled out her makeup kit and started working on his face, applying various cosmetics to conceal his deathly pallor. He couldn't help but think that she'd make a good mortician. Edward hated the process, but he liked Debbie and wanted to keep her happy, so he uttered no complaints. And since his mother had only given a few hours' notice, they needed to work fast.

The timing of the visit seemed odd. His mother kept to such an ironclad schedule that she usually gave two or three days' notice of her visits, sometimes as much as a week. Such departure from her routine had Edward wondering what might be at the core of his mother's urgency. He envisioned her showing up ruffled and bedraggled in a slept-in suit after some magical breakthrough in her plans for his treatment.

Instead, Elizabeth Grey strode into his private hospice room in her customary regalia—navy-blue power suit, diamond stud earrings, perfect hair and makeup, false eyelashes.

So much for bedraggled.

Edward wasn't even the first person she addressed. "How is he?" his mother asked the older nurse, who parroted the usual bit about his condition and that they were doing all they could to keep him comfortable. While his mother grilled Nurse Ratchet, Debbie sat by his side offering quiet comfort, which he appreciated.

Edward's mother then turned to him and flashed her trademark plastic smile, a masterpiece of cosmetic dentistry that, like the green eyes behind it, was absolutely contrived. *Her default look,*

Edward thought with a smirk.

"How are you feeling?" his mother asked as she stepped up, glancing around at the dimness of the room with a disapproving cast.

"I've had better days," he admitted.

"Well, let's get a little light in here, shall we?"

Edward felt Debbie tense at that, but neither of the nurses tried to stop his mother from opening the blinds and flooding the room with a million lumens of sunshine. Edward's pupils contracted painfully to pinpricks, but he didn't complain. His mother did what she wanted; the rest of the world could only deal with it.

"So how are you today, darling?" she asked with a sudden gush of concern as she took a seat beside him.

Edward took in a halting breath and then released it. "You know how I'm doing, Mom. I'm dying of cancer, remember?"

She blinked as if that hardly registered in her mind. "You know the doctors and I are doing everything we can to fix this."

"But you can't, can you? I'm dying of cancer, and even your billions of dollars can't save me."

She winced slightly and pulled back from him. "That's not fair. I have my researchers working on this—"

"And it got to my brain anyway. It's only a matter of time now, Mom. I'm sure they've told you how long I have left."

The answer was two months tops, probably only one.

"I had another seizure the other day, did they tell you about that? And they're going to come more often and get a lot worse, so unless your researchers can magically produce a cure in the next few weeks, I'd rather you skip the pep talk."

Her countenance cycled through several emotions—first affronted, then angry, then forcefully hopeful. She leaned forward and squeezed his hand harder. "Things will get better," she insisted.

"I have the most prestigious doctors and researchers in the world working on this. And we both know that you can beat it. Others have and you can too. I am going to fix this. Do you understand?" She stared him straight in the eye with the same intense conviction she'd shown from his first diagnosis.

By this point, Edward had already heard the same words from her mouth, seen the same look in her eyes, felt the same grip on his hand a hundred times.

And he had grown tired of it. Tired of everything.

His mother had to be going through the motions at this point. Why else would she continue trying to convince him that he was going to survive?

Edward took in a weak breath and allowed her to finish her spiel—her soliloquy, really, as no one else was listening. When she had finished, he replied, "Okay."

She responded with a resplendent smile. "That's the spirit. Keep on fighting, tiger."

But he had no intention of doing that at all. *Let her live in her fantasy world and fight the good fight.* He'd had enough. Capitulation had become logical, and part of him was glad, as it freed him from his mother's expectations of him. Finally, he could simply be himself.

And that was the one thing that he couldn't tell her, though he'd confessed his plan to Debbie after suffering a particularly bad seizure the previous week—the one that confirmed the cancer had invaded his brain. "You know," he'd whispered in the scratchy voice he always got when they tubed him, "I'm actually glad she can't fix this."

Debbie had looked confused.

"She thinks she can save me," he told her. "We all know she can't."

"What are you talking about?" Debbie asked, failing in her attempt to feign innocence.

"I'm going to die. Everybody knows it. And I'm glad."

"Why?"

Debbie hadn't been his nurse for very long at that point. The older nurse's previous partner was a black man who had been dismissed from his care for some reason, probably because he understood Edward's wish without ever having been told.

"Because my life has always been about her, what she wants me to be. I've never been allowed a chance to plot my own destiny."

Debbie shook her head. "I'm sure that's not the case."

"Oh, it is. Believe me. She needs to control everyone and everything around her, right down to the tiniest detail. And if she can't be there to micromanage a situation, she'll assign someone to do it for her. That's what killed my dad."

Again, Debbie appeared confused. "I thought he died in a plane crash."

"I'm pretty sure he was drunk at the time." Edward remained confident in his assumption. His mother could impel a saint to take up the bottle. Hell, his father might even have staged the accident to get back at his mother, to finally gain some control by planning his own suicide.

Debbie looked shocked.

"Trust me. Once you get to know my mom, you'll see what I mean."

And she had.

Edward sat silently while his mother rambled on about new treatments, his favorite basketball team, how he would finish his degree at Yale once he'd beaten cancer. Edward couldn't have cared less about any of it and wondered the entire time if he had the guts to escape his mother as his father had. *It's as good an exit as any,* he decided, *and nothing a sane person could blame me for.* The time had finally come to convey *his* wishes to her—to wrest control of his life from his mother and seize it for himself.

* * *

Elizabeth Grey recited the information she'd memorized regarding LeBron James and Edward's beloved Cleveland Cavaliers. When she finally got a smile out of her boy, she knew she'd gotten the details right.

She hadn't wanted to take time off from her work to visit at a crucial time like this, but it was important to keep Edward's spirits up. She'd read somewhere that cancer was like an ocean, and only positive thinking could keep Edward afloat. *Lose that and you'll sink,* she recalled, gazing deep into Edward's yellowing, bloodshot eyes. *Like a shark drowning because it stops swimming.*

She never stopped swimming, and neither would her son. Sometimes she wondered if he truly appreciated her herculean efforts to keep him alive: how she had strong-armed the boards of several pharmaceutical companies to get him on experimental drugs and shanghaied the most renowned cancer specialists from the best hospitals to treat her son. Just the other day she'd been forced to address this team of doctors, a couple of who were growing recalcitrant regarding the aggressive treatment program she demanded.

They've haven't seen anything yet. Once I have the substance... She thought of the shitshow playing out up in Alaska. Max Ahlgren and his team had a reputation of succeeding when others failed, but Elizabeth could only place so much confidence in anyone, regardless of their stellar performance record. If she wasn't on the scene and running things, she could never be certain the assignment would be carried out properly. She might urge Edward to keep faith, but she hated putting her own faith in the hands of anyone else.

And if Ahlgren enters the ship...

She purged the thought from her mind and concentrated on Edward. Her breath caught in her throat for an instant. *He would have been—no, he* will be *the image of his father.* Edward had inherited his father's blond hair and strapping physical stature. He would regain the latter two once he'd defeated the cancer.

I will kill for him, if that's what it takes, she thought not for the first time. Only this time the thought took verbal form as she whispered under her breath: "I will kill for you."

Edward looked up at her. He opened his eyes a little wider and seemed about to say something when her phone rang. Elizabeth sighed in frustration and vowed to reiterate her orders to Cynthia: no one was to call during her visits unless it was a matter of life or death.

The phone kept ringing.

"Shit," she muttered.

"Mom, I've been thinking a lot—"

"Hold on, darling." She pulled her phone from her purse and checked the screen. Though the number wasn't in her contact list, she recognized it from recent conversations. "Peter?"

"Ms. Grey." Banner's drawl made the two words sound endless. "I have an idea on Alaska, but we'll need to act fast."

"All right. Hold on a minute." She covered the microphone on the cell phone. "This is a very important call, Edward. I have to take it."

"Yeah. They're all important."

"I'm sorry. It has to do with your treatment."

151

"That's what I want to talk to you about."

"And we will talk about it, darling, here in a couple of days when I know a bit more. You must keep faith, Edward. I need you to trust in me for just a bit longer. Can you do that for me?"

Edward stared at her and said nothing.

"A couple more days. We'll have dinner then, okay?"

"Sure." Edward reached for the controller to recline his bed.

"My darling boy." Elizabeth bent over and kissed him on his overheated cheek. "I'll be back soon, and I think I'll have some great news. I love you."

"Yep. Love you too." He was already lying on his back with his eyes shut, and that was how his mother left him.

13

ALL THE BREATH LEFT DR. KUMAR'S LUNGS IN A SINGLE FORCED exhalation when he hit the wall. Max didn't give a damn if he'd broken the old man's ribs. He'd lost a man and he wanted answers—and he would do whatever it took to get them.

"Well!" Max barked into Kumar's face.

Kumar gasped frantically for breath and shook his head. "I signed an NDA and my reputation—"

"Will die right along with you," Max finished. He drew his pistol as he spoke and shoved it under Kumar's chin. "You have three seconds, Doctor."

"Fine, but I really don't know much. It broke out before I had a chance to study it."

"Where did it come from?"

Kumar closed his eyes. "From the ship." He uttered the words with obvious reluctance.

His answer only succeeded in further angering Max. "What ship? What the fuck are you talking about?"

"You really are in over your head, aren't you?"

Max narrowed his eyes at the doctor, but he added nothing further.

Harlow answered for him in a whisper: "It's an alien spacecraft buried beneath the glacier."

Max turned his attention to her, his eyes bulging in disbelief. "You have got to be fucking kidding me. What kind of science fiction bullshit are you trying to sell me?"

"Total bullshit," Red scoffed. "They created that monster, whatever it is."

"I'm inclined to agree." Max nodded. "I'm thinking Elizabeth Grey was genetically engineering some kind of weapon for the Pentagon." It seemed a plausible explanation, considering the creature's capabilities. It also explained Banner's interest in the operation.

"You're wrong," Dr. Kumar stated flatly. "That creature formed out of an unknown substance found on the spacecraft. The scientists working onboard thought it might be sentient, but they didn't have the proper equipment or environment on board to fully study the substance, so they sent it to my lab for testing. Then it broke free." His voice trailing off as the reality of the last few words hit him.

Max could sense the truth in his voice despite how incredible the story sounded. He lowered Kumar back to the floor and holstered his pistol. "How many are there?"

"It's hard to say. It displays intelligence at the cellular level, and the cells seem to be able to organize themselves in any number of ways. They can combine, divide, form different types of tissues and organs. I have only seen the one, but there's more of the substance on the ship. A lot more."

After numerous interrogations over the years, Max possessed a finely tuned bullshit detector. He knew he was finally getting some truthful answers out of Kumar. Answers that bore dread like none he'd collected before. On rare occasion, he'd been forced to retreat from an enemy in the face of hopeless odds. This situation, however, raised the hair on his neck.

You wanna leave? Best do it now before another of your men gets wasted.

He thought of the disabled Sea Stallion sitting on the helipad. Even if they could somehow repair it, which he doubted, attempting to fly it out with no copilot and no hours at the stick in the midst of a raging ice storm amounted to suicide. He then thought of Banner.

What does he know regarding all this?

"Where are the hard drives from your lab?" Max asked Kumar.

"I didn't know they were missing."

"They are. Who took them if not you?"

"There must be survivors on the ship," Harlow replied in a hopeful whisper. "Dr. Jung, maybe Dr. Rogers, or some of her team."

"What are they in charge of?" Max asked her.

"Dr. Jung is head of the overall project. Dr. Rogers was in charge of research efforts aboard the ship, she's something of a lone wolf."

"Sounds like you know her. What's her specialty?"

Harlow laughed. "Being brilliant. She holds a Ph.D. in molecular biology from Princeton and headed the research team Ms. Grey contracted from Stanford. She's kind of a recluse. I've never actually met her."

"And both of these scientists spent all their time on the ship?" Max asked.

"No." Kumar shifted uncomfortably as if he anticipated paying for this betrayal. "Dr. Jung conducted his work in the camp most of the time. Dr. Rogers, on the other hand, I spoke to briefly upon her arrival. After that, she entered the ship and rarely returned to camp. We communicated via email until a couple of days ago. She's had the most hands-on experience with the substance and the ship. Maybe she knows something that could help, assuming she is still alive."

Max nodded, stalling for a few moments while he pondered the team's next move. An actual spacecraft, he wouldn't have believed it, had he not spent the last ten minutes fighting something plainly not of this Earth. If Kumar were his only source of intel, he still might be skeptical. The man kept his secrets close for a university publish-or-perish academic, so Max figured he'd done plenty of government work in the past. But Ms. Harlow seemed genuine and logical. She didn't want to die out here at the hands of the creature.

An alien.

"Have any of you three been on the spacecraft?" Max asked the survivors. None had. The negative responses from Quinones and Harlow weren't surprising, but Kumar seemed too arrogant to let himself be pushed out of the main line of inquiry. "Not even once, Doctor?"

Kumar shook his head ruefully. "No. Access was strictly controlled by Ms. Grey, but believe me, I begged."

"Is there a map of the floor plan anywhere?"

Gable piped up warily, "And why is that important?" His face said he knew the answer already.

"Because we need to board that ship and find Dr. Rogers and Dr. Jung," Max replied, his decision made.

Gable popped to his feet. "Whoa, just a minute, Chief. I didn't come along on this job not to get paid, and according to our contract that dig site is strictly off limits."

"We have no choice," Max stated. "Our contract also states

we're to secure this installation. We need to find a way to kill that thing, and this Dr. Rogers might be our only answer. Besides, we are the only hope these people have."

"Yeah? I don't give two shits about these people and neither do you, so you can drop the fucking Boy Scout act. Who knows if she's even alive? We blasted that thing with seven guns and couldn't kill it. If there's more of them down that hole she's dead sure as sunrise."

"We'll take that chance. There's no other option."

"Like hell there isn't!"

"Well, take it then!" Max stepped up to Gable, nose to nose. "Go on, Johnny; door's right there." He pointed to the gaping hole in the wall. "A couple dozen Greytech security men are lying dead out there, but if you think you can hike out of here on your own and beat this thing with pure Alabama shit-kicker attitude, I damn sure won't stand in your way."

"I've made myself disappear in deserts with no cover for miles around, Chief. You think I can't march out of here and make it back to civilization?"

"Go for it. That thing will sniff you out before you've humped a mile."

"We'll see."

"Nah, Johnny." Sugar reached for his arm. "You can't do it. There ain't no runnin' from this thing."

"I ain't runnin' from shit but an empty bank account and my own grave, not that any of you bastards will be left to bury me." Gable stepped back from Max and addressed the team: "This is a bad decision, and all of you know it. And this ain't the first time you've shoved us into a hornets' nest, Ahlgren. That last mission was a total goatfuck—we're lucky any of us survived. And what about Georgia, huh? We didn't all come back from that one, did we?"

"How the hell could I have seen that coming?" Max asked. "And this is a dangerous job, or have you forgotten?"

"No, I ain't forgot shit. You are the one who seems to have a death wish. Seems like you forgot what happened to your CIA team…"

Max leveled his gaze at Gable, his eyes afire and cut him off. "Don't you fucking bring up missions you weren't even on. You don't know shit about it." Gable's comments stung Max's pride to the core. He hadn't known that any team members knew of his failed Crimea mission.

"I know you lost over half your team before you wisely decided to bug out. Well, I ain't ready to add my name to the Max Ahlgren memorial. I'm getting the fuck outta here, and I bet I'm not the only one. Who's with me?" He ran his gaze over the team members. "What do you say, Diaz? You know we're hell bound if we stay. You've known all along we were facing something we can't beat."

"That's enough, Gable," LT ordered. "We finish what we start. Nobody's going anywhere."

"No. Let him go." Max let his rage simmer. "And anybody who wants can join him."

The team exchanged glances with each other.

"Do any of you really think that thing couldn't have killed these three anytime it wanted to? That it didn't know they were here? You think it's a coincidence that it didn't bust through that wall until we arrived? It watched us sweep the camp, took stock of us, then baited us with the survivors. Once we were all here it struck, and we're a man short because of it."

Red's brow furrowed. "We don't know that for sure."

Diaz snorted. He stared at the floor with wide and empty eyes. "Max is right, the stragglers will be picked off like those poor bastards we found in that clearing. We gotta stick together, or we don't have a chance in hell."

"Agreed," Irish said.

Red nodded. "I don't like our chances of just walking out of here. I've seen how that ends up. Besides, I'd like to tour a spaceship and use a flamethrower before I die." He patted the flamethrower affectionately.

Sugar shook his head, then looked up at Gable. "You and me, we're like brothers. But I can't stick with you on this one. Only way out of this place is down through that hole."

Gable eyed each member of the team, knowing full well he'd been overruled. "Well, fuck it then." He half smiled. "Just let the record show I thought this was a shitty idea."

"Noted," LT replied indifferently.

"All right, we're settled then." Max motioned to the three survivors. "You'll have to come with us; you won't be safe hiding up here."

Kumar cut the positive vibes short. "We won't be safe anywhere."

The others appeared resigned to cast their lots with Max's team.

Max curled his right hand into a fist as he thought aloud. "We're gonna hit the armory before we go in, grab some more ammo and get the three of you some protection." He looked at Harlow. "You actually know how to use that pistol?"

"She does. I show her how," Ms. Quinones boasted. "My brother taught me to shoot guns. He was a *Sandinista*."

Red huffed. "Oh, that's great. We can consider her fully trained. No, really, arming these people is not a good idea."

"Maybe not but it's a necessity," Max stated. "We can't kill this alien and guarantee their safety at the same time. And we need all the firepower we can get."

Kumar unfurled a smug glare. "I don't believe in violence."

"That thing out there doesn't give a shit about your beliefs, Doc.

I suggest you take the pistol we give you. Don't worry, we'll show you how to use it so you don't blow your foot off."

Diaz groused, "I'm more concerned with *this guy* blowing my head off."

Max grinned at him. "Then you can instruct the good doctor in its use, seeing as how you two are already well acquainted."

"Hiking out is sounding *cada vez mejor*," Diaz muttered.

Max ignored his indecipherable lapse into Spanish. "Let's even the score with that thing, gentlemen. Get your shit together. We leave for the armory in five."

The men turned to adjusting their gear and checking their weapons. Some hydrated and grabbed a hurried bite of chow. Those who hadn't already done so reloaded their weapons with full magazines of ammo.

LT approached Max and said quietly. "Got a moment?"

Max nodded. They left the pantry to confer privately in the kitchen. "What's up?"

"You know I've got your back in this, but I think you should reconsider arming those civilians. As nervous as we are, you know they've got to be shitting eggrolls right about now. Give them weapons and you're asking for an accidental discharge and all that goes with it."

"I'm well aware of that. But after seeing that thing kill Thatcher and what it can do, we are going to need every gun we can get. Besides, rescuing any survivors is also a condition of our mission, and we can't ensure their survival and battle that thing at the same time. I don't see where we have much of a choice."

"Okay," LT said with reluctance. "I'll do my best to make sure they know what they're doing. Especially Kumar. Diaz and I will give them a crash course on how to use the G36 assault rifles we saw in the armory and the pistols."

Max nodded. "We need to get Red some fuel for that flame-thrower too. If any man can master that weapon in a hurry, it's him."

"There's some heavy equipment up by the dig. He can siphon off some fuel before we go in."

"Sounds like a plan."

LT released a heavy breath. "This is our ugliest one yet, Max. I hope you know what you're doing."

Max nodded slowly, thinking of his past debacles. "So do I."

14

"YOUR SHOTS ARE HIGH." LT REPEATED, "TRY AGAIN."

Dr. Kumar raised the Glock and took aim at the far wall of the cafeteria. He grabbed his right wrist with his left hand to support the pistol, a typical beginner's mistake.

"No, no, no," Diaz chided. "Your left hand goes under the butt for support, remember?"

The doctor adjusted his grip, put the laser dot on the roof, and fired.

He can hit the broad side of a barn, at least. Max was satisfied. The best that could be hoped for when arming a pacifist professor.

Max had led the team through the dark and the rain to the dig site after plundering the armory for all the ammo they could carry, along with rifles and pistols for the survivors. He had concluded that stealth was pointless with the alien creature out there watching them. All the night and noise discipline he'd practiced over his career wasn't going to hide them on this bleak expanse of glacial ice. Oddly enough, Max felt almost completely safe being so exposed. Like every apex predator, the alien relied on surprise and ambush to take its prey; odds were it wasn't going to attack a large party of heavily armed and wary men out in the open.

Their initial recon from atop the ridge had revealed the most glaring marks of destruction around the dig. They found a small booth by the hole, once a guard shack, with all its windows shattered, along with three more corpses on the ice to make a total of four. Two of the dead were Greytech security men; the others were laborers clad in Greytech jumpsuits. All the bodies were mangled as expected, the creature's usual MO. A search of the intact trailer revealed a fifth corpse in a lab coat but no missing hard drives or survivors.

Max and Gable kept watch on the surrounding area while Sugar stood before the hole with his machine gun pointed into the blackness. Red had poured a bottle of soap into the fuel tank of the flamethrower. Now he and Irish were topping off the tank with several gallons of diesel fuel. No siphoning required; they simply loosened the fuel cap on the overturned bulldozer and allowed gravity to fill the tank.

Dr. Kumar plinked rounds into the trailer roof. The sounds of the striking bullets told Max whether they had penetrated the aluminum or ricocheted off. The ratio of penetration was about seven bullets in ten, and the main reason Max carried a .45 instead of a 9mm. His Glock 21 held fewer rounds; nevertheless, they all would have penetrated that roof.

When the fueling was complete, Red called to Max, "Request permission to finish off this trailer."

"Granted," Max said. "I want to see this."

Red chuckled and took a position about ten yards away from

the partially burned trailer. Kumar stopped firing his pistol. The steady ticking of frozen rain pellets falling on the building roof tops became the only sound.

To activate the system, Red punched numbers into the miniature computer by the weapon's trigger. Older flamethrowers needed to remain lit, the eternal flame on the muzzle acting as a pilot light for ignition. The Mk 42 fired via electronic ignition.

A cone of dull orange flames swirling with oily black smoke spurted from the flamethrower. The ice reflected the glare of the fire and lit the area to twilight brilliance. Red's first burst hit low and arced to the ice just short of the trailer, kicking up a cloud of steam. His second attempt hit dead on, and he kept the trigger down as he sprayed fire along the full length of the trailer. After making one pass, he swept back in the other direction. Team members and survivors shouted their enthusiastic encouragement. Ms. Quinones even went so far as to smile.

Red released the trigger and observed the trailer, now nicely alight and crackling merrily away. "Not bad, but I bet we can do better." He entered numbers on the keypad, faced the target, and fired. This time the jet of flames burned a more brilliant orange, and a wave of blustery heat buffeted Max in the face as Red finished burning the trailer. He had the fuel to the propellant mixture just right or close enough at any rate.

"All right, knock off the hijinks, people," Max ordered. "Save your fuel for the beast."

Red boasted, "Fucker's toast when I see him."

Diaz looked around nervously. "That's likely to be sooner rather than later."

"You keeping the machine gun?" Irish asked.

Red grinned. "Fuck yeah. I can hump them both, and I don't go anywhere without my baby."

"Form it up, single file into that tunnel," Max instructed. "Red, you're on point. I'm right behind you. Then Gable, LT, Irish, you three civilians. Diaz and Sugar guard the rear. And stay sharp back there. Good chance that thing follows us in."

"Last mistake he'll ever make," Sugar assured.

"Light and noise discipline back in effect, that includes you three." Max pointed to the survivors, all of whom had been equipped with night-vision goggles from the armory. "Anyone who speaks better have a damn good reason. We might be able to ambush the creature inside if we keep quiet."

The ice tunnel yawned before Max and Red, a Stygian portal to hell roughly twelve feet in diameter. They donned their NVGs and peered inside. Rubber flooring had been laid down for traction. A length of conduit-wrapped cable ran along the floor to provide electricity for the lights; unfortunately, the generator that powered them was dead.

"After me, Chief." Red still grinned like a kid at a carnival.

Max could have kicked himself. *If I'd known a flamethrower would make him this happy I'd have built one for him years ago.*

The temperature dropped about fifteen degrees Fahrenheit upon entering the tunnel which sloped gradually downward at roughly a five-degree grade. Red stalked forward, his pace a bit fast for the conditions. "Slow it down," Max whispered. Comm had grown so garbled that the radios became useless. The team now relied mostly on hand signals and muttered words. Red nodded acknowledgment though he did not slacken his pace appreciably.

Max considered repeating the order, yet it behooved them to transit the tunnel as quickly as possible, lest the beast confront them in the passage. A blast from the flamethrower in here could melt the tunnel roof and cause a cave-in. Max had overcome his natural fear of death years before, but he didn't particularly want to be buried alive in ice.

Several hundred feet into the tunnel, the ice walls gave way to aluminum shoring, a sign that the tunnel had transitioned from ice into soil. The view ahead brightened through Max's NVGs as they approached a gentle curve. The air grew warmer as they pressed on. Red finally slowed his pace, creeping along with remarkable stealth for a man of his size. The view lightened from green to yellow as they rounded the curve. Max and Red lifted their NVGs. From the apex of the curve, they saw a dimly lit room ahead.

Max heard the whisper in his head again, unintelligible, as if another voice had tuned into his mind. Whether it was taunting him or inviting him, he couldn't tell. He looked around at the team but no one else seemed to react.

Red halted though there were no signs of life visible from this distance. Max wondered if he had heard the same voice, but then understood his hesitation. *We're about to board a starship.* The concept still seemed inconceivable. He'd never doubted the possibility of extraterrestrial life—in an endless universe, there were bound to be other inhabited planets—but he'd never believed that aliens had visited the Earth. Part of him still didn't believe. Perhaps the starship buried in the ice was merely a ruse concocted to disguise the operations of an underground Greytech lab facility. Impossible to say, but the answer lay a mere fifty feet in front of them.

Red finished gawking and moved on, step by cautious step. He located the first bit of carnage a few feet before the room, a tactical boot lying in a pool of blood, the severed foot still inside. They found no signs of the foot's owner, though a trail of blood droplets led on into the room.

Either this alien really gets around or there are more of them.
Max thought of what Dr. Kumar had said regarding the quantity of
"substance" onboard. *Probably a lot more of them.* He noted the car-
bon smudges around the portal and the smell of spent high explosives as he followed Red into the ship.

Though the entry looked sloppy on the outside, Greytech's engineers had bored cleanly through the ship's hull, which was about
five feet thick. *Must have taken them weeks.* Max saw no burn marks
as he walked through the hull, so he assumed they'd bored through
with lasers or, more likely, high-pressure water jets.

Max's first glimpse into an alien spacecraft proved anticli-
mactic. For something so alien, it appeared remarkably suited
for humans. He found himself standing in a long room lined with
alcoves, a wall locker of terrestrial manufacture at the back of each
one. Yellow HAZMAT suits hung in the open lockers, so Max assumed
Greytech uniforms hung in the secured lockers. The room appeared
mundane, yet there were still plenty of signs they were in an extraterrestrial environment. Dim light, ambient yet permeating, emanated from portions of the translucent gray ceiling. Max tapped one
of the dark-gray walls with his knuckles and was surprised to find it
not constructed of metal but rather a lightweight material like hard
plastic resin. There were no bolts or rivets in the walls or floor, and
the few seams visible in the material ran perfectly straight. The room
didn't appear constructed of the resin material but machined from
a solid block of it.

The creature had left its mark here as well. Two portals
accessed the room; both sporting ruined doors as thick as those on a
bank vault, each made of resin. The door at the room's far end hung
askew in its track after taking a pounding from the other side. The
door that had guarded the entranceway lay bent and discarded on

the floor. The trail of blood drops that began at the severed foot ran the length of the room, through that doorway, and on into the ship.

Max dropped back to confer quietly with the survivors. "I take it this is some sort of decon room?"

Kumar pointed to the far door. "That's actually the *decon* room, as you call it, where personnel were sterilized before entering the ship."

"Before entering? You'd think it would be the other way around."

"At first it was, but the initial sweep of the ship revealed no known bacteria or viruses onboard. The environment is remarkably clean from what I've heard, so the cleansing room was used to keep the ship free from contamination by terrestrial bacteria and viruses."

"I'd say its cleansing days are over."

"Good," Red commented. "Those HAZMAT suits are like mobile saunas, and it's already plenty warm in here."

"Yes, it is." Max made an executive decision: "Lose the cold-weather gear; it'll only dehydrate us and slow us down."

The team didn't need to be told twice. They quickly stripped off their excess gear, then folded and stacked the garments by the door in case they had to retreat hastily from the ship.

"That's better," Red said as he resumed point.

"Still too fuckin' hot," Gable lamented.

"Shut up, all of you." Max asked Kumar, "Where do we find this Dr. Rogers?"

Kumar shrugged. "Search me. Never been down here before, remember?"

"Marvelous. Any idea how big this ship is?"

Harlow replied, "I've heard its huge, even bigger than the largest cruise ship. Very little of it has been explored."

"Guess we'd better get looking."

"Where do we start?" LT asked. "She could be anywhere."

"But I doubt she'd be just anywhere. She's a scientist, so she's probably in a lab. I'm pretty sure Greytech posted signs and maps to keep their people from getting lost. For now, let's follow the trail of cords and hoses and see where they lead."

LT nodded his concession. "Good point."

"Let's move out, same order as before."

Red led the way through the cleansing room and into the hallway beyond, a passage as narrow and dark as any in the bowels of a naval ship, with translucent light sources of an unknown origin dimmed low and spaced some fifteen feet apart. Max didn't consider himself claustrophobic, but it was impossible not to feel cramped with the walls so close and the light so sparse.

Red stopped about twenty feet in and pointed ahead into the shadows at a minigun on a tripod, pointed down the hall leading into the ship. He pulled out his LED flashlight and put the beam on it. "Automatic," he whispered. "There'll be a laser trip down the hall somewhere. I haven't seen anything like this since I was stationed at Groom Lake."

Max produced his own flashlight and examined the gun. It was fully loaded, and no shell casings lay on the floor. Yet the hallway smelled faintly of gunpowder. All the situations Max envisioned involved the team retreating back into this hallway to the exit, and someone was bound to trigger the weapon during the chaos.

"Best disable it," Max decided. He removed the ammunition belt and cleared the weapon. For good measure, he then switched off the sensor for the laser trip down the hall. "Let's move on, but keep your eyes open. The next one might be pointing at us."

The scent of spent gun powder grew stronger. At a T-intersection, about forty feet ahead, sat another tripod-mounted minigun. This time brass shell casings lay scattered across the floor at the intersection, winking in the glare of their flashlights.

"Stop," Max ordered. "That thing might be rigged to fire down any hallway. Red, scan the left wall for trips. I'll take the right."

Red nodded, and they pressed on, the bulk of their bodies filling the hallway from side to side. As they moved, a new scent began to compete for their attention: organic rot.

The trip had been hastily rigged, the apparatus glaringly apparent on the ship's smooth walls despite its diminutive sensors. The invisible beam spanned the hall at a height of three feet, too high to step over safely. Red crawled underneath on his belly. Max followed, indicating the laser's location to Gable beforehand. Each man and woman crawled beneath, in turn, having been alerted to the danger by the person in front of them.

Red stopped a few feet past the laser beam. He jerked a thumb toward the left wall and then the right. Two Claymore mines, each detonated, had been rigged at a height of six feet, both pointed at a slight angle to completely cover the last few feet of hallway and the intersection. The sickly sweet smell of gore rotting in the heat fought to overpower the pungent sting of burnt powder. Max had smelled the same scent dozens of times during his career, and it always made him edgy, an expectation that things would get worse before they got better.

"How in the fuck?" Red eyed the floor and walls covered in splatters and smears of black crystalline residue where the creature had been blasted by the mines. It had been headed toward the ship's only exit, yet only a tiny trail of the scattered black drops led in that direction.

Max couldn't suppress a sigh. "Yeah, they're that tough."

"What the fuck? Does it just regenerate like a troll or something?"

Shot up with a chain gun, direct hits from two Claymores, and still running around. We are fucked. "That's pretty much the size of it." Max pointed ahead. "The intersection. Let's move."

The creature hadn't been hit by all fourteen hundred bb's from the Claymore mines. The errant pellets, however, had barely scarred the ship's resin-like interior. They had partially destroyed the directory sign adhered to the wall at the intersection. The remaining half listed points of interest: Cargo Hold, Bridge, Holochamber, Diagnostics, Microbiology, Security, Personnel Quarters, and Services Deck. The half pointing the way to each area had taken the brunt of the blast, leaving it unreadable.

Max noticed that some bb's and the shell casings from the tripod-mounted gun had rolled down the right hallway, yet none had rolled to the left, indicating the ship had come to rest listing slightly. The chain gun had fired about half a belt of 7.62mm ammunition into the creature—Max saw the gleaming blood spatter where it had been hit about fifty feet down the right hallway.

The team and survivors gathered at the intersection.

"Disable the gun?" LT asked.

"Yeah, I'll disconnect the belt and clear the weapon. While it's inoperable, we'll destroy the sensors down each of these hallways. We'll leave the trigger we crawled under intact and reload the gun before we move on. Hopefully, the creature outside will trigger the weapon when it follows us in. It probably won't kill it, but the gunfire might alert us to its presence if we're close enough to hear."

Kumar added, "If it even follows us in."

Max glared at him. "Your opinion is only important when I ask for it. Until then, keep your mouth shut."

Kumar smirked and turned away.

The team carried out Max's orders within minutes. Sugar got

down in the prone position and covered the hallway they'd traversed, and Max wished for the beast to come right now. With the chain gun and Sugar lighting it up simultaneously, they might actually be able to drop the thing. Yet Max knew the timing wasn't right. *No, we're too alert for it to attack right now. It'll wait for us to drop our guard.*

"Form it up," Max ordered when the gun was reloaded. "That way." He pointed down the left hallway. No one questioned his choice of direction since the creature had come from the right. Hopefully, it hadn't dined on Dr. Rogers before getting blasted at the intersection.

The going was slow. Max and Red moved with great care as they examined the walls and ceiling for more traps, yet they found none. There were doors aplenty, some of the sliding variety that automatically opened when someone stood before them, and others apparently controlled by a touch-screen mounted next to them in the wall. All the doors were seamless and constructed of the lightweight resin material. Not surprisingly, the automatic doors revealed rooms that were largely empty and devoid of any signs of habitation. The touch-screen doors could not be opened. When touched a holographic image appeared with strange floating symbols. A swipe of the hand through the image and the symbols would move into a pattern and change colors. Max assumed that they required a biometric reading from someone authorized to enter, but it was impossible to say since the script on the screen was in an alphabet foreign to Earth.

"Greytech brought in four professors just to decipher this alphabet, not that you asked," Dr. Kumar told Max.

"They obviously failed," Max replied.

"Looks Oriental to me," Irish squinted at one of the screens.

"The characters closely resemble ancient Sumerian cuneiform text, so I'm told," Kumar informed them. "I wouldn't know; I slept through most of Ancient History 102."

"Yeah, go figure," Gable grumbled. "Even in college you were useless."

Irish rapped against a door as he passed. "I bet we could blow one of these suckers open."

"No time for that," Max said. "We need to keep moving."

Red asked, "What if she's behind one of them? How the hell would we know?"

"There's nothing living behind them," LT assured him. "They haven't been opened in God knows how long."

"I agree," Max said. "That creature has a thing for tearing down doors to get at anything tasty. There's likely nothing important behind any of them."

They pressed on for a hundred more feet at just below a normal walking pace before stopping to observe something all too familiar: body parts, in this case, the naked lower half of a man lying in front of a closed door, knees broken, the severed intestines oozing blood and excrement.

Someone retched behind him; Ms. Harlow, Max assumed.

Red leveled his flamethrower, stepped over the remains, and stood before the door which slid open quickly to reveal more Greytech casualties. Four dead men lay amongst tables and chairs overturned and broken. Max noted a busted laptop lying in a corner, its surfaces bloody, the weapon used to bludgeon one of them to death. All the corpses lay in twisted positions with necks and backs broken, elbows and knees bent backward. Some were missing portions of limbs, most of which had been gnawed on by the creature and then discarded. The beast had scooped the innards from a torso, the counterpart to the legs in the hallway, and flung them about the place. Papers covered in characters similar to those on the touchscreen doors were scattered everywhere.

"So much for the Four Horsemen of Linguistics," Max commented. "Sugar, Diaz, remain outside with the ladies and the doc. Everyone else, toss the place."

The papers revealed nothing but gibberish; half were illegible with blood. Red found an intact laptop and powered it on. Max watched over his shoulder as he pulled up programs and entered Greytech in the search box, finding a folder labeled Greytech Alphabet Analysis.

"Fuck, it's password protected." Red shook his head.

Max didn't miss a beat. "Don't sweat it; there probably isn't anything here that'll help us anyway."

"Got something here, Chief." LT stood up from the corner he'd been searching and held aloft a black leather daily planner.

"There we go," Max said.

The planner belonged to Lucian Sprague, Ph.D., a professor from Columbia University. It didn't mention Dr. Sprague's area of academic expertise; it did, however, reveal that he'd arrived at the Greytech camp ten days previous and chronicled his various appointments with other researchers since then.

"Bingo!" Max pointed out to LT an appointment entry from four days before: "Dr. Rogers, Holochamber, 8am." He'd scrawled feedback from his appointment below that: "Oddly distracted and supercilious..."

"There's a word you don't hear every day," Max said.

"I thought all professors were supercilious." LT snorted. "The one out in the hall certainly is."

"Whatever the case, we know where to start searching for her." Max rounded up the team, none of whom had found anything else of note. "Be on the lookout for any directions to the Holochamber. Let's move out."

Luck was with the team. The next intersection, a four-way, opened into a round room in the center of which sat a circular elevator. No combat had taken place here. According to the intact sign, the Holochamber was four floors up, on deck eight.

As they approached, the elevator showed up in moments, on its own accord as if it reacted to their presence. Max noted it was made of the same mysterious material as everything else. The team and survivors packed themselves into the round car, an uncomfortably tight squeeze for all. Next to the elevator's holographic controls. Max touched the glowing prompt with the "8" plastered next to it. The weight of the team with their gear would have stalled the elevator in just about any building. But not this tin can. Max felt blood rush from his head down to his boots when the car shot upward as though it were rocket-propelled.

"Know what I'm wondering?" Gable asked. "How the hell is the power on in here?"

"You wouldn't understand," Dr. Kumar sniped.

"That so, Professor?" Gable leaned over Ms. Quinones to get in Kumar's face. "And why is that?"

"Because I don't understand it."

Max had to give Kumar grudging credit. He was probably terrified of Gable—and justly so—but he hadn't flinched when the old Ranger invaded his personal space.

Gable wasn't impressed. "Maybe we should feed you to this fuckin' critter. Buy the rest of us a little more time."

Kumar wrinkled his nose against the onslaught of Gable's reeking Copenhagen breath.

"Just delaying *lo inevitable*," Diaz said. "That thing'll be shitting us all out before this is over."

"Both of you idiots shut your mouths; nobody needs to hear it,"

Max growled.

When the speeding elevator came to a gentle halt, opening on deck eight, everyone flinched. Sugar alighted first to cover the elevator landing. Max followed on his heels and swept the chamber with his rifle's reflex sight. They found the room empty, similar yet not identical to the four-way intersection four floors below. The hallways leading from this chamber were much wider, the lighting brighter, and the atmosphere a comfortable room temperature. A laminated sign on the wall pointed the way to the Holochamber.

Max formed the team up two abreast, and they moved out. The elevator disappeared below as if on cue. About fifty feet into their journey they spotted double sliding doors ajar, from which an amber-orange light poured forth into the hallway. Max halted the group and he and Red crept forward to cover the doorway. The rest of the team moved up silently on Max's nodded signal.

Max peered around the doorway and scanned the room. He could make out what appeared to be a reclining amphitheater seating built into the floor ringed most of the chamber. On the floor, a raised circular platform about ten feet across projected amber light upward to form an abstruse image that Max assumed was a blowup of a molecular structure, complete with notes in the strange cuneiform characters.

Red took in the room from the other side with his NVGs down. He silently signaled that he saw something in the corner of the room. Max motioned the team up and wordlessly relayed the information and, on his signal, they did a dynamic entry into the room.

As they entered, Max could make out a lone female who crouched in the shadows of the room corner. Upon hearing the team approach, she stood up and leveled a Glock at Max and the team.

"Gun," Max yelled, causing the team to fan out. "Hold your fire!"

A standoff ensued, neither party speaking as they sized up the other. Max lifted his NVGs and engaged his rifle mounted flash light illuminating the corner. Max noticed the tatters in her jumpsuit; some of the rips ringed with dried blood. Her pistol arm did not shake with nervousness, and the dark-brown eyes that stared Max down glinted with unwavering determination in the light. He knew the look well and harbored no doubts that she would open fire if she thought it necessary.

"Dr. Rogers?" Max asked, though he doubted this fiery female could be a reclusive researcher. At first glance, nothing appeared professorial about her. She came off as more Lara Croft than Madame Curie. As he slowly approached her, Max was struck by her intense beauty. Of average height, she wore a charcoal gray Greytech jumpsuit that clung to the contours of her taut, toned body, and long raven colored hair hung down her back. He couldn't make out her ethnicity—she seemed to be an exotic mix of possibly many things—but she looked like trouble.

"Who are you?" the woman demanded with cool brusqueness.

"My name's Max Ahlgren, I've been contracted by Greytech to secure this installation and rescue any survivors."

"You could be one of *them*."

Red commented, "He doesn't look like a twenty-foot-tall *T. rex*."

"I see you're familiar with the substance. But that's merely one of its manifestations. How many in your group?" Her pistol remained raised, a Glock 19, the same sidearm the Greytech security personnel had been carrying.

Max understood her wariness but still found it unnerving that she hadn't lowered her weapon. He glimpsed the computer screen and noticed the characters were all in alien script.

"Ten at the moment," Max responded. "Seven on my team and

three survivors."

"Where are you from?"

The question seemed off. "What does it matter?"

"Humor me."

"We're based out of Las Vegas."

"Ok, I wanted to make sure you weren't one of those creatures."

Supercilious indeed. "Are you Dr. Rogers or not?"

"I am, sorry." She lowered the pistol and stepped forward out of the shadows.

"Thanks," Red muttered.

"Dr. Rogers, I'm so glad to see you alive," Dr. Kumar announced upon entering.

She cocked her head and considered him a moment, eyes slightly narrowed. "Yes. And you as well."

Not the warmest of greetings. But Dr. Rogers wasn't the warmest of people. *She's trapped on an alien spacecraft infested with man-eating monsters; cut her a break.*

The survivors sat down in the amphitheater seats, plainly exhausted. The constant toll of being on high alert and having to check every corner and cranny they encountered had taken its toll. Max introduced the team who though also fatigued, remained standing at the ready, with Sugar posted at the door to monitor the hallway.

"Doctor, please allow my medic to have a look at those wounds," Max suggested.

"Not necessary. They're superficial in nature, and I've already dressed them. But thank you, anyway."

"Very well, then." Max pointed upward at the hologram. "So, would that be the substance up there?"

"Yes, it is from a sample I took after it formed into one of the more recent manifestations. Greytech's security force placed all sorts of traps around the ship in the vain hope of killing the creatures. I was able to collect a small bit of its tissue to determine its molecular structure."

Kumar asked, "Did it change after it morphed from the substance?"

"Yes, the cells continue to adapt to whatever stimuli is presented to them."

None of this set Max at ease. "So, there are definitely multiple creatures? What can you tell us about them?"

"It is a polymorphic organism of extraterrestrial origin. The cell structure is very large and vaguely similar in make-up to human stem cells. Its cells can take any form: muscle, nerves, bone, even tissues and organs not previously recorded. However, unlike stem cells, these cells can change shape and composition rapidly, allowing the substance to take almost any form. They regenerate at a frenetic pace. Amputate a large enough chunk, and it will propagate in its own right."

Diaz muttered, "So we've seen."

"Can we kill it?" Max asked.

"It is definitely organic and can be killed if a strong enough external stimulus is directed their way. Crude firepower will do the trick though probably not the most effective means to kill this organism."

"Is it intelligent?" Max wondered.

"They display intelligence at the cellular level that appears to grow along with the creature, a collective intelligence, you might call it."

Kumar glanced up. "It's a shame the notes in the hologram are in alien script. I'm sure they're very enlightening."

"I should think so," Dr. Rogers replied. "But I'm as in the dark as anyone trying to decipher all of them."

"The linguists are dead," Max informed her.

Dr. Rogers shrugged. "That doesn't surprise me. They weren't even close to deciphering the alphabet and were not the sort of men resourceful enough to avoid the creatures."

"And how would you know that, not being a linguist?"

"I talked to one. They did not understand what they were looking at. The characters are only similar to cuneiform; not one of them has been identified as ancient Sumerian. Kind of makes sense actually, considering the cuneiform script was designed for making impressions in tablets of wax or clay."

Max considered that a fair enough answer. "So, has your research given you any insight on how to destroy these things?"

"Not much, unfortunately. This creature appears to be very adaptable and resilient. From what I can ascertain, it is highly evolved. Radiometric dating has put the substance that makes up the creature to be over 5 billion years old, but without more advanced equipment and more time to study and observe it, I can't do much. Samples of the substance were initially sent to the surface for further testing on Greytech's latest equipment. Apparently, it somehow circumvented our quarantine protocols. Now there are several of them running about, likely manifestations from the original."

"Are you saying this thing can reproduce?" Max inquired.

"I don't believe it does in the typical sense. From watching the cells I have studied replicate, I believe as the creature absorbs more nutrients, it can grow in mass and regenerate itself."

"It metamorphosed in my observation chamber," Dr. Kumar said. "Data recorded during the transformation was stored on my console's hard drives, which are now missing. Would you happen to have them, Doctor?"

"No, I do not, though I would love to dig into that data."

"Who could have taken them, if not you? Are there any other survivors on this ship?" Max inquired.

"Not that I know of, but it's a very large ship. It's quite possible there are other survivors."

"What all can this thing morph into?"

"Again, I'm not certain, but potentially almost anything. To my knowledge, it hasn't taken human form yet, but judging from what I've seen, I'm sure it could if it wanted."

"Why bother, when it can turn itself into a dinosaur or some other monster?"

Rogers shrugged. "Camouflage? If it feels threatened, maybe it takes the form of a survivor, maybe it kills you and assumes your identity, Mr. Ahlgren." She smiled for the first time, sly and vaguely vulpine. "But don't worry, it could take your form, but it couldn't take your memories."

It wouldn't want them.

Max realized the implications of her words. "How do we know you're not one of them?"

"Because if even one of these creatures possessed my intelligence, you'd all be dead by now."

Point taken. "Wouldn't doubt it. We need to search the ship for more survivors and locate those hard drives. Apparently, those drives may hold the key to beating these things."

"I've explored the foredecks extensively and found no one. If there are any survivors, they're likely deeper in the bowels of the ship. I could guide you there, of course."

"Yes," Max said without hesitation. "We would appreciate that."

Dr. Kumar would have none of that. "I think we should stay here, Dr. Rogers. Conduct further research while Mr. Ahlgren's team moves on. Even without understanding all the characters, the two of us might be able to come up with something."

Sugar snorted. "While we dumb around this ship and get wasted, old man? Not happenin', and you're coming with us."

"Yes, we should all go," Dr. Rogers agreed. "The creatures will pick off any stragglers they run across. Besides, you'll need me as a guide. This ship has a byzantine layout, and there are certain areas you should avoid."

"Such as?" Max asked.

"The cargo hold. It was secured before Greytech lost control of the site. Not even the creatures can break through the pods, though they've tried hard to do so. Your men have only encountered a small fraction of the substance stored on this ship. Most of the substance is locked up in there; perhaps the creatures feel some sort of familial attraction to it."

"*Tio* Goop *y Tia* Blob," Diaz commented.

Dr. Rogers laughed for the first time, a smile creasing her face. "Funny."

"And best kept to himself," Max reminded him. "Shut up and let the adults handle things, Diaz."

"Jesus, *perdóname...*"

Max turned back to Dr. Rogers. "So where do we begin our search?"

"The ship's bridge is probably our best bet. If I can manipulate the ship's controls, I may be able to close all the bulk heads and attempt to seal the creatures inside, while still trying to leave us an exit route. It isn't guaranteed to work, but it may buy us some more time. There's also an armory on deck R-4 filled with alien weapons. Not sure what the intended use was, but they were there. Greytech kept the place sealed off and strictly off-limits, kept all our resources dedicated to researching the substance. We might be able to figure out how to operate them."

Red rubbed his hands together. "I am so on that."

Dr. Rogers smiled at Red's comment. Max couldn't help being drawn to her. Something about her unflappable demeanor and certainly her beauty put his tortured mind at ease. He'd worked so long for nefarious people in this deadly profession that he rarely trusted anyone any longer. She appeared to have everyone's best interests at heart, single-mindedly devoted to defeating the creatures. She also seemed to be the only glimmer of hope they had. Max felt it was reason enough to trust in her judgment, for now.

Gable had other thoughts and couldn't contain himself any longer. "This is such bullshit, Chief! You want us to go deeper into the ship? She is just trying to get us to do Greytech's dirty work. We went into the ship, we found one of their key assets. We have done our part. This is their mess, let them handle it. It's time to bug the fuck out here and go! Get the real military to handle this."

"You still don't get it do you. There is no one else coming. Even when the Greytech cavalry gets here, they won't be able to stop this. It's up to us."

"That wasn't our mission."

"Our mission has changed." Max replied.

Gable spat a plug of chewing tobacco next to his boot. "Oh, it has now!"

The two men glared at each for a moment, tension and testosterone filling the room.

"What's our mission now?" Diaz said breaking the awkward silence.

Max turned to face the rest of the team. "To survive."

The team exchanged nervous glances with one another. Gable

shook his head and walked away towards the far side of the room, his face still flush with anger.

"So, it's settled, then," Dr. Rogers said. "Bridge, armory, survivors, hard drives, and then we take care of these creatures."

"We are going to find a way to kill these things," Max vowed. "You have my word on that."

"And you have my trust, Mr. Ahlgren."

She locked her alluring gaze on Max, her eyes communicating an unreasonable hope, which bordered on a promise that they would get out alive. Against all logic, he wanted to believe that her research and first-hand knowledge of the beasts could somehow salvage this mission. He found the rest of her quite persuasive as well.

As he could only focus for the moment on Dr. Rogers, Max didn't catch LT surreptitiously shake his head. Irish rolled his eyes. Dr. Kumar disguised his bark of laughter as a cough. Red's ear-to-ear smile heralded a barely audible snort of humor. Sugar merely issued a silent sigh as he turned his attention back to the empty hallway. Had his medic uttered his thoughts on Max chasing skirts while on a mission, Max would likely have shot Diaz dead on the spot.

One of Max's drill instructors at OCS had been fond of saying, *Your authority as an officer ends when laughter begins.* He had always kept the maxim in mind, and it had served him well over the course of his career. Yet one sincere utterance from Dr. Alexis Rogers made him forget those words when he most needed to live by them.

15

WHY DID IT HAVE TO BE A BEAUTIFUL WOMAN? LT ASKED HIM-self. Had Dr. Rogers been male, everything would have been fine. Max would have grilled him for all the knowledge he possessed; after that, he might consult him for advice and directions, but that would be all.

Dr. Rogers would not be out in front right now, leading the team.

LT watched Dr. Rogers stride down the corridor leading from the Holochamber, no hesitation in her step. She moved with almost carefree ease, seemingly unconcerned about encountering one of the alien terrors roaming the corridors. Dusty words little used since college flashed through LT's mind, each vying to summarize her nature: dauntless, intrepid, insouciant. LT finally settled on foolhardy.

And that goes for all of us, except maybe Gable.

LT would never publicly admit it, but the rube Ranger from Alabama had made a good argument. Had they simply hauled ass out of Base Camp right then and there, some of the team might have survived. Or not. *Still better to go down fighting out in the woods than be eviscerated in the halls of a spacecraft—a spacecraft that belongs to the creatures alone.* He found it hard to believe that they were aboard a highly advanced alien vessel, forced to engage the creatures on their home turf. He knew from hard experience this was no way to win a war.

Lack of leadership or worse yet, inept leadership also lost battles. *Do we still have a leader?* LT sure as hell hoped so. He knew little regarding Max's CIA employment or the mission he'd botched in the Ukraine. But Georgia hadn't been his fault, and neither had Mexico. Shit didn't just happen in this business—at times it rained down from the sky in furious hailstorms. Max had a knack for leading the team into shit storms, but he had proven just as adept at leading them out.

But this time? LT had seen Max enamored by women before though he seemed to care for them only in the carnal sense. Whether for love or for lust, LT had never seen him influenced by a woman in the field. His confidence in Max's leadership was slipping, and as the team's second in command, he might have to choose between his loyalty to his friend and his responsibility to the team. LT decided to back Max for now but keep a close eye on this Dr. Rogers. A lone survivor behind open doors, a straggler as she'd said, seemed a bit too convenient for his taste.

The team crowded onto the elevator platform they had ridden up in. Never one to suffer from claustrophobia, LT moved to the back wall of the car. Sugar boarded last, and LT felt the brunt of the squeeze as everyone jammed into the enclosed platform. Dr. Rogers selected deck one on the holographic controls. The door slid shut. Blood rushed to LT's head as the elevator plummeted into the bowels of the ship. The overpowering stink of adrenaline-fueled sweat seemed to fog the air in the car.

"So, these weapons," Max asked Dr. Rogers, "what sort of technology do they utilize?"

"I'm not entirely certain; weapons are not my forte."

"Come on," Red coaxed. "Lasers, plasma, low-frequency sound waves? Gotta be something like that on a spaceship."

"I believe there might be weapons along those lines. I didn't have much time to look at them."

LT pressed for more, "Were you being chased at the time?"

"Something like that."

"It's a yes-or-no question."

"Then yes, Mr. Thompson, I was being pursued at the time."

Being several inches shorter than most of the team, LT couldn't see much through the press of bodies in the car, but Max made sure LT caught his venomous stare. LT averted his gaze, not interested in winning a spiteful staring contest.

"My apologies, Dr. Rogers," Max said. "We are all under a lot of stress." He gazed down upon her with seeming adoration, like some ogre beholden to a benevolent princess.

LT kept a careful watch on the rest of the team. Irish, who to this point had given Max every benefit of the doubt, now looked worried, lips pursed, eyes troubled and downcast.

"Don't sweat the prom queen," Gable muttered to him.

LT had no reprimand for him this time.

The elevator eased to a halt on deck 1. Sugar jumped from the car as the door opened and swept to the left while Max went right. The area judged secure by the time LT exited the car, each corridor covered by a different man. They exited once again in a circular chamber, only this time five narrow hallways converged at the elevator. Adhesive stickers placed by Greytech labeled the tunnels one through five, and a directory of various destinations was posted on the wall. They found the ceiling lower here, only seven feet or so, and the ambient light far dimmer than on the upper levels. Some areas were not lighted at all. Hot air pressed down upon them, soupy with humidity and the noisome stench of rotting flesh that LT knew so well. There had been fighting in this chamber. Splatters of both black residue and red blood blotched the walls and floor by the entrance to tunnel three. A trail of blood continued into the tunnel, which led to the cargo hold, according to the directory.

"Life'll get taken here," Diaz quoted as he took in the environs of the ship's bowels.

"Keep it to yourself," LT muttered back.

"Corridor five." Dr. Rogers pointed the way.

"All right, form up," Max instructed, voice low. "Dr. Rogers and I will take point; Red, follow us. Everyone else, same order as before."

LT stood dumbstruck. *Red should be out front with that flame-thrower. She can stand behind him and give directions.* Others were thinking the same. Even the ever-stolid and reliable Sugar gaped, dubious about that order.

"Will you fucking say something?" Diaz growled at LT.

"It's not my call."

"Well, fuck it, somebody has to say it." Diaz raised his voice and asked, "Shouldn't Red be out in front with the flamethrower?"

Max whirled, eyes wide. "The order will be as I say."

"Because bullets have been so effective on these things, right?"

"Because I am the leader of this expedition, that's why. Now get your ass in the rear where you belong."

"At least I tried," Diaz muttered. "More than you can claim, LT."

You fucking asshole. How could Diaz have dimed him out like that? *You'll pay for that one, Diaz.*

190

Max fixed on LT before he could respond to Diaz. "Do you have a problem with my decision?"

"I think Red should be out front."

"So do I," Red added. "Fire kills everything, at least in the movies. Besides, if she gets offed, we are fucked. How are we going to find our way out of here? No offense, Dr. Rogers."

Dr. Rogers raised her hand for quiet. "I understand your concern, but there are reasons I should be out in front."

"Yeah, why?" Gable demanded.

"The creatures aren't the only danger in this vessel. You'll have to trust me."

"I'm already tired of trusting you."

"Well, you know your options," Max said, weary of the debate.

"There ain't any options at this point."

"Then shut up and try to stay alive. You don't want to be my next buddy in a bag, remember? Now form it up and let's get moving."

LT took his place in the order as they moved into the tenebrous confines of corridor five. *She's moving too fast.* Behind him, he could hear Dr. Kumar panting as he plodded along. The heat, humidity, stench, and a constant high-pitched humming noise served to keep everyone testy. The whining soon took physical form in a vibration LT could feel through the soles of his boots. The floor constantly changed from a solid material into grating that covered access tunnels beneath the floor as well as deeper areas that dropped into pure blackness. Piping and conduit ran seamlessly over the ceiling down here—the ship's power plant, LT assumed.

The team traversed several intersections in their first few minutes of travel and passed dozens of doors secured with the alien handprint readers. Dr. Rogers called a halt about ten minutes into their journey. The lights in the corridor died up ahead, and she stood at the edge of blackness before a holographic image on the wall. Hot air blasted into the hallway like a stiff desert wind, abating the humidity if nothing else. LT and Gable tried to see around Red to what lay ahead.

"What the hell's she doin'?" Gable asked.

"Damned if I know," LT replied.

Max peered over her shoulder as she touched prompts on the hologram. LT considered their proximity inappropriately close, even in such tight quarters.

"Shit, we're followed," Sugar called from behind.

LT whirled around but could see nothing to the rear past the survivors.

Irish pushed Ms. Harlow out of the way as he headed for the rear, slamming her into the wall a bit hard. "Sorry."

LT followed on his heels. Sugar lay in the prone position ready to wreak havoc with his machine gun. Irish and Diaz fell in behind him and took kneeling positions with their rifles. LT remained standing as he swept the dark hallway with the reflex sight on his rifle. He saw nothing moving; neither did the others.

"Where the hell is it?" Irish asked.

Sugar pointed. "It was there, maybe fifty, sixty yards behind."

LT didn't doubt it, but there was nothing to see now. He sensed rather than saw Max come up behind him.

"Status?" Max asked.

"Sugar spotted a creature about fifty yards down."

Max craned his neck and peered down the hallway. Everyone remained silent for several seconds as they tried to spot the beast. "I'm not seeing it, Sugar."

"Me either, but I know it was there."

Max nodded. "Not surprising. Irish, stay back here with Sugar and Diaz. Hit the fucker with the grenade launcher if it makes another appearance."

"Roger that," Irish said.

As they headed back to the front LT asked Max, "What's the word up there, Chief?"

"We're at some sort of drawbridge that's been retracted by someone or something. This is the only way to the R decks, so Dr. Rogers is working on it."

What the hell does she know about those holograms? Something about her ate at LT's intuition. For someone who'd devoted all her time to studying the substance and the creatures that formed from it, she seemed to know a hell of a lot about how the ship operated. *Brilliant for sure, but...*

Dr. Rogers announced, "I think we've got it."

Max peered out into the blackness. "Yeah, here it comes. Great work, Doctor."

"Be careful crossing; there are no railings."

LT heard the bridge slide into place, accompanied by a whirring noise that sounded like an electric motor beginning to spin. Over a period of several seconds the corridor brightened from black to the poor lighting typical of this level of the ship, the glow tinged a light green. Dr. Rogers and Max stepped onto the bridge. Situated roughly fifty feet off the floor, the bridge spanned an enormous room that stretched off into the fading greenish light given off by the several machines that had whirred to life moments before. Each of the conical machines stood twenty feet high and reminded LT of a beehive soaked in tritium.

Red commented, "Killer spot for a lightsaber duel."

"Read my mind," LT whispered.

"Nordic shamanism."

The man is unflappable. Every team member had been forged in the Stoic warrior tradition, yet under the circumstances, most were beginning to crack in some fashion. Red and Irish seemed to be the only others who had retained their bearings: Diaz appeared to be a nervous wreck. Sugar might be having hallucinations and didn't seem himself since first encountering the creature. Max was apparently hunting slash instead of the creatures. He couldn't imagine how long Gable had been holding that intel about Max's escapades into Russia, but a sane man would have known this wasn't the time to bring it up. LT hated even thinking about it, yet he had no choice; he needed to know whom he could rely upon in the event Max died... or became otherwise incapacitated.

Had it reached that point already?

LT wondered about the bridge. Had Dr. Rogers retracted it herself the last time she'd come through, or had someone else? The latter meant there was a good chance that survivors might be in the area. Perhaps there were no creatures on the far side of the bridge if survivors had retracted it to keep them out.

The hallway on the far side of the bridge, previously pitch black, brightened as Max and Dr. Rogers entered. Max issued no order, so once Sugar bounded across, LT halted the column and asked if they should retract the bridge.

Just as LT dreaded, Max asked, "What do you think, Doctor?"

"The bridge controls weren't difficult to decipher, though there are several steps that need to be followed. Nothing I can't do again."

"Good enough," Max replied. "Let's pull it."

"And if she dies, how do we extend it again?" Red asked.

"I'll—we'll see to it that Dr. Rogers doesn't die."

Dr. Rogers offered, "I can write down instructions just in case."

"That might be best," LT commented.

"Won't do us much good if we've got one of those beasts on our tail," Red said. "They're not likely to take a timeout while we read the instructions. Why don't we just leave it extended?"

Max paused in thought. "Good point, Red."

"Yes and no." LT felt the weight of their lives settle like a mantle across his shoulders. "Leaving it down provides a hasty escape route, but it also allows the creatures to follow us."

"They're back there," Sugar rumbled. "I know I saw one. We need to retract this bridge."

Dr. Rogers shook her head. "There are creatures on this side already."

LT finally asked, "Did you retract the bridge last time you were through here?"

"What difference does it make?" Max said.

"Plenty. If she didn't do it, then another survivor did. Or the creatures know how to do it."

"Or maybe the creatures don't have to use the bridge," Max suggested. "I don't think a fifty-foot chasm is enough to stop one of them."

"True enough," LT was forced to concede. "Might as well leave it extended in that case."

"Thanks for seeing things my way," Max said.

LT fought the urge to shout: *You said retract it!* "You should still write down the instructions, Doctor, just in case someone retracts it behind us."

Max glowered briefly at LT before saying, "Very well. If you please, Doctor."

"Certainly," Dr. Rogers said. "And for the record, I left the bridge extended when I passed through here."

The others took a break while Dr. Rogers scribbled the

instructions on a notepad. Sugar had once again taken the prone position behind his machine gun; he stared intently at the tunnel across the bridge, which had gone black after they'd passed through. "Man, I'm tellin' you," he muttered, dropping his NVGs to get a better look.

Diaz joined him in the visual search.

Sugar pointed. "Something back there."

"I don't see anything." Diaz replied. "Wait...it's right fucking there!"

"Let me in there, Diaz," Max said. LT hadn't heard him approach. Max donned his NVGs as he crouched next to Sugar and stared across into the black passageway.

After a minute or so Sugar said, "Right there, Chief. Limit of vision, you see that?"

LT wore his own NVGs but saw nothing.

"I don't think so, Sugar," Max replied. "Looks like shadows, just a play of light."

"Ain't no light in that tunnel."

"Yeah, but there's plenty from those machines down there, light that just happens to glow green. It's screwing with your goggles is all."

"I know what I saw."

Diaz agreed, "Yeah, that was totally one of them."

Max answered Sugar. "I'm not saying you don't. But I am saying it's not there now."

"I concur," LT said. "There's nothing down there right now."

Max got to his feet. "Just stay vigilant. Nobody here doubts you."

Dr. Rogers gave her notes, meticulously written in a graceful hand, to Max. The group formed up and carried on, Rogers again setting the pace too fast. Her zeal caught up with them sooner rather than later. Weak and constantly wheezing, Dr. Kumar could go no further on his own. Though uninjured, Harlow and Quinones were terrified and exhausted and had to be urged along by various team members.

As for Kumar, Max said, "You'll have to carry him, Diaz." His tone remained nonchalant as though he were ordering the man to hump an extra rifle.

Diaz gaped through the crowd at Max. He stuttered briefly as he searched for the proper invectives to hurl at Max. LT began to cut off Diaz's response, but Dr. Rogers beat him to it.

"We should rest for a while, Mr. Ahlgren."

Max pretended to think about it. "Yes, yes, I suppose so. But not for long, and we can't do it here. We need a larger space, easily defensible, where we can all open fire simultaneously on a creature."

"I know a place nearby, a couple hundred yards from here at most."

"Very well. Lead the way, Doctor."

Kumar remained incapacitated. Max and the doctor stepped off. *Does he really think Diaz is going to be able to carry Kumar the rest of the way?*

"Sugar, grab the doctor," LT ordered.

Sugar cocked his head and gave him a quizzical look. "I'm on rear."

"Irish will take the rear. You take the doctor."

"On it."

LT started moving once the team was repositioned. Max, Rogers, and Red were already a short distance ahead. At least Gable had stopped to wait for them.

"LT?" Gable asked.

"What is it now?" LT responded, not in the mood for

redneck wisdom.

"Something's gonna give and damn soon."

LT ruminated upon the several possible meanings of Gable's statement. Was it a mere prediction of things to come—an easy prediction at that—or was Gable planning to do the giving? LT didn't know and wasn't about to ask. He said nothing, dropped his head and continued to march.

* * *

"Wide spot in the road," Dr. Rogers announced as she and Max entered the room. "I hope this meets your requirements as defensible, Mr. Ahlgren."

Dim light flooded the room at their presence. Max evaluated the space with a critical tactician's eye. Roughly fifteen feet wide and thirty feet long, the room had three entrances—the one they were standing in, another on the opposite wall thirty feet away, and the last about twenty feet down the left wall. A sunken floor, three feet deep, ran the length of the right wall before a solid bank of glowing orange hologram monitors, with six built in chairs denoting separate workstations. The ceiling featured two ventilation panels; the floor consisted of solid construction with no gratings.

Dr. Rogers added, "The far exit opens onto a similar drawbridge if that makes things easier."

"Definitely. This will do nicely. Doctor." He turned and addressed the team: "Sugar, Diaz, watch the rear. Two exits to secure. Red, we've got the left; LT and Gable take the far exit. Let's move."

The room lived up to its appearance as an innocuous workspace, at least for the moment. The left hallway lit up, stretching straight on into murky dimness as Red and Max stepped in.

"Clear!" Max shouted.

"Clear!" LT responded from the other exit. "Retracted draw-bridge over here."

The group assembled in the middle of the room. Red cracked some glow sticks to enhance the dim lighting, which the survivors seemed to appreciate. Sugar had a moaning Dr. Kumar draped over his massive shoulders. *I guess ordering Diaz to carry him was a little unreasonable.*

Max issued his orders: "Gable, Irish, rig Claymore mines with a laser trip about thirty feet down those hallways." He indicated the hall they'd entered from and the exit on the left wall. "Two-hour rest period, two men on watch the entire time. I'll take the second hour. Any volunteers for the first watch?"

"Might as well be me," Diaz said. "I have to re-dress his wounds anyway."

"I'll take this side," Irish added.

"Good enough. Make it happen."

Sugar lay Dr. Kumar down in the trough by the workstations, and Diaz turned to cutting off his dressings. The Claymore traps were set up in minutes. They were about as secure as they were going to get.

Irish produced a roll of toilet paper from his pack and pointed toward the far hallway. "If anyone needs to go this spot is as good as any."

Max never ceased to marvel at the professional warrior's abil-ity to fall asleep as though on command, in even the most uncom-fortable of environments. Red and Gable slumped back in the chairs before the monitors and were asleep in seconds. Sugar sprawled out on the floor next to his machine gun. Harlow and Quinones huddled together against the wall a few feet away. The ever-pensive LT sat against the wall vaping and staring into space, eating an occasional cracker from an MRE pouch. Max couldn't see Diaz down in the sunken area of the floor, but he could hear Kumar's grunts of agony as Diaz cleaned and dressed his wounds.

Max and Dr. Rogers sat close to each other in the corner nearest the drawbridge. He remembered well the sequence of events that had brought him here, though the time seemed to have passed in a blur, as though he'd been running on autopilot. *Well, she has been making most of the decisions. She's the only one who knows where we're going.* He had invested his trust in her, something he didn't do easily, and it was paying dividends.

Maybe you're ignoring the team just a little. The thought came unbidden, and Max dismissed it immediately. His men hailed from the world's finest fighting forces—they didn't need to be babysat constantly. *I need to keep up with her, watch her every move. We won't get out of this otherwise.*

And goddamn it, she's easy to follow.

Max liked to categorize people he interacted with, to determine what effect they could have on him or a mission. He considered Dr. Rogers, and she seemed different. She didn't appear to fit neatly into any one category. He decided that she must be a workaholic like he was, consumed by their respective occupations.

He watched her fiddling with some sort of tablet from the ship, its glowing orange screen illuminating features he found mesmerizing: her jaw, strong but not jutting; the flawless proportions of her nose and cheekbones; and her body, lush and sculpted, strong but curvaceous. There was something else about her, a strength and determination he sensed. He felt drawn to her. He wanted to speak to her, but for the moment he contented himself with drinking in her presence as he grew drowsy.

Her hair turned blonde; her eyes became deep-blue pools ringed in dark purple. Russian epithets gushed forth from bruised and swollen lips. She was bound hand and foot to a spindly wooden chair.

"Spare me. I know you speak English,"

She spat a glob of blood in his direction and then shouted more gibberish.

"Hook her up, LT."

LT moved in to attach the electrodes. She growled, leaned forward, and attempted to bite his face, her bloody teeth nearly latching on. LT jerked back from her. "Bitch!" *He drew his Glock and smashed her across the face, the gun barrel opening up a jagged laceration on her cheek. The blow dazed her; she reeled in the chair, head lolling and eyelids fluttering.*

LT rushed forward and seized her head so Max could affix the electrodes to her temples. With that task completed, Max threw a glass of water into her face. She grew somewhat coherent again and stopped screaming. She glared up at Max and awaited a fate that might have been avoided.

Your call, bitch.

"Now, I need to know where the Spetsnaz team took the Americans. Tell me, and we'll detain you until the fighting's done, after which you'll be released. Do you understand?"

"You bastard-faced son of bitch! I say nothing, never!"

"We'll see." *Max flicked a switch and powered on the transformer.* "Last chance." *He grabbed the current control knob on the console.*

"American slime! Fuck your mother in the eyes!"

Max cranked the knob clockwise to a thousand volts, the highest possible setting.

Her body flashed a brilliant light blue for an instant, accompanied by a single pop as loud as a pistol shot. She convulsed instantly as though suffering a seizure; her blue eyes ready to burst forth from their bruised sockets. The wet patch on her shirt sparked from the electric current and caught fire. Her blonde hair crinkled and vaporized, the stench of it summoning bile to rise in Max's throat. She screamed as though speaking in tongues.

"Shut it off!" LT shouted. "She's no good to us dead."

Max turned the knob back to zero. The woman peered all about the room, eyelids and cheeks twitching, her bald scalp singed a sunburned red.

"Tell us," Max coaxed, "and it can end now."

She spat nonsense at him for several seconds before saying, "Never. Never!"

Max cranked the dial yet again to full blast. The interrogation continued for several more rounds.

"This is taking too long!" LT shouted.

Max glanced at his watch. Minutes meant miles now, and miles meant lives for the hostages. "Grab me the bolt cutters."

LT gave him a wide-eyed glance but dutifully retrieved them.

Max went back to work on the woman. Perhaps this will jog your memory. He removed her shoes. She remained defiantly silent. He placed her pinky toe in the teeth of the bolt cutter and snapped down hard. The women let out a piercing scream as the cutter cleanly lopped off her toe. After a single spurt of blood shot from the wound, a metered red ooze pumped from her foot in time with her heartbeat.

"Well?" Max snarled.

Tears welled in her eyes. "Please, no!"

He moved on to the next toe and snapped the handles together again as her screams filled the room.

Max jolted awake, breathing heavily and reaching for his pistol. He saw the bank of hologram monitors and his sleeping team and then remembered where he was. He released his grip on the pistol. He felt Dr. Rogers gaze upon him. Looking over at her, he could see the look of concern and almost pain painted on her face. "Shit." He dropped his head. "I'm sorry. Sometimes I remember things I'd rather forget if I could."

She nodded. "I suppose that's inevitable in your line of work. All the killing, the torture."

Max snapped his head up and glared at her. "How did you know I dreamed of torture?"

"I didn't know. I just assumed you might have been forced to use such tactics in the past."

Max paused a moment before nodding. "Yes."

Didn't save Collins though. The blonde Russian woman had eventually talked. They always did. However, she'd succeeded in buying her associates much-needed time. Unable to intercept the *Spetsnaz* in transport, the hostages were taken back to their headquarters. Max and the team stormed the heavily fortified building and rescued Banner's CIA advisors, but at a price. His medic Collins died laying down covering fire so the rest of the team could escape. Their Georgia debacle in a nutshell.

It should have been me who got planted over there.

And then there was Mexico. *Gable's right—*

A feminine scream cut the stifling air.

"Shit!" Max shouted. "Who the fuck—?"

"Harlow!" Dr. Rogers replied. "She went down the hall to relieve herself."

Max snatched up his rifle, scrambled to his feet along with the rest of the team and ran to the hallway entrance.

He thought he knew what to expect this time.

The beast proved him wrong.

Max raised his rifle and immediately started shooting; but his shots went wide, most of the rounds errant. He couldn't concentrate on his aim, shocked by the nightmarish scene unfolding before him in the dimness.

The creature morphed with astonishing speed from a puddle of the black substance into a large, amoeba-like form. Its snake-like skin swirled with darkening hues as its body contracted and expanded as it took. Max didn't know if it had oozed from a duct or slithered down the hall under the Claymore trap, but at the moment it didn't matter. There was still a chance to save Harlow.

Harlow screamed and struggled. On all fours, she backpedaled from the monstrosity, but her pants were still down around her ankles, inhibiting her movement. The creature continued to morph before Max's eyes. Its extended pseudopods twisted into something akin to a tangle of snakes, their heads circular maws filled with rows of gleaming black teeth appeared, puckering and yawning in metronomic rhythm. A large slit-like mouth formed in the center mass of the creature, as its tentacles reached for Ms. Harlow.

Max continued to fire, seeing some of his shots hit home. One tentacle shot forward and wrapped around Harlow's right thigh, the end of it cracking whip-like against her bare skin, its fangs driving in deep, drawing blood. Another of the tentacles wrapped around her torso, squeezing her body tight as a third tooth filled tentacle came in between her legs and penetrated her in the most gruesome fashion, its mouth open as it slid into her. In twenty-plus years of combat, Max had never heard a scream to match Ms. Harlow's. Her eyes bugged, and Max heard the blood and viscera gush forth from her nether regions onto the floor as the creature worked the tentacle ever further into her body. Another followed its path, stretching her wide and then lifting her up like a grisly hand puppet, smashing her body into the wall. Her screams turned into choked and stifled entreaties for help as the creature dragged her toward its mouth. A gout of blood vomited forth from her lips, followed by the tip of a tentacle.

Max almost couldn't fathom it. *Impaled straight through.* He'd never before witnessed such a disgusting display of human mutilation. Incredibly, Harlow continued to struggle, though her panicked efforts grew feebler as the creature dragged her ever closer.

Sugar moved up beside Max and opened fire with his machine gun. Max found control of his aim and opened up again. The beast retreated rapidly, sucking up Ms. Harlow as it went. She was thigh-deep in the creature's maw, dead, killed either by the beast or friendly fire.

Perhaps seeking more speed for its retreat, the beast sprouted a dozen short and scaly legs. It kept its circular mouth and tentacles and continued to devour Ms. Harlow as it fled. Max expended his ammo and reached for a second hundred-round drum magazine. The beast, already thirty feet down the hallway, would be gone by the time he reloaded, so he grabbed his pistol instead. He emptied it into the creature, all to no avail. Harlow's lifeless face stared Max dead in the eye one last time before she was devoured whole.

"Lemme in there!" Red shouted from behind.

Max ducked out of his way, realizing he could do no more at the moment. He yelled, "Hold your fire!" to Sugar, tapping him on the shoulder.

Red stormed past him, hell-bent on roasting the creature with his flamethrower. Some part of the creature's body rose too high and triggered the sensor on the Claymore mine. Red got lucky; the explosion occurred before he ran past the mine. The concussion dropped him to his knees and left him reeling and dazed.

"Shit," Sugar gasped. He'd just loaded a fresh belt of ammo into his machine gun, and he took off running down the hallway.

Max finished reloading his rifle and ran after him. He heard others running, but he couldn't look back to see who followed.

The beast had turned tail, and Sugar had it running as fast as its stubby legs would permit. He fired in short bursts as he followed. Most of his rounds hit home, blasting off meaty black chunks of gunk.

Max and Sugar reached the corner and found a chunk of the creature congealing into something different. They jumped over the regenerating aberration, trusting that team members following would take care of it while they engaged the larger creature. They rounded the corner, their blazing weapons lighting up the corridor, heralding the beast's demise.

The hallway was empty.

"What the fuck?" Sugar roared.

Max couldn't believe what he wasn't seeing through his reflex sight. He swept the laser dot down the hallway and saw nothing at first.

Then he looked up.

The creature had transformed its solid form back into a liquid substance, oozing upward along the wall into a ventilation duct on the ceiling several feet down the hall. Max and Sugar opened fire, knocking off small globs of the creature but unable to stop its ascent. They could only watch, their smoking guns impotent in their hands, as the last vestiges of the creature slithered upward into the duct.

Max heard Gable blasting away around the corner with his AA-12 shotgun. A pistol joined in moments later. No doubt they were taking care of the part of the beast that had formed from the chunk they had blown off. The firing ceased moments later.

Max shouted, "You get that thing?"

"Yeah," Gable replied. "It's down and out. What about the rest of it?"

"Gone—turned into goo and slipped through a duct."

Silence greeted the news.

"Shit, there's another one *aqui!*" Diaz shouted. "Get it!"

More gunfire ensued. Max rounded the corner in time to see Diaz blast a large black form to smithereens. It appeared to have been trying to form legs and oversized pincers.

LT ran up to Max. "There's bits of that thing all over the hallway, Chief."

"Not for long. Everybody out! Get back to the room now!"

The team double-timed from the hallway. Max, the last to retreat from the tunnel, jumped over a scrap of gore the size of a strip steak that was beginning to take shape, sprouting legs and claws. "Red! Torch the whole fucking hallway!"

Red nodded and jogged forward, still looking a bit woozy from the explosion. Max and Sugar had his back as he slowly moved down the hallway burning up scraps of the beast. When the flames found the creature Max had jumped over, it screeched and writhed, then attempted to charge Red, who finished it off with another blast of fire.

That proved to be the last of the drama. None of the other scraps came to life. Nevertheless, Max insisted that Red incinerate them all.

Max, Sugar, and Red returned to a silent room, the ubiquitous high-pitched whining sound the only noise. Dr. Kumar sat dumbstruck at one of the workstations, while Ms. Quinones sat bawling in the next chair, clutching her rifle. Diaz crouched next to her trying to console her in Spanish, but to no avail.

Dr. Rogers asked, "You burned everything? You're sure?"

"Everything."

Max approached Diaz and put his hand on his shoulder. He

could see that Diaz's nerves already were frayed and trying to console the woman was only wearing at them more. "Go check on the men. Make sure they don't have any remnants of that creature on them."

Diaz nodded and walked off.

Max crouched next to Ms. Quinones, who was still crying hysterically, and grabbed her by the shoulders.

"Ms. Quinones? Ms. Quinones?"

She didn't respond. He slowly removed the rifle from her hands and laid it beside her. Taking her hands in his, she finally looked up at him, her eyes filled with tears.

"She...was...my friend." She said. Her words ragged as she tried to control her sobbing. "The way...she...died." She put her head down and began to cry again uncontrollably.

Max clenched her hands. "Look at me. Look at me!" His voice was stern, but fatherly. Ms. Quinones looked up at him. "We have all lost people today. Good people. But this isn't helping. You need to pull yourself together. I don't know exactly what we are up against, but the only way we stand a chance against these things is if we stick together. We need you. The sadness you feel, you need to channel that into something useful. Can you do that for me?"

Her sobbing lessened in intensity as she nodded her head.

"I need to hear you say it. Can you pull yourself together?"

"Yes." She said meekly.

"We are going to kill these fucking things. Let me hear you say it."

She wiped the tears from her face with her forearms. "We are going to kill these fucking things."

Max wasn't sure they could kill the creatures, but he knew he needed to give Ms. Quinones some glimmer of hope, and that he wasn't going down without a fight. It stung his pride to have lost a civilian in his charge. He had lost hostages before during raids, but never one he had liberated. He stood and addressed the team. "We can't stay here; we need to keep moving."

"Agreed," Dr. Rogers said. "And there are likely to be more of them from here on."

Then he gazed at her and felt what remained of his soul stutter back to life. He needed this woman, but her presence soothed him a bit too much, removed him from his harsh reality when he most needed to be in tune with it. *You're a great help, but you're likewise a huge distraction.* "We'll just have to deal with them. Red, you're back on point."

"Fuckin' A, Chief, it's about time!"

The rest of the team enthusiastically approved.

"Dr. Rogers will be right behind you, giving directions. If she needs to get through, let her by."

"Roger that."

"Good. Eat up, people. Check your ammo. We move out in ten."

16

EDWARD HAD HAD A DREAM THAT NIGHT OF THE STAIRS LEAD-
ing up to the top of an ancient step pyramid. Instead of in the jungles
where they'd been seen before, this was built atop a sheet of ice,
surrounded by howling winds. The pyramid was guarded by heavily armed soldiers clad in black, faceless beneath helmets. Though
the soldiers stood at attention, they were sobbing there, quietly sobbing. Edward, a grown man, happy and healthy looked up at the vast
unknown and around him at these faceless armored men and he
was confused.

"Why are you crying?" he asked them.

The guard pulled back the mask, revealing the face of the older
nurse, who cried and shook her head.

"It was worth it," she said, "I swear it was worth it."

The other kept his mask on and nodded emphatically.

"It is an honor," it said in a garbled voice as if speaking through some sort of garbled radio hidden inside the helmet, "this was all about you."

His mother, dressed in a general's regalia with great big epaulets on her shoulders held the hands of two children, pointedly shoving past Edward and climbing with them up the pyramid. While Edward did not know what it was that was waiting up there, he knew that he did not like it, he knew that his mother was doing something wrong and it would have to be corrected. He followed behind her, hearing in the distance the applause and approval of a studio audience.

"I don't deserve this," he tried to explain to his mother, dreading what she was bringing the children up to.

"Someday when you have children of your own," said his mother, "you'll understand."

"This isn't what I wanted," he pleaded as they grew ever closer to the top step.

"It's what you need," she said.

Edward did not see the top of the pyramid but, still, he awakened with a tremendous feeling of guilt. He did not know what his mother had done for him exactly, but he knew who she was and what she was capable of. He could not judge a parent for loving their child. That should have come naturally and that should have been something he could have felt anytime he'd seen her. That should have been part of his life without having to get terminal cancer.

Edward awakened and he felt like vomiting. The dream reassured him that no, the chemo wasn't completely to blame. His eyes opened and his mother was sitting there.

"I didn't want to wake you," she said.

"I'll have a long time to sleep," he snapped back.

She patted his hand. "I know this past week has been trying for you, darling."

You have no fucking idea, Mother.

"But I need you to hang in there for another few days, okay? You can do that for me?"

This again? "Maybe. What happens in a few days?"

She smiled enigmatically. "We start killing your cancer. Within days my researchers will have a radical new cell-regeneration treatment. This is the break we've been working toward, Edward!" She squeezed his hand harder, dropped her voice to a whisper. "You'll be a trailblazer, the first to undergo treatment by this powerful new method. My researchers say—"

"Oh, well great! Who wouldn't want to serve as a guinea pig for Greytech research?"

"Edward! Don't lose your faith in me now, not when the cure is so close!"

He shook his head in frustration. His mother was desperate, ready to place her faith in any quack treatment that rang with the promise of hope. "Seriously, Mother, where is this cure?"

His gut wrenched. He leaned over the side of the bed and vomited in the pan provided for this purpose. The surge felt as though he were vomiting up his guts, and he expected to see his stomach in the bucket when he was through. An overreaction, of course—as usual he'd deposited only a few measly drops of blood and bile into the can. At this point, Debbie would normally provide comfort and assistance, but she wasn't there.

As if he were leprous, his mother leaned in close but didn't touch him. "There, there, darling, just a few more days."

"Do you mind passing me a paper towel?" Edward asked, gasping and winded. "Seeing as how you chased my nurse out of here?"

"Oh. Of course, dear." She did as he bid. Debbie would have wet the towel and wiped the cold sweat from his brow and the vomit from his lips. But his mother wasn't about to provide such comfort.

Wouldn't want to soil her suit with a little puke.

"Do you need any help?" she asked, sounding uncharacteristically vapid.

"Oh no, I'm just peachy." He paused, out of breath. "Just another day in the ICU." Most of his days there were peaceful but for his ever-present and excruciating pain, which his mother's presence seemed only to exacerbate. She'd opened the curtains upon arrival, the first task she always attended. Thankfully it was raining so the outside light wasn't too intense. She rearranged items on his bedside table unconsciously from time to time as they talked, imposing her own sense of feng shui upon his surroundings, which really annoyed the shit out of him. Sometimes he wished she would just leave him alone to die in this dreary, dismal room.

"Soon, Edward, very soon. You have to—"

"Yes, I have to trust you. Cure is on the way, etcetera, etcetera."

"It is, Edward! Next week at the latest, perhaps as soon as a couple of days."

Edward stared at his mother and found he couldn't help but love her. Perhaps she was a domineering control freak, but always acted in what she perceived to be his best interest. She'd been right more often than wrong.

This time it was different. *Do it now! Just come out and say it!* "Mom, please listen to yourself. 'Perhaps' and 'at the latest'? Those aren't words in your lexicon. Appointments, schedules, commitments: you live a life of order and discipline and expect the same of everyone around you. Yet you tell me to hang in and hope that *perhaps I might be saved. It's not like you to grasp at straws like this.*"

Her painted lips formed a straight and determined line. "I don't have a concrete date yet, that's true enough. But I have more than straws in my arsenal, I assure you. You will live—I will see to it personally. You are not destined to die like this."

Agreed. "Mom, I just can't—"

"No. You can and you will."

"Damn it, will you just listen to me for once?"

"Because I know what you have to say."

Edward wanted to preach his frustration and rage right into his mother's face. He hadn't the energy to do so, however. Rasping and exasperated, he said, "We need to talk about my wishes for once, not yours."

She narrowed her eyes, quizzical. "What do you mean, darling? My wishes are simply for what's best for you."

"No, they're not, because you rarely see fit to listen to me." His brain pounded in a slow and agonizing rhythm, like some monstrous diseased heart ready to seize up at any moment. She had frustrated him to the point where he could barely think. Finally, he raised his head and held up a hand to halt any further platitudes from his mother. "Now, this is what *I* want."

The phone in her purse chirped with an incoming call.

"Seriously?" Edward huffed.

She ignored him and checked the screen. "Damn it! I'm sorry, darling, but I have to take this; it's quite urgent."

Edward laughed—cackled, actually—for the first time in a long time. So typical of her, using any pretense to avoid unpleasant conversations regarding his future or lack thereof. *She probably ordered one of her lackeys to call and rescue her, give her an excuse to return to the office.*

After a threatening glance like one might use to quiet a rebellious five-year-old, she swept out of the room into the hallway to discuss her business. Though the cancer had eaten away at nearly all his vital organs, Edward's hearing remained just fine. He could make out some of his mother's words. Listening intently, he wondered whether the conversation regarded him and the miracle treatments that would *perhaps* commence next week, not that there was any 'perhaps' about it coming too late.

His mother began: "What is it, Peter...? Well, I want assurances in writing that I will have full access to the technology... That long...? Damn the weather, I want in there now! Yes, I will be there. I will take care of things myself this time... Yes, I know what that entails!" Then the cold steel voice of her omnipotence spoke up. Edward knew the tone well and couldn't help but pity whom ever she addressed. "I want the best, Peter, nothing less! We will need total discretion on this! I want this nightmare brought to a close." She sighed. "Tomorrow morning? That's the earliest...? You can't find one pilot who'll fly there now?" She laughed. "Why the hell do I pay taxes then? Look, just get it done. No screw-ups this time!" Edward heard the phone's electronic *beep* as his mother severed the connection. Her high heels clacked on the linoleum tiles as she entered his room.

Edward asked, "So who was that?"

"An important acquaintance, dear, one you've never met."

"Of course not. Anyway..." He bristled at still being treated like a child, an outsider never trusted with all the details of his treatment. The tears he felt coming needed to dry. Crying was forbidden in the Grey household, along with just about every emotion that didn't assist one in conquering the world. "We need to have a serious talk, Mom, the kind that will require you to shut off your phone for a while, if you can bear five minutes of isolation."

"Edward, I can't right now. I have to get back to the office and coordinate some things. It's all about your treatment. Things are finally coming together."

This is a lost cause, even if you told her. She's likely to put one of her goons on the door for my so-called protection. No, not this time, Mother. I've made up my mind, and you're the one who will have to accept it and deal.

"Right," he stated, trying hard to sound upbeat and failing miserably.

"Soon, my darling." She bent over and kissed him on the forehead. "We're on our way, no more *perhaps* about it. Next week we'll turn this thing around, you and me." She smiled and patted his hand, though her quick glance at the door betrayed her wish to be on her way.

Edward kept his tears at bay, though he wasn't sure if he could speak again over the ache of sorrow in his chest. He had to try; these words were important. "Mom, you know I love you."

"And I love you more than anything in the world. Always remember, Edward, what I do, I do for you. Always. I'll be by again in a day or two. I suggest you rest up. Next week will test your endurance, but I know you'll pull through."

Out of words, he nodded and attempted to smile for her. She kissed him again, then departed.

Edward buzzed the nurses' station. Debbie responded within seconds, smiling benevolently down upon him. He never doubted for an instant that his mother loved him and worried constantly over his fate. But only Debbie cared about his own wishes.

"Did you enjoy visiting with your mother?"

"No," he croaked. "She just...she won't listen to me." Now the tears flowed, and Edward didn't give a damn about it. He could express his emotions around Debbie without feeling weak or embarrassed. "I couldn't tell her."

Debbie offered him more genuine concern than his mother

had ever shown. "Edward, this is a huge decision."

A laugh cut off his sob. "The hugest."

"Are you sure about this? I've listened to your mother; she's confident—"

"She's deluded, Debbie. There's only one way out for me. I know it's been done here before."

"Yes, but older people who have no chance at all."

"I don't have a chance either. You know that. Believe me, if my mother could cure me she would have done it a long time ago."

"I don't think she's lying to you."

"No, she's just trying to reinvent the truth. I get that. But I'm an adult, and it's no longer up to her. My decision is made."

A tear rolled from one of her blue eyes and trickled down her cheek. "I'm sorry, Edward. I just wish we could do something."

"You already have. I am so grateful to you."

She leaned over and they embraced. He felt weak in her arms, yet at the same time more masculine than ever. His mother had raised him to be confident enough in his own judgment to follow through with his decisions. He harbored no guilt and would to go to his grave certain of his decision. Maybe his father had felt the same way. In some ways, Edward could now empathize with his father's passing for the first time in his life.

"Only you know what's best for you." Debbie summoned that indefinable quality that the best nurses possessed: the ability to deal remotely with the suffering of others while still carrying on efficiently with her duties.

"It's about time I realized that," Edward said. "Please get the paperwork in order and contact the doctor. I'll also need a pen and some paper."

He was finally in control, for the first time in his life.

17

"THE MAIN ONBOARD RESEARCH LAB IS JUST AHEAD," DR. ROGERS whispered to Max, who nodded. According to her, the majority of Greytech personnel on the ship had worked and lived in this area. The proximity to food, supplies, and living quarters meant a greater likelihood of locating survivors.

"Your men have to be very careful here," Dr. Rogers continued. "Any survivors will be terrified. Perhaps hold your fire—"

"We're always careful, Doctor." Had he not witnessed the demises of Coach and Harlow, Max would have advised his men to carefully assess potential combat situations before engaging. *Not anymore.* They would rescue whoever they could, but Max wasn't about to see his men killed because he ordered them to hesitate instead of shooting. He wiped stinging sweat from his eyes with the back of his Nomex combat glove.

Red paused at a corner and peered around the other side for

several seconds before moving ahead. The team stripped down to plate carriers over undershirts in deference to the oppressive heat and humidity. With his massive tattooed arms and ridiculously long red hair, Red reminded Max of some warrior chieftain in a bad post-apocalyptic movie. Looking back at the team, he saw even more ink and a good half-ton of muscle. He couldn't help thinking they looked like a gang of heavily armed professional wrestlers.

Ms. Quinones brazenly stared at him, as she'd done ever since he stripped down. He couldn't blame her under the circumstances—perhaps having sex one more time was now a bucket-list activity—but she was about twenty years too late for the party. *Survivor Syndrome.* Max had encountered it before. In extreme cases, hostages even had willing sex with their captors.

In contrast, it took all of Max's discipline to not leer continuously at Dr. Rogers, as sex and survival warred in his head. Best not to think about it but impossible when she was so close. In deference to the heat, she'd pulled down the top of her jumpsuit and tied the sleeves around her waist. Her athletic body, covered in beads of sweat, and her breasts alluringly pushed together in a black sports bra, proved to be a major distraction.

Concentrate, asshole, his brain advised. He listened. Training, discipline, and instincts were all that could save his team now. Dr. Rogers could become Alexis once they were safely out of here.

"The double doors at the end of the hall," Dr. Rogers whispered to Red, who scanned every inch of floor and wall as he stalked slowly down the hallway with his flamethrower at the ready.

The hallway ended at a T-intersection. The closed double doors slid quickly open when Dr. Rogers drew close enough to operate the holographic control. "Damn!" she hissed, realizing she'd put Red in danger.

Never one to be surprised, Red charged into the room with Max on his heels. The main lab consisted of a large space crammed with computer equipment, both human and alien. Orange, white, and green light from different monitors mixed with the ambient light from overhead to create a glowing, psychedelic aura. Red broke right and Max left; the rest of the team fanned out and commenced a thorough search of the place.

Max had a bad feeling about this room. Too many nooks where the artful creatures could hide. Besides the monitors, the room held five translucent spheres the size of diving bells. Max guessed were observation chambers. They appeared to be constructed of clear glass, and all glowed a faint orange color that pulsed at the slow rate of an elephantine heartbeat.

Rounding one of the spheres, Max located a sixth chamber. A longitudinal hemisphere of glass remained standing, defying all gravity; the rest of it had been smashed into tiny pieces similar to shattered safety glass. Black blood stained the floor at the sphere's base, but most of the blood drippings and glass lay inside the shattered sphere.

He felt Dr. Rogers's presence as she came up behind him. "Something broke into this thing, not out," he whispered.

"The creature, freeing more of itself," she observed. "This was the only sphere with active substance in it."

After winding their way through the tanks, Max and Dr. Rogers ran across some traditional Earthly lab decor: graphite tables cluttered with chemistry equipment and laptops, along with an anachronistic notepad upon which some scientist had scrawled a byzantine equation.

"What the hell is all that?" Max asked, looking at the problem.

Dr. Rogers glanced at the pad. "Dr. Jung's notepad. He was

old school as you can see." She bent to examine the equation. "And wrong too. But he's not the only one who didn't know what they were dealing with."

The smell of charred flesh led them to the first body, which they found sticking rear-end out from a bank of computer equipment. Max deduced that a creature had picked the man up and hurled him headfirst into the electronics, burying him to the waist. A fire had erupted after the impact and burned some of the equipment above the body. A powdery white residue coated the electronics around the corpse. Max ran his index finger through the powder, sniffed it, then wiped it off on his trousers. "Fire extinguisher residue."

"But is the fireman still alive?" Dr. Rogers glanced around the room.

"Probably not. But it's encouraging to think so."

"Let's move on. Dr. Jung's work area is upstairs in the gallery."

"Upstairs?"

"You'll see."

The murky lighting had obscured the wide stairway leading up to the gallery, situated about twenty feet above the lab's floor. Orange monitors and dull light from the ceiling glowed up there as well, though considerably dimmer than in the lab. These aliens were apparently advanced enough to avoid falling accidents; there were no railings along the gallery ledge or the stairway. Greytech had strung yellow caution tape on either side of the stairs to warn employees of the precipice. A continuous smear of dried blood ran down the stairs and onto the lab floor, trailing off to Max's left and growing fainter as it disappeared into the distance.

Max took a knee and examined the smear, quickly deducing that it was actually two trails of blood. "Looks like two bodies were dragged down the stairs. I don't think the creatures did this."

Dr. Rogers nodded but said nothing.

Max peered around for his team members. The lack of radio communications bothered him, but it was what it was. Hand signals and whispers were the soldier's equivalent of Dr. Jung's scribbled equation: inefficient but effective. Max spotted Gable and motioned him forward. LT saw Gable advancing and followed him to the stairs.

"Anything?" Max asked them.

"Couple of bodies, lab types," LT said. "Mutilated."

"Nothin' important on my end," Gable added. "What's this?" He jerked his eyes up at the gallery.

"Jung's work area. We go up three abreast. Keep close behind us, Doctor. Let's move."

Max noted that Gable and LT remained in top tactical form. Together they moved up the stairs like three wraiths, barely making a sound despite all their gear.

The gallery, a low-ceilinged space about fifty feet on all sides, was a complete shambles of smashed computer equipment, broken furniture, and blood. Of the dozen or so alien computer monitors, only three glowed with life. The lighting did not improve upon their arrival as it had in other parts of the ship. Max noted a spot where a dead body had lain, the origin of one of the blood smears. The central part of the room seemed oddly vacant, as though something large had occupied the space and been moved. Sure enough, twenty feet away, Max made out a large conference table flipped on its side.

Movement, barely discernible above the table edge—

"Show yourselves!" Max shouted, fully ready to empty his rifle into the table if necessary.

"What's the capital of Texas?" asked a voice with a Western twang.

"Austin, now get the fuck out here where I can see you."

223

Two men popped up from behind the table with raised hands. The one on the left seemed a hearty sort, around forty and solidly built with graying blond hair and a mustache. The other man was younger, gaunt and tall, eye level with Max. Blood befouled his white lab coat. He carried a selection of pens and mechanical pencils in his breast pocket, in a pocket protector no less. As if that weren't enough to confirm his geek-god status, he also sported a pair of broken eyeglasses, horn-rimmed tortoiseshell, cobbled together across the bridge of his nose with silver duct tape.

Gable chuckled. "What the hell is this, *Revenge of the Nerds*?"

The geek-god turned red. "Really? You think this is funny?" He pointed to the duct tape on his glasses.

"Among other things," Gable replied.

"Are you Dr. Jung?" Max asked, though he doubted it. This guy was way too young.

The man snorted. "Hardly. My name is Thomas Ruddiman. Though I had the honor and privileged pleasure of being Dr. Jung's chief research assistant."

"Yes, Mr. Ruddiman, so glad to see you've survived." Dr. Rogers stepped forward.

Ruddiman's eyes widened when he saw her. "Dr. Rogers? But how? I saw you get attacked!"

"I got a lucky shot on the creature, just enough to allow for my escape."

"Incredible! I was certain you'd perished." The man sounded genuinely perplexed by her presence yet pleased to see her anyway.

"And who are you?" LT asked the other man.

"Wade Ball, sir, head of mining operations," he responded in a Texan drawl.

"You dig a nice shaft," Max said. Ball's tunnel accessing the ship bespoke of his competence. Max pegged him for a stand-up sort who might be useful in a fight.

"Would never have dug it if I knew what was down here," Ball replied. "I was told we were after some exotic ore lode. Once I found out the truth, it was too late."

"You're not the only one Greytech duped," LT added.

"You men armed?" Max asked.

"Hell yeah," Ball answered. "Got a couple HK rifles here from dead security, some pistols, a few grenades, and as much ammo as we could find."

"Excellent. LT, round up the team and bring them up here."

"On it."

The men recounted their stories as Max waited on the team. Ruddiman had witnessed two creatures invading the gallery and slaying two of his fellow researchers. Dr. Jung went missing during the fight, likely carried off by one of the creatures. He'd presumed Dr. Rogers lost in that fight as well.

What else isn't she telling me?

Ruddiman had managed to run off and hide. Miraculously, he suffered no injuries during or after the massacre. Certain that he was the only survivor onboard, Ruddiman dragged the two corpses down from the gallery and deposited them elsewhere to eliminate the stench of death, both for his own comfort and to keep the creatures from returning to feed on the flesh. He foraged a bit, found some provisions and a pistol, then barricaded himself in the rear of the gallery to await help.

Ball had engaged no creatures. A top mining engineer, he tried to leave camp when he realized Elizabeth Grey wasn't after a lode. Greytech security detained him, and Elizabeth Grey doubled his pay in return for finishing the shaft and cutting through the ship's hull with a hydraulic ram, an old-fashioned mining apparatus capable of powering itself for as long as it had a liquid water supply. After breaching the vessel, Ball remained a Greytech prisoner, though they gave him every possible comfort. Grey promised he would be released once she broke news of the spacecraft and confirmed the existence of extraterrestrial life.

Then the creature broke free from Kumar's lab. Among its victims were the two security men manning Ball's locked door. "That thing tore those boys limb from limb. I saw it all through the little window in my door. Tried to get out and help them. Looking back, I'm glad I couldn't. When I finally did bust out, I grabbed some weapons and food, prepared to hike back to civilization. Then I wised up and started thinking like a hunter. That thing could track me down in those woods. Besides, there's at least a hundred miles of rugged forest and mountains between here and the nearest civilization—practically a death sentence this time of year with the weather. Coming down here to hide and wait felt like my best option."

Ball found Ruddiman barricaded in the gallery. They foraged once for food and ammo but had otherwise stayed in the gallery ever since.

"We're running out of food," Ruddiman lamented. "Only have about two days' worth left. After that, we'd have had to forage. And they're dividing and spawning, these creatures. I doubt we would have made it."

"You still haven't made it," Max reminded him. "Stick with us and do as you're instructed and you just might."

Ball nodded.

"Were you in the military?" Max asked him.

"No, sir. But I've hunted all around the world. I know my way around firearms."

We could have done worse. Max's initial assessment of Ball proved correct, but Ruddiman impressed him as well. He'd put out the computer fire downstairs and saved the lab. And the fact that he'd survived unscathed aboard the ship showed a resourceful cunning that might come in handy. *He's no Dr. Kumar, anyway.*

Max asked Ruddiman, "I take it you've done no further research on the substance?"

"None. I found Dr. Jung's personal journal, but he wrote nothing regarding the creatures that proved helpful."

Ball scowled. "Damn things are likely to take over the world."

LT returned with the team. Max introduced the new survivors and brought his men up to speed on the situation. Kumar immediately started grilling Ruddiman, whom he barely knew, regarding the late Dr. Jung's research.

Max cut him off. "He's told us everything. Now sit down and let Diaz change your wraps. Everyone else take fifteen."

The men ate and hydrated, sharing their provisions with the survivors. He pulled LT and Dr. Rogers aside to discuss strategy. The R-Deck armory remained their best hope to pick up some alien firepower that might kill the larger beasts instead of merely driving them off. They would continue to search for survivors and the missing computer drives along the way. Even LT was onboard with the plan, which pleased Max. Things always ran smoother when they were in agreement.

Red, Dr. Rogers, and Max again took the lead, with Irish and Diaz behind them; then came the survivors, followed by Gable, LT, and Sugar. They wound their way back through the warren of equipment in the lab, ever watchful for any creatures that might have snuck in while they were upstairs.

According to Dr. Rogers, the shortest route to the armory was via a lift close to the ship's reactor. They turned left out of the lab and again took up their slow march, the atmosphere growing hotter and more stifling as they moved. In ten minutes, Kumar was breathing heavily and grunting. *The man's a piece of human luggage.* He proved the maxim that a unit moved only as fast as its slowest man.

Kumar was likewise the first man to scream, his cry reverberating through the hallways.

Max whirled around, rifle at the ready. The team was moving straight through a four-way intersection. Diaz, who wasn't screaming, hung in midair where the hallways converged, suspended from the ceiling by four slimy, black tentacles, each tipped with a hooked black claw the size of a railroad spike. The tentacles entwined around his left arm and leg and his neck. His eyes bulged from the creature's stranglehold. Another tentacle slithered around Diaz's rifle and ripped it from his hands.

Max and Irish put the red dots of their reflex sights on separate tentacles, but the creature dropped from a recess in the ceiling before they could fire. The alien horror they witnessed resembled an octopus: tentacles converging at a mouthful of razor-sharp teeth, a cluster of black onyx eyes in the center of its head.

Kumar cowered in a ball, leaving Irish and Max clear shots on the creature. But it held Diaz aloft before it as a human shield while it glided down the crossing hallway on four tentacles, the talons on each clicking as it retreated.

Machine gun fire erupted at the rear of the column. *Fuck!* Max hoped Sugar was hallucinating again, yet he doubted it. Sugar, LT, and Gable would have to handle whatever had popped up behind them. Max, Irish, and Red took off after Diaz.

The octopus creature retreated with astonishing speed, already thirty feet down the hall when Max and Irish rounded the corner in pursuit. They opened fire, aiming for the walking tentacles. A couple of Max's bullets struck home, yet the appendages stayed intact.

The creature screeched its rage and launched a stream of black liquid from an orifice under its mouth, striking Irish square in the chest. His body armor began to smoke, he stopped in his tracks and yanked the emergency-release handle. The carrier dropped off him in pieces and clattered to the floor as the acid ate through it. Meanwhile, the creature continued to steadily distance itself from its pursuers.

Max heard only a cacophony of gunfire and yelling. A grenade blast from far off punctuated the dissonant fugue. Red now ran by his side. Max held his fire and concentrated on the chase. He would have shot as he ran had the creature not been hiding behind Diaz. Though Max's brain screamed, *He's good as dead!* he couldn't bring himself to fire on the creature. Diaz might not be dead yet, and Max refused to be the one who killed him.

"Fuck, this thing is fast!" Red gasped as they sprinted after it, losing ground with every step.

The hallway widened to twenty feet, and the ceiling rose higher. A large, open portal lay ahead. The creature had already passed through. Despite his single-minded goal of rescuing Diaz, Max still noted the Greytech sign posted over the portal, bold red letters several inches tall, stark against the safety-yellow background: "WARNING! RADIOACTIVE AREA HAZMAT SUITS REQUIRED BEYOND THIS POINT!"

Max and Red ignored the sign and dashed through the portal. The creature had some fifty yards on them and was starting to grow indistinct in Max's vision. They ran on.

It moved faster.

They lost sight of it a hundred yards past the portal. Twenty yards later they came to a three-way intersection. They saw no sign of Diaz or the creature down either hallway.

"Stop," Max gasped, bent double and winded from having sprinted several hundred yards. He'd never run that fast for so long, and yet he'd still failed.

"Dammit!" Red bellowed, smashing one of his beefy fists into the wall.

"Not gonna help." Max felt slightly nauseous, but the feeling passed. He spat on the floor and stood up straight. He saw Dr. Rogers heading for them accompanied by Irish, no worse for wear despite his ruined plate carrier. Far in the distance came Dr. Kumar, helped along by Ms. Quinones. No one else followed them. He heard distant gunfire and muffled shouts as the rest of the team engaged the other beast.

What's the call: Chase Diaz, who's probably dead by now? Or go back for the team and then locate his body? The choice was clear.

"We have to go help the team, then we find Diaz."

Red and Irish glumly agreed.

Dr. Rogers reached toward him. "I am so sorry."

Max reflexively pulled away, regretting that he had done so, but still angered by the loss of yet another man. "Let's go."

An instant after Ms. Quinones and Dr. Kumar passed through the portal, a huge door dropped straight down from the ceiling and slammed to the floor. The impact of the falling door shook the deck. The hallway boomed with its echo.

"Shit! What the fuck?" Max yelled.

The impact of the door dropping put both the Nicaraguan woman and Dr. Kumar on their knees. "I did nothing! We touched nothing!" Ms. Quinones yelled.

"They didn't," Dr. Rogers assured. "It's an automatic safety door that drops in case of a reactor leak."

"Shit, you mean we're gonna be irradiated?" Red asked.

"I don't think so. A core meltdown would be signaled by an alarm as well."

Max reined in his emotions to keep from screaming. "Then why the hell did it drop?"

"I have no idea. There might be a temporary spike in levels; perhaps the creatures have something to do with it. And the vessel itself, sometimes it acts on its own."

"Well shit," Red observed, "we're still in a radiation zone."

Dr. Rogers seemed unconcerned. "Greytech posted that sign for liability reasons. The radiation on this level is mild; I've seen the Geiger counter readings. You'd have to spend days in here to be affected, at least at the reactor's current power level."

Max accosted Quinones and Kumar as soon as they joined them. "What happened to the rest of the team? What did you see?"

"I don't know," Kumar panted. "That...that...thing grabbed on to your man, then someone in the rear started shooting. We ran this way."

Quinones provided an equally useless answer in broken English.

Max keyed his headset. "Ahlgren calling LT, do you copy? Over." No response, only static punctuated by beeps and gurgling noises, as if he'd accidentally called a fax number. He tried again nevertheless and again received no response.

Irish asked, "That door got a control panel? Maybe the doctor can open it?"

Dr. Rogers shook her head. "There are no door controls on this side." It made sense: better to seal off a few people to die during a meltdown than to allow the whole ship to become contaminated.

Irish turned to Max. "What's the call, Chief?"

After a moment of deliberation, Max said, "We press on for the armory and hope that LT finds another route to link up. I'd like to find Diaz along the way. He's likely dead, but I need to confirm."

Diaz had three daughters, and Max dreaded telling his wife that he was gone. But at least death was final; his family would eventually accept it. MIA status would only keep them forever wondering, hoping, doubting, unable to move on with their lives. Max had never reported a man MIA before and didn't wish to spoil that perfect record.

Irish tilted his head. "Diaz had to have bled some. I'll bet we can pick up the trail."

Dr. Rogers released a pent-up breath. "Even without a trail, I have an idea where he might have been taken."

Red rounded on her. "And how could you possibly know that? Hell, how could you possibly know half the shit you know?"

"Easy, Red," Max said. "We need her—"

"For what? All she's done is lead us on a fucking wild goose chase through this ship. We've lost two people since she's been with us, maybe it wasn't such a smart idea to let her lead us further into the ship."

"That's enough—"

"Please," Dr. Rogers said, holding up her hand. "I assure you, I have all of our best interests in mind, and I do know where I'm going. The creature forced us to come this way, not me."

Red started to protest.

Irish cut him off. "She makes a good point, Red. We wouldn't have gotten as far as we have without her."

"Exactly," Max said. "Calm down. Don't let this fuck with your head."

Red said nothing but nodded a few moments later.

"We press on. Now let's find Diaz's trail."

*   *   *

LT liked to think that he didn't personify his occupation—that he was just a mild-mannered hedonist most comfortable at the poker table or a beach resort with a couple of ladies pawing his jock. Life was meant to be lived for such simple pleasures.

And yet, as enticing as these pleasures were, they paled in comparison to the high of battle. He got his kicks in the casino and the bedroom. LT lived for the chase, the fight, the thrill of the kill.

LT always had to make up for his short stature by training harder than everyone else, and it had paid dividends for him yet again. Sugar and Gable each had several inches on him, yet he outran Gable and was right on Sugar's heels as they pursued the creature. Hell, they *owned* this creature. Sugar had detected it and opened fire before it got within ten feet. It turned and fled from the hail of bullets. Gable then scored a direct hit with his grenade launcher, slowing it considerably.

The beast appeared to be larger and stranger than any other they'd encountered. The size of a large bear, its four large multi-jointed like legs converged with a hyena-shaped body covered in some sort of gray membrane, from which sprouted a long snout-like mouth full of gnashing teeth surrounded by about a dozen smaller tendrils, each tipped with long, translucent, scythe-like claws.

LT wasn't sure how long or far they'd run. It didn't matter—this would be the first large creature they bagged, and the effort was worth it.

It scuttled around a corner a few feet ahead. LT and Sugar took the corner, guns blazing, and came face to face with the creature.

Black blood flew as dozens of bullets smacked into the area where the tentacles converged. Sugar bellowed triumphant anger. LT emptied the magazine of his HK rifle, the bright flash from the muzzle illuminating the creature in the dimly lit hallway. Once the bolt locked back on his weapon, he ducked out so Gable could unload on the thing as well.

The creature reared back and raised two of its large multi-jointed appendages to attack, or so LT thought. Instead, they shot upward into a grate in the ceiling.

"No!" LT shouted. "Get it!"

A small tentacle fell off and writhed on the floor. It started to transmogrify and grow, sprouting a single black eye and several crustacean legs. At the same time, the larger creature pulled itself upward into the grate, its body morphing into black goo and squeezing through the bars. It was gone in a heartbeat.

Sugar roared his frustration. A few more rounds might have finished the creature, but he'd run out of ammo as it pulled itself into the grate. Gable switched to his shotgun and put four rounds into the creature on the floor, killing it.

Several seconds passed as they came to grips with what had happened. Ruddiman and Ball caught up to them, their rifles at the ready. Neither man said anything; the lack of a dead creature said it all.

"Had that motherfucker," Sugar growled.

"Gave his ass a run for sure," Gable huffed, exhausted.

LT shook his head. "I thought we had him."

All three men were feeling the inevitable crash in the wake of the adrenaline rush. Dejected silence ruled.

Perhaps it intended to draw us away... "We need to get back and report in. Anybody get a good look at what happened up front?" LT had only seen the tentacles drop from the ceiling and hoist Diaz, but then the other creature attacked from the rear.

"It ran off with your guy, the medic," Ruddiman said. "Last I saw of anyone else."

Ball concurred, "Yeah, that's about the size of it."

"Let's get moving," LT instructed. "Try to link up with the others."

He stepped off in the lead. Navigating back to where they'd been attacked would be easy—just follow the trail of brass shell casings and black blood. Just as LT started walking, the floor rumbled for an instant, accompanied by a single hollow *boom* that echoed through the ship's miles of hallways.

"What the hell was that?" LT stopped and stared at the two survivors.

"Hopefully not the Chief," said Sugar.

"Hell, if I know," Ball replied. "Didn't sound explosive, and I've done my share of blasting."

"Agreed," Gable said.

"Hope it's nothing," Ruddiman offered.

"What does that mean?" LT asked. "What if it's *something*?"

Ruddiman held up a hand. "I don't know, sometimes things just happen on this ship. No apparent reason."

"Keep thinking that," LT grumbled as he resumed walking. *I'm not so sure.*

LT kept the pace slow as they methodically cleared their way back to where the battle began. The trip back took about ten minutes.

"Blood ends here," Gable announced. "That's the intersection where we got jumped."

Max and the others had left the same telltales. They followed blood and brass down the hallway to a closed portal.

LT read the radiation warning sign above the portal. "Shit." A holographic control panel glowed orange next to the blast door. He walked over and tried prompts on the panel, then tried his hand on the biometric reader. "No joy. Guarantee you that noise we heard earlier was this door dropping."

"Should have had her write down how to open doors too," Gable added.

LT keyed his headset and tried Max. Nothing but beeps and static. Several more tries by all three team members produced the same results.

Last-resort time. "Breach it."

Gable tapped a knuckle on the blast door. "Shi-it, this thing's a foot thick at least, I'll wager."

"Do what you can."

Gable shook his head. "Whatever you say, sir."

Ball spoke up. "Y'all shouldn't bother, unless you like wasting your explosives. That door could withstand a direct hit from a howitzer."

"Maybe," LT conceded.

Again, Gable shook his head, disgust on his face. "The fucking thing didn't drop on its own, and Max sure as hell wouldn't have sealed the hallway behind him, so what other explanation is there?"

"Well, it *might* have dropped on its own," Ruddiman reiterated. "Trust me, things sometimes happen aboard this ship, and for the last couple days, the ship has seemed more alive than before."

"*Things*?" Gable asked. "Start making sense, science boy."

"As I said, sometimes things happen: doors open, bridges extend, the elevators run constantly. The ship's computer system senses our presence wherever we go—the automatic lighting confirms it."

"Maybe the creatures did it," Gable suggested. "This is their ship. Maybe they're runnin' the show now."

Ruddiman furrowed his brow with a slight shake of his head. "We don't believe that the creatures we have encountered created this ship. We theorize that they are only the cargo. And they don't seem advanced enough to do that, yet."

"Well, maybe they've stepped up their game. They obviously ain't stupid."

"But they're not smart enough to do that. If they were, they would have killed us already."

Gable packed Copenhagen into his lower lip. "I ain't about to let that happen."

That got LT's attention. "Oh?"

"Time to pack up shop, LT."

"Not your call, Gable." LT stepped up to Gable and got in his face as best he could, though the guy had several inches on him. "After all Max has done for you, you'd just bug out in the middle of the mission and leave him to die?"

"He's dead already."

"You don't know that."

"No, but I do know we're good as dead if we stay on this ship long enough."

"It's your job."

"No, suicide is not in my job description, nor is fighting aliens. They teach you that shit at the Citadel?"

LT threw a right uppercut. Gable blocked with his left hand, steering most of the force aside, but he still took a couple of knuckles on the chin.

Then LT went flying. Landing on his back, he skidded across the floor. He rolled and jumped to his feet, ready to finally put Gable in his place. But Gable was slumped up against the wall gasping for breath. He'd dropped his shotgun as well.

"Enough," Sugar pronounced as if from on high. "I ain't gonna stomach this shit. Now let's figure out what the fuck we're gonna do and then do it."

"We stay," LT asserted. "And you're a fucking coward, Gable."

Surprisingly, Gable turned reflective instead of enraged at the insult. "You think I like runnin' away? You know me better than that, all the shit we waded through over the years."

"You want to run now."

"Because we can't win. You gotta understand that. Best we can hope for is to get off this ship and rendezvous with the Greytech team that's coming tomorrow morning. Have them contact the authorities and get the fucking military in here and nuke these fuckers."

"And just buddy fuck the rest of the team?"

"Might not be any more team," Sugar admitted. "And even if there is, we still can't get through this door."

"We can find a way around to the armory."

"Say we do. That don't mean we can find *them*." Sugar shook his head. "Nah, LT, you got to listen, man. Nobody wanna leave Max and Irish and Red behind, but the chances of us finding them alive are next to nothin'. Johnny's right about this. We need to go."

LT was beaten and he knew it. He hated to admit that Gable was correct. They had expended a shitload of ammo fighting that last creature. How many more could they drive off before they ran dry? *If we even get a chance to shoot next time. Coach, Harlow, Diaz—none of them popped off a single round.*

Yeah, we're well and royally fucked.

Despite the astronomical odds, he still didn't want to leave. Max had awarded him a job on the finest team of operators in the world and entrusted command to LT in his absence. They weren't exactly close friends, but they had enjoyed some damn good times together off duty. *And you're just going to leave him behind?*

"Fine." To LT the word stung with surrender. "We're leaving, for now, but only because you two refused to stay and back me up." He pointed a finger at Gable and then swept it toward Sugar. "If we're fortunate enough to ever see Max again, I want you to tell him that. And the minute we link up with the Greytech team, we're coming back for them."

Gable grinned. "Don't sweat it. Ain't nothin' I didn't say before."

Insufferable ass.

Sugar nodded. For him, at least, the decision to abandon Max was a crushing dilemma. "You know I'll own up to it."

LT heard it all and knew none of it meant anything. *He* was in command, and the ultimate decision was still his.

This will haunt you for the rest of your life.

However many hours that might be.

18

MAX DIDN'T WANT TO ADMIT IT, BUT HE WAS STARTING TO THINK like Red. They hadn't seen any more clues regarding Diaz's whereabouts for some time, yet Dr. Rogers kept on walking, directing Red, Max following along as though on autopilot. Trusting her came easy, perhaps too easy, until Max likewise began to wonder how she could know the things she did. This was not the time for questions, however. She had yet to lead the team astray. Without her they'd be lost, reason enough to keep trusting her.

They strode down a gently curving hallway, the only feature an open door on the right. "Your medic will likely be through that entrance." Dr. Rogers warned, "Be wary. This room is huge, and there are a lot of places to hide."

Red moved to the doorway and peered inside. "Holy sci-fi," he gasped before stepping in. He hadn't given the room much of a once-over from outside.

Max understood when he entered. "Huge" didn't do the room justice—*cavernous* was more like it, a circular space over one hundred feet in diameter, rising to a ceiling of even greater height. Elongated oval pods ringed the curved wall in neat vertical lines separated by ladders. A mini-skyscraper of identical pods connected with ladders and platforms soared upward at the center of the room to connect with the ceiling. The tower and all the pods were constructed of a metal he presumed to be titanium.

The nearest pod, large enough to fit someone human-sized, caught Max's attention. The holographic computer panel built into the head of the pod was currently off. A window comprised half of the pod's top hatch. Max peeked inside and found it empty, just as he'd expected.

In fact, the computer panels on all the pods were powered off, save for one. Perhaps. He couldn't be sure. He thought he espied an orange computer glow through the center tower of pods.

Red asked, "So this is where the aliens ice their meat for the journey home?"

Dr. Rogers smiled. "I suppose they could do that, yes. The more likely explanation is that these are hibernation pods used during lengthy deep-space voyages."

"How many are occupied?" Max asked.

Dr. Rogers hesitated. "None at present. Two aliens were definitely hibernating here, but they've disappeared."

"Two?" Red asked. "There must be five hundred pods."

Dr. Rogers shrugged. "Perhaps they were running a skeleton crew."

"What do you mean, disappeared?"

"You'll see. The open pods are on the other side of the tower."

"Let's check them out. Red, I'll circle right with Dr. Rogers. You and Irish, circle to the left with the survivors. Slowly, people. Those things could be anywhere in here."

Max picked up on the blood trail and found Diaz lying broken on the floor on the other side of the tower. His neck had been snapped at the base of his skull, his left arm ripped off and discarded somewhere. He had most likely died from strangulation before the mutilation—his face bloated and blotched in various shades of purple and dried rivulets of blood ran from his bulging eyes.

Confirmed. It was the best you could hope for.

The others joined them. "Guess these things have taken a dislike to firearms," Irish held aloft Diaz's HK416. The creature had bent the rifle's barrel and rendered it useless.

Max hadn't the time to lament Diaz's passing. "I'll hump the medkit." He and Red stripped it from Diaz's body. He put the kit in his backpack and took Diaz's remaining 5.56 ammo and magazines. "Irish, grab some ammo from Diaz's UMP40 submachine gun for your backup weapon."

"Check these out, Chief." He stood a few feet away by two open pods. One of the pod computers currently functioned, the source of the orange glow. It was empty and appeared to have opened on its own. The other pod's open glass lid was cracked and chipped around the edges.

"Forced open," Max said. "What's the story on these, Dr. Rogers?"

"The pods were like this when the room was discovered. The theory is that one of the pods opened whenever it was scheduled to. The other pod had been forced open by Greytech to gain access to the other alien member of the crew."

"So, where are they?"

"One alien crew member died upon opening the pod. Greytech sent the remains to the surface for further study. We never found any other crew members. It's quite possible the creatures have killed them by now."

Red ran a hand along the smooth surface of the broken pod. "This shit just gets weirder and weirder."

Again, Max tried to find the truth in Dr. Rogers' inscrutable demeanor and cryptic answers. *It might be as she claims.* The ship could have crashed thousands of years ago. The aliens might have awakened, lived, and died while mankind was still holing up in caves. *Or maybe Greytech woke them.* He didn't think she was outright lying, but she knew more about these aliens than she let on. But how best to extract the information from her? Did he even need to extract it? Locating two missing aliens, while fascinating as a concept, was not a part of his mission. *But if they still live, their knowledge could be invaluable in defeating these things.*

Max hadn't survived as long as he had on training alone. His innate sense of danger, an atavistic alarm system that never shut off, went code-red in an instant. He spun around with his rifle raised as the creature dropped from above. It resembled the octopus creature that abducted Diaz, but it had changed its color to a titanium hue to camouflage itself amongst the pods and latticework of the central tower.

Red and Irish, no less attuned to danger, raised their weapons and fired as it dropped. The creature screeched like a keening arctic wind as it absorbed a blast from the flamethrower. Max had to hold his fire as he shoved the falling creature's intended target, Dr. Kumar, out of harm's way.

The burning creature transformed in midair. It hit the floor as a smoldering pile of the black substance. Then, with amazing speed and survival instincts, it flattened and rolled itself up like a carpet, extinguishing the flames. Now a barreling black cylinder, it rolled toward Max and Irish, picking up speed as it went. They poured lead into it to no avail, and Red couldn't hit it with the flamethrower again without incinerating Max and Irish, who jumped straight into the air, each raising his feet as high as possible to clear the rolling beast. Irish caught one toe on the creature and fell forward on his face. Max cleared it, landed on his feet, and turned around.

Already the creature had morphed again, taking on a svelte bipedal form with impossibly long legs ending in curved claws and padded feet. Its elongated head resembled that of a pterodactyl, with a scissor-like beak and prominent pointed crest. It changed shades from jet black to a mottled black and gray that blended perfectly into the dimly lit room. Max and Irish fired on its retreating form, each scoring hits; yet the creature again proved its resilience by escaping. A couple of long-legged strides took it around the side of the tower and out of range. Max and Irish gave futile chase, catching one last look at the creature's back before it ran from the round chamber.

Irish grumbled, "This nightmare is getting too familiar."

"Yeah, but it could have been worse." Max wasn't even breathing heavily after the encounter. The creatures no longer inspired any awe in him, despite their ability to rip a man to shreds within moments. Now they were simply a part of his job, another enemy to be taken down, even though they had yet to kill a full-grown beast. *I'll mount one of these fuckers before this is over.*

Max and Irish double-timed back to the others. Dr. Kumar lay curled up on the ground groaning. Apparently, he'd landed hard and his hip was aching. Max sighed. *I really don't need this shit right now.* He filtered out Kumar's complaints, leaving Ms. Quinones to take care of him while he addressed Dr. Rogers. "We need to move on. Has every bit of this ship been searched?"

"Not even close."

245

"Good. Maybe we'll come across some more clues on how to defeat these creatures. As it stands, we need to continue on to the armory."

"With that blast door down we'll have to circle around to the command center and go from there."

"Whatever it takes."

"The creatures can now camouflage by changing colors," Dr. Rogers observed. "They're learning, adapting. I find that most disconcerting."

"Great," Red said. "They'll be shooting back at us before we know it."

Max motioned to Ms. Quinones. "Get Dr. Kumar on his feet and let's get moving."

She shook her head. "He bruised his hip really bad, Mr. Ahlgren."

"Even if it's broken, you're walking, Kumar. Red, get him on his feet."

Kumar grunted in agony when Red pulled him up by an arm. "I can't walk like this for long." His eyes lost focus, as if he were ready to pass out from pain.

"You walk or you're beast chow," Max told him. "We can't carry you any longer."

As Max had expected, Kumar swallowed his pain and dug up enough fortitude to keep walking. They moved out.

Their new route to the armory took them up three decks via cramped stairwells. The air cooled as they climbed further from the reactor level.

Still on point, Red stopped to examine something he found on the wall. "Some kind of blast mark." He rubbed at a dent surrounded by a black smudge.

"Not the creature's doing, for sure," Max commented.

Dr. Rogers confirmed with a nod. "You'll see more of the same ahead."

The second turn ahead revealed an obstruction halfway down the hall. Approaching carefully, they came upon a defensive mantlet made of the same metal and glass as the hibernation pods, complete with gun ports cut through the metal. The structure had originally spanned the hallway but had been knocked askew at some point. Black blood, desiccated and crusty, smeared the metal. More blast marks pocked the walls and floor down the hall from the barrier. Pools of dried blood splotched the floor at intervals.

"What the hell happened here?" Max asked Dr. Rogers.

"We're not sure; we left this scene as we found it. No bodies, just the signs of a battle. We're nearing the command center, so there are many defensive features located in this sector."

"Aliens versus creatures?" Irish asked.

"So we think," she replied.

"Nothing here now. Let's keep moving," Max mentally noted that the alien defenses resembled human fortifications.

A few minutes later they came upon a hallway, a featureless eight-by-eight chute with smooth white walls that ran about one hundred feet before ending at the bottom landing of a staircase.

"The stairs lead up to the command center," Dr. Rogers said. "I suggest we traverse this hallway quickly."

"Why?" Max asked.

"It serves as a last line of defense for the command center. We shouldn't present a threat, but it reacted violently to the alien substance we tried to transport through it, and after what happened with the blast door downstairs, it would be best not to take chances."

"Understood." And easy enough. The hallway's polished flat walls offered no hiding spots for the creatures. Max stepped off at a normal marching pace, eyes fixed on the stair landing far ahead.

An alarm sounded. Though Max was hard to startle, the blaring beeps were so loud and unexpected that he flinched a bit. Two more beeps sounded after a brief pause. Two beeps, pause...

"What the—Shit!" Irish yelled from the rear as he cut loose with his SCAR on the advancing creature.

A red alarm strobed on the stair landing ahead. A metal door slowly descended. They had only seconds before it blocked off the hallway and sealed them inside.

Max turned around. The rounds popping from Irish's rifle stung his eardrums like whip cracks. Ms. Quinones, screaming, tried to haul Dr. Kumar past Max, who could see little of the creature Irish was battling. He couldn't fire on it effectively with Irish blocking the hallway. He felt someone tugging his arm.

"Run!" Dr. Rogers screamed, trying to haul Max down the hallway. "We can't be sealed in here!"

"Irish, fall back!" Max ordered.

Irish continued firing.

"Now!" Dr. Rogers again tried to drag Max, who didn't resist any longer.

"We can't leave him!" Red shouted.

"No choice! Move it!" Max yelled.

Ms. Quinones squeezed past him and fled in a panic.

Dr. Kumar lay floundering on the floor, unable to gain his feet. Max ran the few feet to Dr. Kumar, grabbed him by the waistband, and ran for the stair landing, dragging the good professor along behind.

Irish ran out of ammo a moment later. Max heard him grunt as he fell beneath the creature, unable to switch weapons quick enough to hold it off.

Ahead the door continued to drop. Four more feet and it would seal them in the hallway. The creature screeched in pain. Max kept running. Red slid under the door first, squeezing by with about three feet to go. Dr. Rogers and Quinones were next.

Dr. Kumar howled in terrific pain as Max dragged him along. Two feet of rapidly disappearing space separated him from safety on the landing. He tossed his rifle under the door and then slid through. One more foot until the hallway sealed. Max heard Irish grunt, and the creature squealed in agony. His guns silent, Irish now fought hand-to-hand.

Reaching back for Dr. Kumar, Max found his wrist and jerked him under the door with barely an inch to spare. The portal closed off the moment Kumar passed through.

Max jumped to his feet. The door had a window, and he peered into the hallway. Every piece of metal Irish carried began to pop and spark. He dropped his fighting knife, but he no longer needed it—the creature had disengaged while running for the far exit. Irish began stripping the metal objects from his body. His grenades went first; he tossed them down the hallway after the creature. He didn't have time enough to pull the pins. Sparks danced all over his body from conductor to conductor. The UMP40 strapped across his back fired once into the ceiling. Irish dropped first his empty FN SCAR assault rifle and then his UMP40. The latter fired on its own, pointed down the hallway toward the retreating beast. The rest of his loaded magazines went off a moment later like so many strings of firecrackers. He took superficial damage from a couple of the bullets as he hurled the popping mags down the hallway.

The creature morphed rapidly into another hideous form, shell-clad with armored limbs, an inappropriate defense and likely the only one its primal mind could devise under the circumstances.

It wasn't working. The beast began to smoke as bubbling lesions appeared on its body. It screeched as its shell dissolved.

Microwaves, Max realized. He grabbed Dr. Rogers by the shoulders and shook her. "Disable it, now!"

"Impossible! It can't be disabled from here."

The lack of a holographic door control told him she was right. Max threw her aside.

Irish thudded into the door, put his face to the window, and yelled words Max couldn't make out. His skin bubbled and melted. Sparking electricity from the few pieces of metal remaining on his body ignited his clothing. He desperately pounded the window with his fists, leaving smears of viscous flesh behind on the glass. Boiling blood poured from his nose. His right eyeball popped in its socket, splattering the glass with red blood.

Max could watch no more. He threw down his backpack and grabbed two breaching charges from within.

An explosion rocked the hallway, followed by five more in rapid succession: McKern's discarded grenades exploding.

Max looked up right as Irish exploded into hundreds of tiny, bloody fragments that blacked out the viewing window. He turned away and clenched his body in rage and let out a thunderous yell from the depth of his soul. "God fucking damn it!"

Max stood there, the breaching charges in his hands now pointless. The sealed hallway had served its purpose, to kill all living things trapped inside. Max heard another loud *pop* from the hallway, though much fainter in magnitude. He couldn't look through the glass, not that he needed to. The creature had exploded.

Red stared blankly at the window, as if his mind was a thousand miles away.

"I am sorry," Dr. Rogers said.

Max looked up at her, anger still in his eyes. "Sorry isn't going to bring him back. Lead the way...doctor."

A seasoned combat leader never doubted in his ability to accomplish a mission, at least never in front of his men. Max wasn't about to do so now in front of his remaining man. Not that it would matter. Despite his sarcastic nature, Red was a pragmatist, and he knew as well as Max did that they were doomed. It was only a matter of time.

*   *   *

Sugar knew he'd lost his edge. Distraction killed; it was really that simple. And Sugar found his mind wandering from their new objective—get the fuck off the ship ASAP—to Max Ahlgren.

He'd met Max in Afghanistan years before when he'd still been in the SEAL teams, and they'd paired up on several joint special ops missions against Taliban insurgents. They worked brilliantly together. Max was a masterful tactician; Sugar possessed killer instincts learned on the streets of Compton and honed to perfection during his time in the Navy. He hadn't thought twice about joining Max's team upon his retirement.

The thought of leaving Max and the other team members behind sickened his conscience. *You never leave a man behind. Traitor, Judas, buddy fucker.* The last two words hurt the most. No insult in the military lexicon was more damning than being branded a buddy fucker. Had he strayed so far from his roots that he was now working for just a paycheck instead of serving his country? *Sad what things have come to.*

Johnny glanced past the survivors back to Sugar. He nodded confidently, assured in his mind that they were doing the right thing.

Sugar refused to meet his gaze. He tried to concentrate on checking their rear every few seconds.

Sweat streamed down his face and into his eyes. The dew rag he wore beneath his helmet soaked through with sweat. This had to be the hottest portion of the ship they'd visited so far.

The survivors trudged along in silence dead ahead of him. *We could have done worse there, anyway.* Max shouldered the burden known as Dr. Kumar. *Should have popped that motherfucker when I had the chance.* He created a distraction that would likely get someone killed. *He's probably dead by now.* Sugar forced himself to forget about the old man, though Max and the team continued to plague his thoughts.

From the front of the column, LT asked, "You sure we're going in the right direction?"

"Pretty sure," Ruddiman responded.

"You best be damn sure," Sugar informed him. *If we're gonna flee like a flock of chickens, we'd best be running out of the slaughterhouse.*

Ruddiman spoke over his shoulder, "Well, it's really impossible to say. The ship's so big—"

Sugar growled, "Don't gimme no fuckin' excuses, kid."

Ruddiman chose not to respond.

Johnny grumbled, "We better find some signs soon."

"Secure it," LT ordered.

Silence reigned. They marched on.

Six hallways converged in a small hexagonal chamber. Greytech had placed a directory kiosk in the room; it now lay on the floor blocking one of the hallways. Each hallway had a number posted above its entrance.

"Flip that thing upright, Gable," LT barked.

The old Johnny would have grudgingly obeyed, bitching and

tossing smart-assed comments all the while. The current Johnny carried out the order quickly and without comment. *He got what he wanted, now he just wants out of here.* If that meant bowing from the ankles at LT's every command, then so be it. Sugar pondered Johnny as he watched him right the kiosk. How could a man come up with the most correct and logical course of action and still be wrong?

Man, fuck it, just stop already.

LT and Johnny searched the kiosk directory for the exit while Sugar patrolled the room's perimeter, gazing as far into each empty hallway as he could. No creatures that he could see; no creatures at all since the encounter where they'd lost Max. Maybe this run of good fortune would hold.

"Here we are," Johnny announced, sounding pleased. "Elevator to A-deck and the exit, down hallway four."

"Fine, let's go." LT set out.

Sugar knew LT still wrestled with the same perfidious demons as he did. LT had made it apparent from the start, and it still showed in the dead-flat tone of his commands.

They formed up again: LT up front, then Johnny, Ruddiman, Ball, and Sugar. After ten minutes and a couple hundred yards, they came upon a cage-style lift of the sort used in skyscrapers under construction, installed by Greytech to replace one of the alien elevators. Fine mesh fencing comprised the four walls; a gate in the front wall granted access to the cage. There was no ceiling. It made sense enough, as no one had ever fallen *upward* from an elevator.

"Our ship has come in!" Johnny unbolted the latch on the gate and boarded the lift.

"You might wanna look up," Sugar warned. "You're in an open shaft."

Johnny realized he'd let his guard down. *He's already back in*

Vegas. He brought his rifle upward and searched the shaft through his sight.

Sugar shook his head. Distractions—the decimation of discipline.

"Clear," Johnny called out a few seconds later. "Least as far as I can see."

Without a word, LT boarded the lift, the survivors following him. Sugar boarded last. The platform ran about eight feet on a side, a tight fit for the five men. Sugar pulled the gate shut and latched it; he then hefted his machine gun and trained it upward into the black elevator shaft.

It all felt wrong. Sugar knew all about vulnerability and how to avoid it, a knowledge possessed by every street kid who survived.

This lift was not the place to be.

"Going up," Ruddiman announced in his best imitation of an old-time elevator operator. He moved his hand over the controls and selected the prompt for A-deck. The elevator eased into motion with nary a jolt and began rising slowly, glacially slower than the enclosed elevators they'd ridden earlier.

The touch-screen control panel provided the only light. Sugar pulled out a green chem light, snapped it, and shoved it into the cage mesh. The illuminated faces around him registered weariness, fear, and apprehension.

Sugar noted an approaching opening in the shaft wall through the green glow. He put his red dot sight on the deck opening as they pulled even with the deck. The hallway leading from the shaft gaped pitch black, only lit for the first couple of feet by the glow from the lift.

Sugar didn't see any creatures as the car pulled slowly past the floor. Then a clicking noise jerked him to full alert. Two massive claws the size of shovel blades punched through the mesh and ripped the fencing from the front of the lift.

Sugar cut loose on the thing. It scuttled into the lift on thick, muscular legs and bowled him over. He fell directly beneath the thing. It had more arms and legs than he could count, and each ended in knifelike claws.

Bellows, curses, screams. The elevator continued its slow ascent.

Someone was shooting, but it wasn't Sugar. He'd lost his window on the creature when it knocked him down. His machine gun now pointed uselessly to the side.

Before he could find his feet, he came face to face with a screaming Ruddiman, his taped-together glasses hanging askew. His scream abruptly cut off an instant later in a gout of blood that erupted from his mouth as the creature decapitated him with one downward thrust of a razor-edged claw. Ruddiman's head landed beside Sugar, his mouth still froze open in scream.

Sugar drew his knees into his chest and then kicked his feet upward into the creature's underside. The blow moved the beast just enough to where he might be able to gain his feet. Instead, Sugar took the opportunity to right his machine gun and fire upward into the creature, which hopped off him immediately as the first bullet struck.

More gunfire, the crack of small arms.

Sugar struggled to stand in the packed elevator. The creature thrashed about and slammed him into the mesh cage as it engaged LT and Johnny, who fought back with pistols. Sugar tried to get a bead on the creature again but found he couldn't risk shooting with three other men in such close proximity. A hornet sting in his leg announced someone had shot him, but he knew from experience that it was a graze.

He finally stood, drew his combat knife, and sank it deep into the beast's back between two appendages that reminded him of large, crooked fingers. The squelching sound the blade made, the spurt of blood as it pierced black flesh—Sugar felt satisfaction. He raised the knife and brought it down again and again, three, four, five times. The creature probed behind itself for him with another of its appendages, smaller but still sporting a claw that could easily eviscerate him. Sugar buried the knife one more time, then grabbed the probing finger-arm in his bone-crushing grip. He found a joint and applied tremendous pressure until it snapped.

The creature forgot all about the others. It spun around at blinding speed, tiptoeing nimbly on its claws despite the chaos and cramped conditions.

Sugar raised his knife for another attack.

This time three arms came at him. He fended off the first with his knife and shoved aside another with his arm. The third arm slashed crosswise and ensnared his exposed bicep with a serrated ridge like a chainsaw. He'd never known such pain, not even the one time he'd been gut-shot in Afghanistan and not expected to survive. It felt as though a train had crushed his right arm just above the elbow, and he let out a bellow that drowned out every other sound in the shaft.

Johnny slashed at the creature with his knife. LT emptied his pistol into the thing. Ball clubbed at it with his rifle. Sugar saw all of it as if he floated underwater, everything wavy and indistinct.

He tumbled backward out of the lift, onto one of the deck levels.

No. He wiggled his fingers—he was certain of it—but they were nowhere to be seen. The blood coursing from the stump of his right arm was tangible enough, however.

Sugar blacked out for an instant and then came to, unbelievably dizzy now. Ball jumped from the moving elevator and landed next to him. LT had exited the lift, which continued rising slowly. Johnny's head poked through the creature's legs. A moment later he slipped out of the elevator and dropped to the deck. The beast barely missed decapitating him with a swipe of one of its claws. Lusting for blood, it unwittingly tried to follow him out of the elevator.

The lift passed the deck. The creature got stuck with half of its body still in the lift and half dangling above the floor, legs and claws slicing the air as it hung suspended. The elevator stopped, began to jerk as the cables strained to lift. Johnny, LT, and Ball cut loose on the dangling creature with shotgun and rifles. The elevator jerked back into full motion, cutting the creature in two in an eruption of black blood and bone fragments.

In a heartbeat, Johnny and LT were on the half that fell into the hallway. It was starting to morph into something else, but it never got the chance. They blasted the thing until their magazines ran out of ammunition. Portions of it still moved, so they finished it off with rifle butts to save ammo. All that remained was a thin black puddle of goo. Taking no chances, they used their boots to swipe the remainder down the dark shaft.

Ball paled at the sight of Sugar's severed, bleeding stump. He took off his belt.

*Be sure...*Sugar tried to say. *Be sure to draw a bloody T on my forehead.* He'd learned that a long time ago in basic training, to always mark a tourniquet casualty with a T so the medics would know at a glance.

"Shit!" Johnny yelped as Sugar heard slaps, felt his face sting. "Wake up!"

Sugar opened his eyes.

Johnny hung right in his face, so close he could make out the tobacco stains on his teeth. "We gotcha, gonna take care of you, don't worry."

"Yeah." Sugar closed his eyes again. He was missing his combat knife and machine gun in addition to his right arm. "You might as well plant me right here."

"No fucking way," LT said.

"Nah, really," Sugar gasped. He knew he'd morphed as surely as the creature they'd battled, only he'd transformed into a burden far heavier than Dr. Kumar. He glared at Johnny. "Just fuckin' leave me. You know how it's done."

He passed out from pain and blood loss.

19

COMMANDERS IN THE FIELD WEREN'T SUPPOSED TO MOURN their dead. Taking the objective was all that mattered; the deeds of the fallen would be remembered after the battle. Max always stuck to that rule. Whether a hard charger or a shitbag, every man who ever served under him had known the risks and volunteered of his own free will. Coach had known he might never see his ex-wife or his girlfriend again. Diaz had known that he might never see his wife or tuck in his daughters. Irish had known that his wife and kids were one day likely to get a phone call to hear that he was never coming home. Commanders weren't supposed to mourn their dead but Max acutely felt the loss of all these men, losses piled onto losses from the past. All he could do was march ahead.

Yet Max couldn't stop envisioning Irish as he climbed an interminable flight of stairs, headed for the ship's bridge. One of the team's original members, a rock-steady man of impeccable bearing and intrepid character. He always had the backs of his brother warriors. Max would have been able to push him to the back of his mind, had he died in anything resembling a fair fight. *Cooked to death in a buried alien spaceship. Try telling that to his family.* Not that Max had any intention of revealing the cause of death. He doubted he'd have the chance to tell them anything. *At the rate we're losing men, we're all likely to be MIA.*

The elevator they encountered couldn't be summoned according to Dr. Rogers, so they took the adjacent stairwell. Despite the alien nature of the ship, Max decided the race that designed this thing must have possessed some human characteristics, though he suspected they were slightly smaller. The cramped stairwell kept going up and up.

Max figured they'd gone up about twelve flights already. He'd stationed Red as rear guard and was now on point, with Dr. Rogers following just behind him. Their pace was annoyingly slow thanks to Dr. Kumar, who demanded a rest after every flight. Max indulged him every five.

Around a corner, Max probed the next flight with his reflex sight and saw nothing. He proceeded. "How many flights more to the command center, Doctor?"

"Only a few more, I believe. I've only visited it a couple of times since access was highly restricted. And never via this route."

Dr. Kumar wheezed, "This being the steepest and most tortuous route, apparently."

"Shut up already." Max had grown tired of him hours ago. "Three good men died so you could live. The least you could do is stop complaining about it."

"Yeah, really," Red muttered. "Secure your whining tongue, or I'll toss you to the next creature we see."

Kumar gulped, panted, and kept climbing.

A few more flights turned out to be eight. The stairs brought them to a narrow hallway with a grated floor running its entire length of thirty feet or so. Electronics and holographic computer monitors covered the walls; most of them dark at the moment. The functioning few glowed the ubiquitous orange.

"Keep your eyes peeled in here, all of you," Max instructed. "We could be attacked from any angle." The beasts possessed both the malleability and camouflage necessary to blend in seamlessly with the computer equipment.

Max stepped into the hall. Looking down through the floor grating he saw at least two more hallways identical to the one they were in. The electronics formed solid walls going down deep into the bowels of the ship.

"Maintenance access hallways," Red muttered.

Good thing we only have to cross one. They made it through without incident, emerging on another stair landing. The flight going up was wide and well lit; the down flight a tenebrous spiral staircase that reminded Max of the ladder wells on naval ships. An open door straight ahead revealed a straight-running hallway. A Greytech directory sign over the door advised that the command center was up the wide staircase, and the computer science laboratory down the hall somewhere. The sign made no mention of the spiral staircase.

Max got his first view of a starship's bridge as he emerged from the staircase into a large antechamber of computers and workstations that opened onto the command center. Functioning computers illuminated portions of the room in sporadic pools of orange. A round elevator yawned open on the right wall, the car lit and ready for the trip down. They'd reached the topmost deck of the ship. Windows of many geometric shapes comprised the ceiling and parts of the walls in an artful puzzle of glass. Unfortunately, only pitch blackness shone through the windows. *Must have been an awesome view when this ship was in space. How many worlds have been viewed through these windows?* Impossible to say, but one thing was certain: one of those worlds had produced the substance.

"I need to see if I can interact with the controls on the main bridge," Dr. Rogers said.

"Lead the way," Max urged.

She headed left at too brisk a pace for his liking.

"Can't wait to see this," Red admitted. "Fuck, I wish I had a camera!"

The glass ceiling vaulted higher, forming a cavernous dome of blacked-out glass. The antechamber floor ended. Two flights of narrow stairs, one to the left and one to the right, led down to the bridge floor, a circular area made up of the usual workstations and computer terminals. Practically all the computers were in operation, their holographic screens flooding the floor in an array of hues. Straight ahead lay the command center, situated atop a round tower that thrust upward from the center of the floor. A circular bank of computers ringed the command tower to a height of four feet and projected upward. The shimmering holographic images formed a round wall of amber light.

The command center was only accessible via a retractable bridge, extended at the moment to allow access. An imposing chair reserved for the captain of the vessel occupied the center of the platform. It faced front for now, but Max figured it swiveled about. He squinted closer and saw a shadow that might have been the top of someone's head poking above the chair back.

Max stopped at the end of the extended bridge. *No, not just a head.* Shoulders too. The man occupying the chair appeared quite large indeed.

With his rifle trained on the back of the chair, Max commanded, "Show yourself! We're Greytech security contractors here to get you off this ship."

The chair swiveled around slowly.

Dr. Rogers gasped.

"I'll leave when I'm good and ready," said the man—no, *the thing*—in the chair.

It wasn't fully a creature. Still bipedal, it possessed a human countenance, bloated and distorted, wrinkled and mottled black in places. Its silver eyes shone through the amber light, catlike, too large and glassy to be human. Jung's body hung suspended, head to toe, in a translucent black skin, a mutated version of the substance that had dissolved his human flesh, exposing the decaying organs exposed. His brain appeared healthy, however—it had grown too large to fit inside any human skull. He'd grown an extra pair of arms just below his original ones. His spidery fingers ended in curling silver, scalpel-like claws, two inches in length. He stood up on lithe alien legs that ended in reptilian feet. The beastly thing towered a good eight feet tall.

"Dr. Jung?" asked Dr. Rogers, dread in her voice.

"Yessss," hissed the half creature. "And you are the one who calls herself Dr. Rogers."

"Don't get any closer," Max instructed Jung. "Stay right fucking there."

"Of course, Mr. Ahlgren." *How does he know my name?* He motioned expansively about the command center with all four of his arms. "Please, join me. We have much to talk about."

"Doctor Jung?" Dr. Kumar asked. "What happened—?"

"Shut it, Kumar," Max ordered.

The invitation was a trap, of course, and Max prepared to open fire. But he stayed his trigger finger and swallowed the order. It would be dicey at best, questioning Jung—and he had no doubt how it would end—but with LT and the others missing, he had to try. Maybe Jung would reveal something to help him reunite his team.

The command center lay on the far side of the extended access bridge, which had no railing against the thirty-foot drop. The tower had obviously been designed to isolate the captain and officers for both privacy and security One of Jung's hands hovered near the holographic control for that bridge, a not-so-subtle reminder he could retract the arch whenever he liked.

"Don't worry." Jung locked his maniacal silver eyes on Max. "I wouldn't kill you like this. You deserve a more heroic end than that."

Either dance with him or shoot him. Max called Red to the front. They stepped onto the bridge, with Dr. Rogers behind them.

"I'm coming too," Dr. Kumar panted from behind. "I want some goddamn answers!"

"Get back!" Max ordered as he stalked forward, never averting his glare from Dr. Jung. "I'll throw you off this bridge if I have to."

"No! I want to hear this twisted thing try to justify its actions."

"Whatever. That's on you." *Let the fool play the righteous researcher.*

Max and Red stepped onto the command center platform and stood face-to-face with Jung, about twenty feet separating them. Dr. Rogers came forward and stood close to Max's left.

"What the hell happened to you?" Max asked.

Jung didn't look the least bit concerned about having three deadly weapons pointed at him. "Isn't it obvious?" He smiled through rough, fishlike lips surrounding an abnormally large mouth with two rows of black-needle teeth. "I have melded with the substance, a symbiotic agreement. Through its generative powers, I've grown new brain cells and increased my IQ tenfold. In return, it has partaken of my knowledge. It is learning to think logically, a process it will pass along to others of its race. Their numbers increase rapidly. Once they gain the power of analytical thought, there will be no stopping us. We will be the master race on this planet within a few years."

"You delusional fuck," Max spat. "What the fuck do you think you are doing?"

Jung coughed out a laugh. "Oh, not a delusion, just a fact. You're seeing it with your very eyes. This is the future."

"Why?" Dr. Rogers asked. "Why unleash these creatures into this world? Why do you want to destroy humanity? Why betray the human race?"

Jung opened his fish mouth and bellowed laughter that reverberated off the glass dome. "Humanity is but a primitive speck in the universe. This alien life form is as old as the universe itself, a collective intelligence that has infinite potential. It does not war against itself, quite unlike humans. It is geared toward one thing only: survival through any evolutionary means necessary."

"You've lost your mind," Dr. Rogers stated flatly.

Jung scratched his chin with his left arm, the upper one. "You of all people should know better. This is both the beginning and the end for humanity. You must understand that. The madness, as you call it, is a mere side effect of melding with an advanced alien organism who, at present, lusts for blood and wants to break free from the bonds of this ship."

"Max, look!" Red pointed to one of the holograms projecting above Jung's head, where an amber-and-black image showed LT leading his men into an elevator.

"Holy shit."

To look backward, Jung rotated his head farther than any human possibly could. "In full color, if you prefer." With his lower right hand, he tapped a touch screen prompt on a computer built into the arm of the command chair.

Max watched with rapt attention. The resolution of the three-dimensional image put HD to shame. Sugar had lost his right arm, the stump tied off with a belt tourniquet. Gable and Ball supported his bulk as best they could between them, ready to walk him into the open elevator. Max saw no sign of the other civilian. Just as LT made to step over the threshold, the curved door slammed shut with a resounding *boom.*

"What the fuck!" LT shouted.

Ball threw his left arm up in frustration.

"Shit!" Gable cried, tobacco juice spitting from his lips.

Sugar's head hung low, his chin on his chest. He shivered once, jerking violently. Half awake, dying from blood loss.

Jung's laugh started low. His lower right hand hovered over the control panel in the chair arm. "You will all die. It is the end and you don't even know it."

Max leveled his rifle at Jung's mutated face. "I've heard enough of this bullshit." And squeezed the trigger.

Red joined in with his flamethrower. The combined force of their firepower blew Dr. Jung through the holograms and off the command center tower. Max ran around the command chair to the other side of the platform, Red running beside him. He didn't see Dr. Rogers or feel her presence as he had before.

Jung appeared again at the platform's edge. He had doubled his mass in mere moments. His face sprouted insectoid features including compound eyes the size of dinner plates and a needle-sharp proboscis two feet long. His legs were breaking and re-knitting themselves, elongating. His fingers extended into long, sword sized claws. A bony, multi-jointed, tail protruded from his thorax, tipped with a stinger that dripped black acid, the fumes burning his nasal passages.

Jung let out a defining roar. It sounded like a demon's in a horror movie.

Movies had never scared Max; however, this aberration struck a primal cord inside him, making his hands feel cold and the hair stand up on the back of his neck. Max learned long ago to control his fear and channeled it into something else – rage. He was more determined than ever to slay one of the beasts.

"Allow me," Red shouted, throwing a column of fire its way.

Napalm flames scorched the creature for only an instant before it scuttled away, dancing deftly across the tops of the computers ringing the platform. Max led it with his rifle and fired, almost every bullet striking home as it tried to circle around to their rear.

This creature was marked for death. Max had never shot so accurately as he did emptying his rifle. Despite its lightweight and advanced design, Max's HK416 rifle was still an ungainly weapon when firing at rapidly moving targets in close quarters. As he grabbed a fresh magazine, the creature hopped from atop the computers.

It charged, dodging Red's stream of fire. As it landed next to him, it swung with its bladed arms. Red blocked the claw aimed for his neck with the flamethrower, but it was fast and another claw raked him across the chest, his plate carrier taking the damage. Red pivoted attempting to avoid the onslaught. The third claw barely missed his shoulder and punched a hole in the flamethrower's fuel tank, the force of the blow knocking him over.

The creature raised up its arms to strike Red again when Ms. Quinones opened fire with her rifle from the retractable bridge. The rounds punching into the creature's head, making it shriek, and temporarily distracting it from finishing off Red.

The creature lunged towards Ms. Quinones as she continued to pepper it with rounds until the bolt locked back on her weapon. She stood paralyzed in fear as the creature towered over.

"No!" Kumar yelled as he yanked her away from the creature and stumbled backwards, landing on his back, his jaw slack with fear, as the creature rapidly closed the gap. The creature's scorpion-like tail swung over its head with blinding speed and jerked spasmodically as it drove its stinger deep into Kumar's abdomen several times. Kumar's organs bubbled and dissolved, the process shrouding him and the creature in a fog of sickly sweet white smoke. He screamed only briefly, then went silent as the acid consumed his lungs.

Ms. Quinones let out a piercing scream as she saw the doctor's body dissolved.

Max slapped a full magazine into his rife, found the creature in his reflex sight, and unloaded into its thorax. Each striking round kicked up a spurt of black blood and pulpy flesh.

"Shit!" Red cried as he removed the leaking flamethrower from his back. The smell of the leaking diesel further energized Max, though he had no idea why. And he had no reason to ask—his aim was dead on, and there was no stopping him.

You are mine, asshole.

The creature jumped off Kumar's smoldering corpse. It swiftly bounded about the domed bridge chamber, defying gravity and all attempts to kill it. Max kept shooting it, but it recovered from the shots so quickly that they barely affected it.

Red reached for his machine gun.

Again, Max exhausted his ammunition. The creature climbed to the apex of the dome and dropped on them. Max hurried to reload, while Red opened fire as the creature dived.

Thunder and lightning came in a single blast that left Max's ears ringing and made his hair stand on end. He dropped the magazine in his hand. The murky chamber went noonday white for an instant. Then a second explosion rocked the bridge as the bolt of energy hit the creature and blew a smoking hole clean through it, the force of the impact propelling it into the far wall of the dome. Max heard its bones shatter over the creature's keening screech. It slid down the glass, leaving behind a snail trail of inky residue.

Max and Red ran to the tower's edge and opened fire. The beast was already regenerating, though not at such a fast rate now. It bucked and jerked as the rounds pounded its body.

Max looked back, Dr. Rogers stood in the entrance to the antechamber. An alien cannon in her arms, a wisp of white smoke curled from its five-foot barrel. And she had a similar looking weapon slung over her shoulder.

"Keep that thing pinned down!" Max ordered Red. He sprinted across the bridge toward Dr. Rogers, hurdling Kumar's corpse, which had rendered down to a pile of smoking meat not even identifiable as human. "Are you all right?"

She met Max's gaze and nodded. Then her eyes registered movement behind Max. "Kill it!" she cried, yanking free the cannon she'd slung over her shoulder.

Max dropped his rifle and picked up the alien weapon. *Christ, practically weightless!* He saw no ports for ammo magazines. The weapon's receiver, though well machined, felt boxy and cumbersome. The power source within comprised most of the weapon's weight. It lacked a true butt stock, merely a composite handle extending upward from the end.

On the side of the weapon near the handle, a small touchscreen computer glowed orange. A bar barely registered on one side of the screen. *Charge indicator?* If so, the weapon was damn near dead.

Max ran back to the command center, holding the cannon at port arms. Red filled the beast with lead, keeping it wounded and on the run, but he needed to change the barrel which was glowing a dull red. Not sure how to maneuver the weapon, Max aimed it from his hip, pointing it at the creature and squeezed the handle. A holographic image appeared above the weapon in front of Max's vision, it reminded him of a heads-up display on a fighter jet. The weapon locked onto the creature, now hopping feebly across the tops of computer stations as it worked its way back to the command center, the hole in its thorax beginning to heal.

Uh-uh, motherfucker!

A bright-yellow circle appeared around the creature, accompanied by a high-pitched chime indicating the lock. Max thumbed the trigger pad on top of the handle and held it down. The initial report sounded like a mini-thunder clap. A blue jolt of solar brilliance hit Max's eyes and blinded him; after that came a loud crackling sound as he kept the trigger depressed. The weapon vibrated in his hand, and the recoil pushed the barrel about a foot upward before he regained control of the bucking weapon, releasing the trigger after a two-second burst.

It took a second for Max's eyes to readjust. When he finally cracked open his eyes, Dr. Rogers stood at his side. She asked with a grin, "Care to view your handiwork?"

Max nodded. His vision had returned to normal, his blindness replaced by a throbbing headache. "Sure. I'm guessing it's safe to look." He peered over the parapet of computers ringing the command center.

The creature no longer existed. The bolt of energy—*Electricity?*

Plasma?—had reduced it back into a puddle of goo from which rose tendrils of smoke that reminded Max of morning mist on the surface of a placid lake. The substance did not move. Apparently, they had finally killed a creature.

"Stay up here and cover us, Red. That thing moves, pop it again."

"Shouldn't be necessary," Dr. Rogers commented.

"Why?" Max asked her.

"The blasts are so powerful that a direct hit kills it on the cellular level. The beasts can only regenerate if their cells are alive."

They jogged across the bridge and broke for the left stairway. "Where did you find that thing?"

"In a small-weapons locker in the antechamber. Fortunately, it still had enough power left to be of use. Those cannons are extremely dangerous—like any other gun, it doesn't discriminate. Any human caught in a blast is as good as dead. The creatures are more resilient—you saw how many times we had to hit it."

"So, it shoots lightning bolts? I didn't exactly get a good look."

"Yes, a concentrated bolt of particle energy. When you fire it, avoid looking directly at the light."

"Are there more in the armory?"

"Yes, but I can't say if they're charged. We'll know soon enough. Be warned that everything in there is incredibly dangerous. A technician was seriously injured when the weapons were first encountered."

They came upon the puddle of substance that had engulfed and melded with Dr. Jung. Max could tell it was as inert as tar cooling on a winter day.

"How's it looking down there?" Red called.

"Dead," Max replied.

"Yes!" Red pumped a beefy fist into the air. "Finally!"

Max climbed back to the command center. "Now let's find LT." He moved to the command chair and pointed to its integral computer. "He was controlling the camera via this computer. Maybe we can figure out how to use it."

Dr. Rogers scanned the holographic displays and worked her way through a series of unintelligible prompts, that led to prompts, that led to even more prompts. Random holograms projected upward and then died out as Max selected new prompts. They saw surveillance images of various hallways and rooms, a scrolling page of data in alien characters that reminded Max of a stock ticker, and diagrams of straight lines and alien characters that might have been technical drawings of the ship's vital systems.

"Christ, you could access anything on the ship from this computer if I knew where the fuck to look," Max grumbled. "There are literally thousands of prompts once you start opening them."

"I'm sorry," Dr. Rogers said. "I wish I possessed the knowledge to help you locate your men."

"That makes two of us. Are you able to access the ships bulk heads to seal off the creatures?"

"No, unfortunately, Dr. Jung has somehow overridden the ships main control systems. We can't access any of the ship's main systems from here now. We now have a more pressing problem. It appears Dr. Jung initiated the ship's cargo hold release procedure. The rest of the creature will be free in a matter of hours."

"What can we do to stop it?" Max said.

Dr. Rogers breathed deep and held it a moment before letting it out. "You two heard what he said: they're multiplying, and he was helping them to evolve into intelligent beings."

"I recall that, yes," Red said.

"We need to destroy this ship. It's the only way we can contain this threat and be certain all of them die."

"And how do we accomplish that?" Max asked.

"I think I know how it might be done from the rear of the ship. The main reactor is there, and so is most of the substance in the cargo hold."

"Uh-huh." Red scratched at his chin. "So, we need to go where there are more of these creatures about to be set free. That is just great! Is there a big red self-destruct button on the reactor as well?"

Dr. Rogers smiled. "It's a bit more involved than that."

"Yeah, yeah, nothing you can explain to mere laymen like us. We'll just have to trust you. I'm getting used to that answer."

"It is what it is," she said with a shrug. "First the armory, though."

"Yeah, I need to pick up one of those cannons to replace my flamethrower."

"You might just find one."

"Then let's move," Max urged.

The three walked across the bridge and back into the ante-chamber where they located Ms. Quinones cowering amongst the electronics.

She shivered, still frightened, but made no attempt to get up and walk.

"Or stay. Completely up to you."

"I go with you," she said.

Red offered her a hand up and jerked her to her feet.

Max took one final look over his shoulder at the only starship bridge he would ever visit. Star Wars *kind of had it right*. Star Trek, *not so much.*

* * *

Max stood on the threshold of the armory. About half an acre of alien weaponry was racked up neatly inside the long rectangular room. Serious firepower waited to be taken: weapons of all makes and sizes obviously designed for humanoids and yet, unlike anything he had seen outside of a movie theater. He couldn't wait to get a closer look.

Red stood beside Max in the doorway and marveled. "I am going to enjoy this." He smiled and rubbed his hands together.

"Keep it in your pants." Max reminded him, "We gotta clear the place first."

"Of course, Chief. You're not dealing with a rookie, you know."

Max noted only a few scattered outposts of orange light. "It's pretty dim in there. Let's hope it gets brighter when we step inside." All the present lighting radiated from small computer terminals beneath a handful of weapons that pointed directly upward, their stocks stuck in the racks for both storage and charging.

"It will," Dr. Rogers assured him. "Unfortunately, those few weapons you see plugged into the active computers are the only ones charged and ready."

"Damn, really?" Red asked.

"Yes. At some point, someone, perhaps one of the creatures, smashed the main circuit board that controls the chargers built into the weapon racks."

"Shit," Max muttered. "But at least there are a few up and functioning. Red, take Ms. Quinones and clear the perimeter. Dr. Rogers and I will take the aisles."

Max stepped inside. The ambient ceiling lights came on. Clearing the aisles would take a while between searching for creatures and checking out the weapons. Some of the weapons resembled conventional rifles of futuristic design, with barrels of varying lengths and differing calibers, though only a handful appeared to use projectiles in magazines. *The rest must be all electronic, right down to the ammo. Hopefully, we'll find another cannon, fully charged.*

He grabbed one of the magazine rifles and took note of its small caliber, roughly the size of a .38. It had an abnormally short barrel, a large drum magazine, and what appeared to be a motorized cylinder built in. Max examined the receiver carefully and found a button that released the magazine. Packed inside were several hundred fléchettes about four inches long. Max examined one—smooth and aerodynamic metallic finish, yet dense and heavy like depleted uranium. *Nice.* He locked the magazine back in and slung the weapon over his shoulder with a thick elastic cord that spooled out from the side of the muzzle and stock of the weapon.

"Can't wait to try this," he whispered.

Dr. Rogers pointed. "There's a test firing area at the far end of the room."

Max and Dr. Rogers continued their sweep of the aisles and located a few more charged weapons. "How about this?" Max lifted a weapon of a submachine gun size that had no barrel but rather something akin to a ribbed porcelain insulator protruding dead center from a concave disk. "Looks almost like one of those old-school portable sound surveillance devices."

"It emits sound, though I'm not sure at what frequency. It might be highly effective against them."

"Try it then. It looks dainty enough for you to wield."

"Wiseass," she muttered but returned his smile.

She grabbed it from the rack, and they moved on. They wouldn't be able to take all the operational weapons with them, but they could certainly test a few before choosing what they wanted. Ten lightning cannons lay racked up in the final row, most of them on very low charge. Max grabbed one before moving on.

They met up with Red at the rear of the room before the mouth of a twenty-foot-diameter tunnel built into the wall. Red and Max shined lights inside the ballistics tunnel, spotting no creatures secreted within. However, the tunnel continued past the effective range of their flashlights.

Red jerked a thumb over his shoulder. "There's an open vault with some ordnance along that wall. Found mines of some sort, some ammo cans too. I left them over there for now." He pointed to the cannon. "Did you pick that up for me?"

Max grinned. "All yours. If you can handle it."

Red snorted in mock derision. "Need you even ask?" He took the cannon, checked the power on the computer screen, and admired the weapon. "Un-fucking-real. It's like an ACME-brand disintegrator!"

Max grunted, almost a chuckle. "Too bad we're not here to kill Roadrunners."

"How about a test shot?" Red sounded like a kid with a new BB gun.

Max shook his head. "We already know what it does, and we have to conserve battery life. I'm guessing that cannon has about a minute of power tops, probably not even that. Let's try out these other two."

Dr. Rogers stepped up to the tunnel mouth with the sonic weapon, powered it on, and pulled the trigger. An orange light on the receiver illuminated while the trigger was depressed. She expended no great physical effort keeping the weapon on target. It appeared to do nothing, however, emitting neither sound nor light.

"Well, that looks weak," Red commented when she was through.

"Looks mean nothing in this case," Dr. Rogers informed him. "This is a sonic disruptor, low frequency I believe, judging from the faint vibrations I felt. It shatters cell membranes with a bass vibration so low the human ear can't hear it."

"Makes sense, actually." Max considered the disquieting bass vibrations produced by massive subwoofers, one of the most unnerving sounds he could recall.

As Max readied the fléchette rifle, Red asked, "Gonna pop some squirrels with that, Chief?"

"Nah, but I could if I wanted to." He dropped the drum magazine and passed one of the fléchettes to Red.

"Suits your prickly personality."

Max slapped the magazine in, the cylinder spun automatically. *So similar to a chain gun.* Red and Dr. Rogers assisted him in figuring out the rifle. They took several minutes loading the weapon and then deciphering the alien computer prompts before Max finally stood to test the weapon.

The rifle barely kicked at all, like shooting an airsoft gun. A barely audible chattering sound and a tiny blue muzzle flash accompanied each shot. Sharp firecracker reports echoed back down the ballistics tunnel when the darts hit the far wall and, to Max's astonishment, exploded.

He admired the aliens' innovation. The darts would sink deep into any creature before exploding, likely doing ten times the damage of normal bullets. The rifle's loaded weight proved to be its only drawback, as the drum magazine weighed around twenty pounds. Still, Max felt confident he could wield it effectively in the thick of combat.

Red commented, "Be nice to have some targets down there."

Max turned and saw a dead computer kiosk about fifty feet away. He motioned Ms. Quinones to one side and opened fire on it. The fléchettes punched through the computer cabinet and blew the machine apart from the inside out. The screen shattered into tiny faux diamonds, and tendrils of oily black smoke leaked from the holes in the cabinet. Noxious fumes from smoldering plastic filled the air.

"Hardcore enough for you?" Max asked.

Red nodded. "I feel the momentum shifting in our favor."

Max silently agreed, reminding himself likewise not to get carried away. Going into battle with an unfamiliar weapon was ever a tricky and perilous proposition. "You see any ammo for this in the vault you found?"

"Don't know, didn't open any crates. Let's check it out."

The vault door, about a foot thick, stood wide open. A jumble of metal crates and canisters lay strewn across the floor. A box half-full of circular objects the size of hockey pucks sat open on a metal table. Each disk had a dial recessed into its surface. The two symbols below the dial corresponded to a dead indicator light. Max guessed the small black window above the dial was a blank digital readout. He noticed several tiny holes spaced at intervals around the circumference. Another hole on the other side of the disk housed what appeared to be a black button.

"What's your take on these?" Max asked. "Other than mines of some kind."

Red let out a breath. "The dial is likely a timer mechanism. Maybe it can operate via sensor as well—maybe that's what the holes are. Hard to say."

Max nodded. "Let's take some out and play." He gave the order with much reluctance. *Did you come all this way just to blow yourself up?*

"I'll come with you. I have an idea," Dr. Rogers said.

"Fine. You stay here," he instructed Ms. Quinones.

"I pray for you," Ms. Quinones said as they headed back to the tunnel. She ogled Max once again with her wanton cougar's eye.

You'd better. Without us, you're beast food.

They brought two mines with them. Dr. Rogers held out her hand, and Max placed one in her palm. Dr. Rogers pointed out one of the markings on the mine. "Okay, the symbol here is identical to ones I've seen on other alien weapons. It designates the operation time remaining concomitant to the power supply."

"And the other symbol?" Max asked.

"No idea."

"And what's up with that button on the back?" Red asked.

"Bet you it arms the mine," Max said. "Only one way to find out."

"I'll do it, Chief."

Max nodded. Red said it with no reluctance whatsoever. He was a weapons expert, and it was part of his job. He stepped into the tunnel. Dr. Rogers and Max took up positions to either side of the bore, safe from the anticipated explosion.

After a few seconds in the tunnel, Red announced, "It's not a button at all. It's a magnetic sensor that pops loose from the mine when depressed. The arming button is on the other side of the sensor." Max heard the soft metallic *clank* of a magnet grabbing metal. "Yeah, I get it now. Be right with you." Red's footsteps walked down the tunnel, followed by the same *clank* of magnet on metal.

"Okay, here goes nothing!" Red shouted. A *click* indicated it was armed, then Red's footsteps pounded as he came running from the tunnel.

Max asked, "What have you accomplished exactly?"

"The mine is attached to the floor about a hundred feet down. I placed the sensor on the wall twenty feet inside and pushed the button, which I'm thinking arms the sensor after a period of time has passed, probably just a few seconds if the aliens knew what they were doing. Now we just need to trip it. Can you spare a few needles from your rifle?"

Max popped out the drum magazine and offered it to Red, who pulled out a handful of fléchettes to toss down the tunnel. Max and Dr. Rogers took up positions with their backs flat against the wall next to the tunnel, fingers in their ears.

Red flattened against the other side. "Hope these mines aren't nuclear." He cast the darts into the tunnel.

The explosion shook the deck. A horizontal column of white-and-blue flame shot from the tunnel into a rack of dead weapons thirty feet away. The non-metal parts of the various guns began to smolder, black polymer grips and stocks melting down to puddle on the floor.

Red nodded in satisfaction. "I think I'll replace my Claymores with a few of these high-tech alien models."

"Me too," Max concurred. "It appears we've found a better mousetrap."

"We should learn how to use the timer function as well," Dr. Rogers suggested.

That proved easy. The timer activated when the user pressed down on the dial and turned it clockwise. The digital readout came alive with unintelligible alien numbers, so Red spun the dial until the number changed thirty times. He released pressure on the timer dial, and the time indicator light illuminated. The numbers started counting down. Red threw the mine far into the tunnel. They braced for the explosion as before. Max counted down with his watch. The mine exploded twenty-seven seconds later, the flames again shooting from the tunnel to fry the rack of weapons. The barrel on one of the lightning cannons drooped over like a wilted flower.

"That answers that," Max said after the echo died down.

Red grinned. "Ah, I love incendiaries."

Back at the vault, Max found three crates of fléchettes along with a second drum magazine, which he loaded. Twenty pounds of explosive darts—God only knew how many individually. He hoped the weapon retained enough charge to be able to utilize all of them. Max pondered leaving his HK416 behind to lighten his load, but after a few seconds of hard deliberation decided against it. The 416 was low on ammo and not particularly effective against the creatures, but he knew the rifle intimately, and he needed a reliable backup weapon. He inserted his last remaining hundred-round drum and released the charging handle on the weapon.

Red dumped his UMP40 and its ammo but refused to part with his machine gun. Max didn't approve of his decision—two bulky weapons would slow him considerably—but he let it slide. Nobody knew Red's limitations as well as Red. If he thought he could hump the two heavy weapons, he was welcome to try.

The mines at least were tiny. Max, Red, and Dr. Rogers took five each.

Max thought he was finished arming for the journey ahead; then he remembered the half-dozen M576 grapeshot rounds he'd brought along for the custom-built 40mm grenade launcher he carried on his back. He'd been introduced to the round while he was doing black ops missions for the CIA. He'd never used such grenades before then and didn't remember them being in the arsenal during his time in the corps. Designed specifically for close-quarters combat, they would likely prove useful in the close confines of the ship. The grenades dated from the Vietnam Era and had been slated for destruction. Max didn't consider their age a big deal—he'd trained with ordnance produced as far back as the Korean War and had never noticed a preponderance of duds in the older munitions. He ejected the high explosive rounds from the launcher and replaced them with the grapeshot grenades.

Contrary to Red's earlier statement, Max didn't think the momentum of battle had shifted to their favor—that remained to be seen—but morale was high, their attitude confident. *Drop a man in a war zone with inferior gear and he'll defeat himself long before the enemy kills him.* They'd suffered through that scenario since boarding the ship. *That's over. We're good to go now, as strapped as we're likely to get. But is it enough?*

The creatures would decide that.

20

LT PEERED UP THE FLIGHT OF STAIRS AND ATTEMPTED TO CALCU-late whether he had energy enough for the climb. He ran equations in his head as he often did, but he faced a lot of unknowns, the first being how far they would have to climb. The stairs ran thirty feet before turning to switch back. *How many flights? How much does Sugar weigh? How much of him am I supporting?* LT and Ball supported Sugar between them.

Gable watched their backs. "You gotta be shittin' me," he grumbled when he saw the stairs.

"You got a better idea?"

Gable spat a stream of tobacco juice on the floor. "There's gotta be other elevators, you know. We're dead if we get jumped by a creature in this stairwell."

"But the elevators are safe, right?" LT snorted. "Just keep your eyes open and watch our ass."

"Lots to watch back there. I'm seeing things, but I know I'm *not* seeing things, you know?"

"Not really."

"I know," Sugar rasped. "Need some water...before we climb."

"Anything you need, buddy." Gable poured water from his canteen down Sugar's throat.

Sugar took four massive gulps and gagged on the fifth, resulting in a coughing fit that ended in a bout of chilled shivering. He could barely stand on his own, too weak to walk unassisted. *Feverish, dehydrated, he didn't bleed long, but he bled long enough.* LT consulted his watch: 06:42. *The Greytech detail should be here any time now. Maybe they're here already.*

LT and his men might have been outside already if not for the last elevator slamming shut in their faces. He couldn't stop thinking about some puppeteer behind the scenes, pulling their strings by manipulating the ship's functions. Things happened for a reason. He didn't believe the ship acted on its own, no matter what the esteemed Dr. Rogers claimed.

After a final moment of mental preparation, LT hoisted Sugar to the first step. He'd felt two faint rumblings about an hour earlier that might have been anything: earth tremors, explosions caused by a creature or perhaps something Max had done. Though he had no way of knowing, LT sensed Max still lived. He could only wonder what Dr. Rogers had him chasing now. *She has her own motives. He should have seen that.*

LT nodded to Ball. They got Sugar moving and started the climb. Sugar didn't take it well. A half-dozen steps up and he was winded. His intact left arm draped over LT's shoulders, forcing him to bear the brunt of his weight. Ball did what he could on the right side, but the severed arm kept slipping off his shoulder, causing

Sugar to groan in pain.

It took twenty minutes to climb five flights of stairs. LT saw an opening at the top of the sixth flight and hoped to see signs up there pointing the way to the exit. The stairs kept winding upward, but he didn't think Sugar could handle another six flights.

LT and Ball urged Sugar onto the last flight of stairs.

Halfway up Gable muttered, "Shit!"

"What's going on back there?" LT asked, unconsciously trying to drag Sugar up the stairs faster.

"What the fuck do you think?" Gable responded.

A clanking sound came from the rear: a hard object bouncing down the stairwell and caroming off walls. Gable's tossed grenade exploded five seconds later. A blast furnace wind shot up the stairwell, but the switchbacks eliminated the concussive effects. Another grenade went bouncing down the steps. Sugar started climbing faster, using what little gas he had left to get them up the steps. He'd picked up the pace for their sake, not his own.

The second grenade detonated; a piercing screech echoed up the stairs and bored into LT's ears. Sugar was heavy but getting him the fuck away from whatever it was down below was a priority. Using what little strength he had left, he and Ball had Sugar moving at top speed now, already halfway up the flight of stairs.

Gable shouted, "Keep moving; I got this!"

He didn't need to say it twice. Sugar unleashed a groan of agony when they reached the landing a few seconds later. LT peered out the exit into a three-way intersection. Straight ahead and to the left ran long corridors lined with the typical closed doors. *There!* He saw another intersection fifty feet down the right hallway. Another kiosk directory stood at the junction.

"Hang on, Sugar," LT urged. "We're getting there."

They stepped into the hall and hobbled for the kiosk.

The third explosion sounded muted compared to the others.

"That'll fucking teach you," Gable shouted as he emerged from the stairwell.

"WP?" LT asked, his eyes still on the kiosk.

"Yep," Gable said.

"Good call." White phosphorus munitions caused severe burns and produced thick volumes of smoke. If the creatures needed oxygen to survive, they would have a difficult time continuing the chase up the stairs. LT doubted they did, but perhaps the incendiary would stall the creatures and buy them some time. *Just show me the way out of here.*

Miraculously the kiosk hadn't been upset in any manner. "How we looking back there, Gable?" LT asked as he scanned the directory.

"It ain't come out of there yet."

"E-Deck Elevator/Exit." LT found the arrow: left hallway. "Let's go!"

The elevator waited only about thirty feet down the hall at a T-intersection. LT called the car via the orange holographic computer. He considered for the first time that they hadn't had to wait for an elevator until now. *Will it even show up?* The puppeteer—if such an entity existed—hadn't granted them any mercy thus far, why start now?

The car arrived within seconds, its curved door hissing open in invitation. Ball looked apprehensive about entering, likely afraid the door would slam shut on them.

LT figured that was the least of their worries. "Let's go. Get him inside."

Gable shouted, "Y'all better, like right fuckin' now!"

They crossed the threshold with Sugar and stepped inside.

A black flood poured down the hallway from the kiosk intersection. In a liquid form, the beast flowed effortlessly toward them like a massive blob of mercury.

As Gable jumped into the elevator, LT glared at the glowing orange gibberish on the control screen. One of these buttons had to close the door.

"Go, go!" Gable shouted.

The door didn't close. Only a few feet away, the flowing beast began a transformation, a fanged mouth taking shape and five pincers sprouting from random locations.

"Fuck me!" LT jammed an index finger into random prompts and hoped he would hit the right one.

"Hurry the fuck up!" Gable opened fire with his rifle.

The beast grew two plated scorpion-like tails. It whirled them once through the air to gain momentum and then shot them forward to strike.

The door slammed shut. An instant later it buckled inward with a *bang* as the tentacles struck full force. Then the car shot upward, leaving the creature behind. LT released a sigh of relief.

"That was hairy," Ball said.

LT nodded. "Just hope it's the last one we see."

Gable smiled sardonically and looked ready to say something. The words never came. *Good. Keep your mouth shut and don't jinx us.*

The elevator stopped at E-deck. The buckled door opened about two feet and stopped, too bent to open any further. It was just enough. LT and Ball carefully maneuvered Sugar through the opening and into a four-way intersection. A directory sign stared them in the face. LT followed the arrow for the exit.

After negotiating two turns and a few hundred feet of hallways, LT saw the first indicator that they were near the exit—the dull gray gleam of a few bb's lodged where the floor met the wall. They walked another twenty feet to a right turn where several dozen bb's had come to rest in the corner. He saw the brighter gleam of brass shell casings on the floor ahead and smelled putrefaction in the air.

"I think we're getting close, boys," LT said as he turned the corner.

About fifty feet down the hall he identified the tripod-mounted chain gun guarding the three-way intersection they'd traversed what seemed like decades ago. Brass shell casings and bb's littered the floor. Sticky black residue coated the deck at the point where the chain gun had blasted the creature. LT felt like a cartoon character walking through a puddle of glue.

"Still a live sensor in the exit hallway," Gable reminded him.

"I haven't forgotten," LT responded.

The chain gun was still loaded and ready to fire. The creature they'd battled outside had either slipped beneath the sensor or hadn't followed them. Sugar would never get over or under the sensor in his condition. LT pulled the ammo belt from the machine gun, then discharged the round in the chamber. "Let's get the fuck out of here."

They made it to the cleansing room without incident. Suiting up Sugar in his cold-weather gear seemed to take forever.

"Y'all go for help." Sugar waved them onward with his remaining arm. "You don't need me slowing you down. Leave me with a gun and some grenades."

"Not happening," Gable stated. "We all leave together."

Sugar gazed down at his right arm. "Not all of us." The stump had stopped bleeding a while ago; the flesh below the tourniquet now purple from lack of circulation.

Gable seemed poised to say something encouraging, but he swallowed it.

They emerged from the tunnel into the gathering light of pre-dawn. The storm had passed. Not a single cloud marred the still star-filled sky. A blustery wind buffeted the men, seeking any opening it might find in their gear.

"Listen," Sugar gasped, barely audible.

From the direction of Base Camp came the unmistakable sound of whirling helicopter rotors.

"Bird is the word!" Gable hollered.

"Be careful!" LT said. "There are likely still creatures out here."

"I got our backs. Lead on, sir."

They walked from the tunnel, around the flipped and burned trailers, and past the mutilated, frozen corpses. And away from Max. *Be right back for you, Chief.* Their fee was likely forfeited because they'd entered the ship, but LT didn't give a shit. They were alive, and now they had the necessary backup to bring out Max and hopefully find a way to destroy the ship. They'd lost Coach for sure and Diaz most likely. But Sugar would live. *At least you can be proud of that.*

Gable called, "Y'all just concentrate on walking the big guy to the chopper pad. I'll take care of the rest."

As they trudged down the hill and back into Base Camp, LT saw no Greytech personnel or any sign that they'd ventured into camp. All the action clumped around the helipad, where a CH-53 Sea Stallion had landed and shut down, its rotors now still and silent. LT made out bodies in formation next to the helipad—a full complement of heavily armed Greytech security men.

"Finally!" Ball gasped.

"Over here!" LT frantically waved to them with his left arm. He was ready to drop after supporting Sugar for so long. He glanced back and saw Gable, about thirty feet behind, poking his nose and shotgun through the side of a trailer ripped open by a creature.

"Gable!" LT motioned for him to join them.

Gable held up a finger and stalked off onto a side street.

Shit, are the beasts still running around up here?

"They're coming!" Ball yelled.

A squad of ten men marched toward them. Eight were rank-and-file security men holding their rifles at port arms. A ninth man carrying a pistol led them forward, obviously their commanding officer. The tenth man held no weapon, though a holstered automatic pistol rode on his belt.

"We're good for now," LT said to Ball. "Let's lay him down until they bring a stretcher." They gingerly lowered Sugar to the freezing earth.

"LT," Sugar whispered, his eyes shut.

"Right here, bro."

"Go back for Chief. He's still alive."

LT nodded. "I know he is. We'll head in as soon as we get squared away with the Greytech team. You just relax and concentrate on recovering."

"Can't concentrate...on shit right now." His jaw suddenly went slack as his head lolled. His breaths were rapid and shallow, but it was enough that he was breathing considering his injury.

The squad arrived, their officer calling a halt about twenty feet away. They wore the latest in body armor. High-speed comm gear, optics, and grenades adorned their bodies. The troops carried HK G36 rifles; the officer a Glock 21. They might be working for Greytech at the moment, but up close, LT could tell by their bearing and dead countenances that these were more than mere security goons. *Battle-hardened, these guys have seen some shit.* LT was pleased—they had the skilled backup needed to go back inside and rescue Max.

LT's confidence wavered when he saw the tenth man, who

stood out from the security detail in brand-new pristine gear. He was a couple inches over six feet and sported a mouthful of perfect teeth smiling incongruously in his creased and weathered face.

Banner. CIA. LT had met him once several years before at a mission briefing. Max knew him intimately and had nothing good to say about the man.

"Man, are we glad to see you guys," LT said to the commanding officer. He then nodded at Banner. "Sir."

Banner kept his smile beaming. "Ah, Thompson, isn't it?"

"Yes, sir."

The commanding officer with the pistol smiled as he slid his goggles up onto his helmet. LT recognized Michael Stewart, chief of Greytech security. He cocked his head and looked quizzically at LT. "Looks like matters have gotten out of control."

"Yes," LT admitted. "We've got a real situation on our hands. The creatures—"

"Where's Ahlgren?"

There was no getting around it. "Aboard the ship."

"I see. Men." The final word was his order. Michael Stewart turned his back on LT and started back to the helipad.

Eight rifles came to bear on LT and Ball, who yelled in surprise and fumbled for the rifle slung across his back. Banner's smile brightened as he watched, never drawing his weapon, only observing. He obviously liked what he was seeing, appeared to enjoy the spectacle, in fact.

A hyper shot of adrenaline poured into LT, whose rifle was likewise across his back and out of reach. He saw muzzles flash, heard the brief and deafening roar of massed gunfire, and felt the bullets as they punched into his body.

* * *

One of the demon creatures inadvertently saved Gable's life. He glimpsed it as it ducked around a building and went to investigate, locating some fresh tracks. As he ran back into the camp's main street to report to LT, gunfire erupted. He took in the massacre for a heartbeat before springing into action, spraying the area with his SCAR and hitting a couple of the Greytech men. Then he popped a smoke grenade and lobbed it toward the detail, cover so he could check if anyone had survived the slaughter. He abandoned that plan when the Greytech men unleashed a hailstorm of return fire.

In that instant, when he saw LT and Ball gunned down mercilessly, Sugar murdered on the ground where he lay defenseless, just barely alive, Gable's fate flipped a hard one-eighty. The implications were clear enough: the mission was officially doomed. Survival became his only priority, all other objectives rescinded.

Attempting to flee Base Camp before the imminent Greytech occupation, he hit up the armory, stocking up on MREs, water, and ammunition for the long wilderness trek back to civilization. He had no time to lose. Though he couldn't hear the Greytech men securing the camp, they were certainly doing just that, and their orders didn't call for taking prisoners. Gable got out of the armory fast and made for a trail he'd seen leading off into the woods.

Just short of the forest path, he spied the tunnel entrance about a hundred yards ahead across the ice. LT and Sugar had believed Max still lived. Gable remained skeptical. *But if he's alive, you need to warn him. You owe him that much and more.* He hesitated and then broke for the tunnel instead of the woods, knowing full well he would likely never see sunlight again.

He thought he'd seen the last of the vast, labyrinthine spacecraft.

292

Now, lost once again in the bowels of the ship, he realized just how little of it he'd seen in the first place.

And the fucking creatures were everywhere. Within a few minutes of boarding, one chased him into an elevator. The lift deposited him on what he took to be the ship's lowest deck. He hoped that his relocation had been a fortuitous occurrence since Dr. Rogers had talked of the substance in the cargo hold. Max might be alive down here somewhere. If not, perhaps he would at least locate a clue of his demise and then be free to bolt for the surface.

He avoided several that he'd glimpsed, but one tailed him now.

Gable waited around a corner where two passages met; the narrow hallways more like crawlspaces cut through miles of machinery and electronics. He couldn't stand fully upright beneath the hallway's ceiling. Stifling air pressed down upon him, hotter than an Alabama July. The entire sector so far had been a warren of dead ends, tight spaces, grating, ductwork, ladder wells, and bridges spanning deep chasms lined with blinking orange super computers. The constant whine and hum of machinery vibrated through the deck and walls. Gable wondered if the noise helped to conceal his presence.

Don't kid yourself, boy. Hearing comprised only one of the predator's senses. *He'll come. He's got your scent.*

As he waited Gable thought of Sugar and LT lying out there dead, their blood thawing the frozen earth.

Johnny Gable was raised to be a God-fearing man, instilled with the righteous beliefs of the Pentecostal Church. He still believed in a Creator—but he hadn't prayed since the first Gulf War. Why bother? The Holy Ghost never appeared on the battlefield, though demons aplenty ran amok. He killed them; he served with them; he brought them home, and they possessed him. Prayer had proven about as pointless as jerking off into a rubber.

Yet the prayers came, unbidden and unconsciously, the remnants of his righteous youth.

You're fucking losing it, Gable!

His brain responded with Romans 14:8: *If we live, we live for the Lord; and if we die, we die for the Lord. So, whether we live or die, we belong to the Lord.*

Sugar would have approved. *Now there was a righteous man. Never abandoned his faith, even after all the shit he witnessed. He was a stronger man than me in every way.*

John 15:14 flitted through his mind: *You are my friends if you do what I command.* He considered the passage fitting for LT. *A little rough but not inaccurate.* On a good day, LT had the bubbly personality of a snapping turtle hooked on a trotline. But he'd been damn good at his job, a fine executive officer. Gable had truly respected him. *Not a natural leader of men, but he never let that stop him.*

He thought of Max, the cement that held the team together for so many years. *You better be alive down here, you bastard. And I better sure as hell find you.* Max had hired him at the lowest point in his life, right after the Army kicked him out for drunk driving. His first offense—the brass wasn't forgiving of such transgressions in the modern military. They made an example of Master Sergeant Gable by giving him the boot a mere four months shy of earning his twenty-year pension. He could have accepted it had he been a shitbag habitual fuckup, but he was not.

No, you're just a loudmouth who had money coming to you. One fuckup was all they needed to hang your ass.

Gable told Max his DUI had been an isolated incident. Max took him at his word and hired him. Gable, Sugar, Irish, and LT had been on the team from its inception. He owed Max for believing in him, a debt that still demanded payment.

A shrewd grunt never relied on luck, but likewise never shunned fortune when it smiled upon him. Gable had nothing to lose, so he powered on his radio and gave it a shot. Maybe the reception had cleared. Perhaps Max was close enough to read him. "Chief, this is Gable. Do you copy? Over."

High-pitched sonic feedback sliced into his eardrums. He reached down to adjust the reception and heard, "Copy—" Static, then, "—there, Gable?"

"Affirmative," Gable replied. More static, he waited for Max to continue. When he didn't respond, Gable tried him again. Nothing.

Pitch blackness entered the limit of his vision. He had his SCAR ready and pointed down the hall. Even from this distance, he couldn't miss. The creature oozed forward, a thick substance forming a massive blob of black that plugged the hallway floor to ceiling. It amazed Johnny that they could move so quickly in a liquid state, though this one could have moved faster, as others had.

Cautious. Perhaps they'd tangled with this one before; it seemed to have a healthy respect for both firepower and the convoluted terrain, which offered plenty of hiding spots for its prey. *How right you are.* He'd rigged a Claymore mine on the ceiling about ten feet down the hallway. It pointed downward, one sensor rigged at floor level and one three feet up the wall. The mine was a decoy, an appetizer.

So was Gable.

"Let's go, fuck knuckle!" Gable shouted. He squeezed off a burst from his SCAR. The reports echoed sharply through the cramped maze of tunnels.

The creature doubled its speed.

Gable keyed his radio and tried Max again, not expecting anything.

"Where the fuck are you? Over," Max responded, the reception just clear enough to make out his words.

"Lowest deck. Greytech's fucked us over, killed LT and Sugar—"
Gable had to break off, the creature now only a few feet away.

"Stay there. We'll come for you!" Max stated frantically.

"Don't bother, Chief. You know me. I'll be ok."

Gable stood transfixed, watching the creature transform into the serpent-like thing that had run off with Ms. Harlow. It had detected his mine sensors and taken to the ceiling to avoid them, crawling upside down. The long tentacles sprouting from its armored, bullet-shaped head preceded it, reaching out for Gable. The new monstrosity moved at inhuman speed, scurrying along the ceiling on its many legs, effortlessly defying gravity. Once it passed the decoy mine, it doubled its speed again.

A tentacle whipped toward Gable, nearly striking his face as he ducked back around the corner. He had anticipated the creature would sense the decoy mine and sensors and take to the ceiling. He'd rigged two more Claymores on the floor just around the corner, pointing upward, the laser sensors positioned on the walls at ceiling level. Gable ducked past the sensors. He ran a few feet and turned with his rifle leveled just as the two mines exploded with a concussion that left his ears deaf and ringing.

The creature, cautious as it stalked him, had become as voracious as any other predator once it thought it had cornered its prey. The blast from the mines turned the first few feet of its body into a mess of pulpy black goo. Its legs lost traction on the ceiling, and it crashed to the floor, apparently lifeless.

None of that jibed with what Gable knew about these creatures. Were simultaneous direct hits from two mines really enough to kill one of them?

The black remains bubbled for a heartbeat like grease being

heated in a skillet. Then it reassembled itself, pieces of it beginning to re-take the serpent-like shape. Gable poured bullets into the thing, but they had no effect. The creature re-formed in under eight seconds, new and improved, its tentacles now tipped with thorn-like stingers that dripped black acid.

Gable put one last burst into the thing and ran for his life.

He had recon the area before setting up his trap and knew the hallway led to a bridge extended over a chasm of unknown depth. He sprinted faster than ever before down the cramped hall, leaning forward both for speed and to avoid the low ceiling. Something struck him in the back, nearly knocking him forward onto his face. Nothing pierced his skin; the body armor had done its job. Gable didn't dare look back at the creature as he ran from death, a futile and terrifying chase.

Sweat poured down his face and soaked his body as he ran onto the bridge, only a few steps separating him from the pursuing beast. The hallway on the far side loomed a few strides ahead. With his left hand, Gable grabbed a grenade off his plate carrier, pulled the pin and dropped it as he entered the hallway. The beast tailed him so closely that it ran over and past the grenade before it detonated. Shrapnel must have struck it in the rear; it screeched and halted for a second as it regenerated. Gable figured he gained maybe twenty feet on the thing now, perhaps enough to turn imminent death into yet another close call.

He turned hard right into another passage and kept sprinting, running faster than the overhead lights illuminated. A glowing orange computer terminal beckoned ahead. Gable reached it. He glanced right and left for a hallway. A dead end, he turned around.

The creature stood motionless, about ten feet away, waiting, as though savoring every morsel of his fear.

Gable thought of his two grown daughters, Rachel and Jenny. Jenny had married a Ranger only four months before. *Worst mistake she ever made.* But he was a good guy and would take care of her. *For as long as he stays alive, anyway.* Gable had been looking forward to grandchildren.

Nope. He opened fire on the beast. Ten shots emptied the magazine. No time to reload.

The creature lashed out with a tentacle and missed, the acid-dripping claw burying itself into a wall display. A single loud *pop* emanated from the device as it caught fire. Ozone reek filled Gable's nose.

He ducked another tentacle as he backpedaled, dropped his useless rifle, and then stood, fighting knife in hand.

Time to dance with the devil.

21

MAX TRIED TO REACH GABLE THREE MORE TIMES BUT RECEIVED only static and beeping for his efforts. So he did what any capable military commander would to reopen the lines of communication: he dumped the radio on his comm guy.

"Gable, this is Red. Do you copy? Over." Red hadn't any luck using his own radio, and Max's was proving equally uncooperative. "Let's try rolling freaks..." Red muttered as he switched to one of the team's two designated backup frequencies.

"Good idea," Max said, though they both knew it wasn't likely to work. Comm had been screwy from the get-go. Gable raising him by radio had been a freak occurrence, not likely to be repeated, but they had to try.

"Shit," Red muttered as he returned the radio to Max. "But at least Gable's alive."

"Five minutes ago, anyway."

Neither man repeated the most disturbing detail: LT and Sugar were dead. *Fucked over by Greytech.* That came as no surprise, but the reality and unjustness of it roiled in Max's gut. *I don't give a shit how powerful you are, you'll answer to me for killing my men.*

Gable was a wiseass bug eater who'd needle you all day long if he had the chance, but he was no liar. He might have been mistaken, however. Banner had his shitty fingers in this after all, and he'd cultivated a well-earned reputation as a treacherous, sadistic fuck over the years. Maybe he was up top; maybe his men had murdered Sugar and LT.

Either way, somebody up there had some explaining to do if Max ever got off this ship. Banner, Liz Grey, perhaps both of them—somebody would die for killing his men.

"Well, we're headed down there anyway, maybe we'll bump into him." Red flashed his most positive false smile.

"Pray to your gods that we do."

Red laughed. "I've prayed for the aid of several different gods."

Your pagan deities don't give a shit about us, no more than God does. "Let's move. We have an elevator to catch."

As they left the armory, Max took point with the fléchette rifle, Red took up rear guard with the lightning cannon. Between them with Ms. Quinones, Dr. Rogers instructed them to hang a right, and they marched briskly off, no longer burdened by Dr. Kumar. Max wasn't pleased about Kumar's death, but he could live with it, especially if his absence kept the rest of them alive. *He was warned. The stupid old goat had it coming.*

"Straight ahead." Dr. Rogers pointed to a large circular elevator.

"I see it," Max said, eager to get downstairs and try Gable again. He hoped, with their radios in closer proximity, they might be able to contact him.

Red grinned. "Hey, this elevator has me thinking of a great lawyer joke. Wanna hear it?"

Max narrowed his eyes and glared at him. "What the fuck is wrong with you? Am I sharing an elevator with the Joker?"

Red laughed. "I prefer the Jester, actually. I'm a good guy, remember?"

"It's easy to forget sometimes."

Red had always been batshit crazy, but Max could tell the ship and the mission were eating away at what little sanity he possessed. *Might be a good thing.* Red worked best when he was relaxed. His noise discipline was slipping, but did it even matter? Silence was golden when fighting against men. These creatures seemed attuned to their prey on every sensory wavelength at all times. *Hell, they can probably feel the vibrations of our footsteps.*

Their elevator ride ended at the center of a low-ceilinged round chamber about thirty feet in diameter. Max stepped out with the fléchette rifle at the ready. He and Red performed a quick sweep of the room. The ambient ceiling lights shed little illumination. Grating covered the room's entire floor space, the blackness beneath glowing orange or amber in spots corresponding with computer terminals on a lower level. A couple of terminals in the wall likewise glowed orange, but most of the machines had been destroyed. One had even been torn from the wall and hurled across the room.

Red shook his head as he observed the busted computer. "They aren't very tech savvy, these creatures."

Max scanned the room. "The fact that they're even taking an interest in electronics worries me." Judging the room free of creatures, he waved Dr. Rogers and Ms. Quinones from the elevator.

A Greytech directory sign pointed the way to the cargo hold through one of the room's five exits.

Red pointed down one of the other hallways. "I suggest you make it snappy. We need to move."

One hundred yards distant, the overhead lights brightened, set off by a creature in liquid form beginning to take a more sinister shape, picking up speed as it moved along. It had apparently noticed their presence.

"Let's go, people!" Max yelled. He took off for the hallway to the cargo hold, which ended in a T-intersection sixty feet later. No sign pointed the way.

"Right," Dr. Rogers advised.

Max peered around the corner and saw more lights illuminating over another wandering creature, the largest he'd seen so far. *Might be two of them. Hard to tell at this distance.*

Something clanked, and Max turned to see Dr. Rogers pulling up a hatch in the grated floor. "We can travel via the service passage," she whispered. "If we're quiet enough, we might be able to avoid detection."

If there aren't already creatures down there. "What do you say, Red?" Max asked.

Red kept his mouth shut and nodded.

Max started down a short ladder into the service passage. The hallway above felt cramped enough; the passage beneath resembled a rat warren with five-foot ceilings and machinery jutting out of the walls. It took Max a good minute to squeeze into the hatch and lower himself into the tunnel. He oriented his fléchette rifle forward and moved to make room for the others. The two women, unburdened by cumbersome gear, dropped in without issue.

"Aw, dammit," Red muttered as he climbed down. "I barely fit in here."

"Face backward; you will have to act as rear guard," Max

instructed. Red would have no room to turn around with the lightning cannon once he entered the service passage.

Ms. Quinones helped him down by taking his machine gun and ammo belts and then the cannon.

"Could you move any fucking slower?" The delay left Max peeved, his lower back already aching from having to stoop beneath the grating.

"I'm in," Red whispered as he finally dropped in and pulled the hatch closed behind them. "Creature just entered the hallway down by the elevator."

"Nobody talks but me and Dr. Rogers. Move out."

Max had read voraciously on subterranean combat. Tunnel rats fascinated him; due to his large stature, theirs was one of the few combat jobs he felt unqualified to perform. No sane commander would have sent him on such a mission, yet as master of his own destiny, he'd chosen to be a rat. *Maybe I should crawl; it would be a hell of a lot less painful.* His back muscles spasmed with fire, but he ignored the pain as he duck-walked beneath the grating, inching the party forward. His gear snagged constantly on conduits, machinery, and electronics. The high whining of whirling machinery grew louder as they moved along. *Generator, maybe.* It helped conceal their presence, whatever it was.

The service passage widened into a small square room; the walls lined with control switches and buttons. The floor dropped two feet. Max relished being able to stand upright, knowing the feeling wouldn't last long. The machine whine emanated from a large metal cylinder protruding halfway out of the wall. Speech was impossible without yelling in someone's ear, but Max had no verbal orders to convey. He ordered a stop by stopping. The women entered and sat on the floor. Red winced as he stepped down into the room, his back likewise killing him. This room provided an ideal spot to rest, something they might not run across again down here.

The room darkened as a creature walked over the grating above on six legs. Max couldn't make out any more of the thing than its elephantine skin and large padded paws, the toes tipped with black razor claws that protruded into the grating with each step. Max and Red watched it slowly stalk overhead.

The machine whine had concealed them. They would be golden so long as they stayed completely quiet and still.

As the beast passed over them without stopping, Ms. Quinones white-knuckled a string of wooden rosary beads, silently kissing the crucifix once the beast had gone. Max had to give Jesus grudging credit; he'd done a fine job keeping Ms. Q from panicking and giving them away.

After a couple minutes' rest, Max moved into the next tunnel, which, to his dismay, shrank in height after a few feet. He got down on his knees and started crawling. No creatures appeared overhead, and he took for granted that the others in his group would keep up, crawl like their lives depended on it. *That shouldn't be hard.* He stopped frequently to unsnag his gear from various protuberances in the tunnel. Still, they made fine headway for the first twenty yards or so.

The machine whine lessened with every foot they put behind them, but Max figured it to still loud enough to cover their movements for a while. *It can't last.* Half blind in the tenebrous tunnel, Max almost crawled headfirst into a closed door. An orange holographic screen covered in prompts appeared before his face. Too big to turn around, crawling out backward would be pointless since they'd yet to pass any exits from this tunnel. With considerable discomfort, he rolled onto his side and motioned Dr. Rogers forward to open the door.

She crawled forward and wedged herself into the tunnel next to him, their bodies filling the tight passage. She was all business, sparing Max only a glance before going to work on the door. Their faces were pressed together, ideal kissing distance, but the doctor had eyes only for the control panel. Being pressed against Red or Ms. Quinones in a tight space would only have annoyed him, but the curves and fine musculature of Dr. Rogers's body seemed to meld perfectly to his own. His arousal increased as she shifted her body against his in exertion as she worked to open the door.

A faint metallic *clank* followed by a dull *thud* emanated from above as a creature dropped from a duct onto the grating overhead. Alarmed, Dr. Rogers stared into Max's eyes and pressed herself closer to him. She didn't breathe, didn't move at all as they waited for the creature to either detect them or move along.

The beast seemed developed differently compared to others, taking on a simple insectoid form. Max could see only its legs, belly, and a silhouette of massive mandibles. It started walking off down the hallway they'd just traversed. As Max watched it depart, he glanced to Ms. Quinones—hyperventilating, rosary beads in hand. He would have raised a finger to his lips had it been possible, but his arms were pinned against Dr. Rogers. *Thank God we have that whining—*

The machinery stopped, suddenly and inexplicably. The hallway went dead silent but for the clicking of the beast's insect legs on the grating above.

Max watched Ms. Quinones's eyes bug wide as she peeked up at the beast a mere two feet away. *Keep it together!* he silently implored. *Just a few more seconds!*

Ms. Quinones whimpered faintly as the creature passed over her—then sobbed once as fear and claustrophobia cracked her composure. Not a loud sound, but she might as well have announced their presence with a fanfare of trumpets.

The beast stopped.

Fuck!

One insect leg morphed into a thin tentacle and shot downward through a small portal in the grate, perhaps a foot square. The tentacle cracked like a whip, wrapping itself several times around Quinones's left ankle. Dr. Rogers screamed in Max's ear, drowning out Quinones's banshee wails and Spanish entreaties to Jesus, begging his mercy one final time. The men cursed and tried to bring their weapons to bear in the tight quarters.

Ms. Quinones's ankle snapped as the creature yanked her leg upward through the grating. It kept pulling with tremendous strength, forcing her body through the small port, pulverizing her bones and ripping her skin off in a downpour of blood. The sound of her pelvis being crushed reminded Max of someone chewing on a mouthful of ice cubes.

Red rolled on his back and pointed the lightning cannon straight upward.

"No!" Dr. Rogers screamed. She had a point: the lightning bolt would strike the grating. It might electrify the creature, but it might fry them as well. Back at her work, she jabbed at the prompts on the hologram.

The door slid down into the floor and Dr. Rogers crawled forward into the next passageway.

They couldn't do anything for the old girl now, Max considered crawling away. Instead, he stuck the barrel of the fléchette rifle upward through the grating and cut loose on the terror above. It screeched as two explosive darts punched through its skin and detonated. Then it ran off down the hallway, taking most of Ms. Quinones with it, leaving behind only a few scraps of flesh, shards of bone, and her rumpled, bloody suit of skin.

Max shook his head. He'd kind of liked her, though not in the same manner that she'd liked him. For a lunch lady, she was a pretty tough old girl.

The report of Red's lightning cannon startled Max. Another creature wailed as it oozed out of a duct they'd passed about fifty feet back. Max looked on in satisfaction as blue electric current crackled and sparked over every inch of the creature. The energy dissipated, but the creature still moved.

"Fuck you!" Red cried and blasted it again.

The creature popped as if it had been cooked too long in a microwave. Red howled in triumph. Max kicked Red's leg to get his attention. They needed to keep moving. Max squeezed through the service tunnel door and crawled onward following Dr. Rogers.

Red's lightning cannon erupted three more times as they moved. Max had no idea if he was killing creatures or just holding them off. His only concern was finding another hatch to get them out of the tunnel before another creature skinned someone else.

Max rounded a corner and saw a ladder on the wall a few feet away. He stood, pushed open the overhead hatch, and laid it aside. As he squeezed out of the hatch, he realized he should try to radio Gable while the others exited the service tunnel. Nothing but the usual static and beeps. Max regretted his instruction to stay put from their previous conversation. *Get the fuck off this ship, Gable. Take to the woods. If you're still alive down here, you won't be for long.*

He emerged at one end of a hallway that might have stretched to infinity. No computers stuck out from the walls, but several closed doors lined either side of the hall.

"How far?" Max asked Dr. Rogers.

"Not much further. There is a security door halfway down the hallway, then a control room at the end with a bridge beyond. The cargo hold and reactor are on the other side. The going is rougher over there—narrower halls and six-foot ceilings."

"My back can't wait." Max stepped to the corner and peered down the hallway they'd just navigated. Visible creatures dimmed everything to blackness not far in the distance. "Let's go, Bergman."

Red passed the lightning cannon up to Dr. Rogers. "I'm moving, Chief. It ain't easy being this hardcore." He shoved his machine gun through the hatch.

"Move your ass, or you'll have more action than you can handle in the rear."

Red emerged from the hatch. "Hope I've got the firepower to do it." He showed Max the screen on the cannon. Four shots had reduced it to half power. Max's estimate of a one-minute power reserve had been ridiculously optimistic.

"Marvelous. Thank God you like to hump too many weapons." *Not that your machine gun is likely to kill one of them, but it's a fair deterrent.*

They started down the hallway. With the possible exception of his first engagement, Max had never walked into a combat situation feeling so tense, even though the hallway ahead appeared to be clear. They could walk upright for the moment, and Max marched off as though leading his old infantry company on a training hump. Speed was their ally for the moment, as they needed to traverse this hallway quickly. Shoot, move, communicate, as the old maxim went. Two out of three would have to suffice.

Red unleashed the cannon on a creature tailing them. They hadn't even traveled one hundred feet, and the hallway wouldn't end anytime soon. Max didn't bother asking Red if he'd killed the creature. Instead, he stepped it out, marched a little faster, and watched for any signs of beasts trying to blend into the hallway. He still had to worry about creatures down in the maintenance tunnel as well. No way could he possibly be wary of all the dangers that might lurk in every crevice around him.

Again, Red fired. The pungent scents of burnt flesh and ozone pervaded the hot, sticky air. Red howled and hurled another jolt of lightning. Max glanced over his shoulder and saw the bolt blast a creature that had taken an armored reptile-insect hybrid form. The hit knocked it several feet back down the hallway. It landed on its back, its serrated insect legs flailing at the air.

Another creature rounded the corner, its exact form indistinct from that distance.

Max had seen enough. Red had one shot left with the cannon, two at the most. Since no creatures were visible ahead, Max switched places with Dr. Rogers as they retreated from the pursuing beasts. He wouldn't be able to get a good shot around Red in the narrow hallway, but he had to be there to back up his man, just in case. They jogged backward, keeping the creatures in sight at all times. The beasts were closing in, but Red let them come for the moment. The cannon was more effective at close range, and he had to make his last couple of shots count.

"We clear up there?" Max called to Dr. Rogers.

"Yes. I see the end of the hallway!"

Red shouted, "'Bout fucking time!"

They kept retreating. The lead creature, an aberration with five scuttling legs ending in spade-like claws, had closed to within fifty feet. *Wait for it, Red!*

They had nearly reached the security door, where Dr. Rogers stood poised to close the portal off behind them. Max glimpsed another of the small ports in the grating after he'd passed it. Red came abreast of it and paused to take a shot with his cannon at the lead creature, now within forty feet.

Max sensed the lurking creature an instant too late. A tentacle shot out of the portal and wrapped around Red's ankles, yanking him off his feet. It pulled him knee-deep into the hole, skinning the flesh from his calves. His exposed bones scraped steel as the beast attempted to pull his bulk through the tiny aperture. Red's echoing bellow of pain might have been heard back in Base Camp.

Max shoved the barrel of the fléchette rifle down through the grating and fired, pumping the heavy explosive darts into the beast below. The sounds were nearly enough to drive him insane: Red screaming in agony; the creature wailing beneath the onslaught of darts; the rip of cartilage and muscle being torn apart; the motorized whirl of the fléchette gun's cylinder as it fired at a thousand rounds a minute.

The creatures were damn near immune to bullets, but the exploding fléchettes seemed to disrupt their regenerative properties. The thing beneath the floor started to smoke as the darts sank deep into its flesh; then it imploded, deflating into an inert puddle of the substance.

Red lay writhing on the floor, vermillion blood coursing from the stumps of two legs severed at the knee. Max opened fire on the lead beast in the hallway, a mere twenty feet separating them. As the darts pierced its body, it screeched and backed away at top speed.

Max pulled Red through the security doorway, which Dr. Rogers closed behind them. He got to work on Red while Dr. Rogers moved on to open the door at the hallway's end. After Max pulled Red's tourniquet off his vest, he grabbed another one from his own calf cargo pocket. The beasts had retired far down the hallway for the moment to heal their wounds. *They won't be gone for long.* He ripped open the cravat package with his teeth and started tying off Red's left leg.

"I'll get you out of this," Max vowed. He hadn't been able to save Irish, but he would get Red out of this hallway somehow.

Red's bleeding subsided from a garden hose spray to a steady trickle, and then degenerated to a mere ooze as Max cinched the tourniquet tight above one bleeding stump.

"Stop it, Chief," Red said raising his hand.

"Nah, you're coming with me."

Red shook his head in frustration. "Don't play hero on my account."

Max dismissed his concern and started tying the second tourniquet.

A doorway about twenty feet down the passage opened; out stepped a thick-legged muscular beast in semi-humanoid form, with absurdly long arms that ended in hooks the size of sickle blades. A pit viper's pointed head surmounted its three-foot neck, topped with a thorn-like crest that could easily impale a man. It ran at the security door and jabbed its hooks into the control panel.

Max looked at the aberration through the viewing port in the security door.

Can they open doors now? Have they evolved that much? Max wasn't going to stick around to find out.

He grabbed Red by the drag handle on his plate carrier and started dragging him down the hallway.

The security door slid open a few seconds later. Max's brain barely had time to process the dismaying development before the creature crouched on its brawny back legs and sprang forward.

Red blasted it in midair just before it pounced on them, sending it tumbling back down the hallway in a whirling tempest of flailing arms and legs crackling with blue electricity, its scream an assault on the ears.

"Shit," Red whispered. "Dead." He meant the lightning cannon, not the beast, which calmed its sizzling body and started to recover. Red dropped the dead cannon. "Give me the MG!"

Max paused long enough to put Red's beloved machine gun back in his hands.

The beast stood again and advanced, the two other creatures right behind it. Max leaned back and pulled, drove with his legs, used all his strength to get Red's bulk moving again.

"Come on, you motherfuckers!" Red shouted as he sprayed lead down the hallway.

Snakehead absorbed the bullets and continued to march, though the shots slowed him considerably. Max raised the fléchette rifle with his right hand and fired, grateful for the weapon's lack of recoil, which allowed him to drag Red simultaneously. Several darts struck the creature's snake head, blasting it to pieces. The thing dropped to the grating. *Not dead but seriously fucked up.*

Another creature in centipede form—perhaps the same one that killed Harlow—slithered right over the other obliterated creature to continue the chase.

"You want some, Mr. Caterpillar?" Red fired a burst at it. "Come and get it!" He pulled the trigger and squeezed off more lead. He ran out of ammo a second later.

Max shot it up with a short burst from the fléchette rifle. The creature turned and began to flee. The rifle's BB gun kick then abruptly stopped. The cylinder continued spinning, its chambers empty. Knowing he didn't have time to reload the fléchette rifle, Max traded it for his HK416.

The worm creature turned hard about and took up the chase

again. Max looked over his shoulder and saw Dr. Rogers about a hundred feet away. She'd reached the end of the hallway. Max emptied his rifle into the creature as he dragged Red the last thirty yards. The bulk of the rounds struck home; several more sparked as they ricocheted off the creature's armored head. The rifle's bolt stopped at the loading position. Empty. With no more ammunition, he dropped the rifle and drew his pistol, firing vainly at the approaching horror.

Max grunted as he tried to drag Red even faster, every muscle in his body burning under the strain. The beast sensed their defenselessness and charged forward on its dozen-odd legs, closing the gap. In a few moments they would be in tentacle range.

We're not gonna make it.

"Chief, I got this!" Red held up his hands, an alien mine in each massive palm. He held down the timers with his thumbs, not bothering to turn the dial to set a time. They would detonate when he released pressure. "See you in Valhalla."

Max met his eyes and nodded. Nothing further needed to be said. He wanted to stay there and die fighting with Red—and would have if the fate of the human race weren't riding on his shoulders.

He let go of the drag handle and fled, his panicked instinct to survive suppressing his self-loathing at abandoning Red.

"Hurry!" Dr. Rogers shouted from just inside a doorway.

From down the hallway came unintelligible war chants uttered in the ancient tongue of the Norse. Red's only academic pursuit had been researching every aspect of Viking culture, right down to learning Old Norse from a noted Norwegian scholar. The berserker would die fighting to his last breath, just as his ancient forebears had. Max didn't need to understand Red's shouting to recognize his last words as curses upon the creatures.

The mines detonated simultaneously, the blast so forceful in the cramped hallway that it might have been measured in megatons. Max dove toward the open door, arms outstretched like a runner trying to steal second base. The shockwave ahead of the flames propelled his flying body forward at tremendous speed. He felt the heat on his legs as he sailed through the doorway, which slammed shut an instant later, shielding him and Dr. Rogers before the flames roasted them alive.

22

MAX LAY SUPINE ON THE FLOOR, STARING BLANKLY AT THE CEILing. A wave of exhaustion crushed him. He felt immobile as though an elephant crushed his chest. *Fuck, this is futile.*

Dr. Rogers appeared, squatting over his inert form. "Max!" She shook him.

"Yeah."

"We need to move. We've nearly reached the reactor."

Max continued staring upward as he considered her words. *Nearly* didn't cut it. The ship was teeming with creatures; he doubted they would reach the reactor. He pounded the floor once with a fist. "No. This isn't gonna work." He hated to say it. He hated losing, but they'd been bested. Eight men had fast-roped off a helicopter two days previous. Seven were now dead. Max knew he would soon join them.

"It will. I'm certain I can initiate the reactor's

self-destruct sequence."

Max sat up. "Be pretty hard to do if you never reach the reactor. And with no additional firepower to support us I doubt we can make it."

"We need to—"

"No, Gable was right. We need to do is get off this ship and contact some proper authorities. I still have connections in the military, a two-star who works at the Pentagon. If I can get out of here and contact him, he might be able to put boots on the ground, get Greytech off the site and seal up this vessel for good. Maybe even destroy it with tactical nukes. It's our best alternative."

"Greytech isn't about to let you call in any sort of assistance. Even if you did, do you honestly think the government would destroy it? They would try to contain it and study it."

"I don't plan on asking them. I'll hide in the camp, steal a radio, and notify the military to come in and mop this up. We have to-"

She shook her head. "There isn't time for that! These creatures represent an existential threat to humanity, to all life on the planet. If we don't stop them now, it will be too late."

"Maybe it already is. You've seen these things butcher my men, and we'll be next if we make for the reactor."

"We stand the same chance of dying if we try to escape the ship."

Max conceded her point with a reluctant nod. "True enough."

"If you want to leave and try contacting the military, I understand. This is my responsibility, and I'll handle it alone. I *will* destroy this ship and all the creatures onboard."

"And sacrifice yourself as well?"

"Absolutely."

Max nodded. *She's determined to see this through to the end. Why aren't you?* He thought back to his training at OCS Quantico, a long time ago. The Marine Corps' legendary sergeant Dan Daly crying, "Come on, you sons of bitches! Do you want to live forever?" before he led the charge at Belleau Wood. *That's how you've always operated. And living forever sounds overrated, especially when you have nothing left to live for.* Seven good men had died on this mission; he could at least attempt to make their sacrifice count for something.

"Very well. I'm coming with you. Two is one, and one is none. I need to make sure you execute your plan."

She smiled at him. "You don't trust anyone, do you?"

"I trusted my men. They're dead now."

"You can trust me."

"Perhaps I can, but I'm still coming with you. Trust but verify."

* * *

"Just ahead," Dr. Rogers whispered. "Almost there."

They stood at ceiling level on one end of a cavernous room several stories in height. A narrow catwalk before them hugged a sheer wall of computers over one hundred feet above a floor crowded with glowing, whining machinery. Like the bridges they'd traversed, the catwalk had no railing. The reactor control room lay behind a closed door at the other end of the catwalk, below a yellow warning sign emblazoned with a black radioactive symbol. A corpse in a shredded, bloody HAZMAT suit lay sprawled on the walkway outside the door.

Max paused for a single breath to center his mind on the job at hand. He peered down into the glowing machinery, scanning for any creatures. None stood out ahead, but at least one was following them. "Let's do this."

They'd only traveled a few hundred feet since escaping the long hallway where Red had dispatched himself to Valhalla. In that time

Max had emptied most of the second drum of darts he'd brought from the armory, driving off three creatures to clear their way. The fléchette rifle felt feather light now. When it ran empty, he would be left with only his Glock and the grenade launcher strapped across his back.

Dr. Rogers strode onto the catwalk with Max right behind her. The control room door beckoned about sixty yards distant. He kept alert for any signs of creatures but made no attempt to slow Dr. Rogers. *The sooner this is done, the better.* Miraculously, they reached the far door without incident.

"WARNING: FUSION REACTOR CONTROL ROOM. ACCESS STRICTLY FORBIDDEN!" read the sign posted over the door. The Greytech guard had been sliced and pierced by claws at least two dozen times, but the wounds all appeared superficial. Max figured he'd bled to death, probably while his assassin watched in sadistic glee. The dead man's rifle was missing, but Max took his 9mm pistol, still holstered and fully loaded, along with two mags of ammo.

Dr. Rogers stepped over the corpse and stood before the closed door. She wasted no time accessing the holographic computer that controlled access. She could only open some of the doors throughout the ship, and Max had no idea if she might open this one. A portal guarding such a critical facility would likely feature an abundance of additional security features. Max took up a defensive position about twenty feet down the catwalk from her, so he would have a clean shot with his rifle if a beast appeared near her. He watched for creatures as she worked. Nothing appeared at the catwalk's far end, but Max knew they hadn't given up the chase.

A viscous stream that reminded Max of filthy motor oil poured down from a small ceiling duct onto the catwalk. He waited for it to ooze into a full puddle before opening fire, cutting loose as it rapidly took shape. The darts hammered it hard, made the thing squirm and bubble as they exploded. Never fully forming, it capitulated, flowing straight down through the grated floor. A temporary victory at best; it would climb back up to re-engage at some point.

Dr. Rogers screamed.

Max spun with the rifle leveled and saw the large humanoid creature that had taken Thatcher. It let out a deep growl as it flipped up onto the catwalk between Max and the doctor. The creature paused and seemed to consider her, then reached out and grabbed her with its prehensile arm. It clutched her throat and lifted her off the deck, her hands grasping at the creature's unearthly strong hands.

"No!" Max yelled as he sighted in on the beast. He knew he might kill Dr. Rogers while trying to slay it, but she would die for certain if he held his fire. He blasted at the alien's legs with the fléchette rifle, the darts tearing into the creature, black gore flying.

Then the tapping recoil stopped; the empty cylinder spun impotently. Max dropped the rifle and reached back for his grenade launcher as he began sprinting toward the creature. He waited until he was sure he wouldn't hit Dr. Rogers with the spread, then pumped three grapeshot rounds into the creature's lower back thorax. Smoking substance oozed from its shredded body and the pellets sent chunks of the creature spinning off into the bright, cavernous abyss.

The beast roared, dropped Dr. Rogers and turned towards Max, who threw down the now-useless weapon. He leaped forward to meet the creature and caught it off guard—it hadn't expected him to attack hand-to-hand. He launched his body and slammed into the thing. It felt like he'd slammed into a brick wall, pain shooting through his shoulder as he made the tackle. His old college coach would have been proud. The beast creature's center of gravity offset, it fell hard to the catwalk with Max on top of it.

Then the creature flipped over, and they rolled off the catwalk in a death embrace.

Max stuck out his left hand and grasped for the edge of the catwalk. His gloved fingers found temporary purchase on the lip, his grip slipping fast.

The creature dangled next to him, one arm hooked on the edge of the walkway. It slashed at him with the other arm and narrowly missed. Max pulled the extra pistol from his belt and fired several rounds into the joint on the arm from which the creature dangled. The beast screeched and dropped, flailing its arms in an attempt to take Max down with it.

The pain hit him like a sword slash across his right side. A gash opened just below his ribs, several inches long and bleeding profusely from where the creature's hooked claws had sliced through his ceramic body armor to embed itself in his side. He screamed in agony as he dropped the pistol, grasping desperately for the catwalk ledge.

The creature's lower body fell away, its way of sloughing off excess weight, but its torso and arms remained. The beast dug its embedded claws deeper into Max as it began to morph into something else. His fingers failed, slipping, unable to keep the weight of his body and the creature suspended any longer.

Two strong hands grasped his left wrist and began to pull. Dr. Rogers stared down at him, saying nothing as she leaned back, her feet braced against the lip of the catwalk, putting her entire weight into the effort. Her terrific strength astounded Max. The creature attempted to climb up his body, and his muscles twitched under the strain of being stretched between the beast and Dr. Rogers. He reached down with his right hand and grabbed the release handle on the plate carrier.

"Drop dead motherfucker!"

With one swift yank, the creature howled and fell away into the abyss below.

Dr. Rogers kept pulling, her assistance enabling Max to swing his left boot onto the catwalk. His wound throbbed and burned as though packed with salt, but he overcame the agony for another few seconds, just long enough to climb to safety.

"Max!" Dr. Rogers gasped.

He peered down at his gaping wound. "Leave me. Finish the job." His consciousness faded.

The door to the reactor control room stood open. She bent down, grabbed him by his ankles and dragged him inside. The door slammed shut behind them.

An incongruous mix of light and fog permeated Max's mind. His mind's eye cleared and focused on a sunny sky above an endless field of cropped green grass. A towheaded boy, reed thin, stood before him holding a football. "Dad!" David called in enthusiasm and happiness at seeing his father again after one of his lengthy trips away from home.

"Go deep, Davey! Let's see what you got!" Max urged.

David pitched him the football and ran off laughing toward an imaginary end zone. Max watched him run on skinny legs. Awkward but fast, once he grows a bit he'll make a hell of a receiver.

Man and boy played in unrehearsed synchronicity, Max releasing the ball when he knew the time was right. The ball spiraled through the air with nary a wobble as it rose, arced, then started to drop. David gazed over his shoulder and stretched out his arms, fingertips grasping the football an instant before it would have dropped incomplete. Max watched his hands but also his eyes, bright blue even at this distance. My boy. Max remembered the day David was born, how he couldn't help thinking he was the luckiest man in the world.

The sun brightened, forcing Max to shield his eyes. "David?" he shouted, daring a peek through his fingers at the nearly blinding light, which seemed oddly divine. Whether a light of blessing or punishment, he couldn't say.

The divine light disappeared, replaced by a subdued glow he recognized as the ambient lighting in the space vessel. Max felt a warm, soothing sensation in his side. He gasped and came wide awake. He peered into Dr. Rogers's brown eyes as she knelt over him. She had her hands pressed to the wound on his side...

Or, more accurately, what had been a wound. It was completely healed, no scarring, as though nothing had happened.

"I was dead," he breathed. "I should be dead."

"No," she told him. "I couldn't allow that. You're alive."

He stared up into her face as she stood and reached out to him. He took her hand, feeling her strong grip as she helped him back to his feet. His outfit hung on him in tatters, but somehow, he was healed.

Dr. Rogers met his gaze. "Was that David?"

"Who...? What the hell are you? How do you know about David?"

"I am the only remaining member of this exploration ship's crew."

"The crew?" Max tried to still his spinning brain. The revelation momentarily stupefied him, but the pieces locked neatly together in his mind: her astounding strength, her knowledge of the ship and its alien weapons, her ability to sense his thoughts. He realized he had perhaps known it all along in the back of his mind, but her saying it made the reality of it finally set in.

He reflexively drew his pistol and pointed it at her, his mind still trying to digest the revelation. "Tell me. You need to tell me everything, starting with who you really are."

She pushed the weapon aside and stepped closer to him, grasping his forearms. "Max, there isn't time."

"What happened to the real Dr. Rogers?"

"The creatures got to her. To stop them, I had to infiltrate the Greytech research party, and when I found her dying, I had my chance. Granted, I don't have the shape-shifting abilities of these creatures, but I am able to project a human form in people's minds. They saw what they wanted to see, and I read most of her thoughts before she passed."

When she released him, he clung on to her. "What are you?"

She smiled. "I think you know by now. And you know that some things are universal, no matter how different we are." She paused as she gauged his reaction. "How do you feel?"

"Good as new." Not completely the truth, he felt weak and slightly dizzy. But he could feel his condition improving with each passing second, pretty remarkable for a man who'd just been sliced open by an alien.

"Liar," she said with a laugh. "Let's finish this."

She pulled away and walked across the bridge toward the reactor core airlock, the bright light from its window creating a halo around her. The reactor core control room was a broom closet when juxtaposed to the grandeur of the command center. There were workspaces for only ten people, eight of which were located in a pit accessible via a spiral staircase. The crew in the pit would see nothing but their workstations. An extended bridge led to a small control tower with two more work stations, far above the other crew, before a smoked-glass observation panel with a door that looked into the reactor chamber.

The reactor consisted of a huge cylinder about sixty feet high and thirty feet in diameter that glowed white-hot. Eight slim, skeletal towers of gray metal surrounded the reactor, each with a glowing orange control station at its spire. Square cantilevered bridges of gray metal packed with conduits and piping connected each tower to the reactor. The facility was impressive enough though something of an anticlimax.

"So how are you going to destroy it?" Max asked.

She turned. "I will disable the reactor core's magnetic gravity field, which will cause the core to go thermal and initiate the ship's self-destruct mechanism."

"What will happen to you?"

She glanced back at the chamber. "I will cease to exist."

"No! Why don't you initiate the self-destruct and leave? You could come with me, and with your abilities, you could do a lot of good in this world."

"You know I can't, Max. I wish I could have saved the others. But there's one thing left I can do. This ends with me, and it ends right now." She turned and opened the airlock to the reactor core.

"I'm coming with you," Max stated solemnly.

Dr. Rogers didn't respond. She gazed into Max's eyes, reached up to touch his face, and kissed him.

Max felt her lips against his, and the world suddenly stopped. He felt as though he were awakening from a long night of uninterrupted sleep, a sensation he hadn't known in over twenty years. He then felt a strong shove against his chest, like an invisible hand, forcing him to take several steps back. Momentarily stunned, Max watched as she opened the airlock hatch that accessed the reactor core chamber.

He tried to reach for her, but his legs weren't quite there yet. Instead, he had to lean against the wall for support and lifted his other hand to block out the brilliant light pouring through the air-lock's windows. It glowed red through his flesh before darkness swallowed the corridor once more.

Max reached the inner airlock door, the thick, tinted window separating him from her. The fulgent light from the reactor core now cast a halo around all of her.

"Alexis, no!" he shouted, banging on the glass.

Her thoughts entered his head. "Forgive me, Max. It isn't your time. I hope our paths cross again in another life."

"Wait!" he called after her. Wanting more. Wanting to know more.

But she didn't look back.

She reached the base of the tower and turned her attention to the control panel. Her hands moved like a conductor's, holographic images quickly shifting left and right as she accessed the panel. The light in the room became brighter, more intense, even through the dark-tinted glass.

Max banged on the window and shouted her name again.

This time she turned and regarded him. The skin on her face had turned bright red as it began to fissure in the heat. But her brown eyes were still bewitching, and she could still smile at him.

Max closed his eyes for a moment, wiped them clean, and waited a moment before trying to peer into the brightness again. She'd moved out of sight by that time. *What? Where is she? Is the energy too much, even for her?*

A shadow moved in front of the door, blocking out the light. His vision went black; his eyes couldn't adjust fast enough. He blinked, rubbed his eyes, tried again to see. With great difficulty, he identified her face—her features shaded by the brilliant light from the reactor. She had her hands pressed against the door. Her flesh cracked, but her eyes were still brown, still penetrating. He could feel the reactor's heat even through the barrier. She smiled at him.

Her voice then filled his head, *Go home, Max.*

Home?

Again, she stepped back from the glass screen. *Go now. Leave this ship and live.*

Max finally nodded, causing her to smile one last time.

Suddenly a halo formed around her, bright blue and green, like the bottom of a gas flame. He saw her silhouette, watched as it transformed in the light, until he saw her true form revealed. It was beautiful. Just as the thought came to him, her body disappeared in a burst of bright white, the brightness too much to bear. A brightness that was too much to bear because for so long he was dead inside, and maybe, somehow, in spite of all the blood and the mistakes and the lies and the pain and the hell that he'd endured, maybe, just maybe he had found his way to atone for his deeds. There was a brightness that was too much to bear and like all other burdens that he had lived with, he bore it.

She was gone. Whatever held him to that door was gone too.

And just think, you're probably the only man on Earth to ever have his heart broken by an alien.

He heard a thumping at the entrance door and through its window saw three creatures awaiting him on the catwalk. One was jabbing the holographic control with an appendage that ended in a hand that looked almost human, examining it, attempting to gain access. *He might just get it, but I'm fucked either way. Unless...*

Another door led from the control room. He smiled and shook his head. *She wouldn't leave me in the lurch like that. I should have known.* The door opened when he approached, just as he knew it would.

Max knew he needed to follow her instructions. He had a mission to finish.

23

LUCKY PEOPLE DIED THE EASY WAY: HEART ATTACKS, CAR ACCI-
dents, shot in a holdup or on a battlefield. Edward Grey envied them
that. *No planning, shit just happens. And there's nothing to think
about until it happens.* And by then, of course, it was too late to stave
off death.

Edward had nothing to do *but* think about his imminent demise.
He looked at the three pills in the orange prescription bottle, the
potent barbiturates that would lull his body into permanent sleep,
and realized his time had finally come. He'd gone through a great
deal to obtain the drugs: paperwork, finding two friends to witness
his signature on the assisted suicide forms since family and hospice
staff were not allowed to serve as witnesses, and locating a doctor
to prescribe the lethal drugs. The hospice staff were not allowed to
interfere with his wishes but were likewise prohibited from helping him to carry out the deed. Edward would have gotten his scrip

from an outside doctor anyway; despite confidentiality laws, he didn't trust the doctors at the facility to keep his decision from his mother, who would most certainly interfere. Edward wouldn't allow that—he'd had enough of her entreaties to stay positive, as well as her whimsical promises that she would find a cure. *It's over. Today.*

And it's about fucking time.

Two days were nothing to the average person, but to a cancer patient, they could seem like decades. Even Edward was astounded at how his condition had worsened in only forty-eight hours. He suffered two more seizures and started pissing blood, in addition to the other various and arbitrary symptoms he'd accumulated over time.

"May I have the mirror, please?" he asked Debbie, who sat at his bedside.

She produced the handheld mirror which was the only mirror in the room and held it up in front of him.

Edward had demanded the mirrors in his suite be taken down so he didn't have to look upon himself. Now he wanted to take a good long look at what he was about to leave behind. *A monster, some horror-movie ghoul who just clawed his way out of a grave.*

As always, he first noticed the premature aging: the bags under his eyes, the faint age spots starting to speckle his bald head. He embodied the general and repressive weariness that the aged took on as they fought through the trials of everyday life, ever mindful of their ineluctable fate. The lesions and purple blotches on his face also had their say, tacking on another twenty years of unlived life. His sallow, bloodshot eyes belonged on a basset hound, not a nineteen-year-old man. He wasn't surprised to see blood on his tongue when he opened his mouth wide.

Fucking gross. Enough of this already.

Edward handed the mirror back to Debbie and said, "It's time.

I can't take this anymore."

She wept but nodded her understanding. "You should call your mother first."

"I already did."

"Try her again. She's your mother. Don't deny her one last talk with her boy."

Edward sighed. "Very well." He suddenly felt guilty even though he had done no wrong. He'd called his mother's cell earlier and received no answer, so he forwarded his call to Cynthia's phone. She'd promised to give Ms. Grey his message, and Cynthia's word was good as gold. His mother had yet to return his call, however.

Debbie dialed the number and handed him his cell phone, which rang six times before he heard his mother's voice again recite: "You have reached the voicemail of Elizabeth Grey, President of Greytech Industries. Please leave a message, and I will return your call as soon as possible. If you require immediate assistance, please press one to be connected with my personal assistant, Cynthia Hilliard." The recording stopped, giving Edward about three seconds to dial one or wait for the beep to leave a message.

He chose to end the call though it didn't bring him the satisfaction he'd hoped. In truth, he wanted to speak to his mother one last time, preferably as he was swallowing his lethal dose of drugs when it would be too late for her to interfere. He desired to inform her of his decision with no goddamned interruptions this time. And he definitely wanted to say goodbye.

You could call back and leave a message, tell her one last time that you love her. But he decided not to. She would never erase it; it would haunt her for the rest of her days.

That last thought crushed him, made him shiver. He loved his mom, and deep down, he appreciated all she'd ever done for him, even all the annoying shit she'd put him through. *It's just her way. She holds the whole world to her impossible standards; she can't help it.* And she would continue to do so, only he would no longer be subject to her whims and manipulations.

He twitched as some synapse in his brain misfired. Such episodes always preceded his seizures, and he didn't desire to suffer through another, especially when he didn't have to.

"It's time," he said.

Debbie nodded but made no move to help him. Washington State's assisted suicide laws for the terminally ill stated that he had to end his own life, that no one else could administer the lethal drugs or provide any assistance.

Edward was now truly on his own. And he was just fine with it.

So weak that he could barely press down and turn the safety cap on the prescription bottle, he managed it after a few seconds of trying. The meds looked innocuous enough, the sort of standard capsules that might deliver cold medicine or cure heartburn. He was ready to tip the pills into his hand but stopped.

"There's a playlist of songs on my iPod," he said. "It's just labeled 'favorites'. Can you turn it on, please?"

"Yes," Debbie muttered, the word nearly unintelligible through her sobs.

Edward listened to X Ambassadors belt out "Jungle", a song he'd listened to many times while pondering his fate. No one truly wanted to die—it went against every basic tenet of human nature. But he wasn't the first to commit suicide or to know that he would be dead in a few minutes. Only now he knew what it felt like. *Resignation. Things have happened to me, terrible things beyond even my mother's control.* He swallowed once, his throat aching with sadness. *I don't want to die.*

And yet he had no choice.

Moving faster than he had in weeks, Edward grabbed the open pill bottle and upended it into his mouth, chasing it with a glass of water. He felt no different.

That was about to change. Debbie lay down next to Edward and took him in her arms. "Jungle" ended; "Hands" by Barns Courtney took over. "This song is for you," Edward explained.

He didn't feel his breathing growing imperceptibly shallower and shallower. He held Debbie and wept along with her as he stared out the window into another dreary Seattle day.

"Thank you," Edward whispered to Debbie as he felt himself falling asleep for the last time. "I love you... Wish you all the best... I remembered you in my will... You're a very rich woman."

The day grew darker; light faded in and out, then burst into blossoms of color behind his eyelids as they closed for good.

He died as the Lumineers played the opening bars of "Ophelia".

24

THE CREATURE WAS BACK, AND HE'D BROUGHT COMPANY.

Max turned and squeezed off a couple of pistol shots, hoping that it would somehow slow the creature, then kept running as fast as the low ceiling and dim lighting allowed. The creature's six legs clicked on the floor as it ran, the sounds growing ever closer. As he struggled to stay ahead of the creatures, he glanced back anxiously every couple of seconds. When he looked, Max couldn't see the nightmare chasing him, just blackness and flailing shadows. His heart pounding in his chest like a sledgehammer as he sprinted on.

Got to stop them. They'll run me down.

The deck rumbled from an explosion in the reactor chamber. Max leaned into his stride, mindful once again that he wasn't only racing those creatures for the exit; he had to beat the ship's self-destruct as well. He needed to gain a tactical advantage against the pursuing creatures if he wanted to see the surface again.

I may die today, but not until I see the surface.

Max came to a corner, scanned the continuing hallway and saw no creatures ahead. He pulled one of the alien mines from a cargo pocket and depressed the magnetic sensor on the back, which fell free into his hand. He attached the sensor to the wall at the corner, pressed the arming button on the mine, and stuck it to the wall next to the sensor.

Then he ran. *Only fools stick around for the fireworks.* It was one of Gable's old catchphrases, rather appropriate under the circumstances.

The clicking of insect legs grew louder when the beast turned the corner. Max kept running. As he'd hoped, the beast was so bent on taking its revenge it tossed caution and common sense down the shitter, like any typical, intelligent creature. The mine detonated; the concussion knocked Max forward onto his face and singed the hair off the back of his head. A shriek erupted like the sound of steel raking against steel. Max wasn't sure if it was the creature screaming or the ship starting to fall apart. He didn't have time to care. But, as he got up to run, he couldn't help sparing a glance back. No sign of the ant creature or the one following it, just a lot of noisome smoke and black gore spatter.

A blown-off portion of ant-thing's mandible lay on the floor near Max's feet. The chitinous appendage swelled and then popped open. The black iridescent substance inside bubbled as it reformed. Tiny insect legs sprouted at an alarming rate. The transformation sounded like someone crinkling a newspaper. Max blasted it point-blank with his pistol, stopping the transformation and sending the dead spawn skittering across the floor.

Max took off and didn't look back until he reached a four-way intersection. Another creature now tailed him, and it appeared to move much quicker than the ant-centaur. Two more creatures lurched down one of the other hallways, traveling away from him.

Greytech had posted a directory sign. Max took a right down the hallway toward the E-deck elevator and the exit. Neither appeared anytime soon. Max sprinted as fast as he could beneath the six-foot ceiling, legs and lungs on fire, refusing to acknowledge that the creatures were finally wearing him out. He glanced back and saw the trailing creature enter the passage from the four-way intersection, barreling after him at greyhound speed. A cross of alligator and insect, it had six legs, a shining exoskeleton, and a large armored head with an elongated snout. A long tail tipped with a stinger whipped behind it as it ran.

The ship continued to vibrate and tremble beneath his feet, and a whirring turbine sound came from the aft of the ship, growing in intensity and pitch. The lights in the passage flickered, died for an instant, then turned on again. Two doors, one on either wall, suddenly popped open and remained that way. The hallway opened on a chasm of machinery about a hundred feet ahead; the area illuminated brighter than any other he'd seen on the ship. The bridge across was extended.

You'll never make it across at this rate.

He wanted to glance back at the creature but knew it would only slow him down. He unclipped a white phosphorus grenade from his belt, pulled the pin, and tossed it over his shoulder. The bridge still loomed a few feet ahead when the grenade detonated. Max wondered whether it had slowed the beast. A hot wind hit the back of his neck—not the grenade's concussion but rather the creature's breath as its jaws snapped together right behind him.

Shit. Max rummaged frantically through his bag of dirty tricks that he'd collected over the past twenty-plus years and came up empty. None of his experiences could save him now.

You're not dead yet. One last chance...

Sweat poured down his face and soaked his body. The extended bridge beckoned, but it would do him no good if he couldn't retract it. The orange holographic control panel sat to the right, the alien prompts a mishmash of orange scrambled eggs. Max extended the fingers on his right hand and reached for it, hoping that one of his digits would find the prompt that retracted the bridge. Something slammed into his helmet, knocking it from his head. It tumbled off into the chasm.

The bridge started to retract toward the far side, about thirty feet away.

Max jumped for the end of the bridge. Though his right hand was empty, the pistol in his left hand had to go. He tossed it out into nothingness and reached with both hands for the end of the bridge. Far beneath him two of the strange beehive-looking machines glowed white-hot, lighting the chasm to noonday brilliance. His fingers caught hold, then slipped. A brush of firmness instinctively curled the fingers, and they found one of the horizontal cylinders that locked the bridge into the wall when extended.

He twisted his body to glimpse the beast hung in midair, its six-legged form useless. It clumsily flailed at Max with its front legs before plummeting into the chasm. Max knew better than to breathe a sigh of relief. He had to vault into the hallway before the bridge retracted fully into the wall, consigning him off.

Five feet. Exhausted, the ache in his arm intensified as he white-knuckled the cylinders. He swung his legs forward for momentum, then backward as he let go of the cylinder and attempted to backflip into the hallway.

The sunlit underworld spun before his eyes. Too exhausted, he doubted he'd been able to generate the momentum necessary to flip up into the passageway. After dodging thousands of bullets over his long career, he would die the instant he hit the floor. If he were lucky. The creature down there would still be alive, and Max didn't want to be conscious when it tore into his flesh with that savage maw.

Mercs die. You survived longer than most.

The small amount of inertia he'd gained when he flipped dissipated. No question now, he wouldn't make the hallway.

White light blasted his face from far below as one of the beehive machines exploded with tremendous force. Max felt himself propelled forward as the shockwave hit him. Then the other glowing beehive exploded.

Max tumbled head over heels into the hallway. For a moment, he lost all sense of reality and couldn't tell if he was conscious or unconscious. He couldn't see, couldn't hear, felt as if he'd baked in the Middle Eastern sun for the past few hours. He lay there helpless and hoping that his senses would return. Such an ironic coincidence, surviving the trip across the chasm only to be killed by a beast while he stumbled around deaf and blind.

Come on! He blinked his eyes, slapped himself across the face. Nothing worked but time. After a minute, he regained fuzzy vision and a negligible sense of hearing. It was enough; it had to be.

He drew his Glock and proceeded down the hallway as another explosion rocked the ship.

Within three minutes he regained his full vision and most of his hearing. Two turns in that time put him into a new hallway with an eight-foot ceiling as he departed the engineering section of the ship. He came upon a four-way intersection in a small room, an upright directory kiosk at its center. The E-deck elevator and exit were down the left hallway. In that direction, the elevator beckoned from a T-intersection about thirty feet ahead, its crumpled doors opened about two feet wide.

A creature moved past the elevator yet didn't espy Max down the hallway. *The car is there. Just sneak in and go.* With so little left to lose, it was the best plan he could cobble together.

A conduit sparked over Max's head; he moved on just before it popped and started burning, filling the air with ozone and the scent of scorched plastic. The strongest explosion yet rumbled through the ship.

He sprinted to the intersection at the end of the hallway, the elevator straight ahead. The left hallway looked clear; to the right, one creature stood about twenty feet away.

It sensed him and turned around on five legs ending in elephantine feet. The alien monstrosity reminded Max of an oil-drenched sunflower, featuring eight muscular appendages tipped in black spade claws instead of petals, converging around a round mouth packed with hundreds of needle-sharp teeth. The beast came for him, not as fast as the six-legger that had chased him onto the bridge but likely fast enough to reach him before he could seal the elevator.

Max almost reached for an alien mine, then thought better of it. He unclipped his other white phosphorous grenade.

A pipe in the ceiling burst a few feet down the hallway, spewing scalding water. Steam obstructed Max's view of the oncoming creature. He considered bolting for the elevator; perhaps he could roll the grenade down the hallway through the steam and make it inside before the creature recovered enough to give chase.

No. Get it right this time. He pulled the pin on the grenade, held down the spoon and waited, backing up to avoid being trapped in the cloud of steam.

The creature emerged from the steam five feet in front of him, four spade claws raised high, poised to eviscerate him. Round mouth opened wide, it hissed in triumph. Max tossed the grenade inside its maw and tumbled toward safety. One of the spade claws grazed his thigh, drawing blood as he escaped, but the others thudded solidly into the floor.

Max rolled to his feet in front of the elevator door, the grenade exploded with a dull *pop*. One of the creature's arms was blown off, it screeched, belching fire and acrid fumes from its round maw as it began to spontaneously combust. It jumped straight up in the air, smashed into the ceiling, dropped back to the floor and took off running through the steam down the hallway, leaving a cloud of oily smoke and acrid fumes in its wake.

Max peered into the elevator, judged it clear, and squeezed inside. He hit the prompt he recognized as 'up'. *Almost there. Stay sharp and you might just get out of this.*

A creature had dented the elevator door, likely to get at LT and his men. He saw several bloody boot prints in size sixteen. *Sugar.*

Max shook his head. *Dead, all seven of them. You sure know how to fucking pick a mission, Ahlgren.* The fact that he couldn't possibly have known what awaited them in Alaska offered no consolation at all. *So many red flags, starting with Banner. It sounded too easy from the start, too good to be true.*

Then the most disconcerting thought hit him: *You jumped at the easy money, and your team paid the price.*

The elevator jerked to a halt. The lights faded dead and plunged the car into pitch-blackness. He pulled his flashlight just as the car started moving again, lights back on. *Fuck, just get me to the top.*

He got his wish several seconds later when the car arrived on E-deck, opening on a four-way intersection with a directory sign on the wall. He squeezed through the crumpled door and headed for the exit down the right hallway, which appeared to be clear of creatures.

BBs and brass shell casings on the floor told Max he'd nearly reached the exit. He strode toward the three-way intersection guarded by the tripod-mounted minigun and saw that the weapon had been unloaded and cleared—LT's doing. *No need to worry about that sensor down the exit hallway.* Max had disabled the other minigun on the tripod near the cleansing room.

Straight ahead the hallway went black, the light blotted out by the oozing creatures.

Max jogged into the three-way intersection and turned left, wondering if he had another sprint left in him. At least he saw no creatures ahead. Adrenaline flooded his bloodstream, pushing him on as fast as his legs would carry him. He knew it wouldn't be fast enough.

Max reached the minigun on its tripod, the big steel can of chain-linked ammo still sitting on the floor next to it. The creatures behind him emerged from the shadows and surged toward him. He had to slow them down if nothing else. No way he would be able to beat them out of the ship in his current condition.

Though the minigun had been rigged to fire electronically with a trip sensor, it also featured a manual trigger. Max acted fast, with practiced precision, loading the ammo belt and charging the weapon. The beasts came on, three or four of them, thirty feet away and gaining several feet every second. Eschewing the tripod, Max hefted the minigun, leveled it down the hallway and cut loose. The minigun burping its deadly tone of destruction. Even a full box of ammo wouldn't last long with the gun's high rate of fire, so every shot had to count.

The nearest creature leaped for him, and he opened up on the armored, lizard-like monstrosity with a spiked ball at the end of its tail. Max filled its extra-wide yap with bullets, shooting it down in midair, its body disintegrating under the withering fire. What remained flattened to the floor and attempted to continue the chase by staying low.

A spade-clawed creature ran over it as it recovered, wailing a screech of anticipated victory. Max lit it up, watched black chunks of flesh fly and splatter. He continued sweeping the hallway with bullets, left and right, the muzzle flash illuminating the area. Unable to regenerate at a pace equal to their destruction, the creatures reverted to liquid forms and oozed away down a duct, beaten for the moment.

Another creature in yet another fantastic form of deadly appendages rounded the corner at the three-way intersection. Max couldn't make out specifics on the beast and didn't care to. He emptied the minigun at the thing. The creature looking like a macabre dancer in the strobe-like muzzle flash. Most of the bullets that didn't score direct hits still struck home via ricochets off the walls and floor. He sheared a leg off the thing and sent it retreating around the corner just as he exhausted the box of ammo, the barrel spinning empty as the remaining brass tinkled to the deck.

One pistol and two exhausted legs were all Max had left. He drew his Glock and fled from the hallway into the cleansing room. He could only pray there were no creatures in the room, and God grudgingly cooperated.

Three suits of cold-weather gear were missing.

Max grabbed his suit as he ran for the exit. An explosion somewhere in the ship shook the deck violently enough to knock him off his feet. He got back up, ran into the access tunnel and kept running until he reached the surface, never looking back.

The sun had yet to break the horizon, but Max had to slow his pace as he neared the mouth so his eyes could adjust to the brighter light. He shielded his eyes with his off hand as he walked from the ice cave into the arctic predawn.

When his eyes had adjusted, he dropped his hand.

And found himself staring directly at Banner, who stood tall in pristine, new combat gear at the center of a group of eight men surrounding the tunnel entrance. Six troops, hired by the CIA no doubt, trained rifles on Max, the red dots from their laser sights swirling over his chest. Greytech Security Chief Michael Stewart stood next to Banner, impassive. Neither man had drawn his pistol.

"Ahlgren!" Banner shouted. "Get your ass over here, son!"

He stood about ten feet away. Max dropped his cold gear before walking up to Banner. He didn't bother raising his hands.

Banner's weathered, cowboy face creased like an old roadmap when he smiled at Max. "Well, Max, seems you've left us quite a mess to clean up."

"Seems appropriate. You are a part of it."

Banner laughed. "Ah, Max, you never will understand how the world really works." The earth shook for an instant. "What the hell was that?"

"Wouldn't you like to know," Max retorted.

Banner drew his pistol and pointed it at Max's face. "Get on your knees, asswipe."

Max obeyed.

"You know, I always liked you, Max. You were a damn good egg, very useful when you wanted to be."

"Then I wised up."

Banner laughed as though Max had told him a ribald joke. "Not soon enough, hoss."

One shot. They hadn't disarmed him—why bother when they could kill him the instant he reached for a weapon? *Just give me that chance.*

"You remember that last mission you did for me? The one in Georgia?"

"How the fuck could I forget?" The blonde Russian agent, the electrodes, the bolt cutters, the screams, Parrish being cut down as they made their extraction—Max couldn't escape it.

"Yeah, I underestimated you on that one, Max. I didn't think you'd kill her and then go rogue into Russia after they captured me."

"I didn't do it to save you, asshole. Those hostages were your men, but they were under my command. I don't abandon my troops, even company men like these." He jerked his head toward Banner's men.

"Heroic. Yet unnecessary. You fucked up when you killed her. She was my way out. I was going to hand deliver your men back to the Russians as proof of American involvement in the conflict. But you had to go and fuck everything up, you and that dipshit Vietcong you used to work with."

"The unarmed man you cut down an hour ago?" *He was half-Thai, you jackass.*

Banner ignored the question. "That Georgia mission cost you a lot, didn't it?"

"I lost a good man and my reputation with the Agency." *And a few hundred hours of sleep.* "Why are we discussing this now?"

Banner laughed, a false bonhomie that bored Max. "You never could see the big picture, Max. That wasn't all you lost. You seem to forget what was not awaiting you when you got home."

Max didn't have to be reminded of what hadn't awaited him. Though his disciplined mind shielded him from facing the agonizing truth headlong—rejecting the thought, shoving it from his conscience before it could break him down—the full circumstances of his loss fell into place, completing the picture. He'd had suspicions that it hadn't been an accident but never any solid proof to act on. Banner's revelation—his confession—sent Max into a quivering rage. His nostrils flared; red spots flickered before his eyes.

One shot!

Max was dead already, no question, but damned if he wouldn't take Banner to Hell with him. In that perfect moment, Banner's vigilance slipped, his gun no longer trained on Max's face. His jaw fell open as he yelled, eyes wide and white with fear. He gazed past Max; something else had caught his eye.

Max reached for his Glock with a gunfighter's blinding speed. He pulled the trigger.

A freight train blow impacted his right shoulder the instant the gun fired, the blow ruining his aim and knocking him to the snowy ground. His shot went wide past Banner's screaming face. Banner's men fired their rifles in a panic, all guns pointed in Max's general direction.

But Max knew damn well what they were shooting at. He ducked and rolled past Banner, a heartbeat before a spade claw would have taken his head off.

The CIA team forgot about him as the creatures poured forth from the tunnel and set upon them. Max had no intention of sticking around for the battle. Instead, he rolled to his feet and sprinted from the melee. He found himself behind Banner and his men now, on the Base Camp-side of the glacier.

Time to leave.

Like Lot's wife, he couldn't resist a glance back.

Four creatures made short work of the CIA team. In the pre-dawn light, Max could see the true alien horror the creatures represented, as they tore apart Banner's men. Their screams and wails filling the arctic air. The primitive camouflage they had used to blend into the ship's interior had evolved. Two of the beasts were snow white. A third appeared mottled white and gray. The fourth's colors continued to change and blurred like a mirage. When stationary, this fourth beast would be barely detectable.

One of the white creatures looked like the spade-clawed beast Max had fed a grenade. It vented its wrath on one of Banner's men, slicing through his neck as though it were a warm stick of butter. A geyser of blood spewed upward as he dropped. The mottled beast resembled the six-legged creature that had chased Max onto the bridge, though he doubted it was the same one. It lost its mottled colors in a heartbeat, turning completely white to match the glacier. One of Banner's men unloaded a magazine into it as it charged. It took him down in a bone-crushing tackle. Its mouth came up bloody, trailing guts, skin, and shredded tactical clothing, which it devoured in a single gulp. A white tentacle from another beast wrapped around a man's rifle and jerked it from his grasp; another tentacle whipped around his neck and snapped it like a toothpick.

The creatures would eat Banner's team for breakfast and have Max for seconds. Nevertheless, he stayed long enough to see a transparent creature charge full-speed into Banner and knock him dazed and bleeding onto the ice. Banner shook his dizzy head, raised his pistol and shot it several times in its sleek, armored pterodactyl head. The bullets ineffective against the massive creature. Banner dropped his now-useless weapon and crawled away in panic from the oncoming terror. He wailed like a eunuch as the creature's beak crunched down on his leg, severing it from his hip and sending it whirling off into the snow with one shake of its head.

"Max!" Banner yelled as the creature pulled him toward its open jaws.

Max had his weapon raised, finger poised on the trigger, ready to take his vengeance on Banner. Then he thought better of it. *Son of a bitch deserves no mercy.*

Banner clawed futilely at the ice, his screams filling the air.

Max fled toward Base Camp and the chopper pad, eager to be airborne before the creatures finished breakfast. Evil had conquered evil, and in some twisted fashion, justice had been served. Though Max wasn't foolish enough to believe the enemy of his enemy was his friend—*not in this case, anyway*—he felt some satisfaction at Banner's demise.

He still had to deal with Elizabeth Grey.

25

THE CREATURES THAT HAD SO CAGILY STALKED MAX AND HIS team, planning artful ambushes to pick them off one by one, lost all the restraint they had shown in hunting his men. And no wonder—Base Camp had erupted into panic, chaos, and, above all, fear, an ideal feeding ground. Bursts of automatic fire from Greytech and CIA personnel echoed through the camp, mixed with the screeches of marauding beasts and the terrified wails of men about to meet their maker.

Max ducked through the predawn shadows from building to building as he made for the chopper pad, dodging beasts and men alike. He felt the sting of the keening wind beneath the cloudless cobalt sky and cursed Banner one more time for making him drop his cold-weather gear. Exhaustion sapped his speed and strength. Trying to adjust from the ship's heat to intense cold only enervated him further. Even his wits were worn out. Two straight days of dodging demon spawn in a desperate attempt to survive and save humanity would take its toll on even the heartiest of men.

Face your fate. Your men did.

Down a street he saw a Greytech man assaulting a beast with a flamethrower, advancing as he drove the thing back beneath a fountain of fire until the creature, screeching and engulfed in flames, unexpectedly sprang thirty feet through the air and landed on him. They tumbled through the snow, a ball of fire rolling through a cloud of steam. Max didn't stick around to see the *coup de grâce*, but he heard the flamethrower's tanks explode, accompanied by a triumphant pitch in the creature's screech. The thing would regenerate and be killing again in a matter of seconds.

Max kept up his steady progress, using the creatures' assault on Base Camp to cover his movements. He'd nearly cleared the streets of Base Camp, could see the chopper pad a couple hundred feet ahead.

A Greytech man rounded a corner and came face-to-face with him, his face ash gray with fear. Max shot him before he could raise his rifle, then sprinted for the chopper pad.

No one guarded the three helicopters on the pad: two Sea Stallions and an upgraded Bell Ranger 407, gloss black and emblazoned with Greytech's silver sun-and-doves sigil.

Her Highness has arrived.

None of the pilots were present, probably hiding from the creatures or looking to see what the commotion was in camp. Had they any sense they would have fled, but Max knew Liz Grey's minions operated on unquestioning loyalty as opposed to common sense. Her security personnel had likely been ordered to cleanse Base Camp of creatures. Both facts worked to Max's benefit, and he wasn't about to question that elusive bitch known as Lady Luck.

Arriving at the pad, Max dove beneath a cylindrical fuel tank between a Sea Stallion and the Ranger. His initial assessment proved accurate: no one tended the helicopters. The pad lay well clear of Base Camp buildings, though the flipped and sundered shipping containers his team had inspected upon their arrival sat nearby. Something exploded with a roar back in camp. Gunshots and human cries grew scarcer by the minute while beast screeches and explosions were on the rise. The earth trembled, another rumble from the self-destructing ship.

Nothing to it but to do it. Max pulled himself up through the Ranger's side door, pistol in hand. A partition, currently lowered, separated the cockpit from the passenger compartment, which featured four plush chairs with integral computer terminals. Max wasted no time donning the pilot's helmet and taking his seat. He scrutinized the controls and located key functions. Though larger than the birds he'd trained on, Max felt confident he could competently fly the custom Ranger back to civilization.

Pre-flight checklist his brain said, but there was no time to do things by the numbers. He started the engine, still warm from the flight in. The rotor kicked slowly to life and revolved ever faster, blades thumping over the engine's turbo whine.

Go! Take off already!

A loud *pop* from his left startled Max. The Doppler radar display on the dash console exploded in a shower of glass and sparks. He looked over and saw a spider web of cracks emanating from a bullet hole in the window.

"Shut it down now!" Elizabeth Grey screamed. She stood on the tarmac beneath the shattered window, clad in a skin-tight, black tactical jumpsuit, fully looking the part of an evil witch. Though she appeared unharmed, by the looks of her she had seen some of the action unfolding in Base Camp.

Max stared into the barrel of the Sig Sauer .380 pistol she pointed at him and slowly moved his hand to the Glock holstered on his right side.

"Don't you fucking even!" she shouted over the engine noise, smirking despite the malice in her voice. "Now shut it down!"

Max put up his hands where she could see them before dropping them to shut down the engine.

"Get out of the helicopter and keep your hands where I can see them. Don't think for an instant I can't waste you with one shot."

Max knew she meant it. He also had plenty of vital points exposed for her to shoot; she could put a bullet through his neck or even the pilot's helmet at this range. He opened the door and slowly climbed down from the cockpit.

She gave him a once over. "Put your gun on the ground. Now. Slowly."

Max placed the Glock on the tarmac. "You're making a huge mistake. You've seen what's out there, what's happened to your camp. It's over."

"No, *I* decide when—"

"No," Max said, shaking his head. "It's over and done. All those tremors you're feeling are from the ship. It's in self-destruct mode."

She laughed. "No worries, Mr. Ahlgren. My engineers are already working on it."

And you're outta your fucking gourd. "Banner's dead. And I guarantee none of your people can stop it from happening."

"But we will! This site will be secured and preserved, and we shall learn the secrets of these beasts and their healing powers." She sobbed, then smiled. "My son awaits a cure for his illness, and I will save him! I don't care what they say!"

Insane.

Max found no other word for her. He hadn't been aware she had a son who was terminally ill, but it explained this failed expedition. Well, that and the billions she thought she could make creating pharmaceuticals. For an instant Max felt sorry for her, knowing how painful it could be to watch one's child suffer.

Then he glared into those maniacal green eyes and wondered what he'd ever seen in them.

"You're finished, Ahlgren. Time for you to join your team." She leveled the pistol at his eye.

Max pondered his next move. If he didn't get the jump on her now, he was finished. But she stood hyperalert, always several feet from his grasp. The creatures had proven unlikely allies; perhaps one would provide a distraction. Then he would close the distance and kill her.

Max grinned at the thought. "Then I'll spend eternity with the finest group of men I know."

She smirked. "Oh, that's touching. You're a regular warrior-poet, aren't you? Now turn around."

"Not so easy when you have to pull the trigger, is it?"

"Do it!"

Max tensed his leg muscles, ready to pounce on her despite the distance between them. He doubted he'd survive the charge. *Doesn't matter anymore.* His work here was complete: the ship would explode, hopefully wiping out all the creatures in a heartbeat. He could die and join his men with a clean conscience knowing he had accomplished his final mission.

"No." Max stood firm, determined to make his death as hard on her as possible. "I won't do it. Shoot me, you fucking cunt. I've been ready for this for a long time."

She seemed taken aback for a second but gritted her teeth.

The pistol aimed at his face, Max could see her finger tense on the trigger, beginning to squeeze. He was ready for the shot. In some ways, he had been anticipating this shot for years, resigned to his fate.

The camp's chaos went oddly quiet for a moment. A single shot stood out in the calm.

Max never felt the bullet.

A look of astonishment crossed Elizabeth Grey's face. Her body jerked once, violently, a spray of blood erupting from her chest. Her knees buckled, and she collapsed onto her back. Her .380 clattered to the tarmac beneath the bird. Her eyes went blank as her vibrant life force steadily departed her body. Dark blood pooled on the cement beneath her corpse.

"What the hell?" He peered into the distance, behind where she'd stood.

A man with a rifle lay prone in the snow and frozen muck about fifty feet distant.

"LT!" Max ran to him, saw the trail of blood he'd left behind crawling toward the chopper pad to save him from Elizabeth Grey. They'd shot LT at least a half-dozen times, yet somehow, he still lived. "You always had good timing!" Max dropped to his knees next to him.

Crusty, drying blood ran from the corner of LT's mouth. His eyes were glassy; his complexion bone white from blood loss. Max didn't know if his XO would survive the flight out, but he was getting on the chopper.

When Max reached down to lift him up, LT gasped, "Nah, Max. Last mission."

Max pulled out his hydration bladder and poured the last sip into LT's mouth. He spat most of it up but gulped down what he could. Max didn't know what to say. LT wouldn't survive the trip—that much was apparent—but Max hated the idea of leaving him behind.

"Remember...Afghanistan?" LT asked.

"Yeah, I remember." Still in the military, on their second mission working together, LT's squad got pinned down in an area of sparse cover by a Taliban machine gunner. Max charged the machine gun nest single-handedly and took it out with a grenade tossed from close range. It seemed like an eternity ago.

"Always wanted"—he coughed up bile mixed with a few drops of his remaining blood—"to pay you back."

"You have, man. I owe you one." While the earth rumbled, at least a six on the Richter scale, Max grabbed LT's hand and squeezed.

LT responded with a weak grip. A fulgent beam of light struck their eyes as the sun crested over Boundary Peak 171. "Hell of a view," he commented as they stared into the sunrise.

Max felt the strength depart LT's grip as his soul slipped from his body. "It sure is." Max turned away from the dawn and closed LT's eyes for the last time. "Goodbye, my friend."

Again, the earth shook, followed immediately by another powerful tremor. Four Greytech men raced down Base Camp's main street, three creatures in pursuit. Max ran for the bird and fired her up. As the engine came back to life, he watched a white creature shoot out a tentacle and wrap up a man's legs. He went down like a roped calf at a rodeo. The creature fell upon him and started mangling his body. As Max watched, the creatures began to morph together into something much larger and more menacing. He didn't know how large or powerful this new terror would become, and he wasn't about to stick around and find out.

Max throttled up to full power and took off, pulling the stick hard to the right as he raised the collective. *Hope nobody's alive down there with a grenade launcher.* He then pushed the stick forward and nosed the helicopter down, the blades pulling it through the air as it rapidly picked up speed, just missing the tree line as he pulled clear of the landing pad and started gaining altitude.

26

THE CONTROLS ON THE BELL RANGER WERE ARRANGED A BIT DIF-
ferently than the training choppers Max had flown, but he got the
hang of them quickly enough. He kept the bird in a steady climb,
turning it for the airport, the location already a known point in
the GPS.

Max caught a flash in his peripheral vision: a gout of fire
erupting from the ship's entrance tunnel as the ship's self-destruct
sequence neared its climax. He pushed the stick forward and gained
altitude and distance as fast as the bird allowed.

The world turned blindingly brilliant before he cleared the valley's southern ridge. Max knew he would truly be blind had he been
looking backward.

Shockwave!

He dumped altitude on the chopper and hurtled downward into
one of the narrow gorges they'd crossed humping into Base Camp.

The shockwave boomed out of the valley and over the ridge which protected the helicopter from the worst of the blast. Even so, the noise was akin to a close-quarters cannon blast on unprotected ears and drowned out the engine's whine and the thumping of the rotors.

The bird hurtled down into the thickly wooded gorge at over a hundred and fifty miles per hour. Sweat ran down into his eyes as he strained at the flight stick, trying to bring the chopper level again before he started mowing treetops.

A half-frozen waterfall down in the gorge glistened under the morning sun. *Last beautiful sight you'll ever see.*

The Ranger's nose began to rise, but not quickly enough. Evergreen treetops approached; another hundred feet and Max would be a corpse, consumed in burning wreckage. He held the stick steady, afraid to overcompensate.

Max sheared off the top limbs of two exceptionally tall treetops, but it pulled out of the dive as he pulled violently on the collective. Its belly raked over several other trees as he fought to bring the chopper level. Then it started climbing again. The rotors hadn't hitched a bit slicing through the narrow trunks atop the trees, and the bird remained airworthy.

Max wondered if he could make the same claim. His trip back to the airport would be his answer though he didn't foresee any further problems.

Then he noticed the fuel gauge.

* * *

An air traffic controller radioed, "Inbound helicopter identify. Over."

"Greytech helicopter. Landing. Out," Max responded, not

interested in call signs and landing clearances at the moment. The low-fuel alarm blinked red, just as it had the previous ten minutes, and the engine sputtered for the first time. He dropped to fifty feet with the airport still a mile distant.

"Grey1, come in. Over," requested a deeper voice.

"Shut up," Max grumbled absently.

The engine sputtered again, costing him another ten feet of altitude as he approached. He thought of putting down into the lake that abutted the tarmac, but he didn't know how deep the water might be. In shallow water he would probably be fine, but if the water was deeper, the chopper would smack the surface and promptly flip belly-up due to the weight of the engine below the rotor.

"Say again. Over." The tower was not amused.

"You might wanna send a crash truck," Max suggested. "Again: out."

When the tower asked another question, Max turned off the radio to ride out the last half-mile.

The bird's engine stopped just as Max cleared the lake. He attempted to land via autorotation but ended up coming in too low and too late. The chopper smashed down hard on the concrete with a jolt that rattled his head, making him bite his tongue.

Could be worse.

He unbuckled from the pilot's seat and exited the aircraft, every bone and muscle in his body moving reluctantly in aching protest. Dizzy, he leaned against the helicopter and vomited up a few strands of caustic bile. He couldn't remember the last time he'd eaten.

Max groggily refocused on the airport.

A white pickup truck pulled up next to the chopper. From it alit a tall, gangly man wearing sports goggles. A small fire truck barreled down the runway toward him, red lights flashing.

The tall guy didn't bother asking if Max was okay. "Hey, you're not the pilot!" He pointed an accusatory finger at Max.

Max's head cleared. "The fuck I'm not," he growled into his face.

The guy backed off with his hands raised in placation. "Okay, whatever you say. Jesus, what the hell happened to you, anyway? You get mauled by a grizzly or something?"

Max didn't answer. He walked to the pickup truck and climbed inside.

"Hey, you can't do that!" The man recognized his imminent death in Max's gaze as they stared each other down. "Hey, whatever you want, jack. Is there anyone riding—?"

Max drove off with his pickup. The men in the fire truck stared at him as he gunned the engine, bound for the hangar where the private jet hopefully still awaited.

Max almost started to believe in karma when he saw his plane in the hangar, cabin door open and ladder extended. In a screech of brakes, he stopped the truck on the smooth concrete floor. The pilot appeared in the doorway as Max marched to the plane.

"Mr. Ahlgren?" the pilot asked, not entirely certain with whom he was speaking.

Max understood, knowing he looked his part as the sole survivor of a mini-apocalypse.

"This thing topped off?" Max asked as he climbed the stairs into the cabin.

"Yes, sir."

"Good. Get us out of here. Now."

"Anyone else coming?"

"There is nobody else."

The pilot gulped. "Uh, all right. I'll start pre-flight inspection immediately."

Max shook his head. "No time for that. Fire this thing up and get us airborne while you still can. Before the FAA grounds all flights out of this state."

"Why would they do that?"

Max pointed out the cabin door toward the northeastern horizon. The gray mushroom cloud had risen to the height of the stratosphere over the last hour. The debris was beginning to disburse in to the jet stream which could potentially carry radioactive particles all over the US and Canada. Innocent people would die from the radiation, though the vast majority of the population would live on, free from the threat of alien genocide.

As ever, collateral damage was unavoidable in war.

"Get the picture?" Max asked.

The pilot nodded dumbly. "Where to?"

"Henderson Executive Airport, Las Vegas. Don't request clearance for takeoff. Just go."

* * *

The luxurious jet featured many conveniences, among them a shower Max could barely squeeze into. He spent the first hour of the flight downing several bottles of water and part of a sandwich, bathing, and then dressing his many wounds, a couple of which would need stitches to heal properly. Anticipating infection, he would get himself looked over by a physician upon returning home. Considering what he'd gone through, the puissant foes he'd defeated, he figured his body had gotten off easy.

Seven other men hadn't been so lucky.

He alighted from the lavatory in civilian clothes. He put his tactical uniform, the tatters soiled with the blood of man and beast alike, in a plastic trash bag and exhorted the stewardess to have it incinerated when they landed.

Max wanted nothing more at that moment than to crash in one of the leather lounge chairs with a can of Diet Mountain Dew. Every quarter of his body demanded rest. His aches and pains would have their due soon enough. First, he had to look into something.

His leather duffel bag was stored in a compartment at the front of the cabin, along with the rest of the team's luggage. The sight of their belongings hit him like a boot to the gut, a reminder of his men and the devastating news he would have to deliver personally to their loved ones. Max placed his bag on the floor, then reached blindly inside the compartment for another, coming up with Sugar's old green sea bag. He opened the top and saw a gallon-size plastic zipper bag containing the personal effects Sugar had stored when cleansing for the mission—pictures of his wife and family, a battered leather wallet, and a gold Rolex watch that had been one of his most prized possessions.

Gulping down the ache of sorrow in his throat, Max sorted through the rest of their belongings, not to snoop but rather to remember. They had all been reborn as fighting men during their military training decades before, their individual personalities subdued and then flattened into non-entities as they learned to work as one with their peers. Their training never ceased; it simply became more advanced, tailored to a specific job. As the years passed, each man had cultivated a new individuality able to coexist with his military mindset. The personal items Max sifted through represented not only the men he'd known, but in some cases the men they had been before taking up the warrior's life: LT's Citadel ring, class of 1999; a worn 1978 silver dollar in Diaz's belongings that Max never knew he carried; a thin tablet Red had picked up straight from Japan that he had been trying to hack and modify, the characters were Kanji; Gable's first parachute badge, pinned inside his wallet for luck; a picture of two pretty, teen-aged girls in clothes from the 80s, found in Coach's belongings; the bone-handled Böker lock-blade Irish kept clipped to his belt.

Just tokens now, artifacts. But at least their families will have something.

Max could look no more. He zipped and closed his team's luggage and returned it all to the locker. Bringing his own bag back to his seat, he settled in with the finest-tasting Diet Mountain Dew he'd ever had the pleasure of drinking.

His body begged for sleep the moment he sat down, but one final item of business remained. Max powered on his laptop and logged in. His home screen was nothing special, just a stock photo of a tropical waterfall. He'd stopped using pictures of his wife and son a while back, and now he was glad he had. He didn't think he could handle another shot of loss and regret.

Max clicked into the documents and opened a password-protected file folder titled "ALASKA". Several files within detailed all aspects of the Greytech expedition that Elizabeth Grey had deemed relevant. He clicked on a PDF document labeled "ON-SITE PERSONNEL", a simple listing of names and occupations with accompanying identification photos, and scrolled down alphabetically.

Max groaned when he reached "KUMAR, DEAN Ph.D." with his cantankerous, Abe Lincoln countenance. He was about to scroll past his profile completely yet forced himself to keep reading. "NEXT OF KIN: None." *And no students or faculty are likely to miss him, I'll wager.*

Max scrolled through more profiles until he reached "ROGERS, ALEXIS Ph.D.".

The real Dr. Rogers resembled the alien Dr. Rogers, but Max

could tell them apart in an instant. The real doctor, relatively attractive, showed early signs of aging poorly. The alien Dr. Rogers's facial features were better defined, more vibrant. The real Rogers had a desk-commando's soft body that spoke of crash diets and birdlike eating habits to keep her weight in check. Though two different people, he could see how even her close colleagues would have accepted the alien as legitimate. As the Alexis he'd known had pointed out, people saw what they wanted to see, what they expected. She might have received a couple of odd stares from her colleagues, but no one had suspected Dr. Rogers had been replaced by an alien simulacrum. She had performed the perfect infiltration, and Max admired her for it.

Took her few thousand years, but she accomplished her mission.

And so had Max, who closed the laptop and put it aside. They would not be flying to Vegas just yet, he decided. He keyed the cockpit. When the pilot answered, Max announced, "Change of plans. Take us to Minneapolis."

"Yes, sir," the pilot responded. "We'll lay in the course now."

Max finally allowed himself to drift off to sleep. He didn't remember the dreams that followed, but none were nightmares.

27

WINTER HAD DESCENDED ON MINNEAPOLIS IN TYPICAL AND timely fashion. The leaden-gray sky spat the occasional snow flurry, and weather reports predicted a coming storm would dump six inches overnight. Enough snow to paralyze a city like New York, it wouldn't slow Minneapolis in the least.

Max strode the weekday streets amongst throngs of professionals departing work for the day. Traffic trickled along. Horns blared, and Max marveled at how overcrowded the city and its surrounding area had become in his lifetime. Still, it was nothing compared to Las Vegas, that place he had falsely come to regard as home.

No, you just lived there. It was your refuge but no more.

Max was ready to return to his family—to come home forever.

Suddenly, he wanted a beer, just one, as he'd never been much of a drinker. He gazed through plate-glass windows into a couple of bars at the happy hour crowds of smiling, clean-cut yuppies and decided to move on. He had nothing against them, but they likewise shared nothing in common. Their lives were all presentations and paychecks, Starbucks and social media. They had no inkling of the diabolical forces at work across the world and within their own government, of how the powerful manipulated society and perpetrated heinous acts to satisfy their every want and whim.

Max entered a chain sporting goods store and bought a football, regulation size. Then he moved on to a florist's shop and purchased an arrangement of half a dozen white lilies, Janet's favorite. He hailed a cab driven by a gray-bearded Sikh in a black turban and told him the destination. Darkness descended as they departed downtown for the suburbs. Snow fell in fat flakes, growing steadier and heavier by the minute. The cabbie drove like a native, unfazed by the snow, deftly navigating the slippery streets.

"Right here is fine," he told the driver.

"Should I wait for you, sir?"

Max shook his head. "No, my boy loves the snow."

The driver gave him a bewildered look as he accepted the fare and a generous tip. He gave Max a company card. "Thank you, sir. Do call our dispatcher when you are ready to return."

Max said nothing, got out, and closed the door.

The Sikh drove off through the snow, back to the city.

Max walked through the wrought iron gates and up the drive. He knew the way by heart and two inches of snow couldn't hide the headstone from him. He could have found it under two feet of snow.

He dropped to his knees before the stone and felt the wet snow soak through his pants. "AHLGREN" inscribed boldly across the cold gray granite. Max used his index finger to trace the epigraphs below: "David James 1998-2008"; "Janet McGrath 1976-2008". Max placed the football and flowers before his family and reminisced.

It had all seemed so open and shut, tragic and yet routine: a fatal collision on a rainy night. The driver of the other car, a stolen vehicle, fled the scene and was never identified. Such things happened all the time.

I should have known Banner was behind it.

Why the fool had been trying to start World War III by exposing covert American involvement in the brief Russo-Georgian War of 2008 still eluded him. But did it even matter now, kneeling at the graves of his family?

Max shook his head as he considered his late wife. *I did nothing but fail you.* The long, multiple deployments; all the ghosts that hitchhiked home with Max from around the world, she'd dealt with it all and then some. And when she couldn't take it any longer, Max kept heaping more on her. Mass military deployments to the Middle East were usually scheduled, but Max's team stayed on call, ready to deploy at any moment. He remembered eating breakfast one day with his family and promising David they would go to the park and run some plays after school.

I was in Venezuela when he got off the bus that afternoon. Max remembered the job, his second mission leading his own team, ordered to rescue two Haliburton executives from one of Hugo Chavez's jails. They fought their way into the place, freed all sorts of random political prisoners. Yet one of their objectives disemboweled, and the other hung by his thumbs from the ceiling, skinned from the neck down. Max didn't remember their names, but they still invaded his dreams regularly.

Banner had recommended him for that job as well. He wondered now how if those events were somehow connected.

Janet left after that and took David with her.

I failed at the only mission that mattered...

Memories flooded his mind: the first time he met his wife, the night he asked her to marry him, making love to her, the first time he held his son, rocking him to sleep as a toddler, wanting to savor every moment with him when he was home, playing catch on the back lawn.

Then he remembered receiving the news of their deaths.

Max's Glock found his hand, the cold barrel pressed to his temple. He didn't remember drawing it, but there it was, right where it needed to be.

Dad! David's voice cried in his mind.

Max swallowed and choked back tears. Adrenaline filled his system and his stomach knotted. Now armed with adequate courage to finish the deed, he contracted his index finger, a couple pounds of pressure on the trigger. "I'm coming home, guys. For good this time."

Tears streamed down his face. He gazed up at the night sky. He wasn't sure how long he'd knelt before the headstone. The snow had stopped and the clouds had passed for the moment.

Dad, wait!

I can't wait any longer, son. Another pound of pressure on the trigger.

Max saw them in the sky, David and Janet, peering down upon him like living constellations, and then, for a moment, he was among them in the stars.

Max didn't lower his right arm, he felt it pushed gently downward. Janet's touch, her love. He'd loved it—would never forget it—and here it was again, even if he could only sense it. He likewise sensed her kiss on his lips and knew her soul lingered there beside him.

Not yet, Max. It's not time.

When Max looked back to the sky, David and Janet had gone.

The stars had advanced and tendrils of cloud had moved back in, vanguard of the coming storm. Max's Glock lay in the snow next to the football. He stared at it for a second, examining it, as if the familiar tool would provide answers. Finally, he blinked. He wiped the snow from the pistol and holstered it, then stood, feeling the stiffness of kneeling too long.

Their bodies remained buried here, but their spirits had departed once again. Max didn't know if he would ever sense their presence again while he still lived, but it didn't matter.

They will always be with you.

Max had come to terms with their death, but it didn't give him the peace he sought. Instead, the wheels turned in the back of his mind about the orchestration of their demise. His body no longer cold, it felt warm in fact, as if a fire had been lit inside him, and his mind was suddenly crystal clear from the epiphany on what needed to be done. At the thought of it, his eyes narrowed like hooded slits.

This isn't the end. This is only the beginning. Whoever did this to you will pay.

Max bent forward and kissed the top of the headstone. For a moment he stared deep into the distant shadows, his mind drifted back to his brothers in arms, and the private hell he had just endured. He turned to face the darkness that lay ahead. As he walked away into the night, he glanced at the heavens once more, no longer feeling so alone.

A Final Note

This book is a work of fiction, but the pain many veterans experience is very real. The brave men and women of our armed forces endure much in the service of our country. The wounds they suffer, both seen and unseen, stay with them often long after they have served. Veterans often return home feeling disconnected from the society they sought to protect. The feelings of isolation and carrying the sense of guilt knowing they survived when others did not, causes many veterans to turn to suicide.

To my brothers and sisters in arms, you are not alone. If you or anyone has thoughts of harming themselves or others, please talk to someone. If you don't feel like talking to a family member or friend, contact the number below:

National Suicide Prevention Lifeline 1-800-273-8255

Suicide is a permanent solution to a temporary problem. Please don't waste the limitless potential inside of you. You alone decide how to write the final chapters of your life.

Semper Fi,

Ryan W. Aslesen